Praise for Stephen L. Carter's

JERICHO'S FALL

"Carter meticulously ratchets up the tension."
—Chris Bohjalian, *The Boston Globe*

"*Jericho's Fall* is that rare thing: a page-turner that grips the reader's attention as they plunge into a vortex. . . . A thrilling roller-coaster ride until the very last page. . . . Carter is a masterly novelist."
—*San Francisco Chronicle*

"An intricate spy thriller that proceeds at breakneck speed. . . . Graham Greene's readers, who savored [his] novels' unselfconscious erudition and matter-of-fact moral complexity, as well as their engaging plots, are likely to feel themselves on familiar ground here."
—*Los Angeles Times*

"A simmering page-turner about the murky underbelly of intelligence and finance."
—*The Seattle Times*

"Carter writes graceful prose, and he understands the mechanics of suspenseful storytelling."
—*The Washington Post*

"One of those novels that people linger over and re-read simply for the experience and pleasure of analyzing how the author worked his magic. . . . Stephen Carter is possessed of a sharp and subtle wit. . . . This is the sharpest manifestation of his talent to date."
—*Bookreporter*

Stephen L. Carter

JERICHO'S FALL

Stephen L. Carter is the William Nelson Cromwell Professor of Law at Yale University, and the author of seven nonfiction books. *Jericho's Fall* is his fourth novel. He and his family live in Connecticut.

ALSO BY STEPHEN L. CARTER

FICTION

The Emperor of Ocean Park

New England White

Palace Council

NONFICTION

God's Name in Vain:
The Wrongs and Rights of Religion in Politics

The Dissent of the Governed:
A Meditation on Law, Religion, and Loyalty

Civility: Manners, Morals, and the Etiquette of Democracy

Integrity

The Confirmation Mess:
Cleaning Up the Federal Appointments Process

The Culture of Disbelief:
How American Law and Politics Trivialize Religious Devotion

Reflections of an Affirmative Action Baby

JERICHO'S FALL

a novel

Stephen L. Carter

VINTAGE CONTEMPORARIES
Vintage Books
A Division of Random House, Inc.
New York

FIRST VINTAGE CONTEMPORARIES EDITION, JUNE 2010

Copyright © 2009 by Stephen L. Carter

All rights reserved. Published in the United States by Vintage Books,
a division of Random House, Inc., New York, and in Canada by
Random House of Canada Limited, Toronto. Originally published in
hardcover in the United States by Alfred A. Knopf, a division of
Random House, Inc., New York, in 2009.

Vintage is a registered trademark and Vintage Contemporaries and
colophon are trademarks of Random House, Inc.

This is a work of fiction. Names, characters, places, and incidents either are the
product of the author's imagination or are used fictitiously. Any resemblance to
actual persons, living or dead, events, or locales is entirely coincidental.

The Library of Congress has cataloged the Knopf edition as follows:
Carter, Stephen.
Jericho's fall / by Stephen Carter.—1st ed.
p. cm.
I. Title
PS3603.A78J47 2009
813'.6—dc22 2009003814

Vintage ISBN: 978-0-307-47447-6

Book design by Virginia Tan

www.vintagebooks.com

Printed in the United States of America
10 9 8 7 6 5 4 3 2 1

Once again, with love, for Enola

And it came to pass, when Joshua was by Jericho, that he lifted up his eyes and looked, and, behold, there stood a man over against him with his sword drawn in his hand: and Joshua went unto him, and said unto him, Art thou for us, or for our adversaries?

—Joshua 5:13

JERICHO'S
FALL

The Return

On the Sunday before the terror began, Rebecca DeForde pointed the rental car into the sullen darkness of her distant past. The Interstate was behind her. So was the chilly rain that had slowed her progress. The county road wound through thick Colorado forest, now snuggling along mountain peaks, now twisting among glowering trees. Here and there a distant flicker marked a farmhouse, then was gone. Fog enclosed her like sudden blankness. There was no moon. There were no stars. Street lamps had overlooked this corner of America, and so had the programmers of the car's GPS. The road was curvy and unkempt and, in mid-April, icy in places. Still, Rebecca drove very fast, the way she always did. She did not know whether she was running away or running toward. She was thirty-four years old and for most of her life had felt as if she were running sideways, a cheerleader watching others play the game. She had grown accustomed to her role, and hated to be dragged onto the field. She had not wanted to make the journey, but she had no choice. Jericho Ainsley was dying, and although hardly anybody remembered nowadays exactly what Rebecca and Jericho had been to each other, everybody agreed that they had once been something. Beck herself had trouble recalling the precise details of their eighteen months together, even though, once upon a time, she had given interviews about it.

"Come on," she urged the poky car as it struggled up the slope. Like many lonely people, Beck was on terms of easy conversational familiarity with the objects around her, and, often, with herself. "Come on, you can do this, don't quit on me."

The car seemed to grumble back at her.

"It's okay." Patting the dashboard as its screens glowed sullen rebuke. "It's okay. You can do this."

The car finally upshifted, and picked up the pace. Rebecca smiled, although another part of her would happily have missed the trip entirely.

Jericho was not supposed to die. Not yet. He and Beck were supposed to—what? Reconcile? Apologize? Have an ordinary human conversation? There was some ceremony left, anyway, and they were supposed to have all the time in the world to perform it.

"Guess not," she muttered.

Beck had learned of Jericho's condition not from his family but from an enterprising reporter, who had tracked her down in Boston. The reporter called not the BlackBerry she used for business but her personal cell, a number known to perhaps a dozen people. It was Saturday. She liked weekends, because the stores were crowded, and you could observe the flow of customers, looking for bottlenecks and underused spaces.

I'm updating Ambassador Ainsley's obituary, the reporter had shouted, because Rebecca was walking the sales floor and could hardly hear over the din. *Not the national-security angle,* the reporter explained. *The personal side. The scandal. In case he dies this time.*

And wondered whether she would care to comment.

Beck had said something rude and unprintable. Hanging up, she had called the house, the number she never forgot although she had not used it in years. She feared and half hoped the number had been changed, but Audrey answered on the second ring and said that Jericho had been asking for her: Audrey, who never went anywhere. If Audrey was at the bedside, things were grim indeed. *The doctors have surrendered,* she said. *My father's future is in God's hands,* added Audrey, who preached that all things were.

Beck promised to come at once.

At once proved complicated. She arranged for her conniving deputy to take over the semi-annual inspection tour of the nineteen New England stores owned by the retail conglomerate that employed her, then called her boss, an acerbic little man called Pfister, who grumbled and fussed and told her that this was a really lousy time to take family leave. Had Rebecca finished college, she would be Pfister's boss rather than the other way around: they both knew it. He scolded her all the harder as a result. But when Rebecca for once stood her ground, Pfister, astonished at his own generosity, told her that she could have three days, no more. He needed her back in time for the regional managers' meeting, set to begin Friday morning in Chicago. Beck promised she would be there.

Actually, she would not.

By Friday, Rebecca DeForde would be running for her life.

SUNDAY NIGHT

CHAPTER I

The Mountain

(1)

Darkness bore down on her as the car shuddered up the mountain. Distant lights danced at the edge of her vision, then vanished. Beck wondered how bad it would be. In her mind, she saw only the Jericho she had loved fifteen years ago and, in some ways, still did: the dashing scion of an old New England family that had provided government officials since the Revolution. One of his ancestors had a traffic circle named for him in Washington. A cousin served in the Senate. The family's history was overwhelming; the Jericho for whom Beck had fallen had certainly overwhelmed her. He had been brilliant, and powerful, and confident, and fun, ever ready with eternal wisdom, or clever barbs. She did not like to think of that mighty man ravaged by disease. She had no illusions. She remembered what cancer had done to her own father.

Whatever was waiting, she had to go.

On Saturday afternoon, having cleared her decks with Pfister, Beck took the shuttle from Boston to Washington. She lived in Virginia, a stone's throw from Reagan National Airport. Her daughter was at a church retreat, church being a thing that Beck did because she had been raised that way, and her mother would be offended if Rebecca dared differ. Beck decided to let Nina stay the night with the other kids. The two of them could ride together to the airport on Sunday, then enplane for their different destinations. Rebecca's mother, Jacqueline, had been after her for weeks to send Nina for a visit, and maybe this was the time. The child was only in second grade; missing a few days of instruction would do her no harm. Beck hesitated, then made the inevitable call to Florida, to ask if her mother could look after Nina. The conversation soon turned into a battle.

I don't know how you could even think about taking a six-year-old to visit a man like that.

I'm not taking her, Mom. That's why I'm calling you.

You said you decided not to take her. That means you thought about it. I don't understand how your mind works sometimes.

She tried, and failed, to remember a time when she and her mother had not been at odds. Because, in the eyes of her eternally disappointed mother, Beck would never be more than ten years old. Certainly their animosity predated Jericho; and perhaps it had played some sort of role (as every one of the therapists Rebecca had consulted over the years seemed to think) in her falling in love, as a college sophomore, with a married man thirty-two years her senior who tossed away his remarkable career in order to possess her.

I appreciate your help, Mom.

Oh, so you appreciate me now. Does that mean you'll call more often?

But Beck rarely called anybody. She was not the calling sort. She lived in a cookie-cutter townhouse in Alexandria, along with her daughter and the cat, and when she was not homemaking or child-rearing she was working. Her mother had married young, and was supported by her husband until the day he died. Beck's marriage had lasted less than two years. The thing with Jericho had ruined Rebecca for men, her mother insisted; and maybe it was true. Her mother was full of certitudes about the errors of others, and for the next few days would fill Nina's mind with her fevered dogmas. Hating herself, Beck had put her daughter on the plane to Florida anyway; and Nina, cradling the cat carrier, had marched regally into the jetway, never turning her head for a final wave, because she was a lot more like her grandmother than like her mother.

Or maybe not. Rebecca herself had been a feisty child, curious and willful and prepared at any moment to be disobedient. She had always pretended that she was fine without her mother, perhaps because her mother spent so much time insisting on the opposite. Her rebelliousness had led her into trouble all her life, including at her pricey private high school, where a protest against the dress code had led to a suspension; and at Princeton, where a star wide receiver tried to have his way with the reluctant freshman and wound up with a broken nose for his troubles, missing half the season. A year later, she had wound up in Jericho's bed. Maybe Nina was not like her grandmother at all, but simply a younger version of Beck—a possibility too scary to contemplate.

(11)

Lights on her tail. Was she being followed?

A wiser woman, Beck told herself, would have dismissed such a notion as the sort of nonsense that always sneaked into her head when she thought about Jericho. In the chilly night hours on a lonely and lightless mountain road, however, when the same pair of headlights kept slipping in and out of the fog, it was easier to be fearful than wise.

She accelerated—no easy matter for the little rental car—and the headlights vanished. She slowed to round a curve, and they were behind her again.

"How do you know they're the same headlights?" she sneered.

She just knew. She knew because the years had slipped away and she was back in Jericho's world, a world where a canoodling couple at the next table in a restaurant at a resort in Barbados meant you were under surveillance, where the maid at the Ritz planted bugs in the bedroom, where unexpected cars in the middle of the Yucatán were packed with terrorists ready to exact revenge for your earnest defense of your country.

She reminded herself that Jericho's paranoia no longer guided her life, but her foot pressed harder anyway, and the little car shuddered ahead. She shot down into the valley and passed through half a town. It began to snow. She climbed again, breasted the rise, went around a curve, and suddenly was suspended in nothing.

No headlights behind her, no road in front of her.

Then she almost drove over the cliff.

Things like that happened in the Rockies, not metaphorically but in reality, especially in the middle of the night, when you daydreamed your way into an unexpected nighttime snowstorm—unexpected because in Beck's corner of the country, the worst that ever happened in April was rain. At ten thousand feet, as she was beginning to remember, the weather was different. One moment, hypnotized by the cone of her headlights as it illuminated the shadowy road ahead and the dark trees rushing by on either side, Beck was gliding along, totting up the errors of her life; then, before she realized what was happening, heavy flakes were swirling thickly around her, and the road had vanished.

Rebecca slowed, then slewed, the front end mounting an unseen verge, the rear end fishtailing, but by then her winter smarts had returned, and she eased the wheel over in the direction of the skid. The car swiveled and bumped and came to rest ten yards off the road. She sat still, breath hitching. No headlights behind her, or up on the road, or anywhere else.

"False alarm," Beck muttered, furious at herself for having let Jericho back into her head, gleefully whispering his mad cautions.

She set the brake and opened the door and found, to her relief, that she was not in a ditch or a snowbank. She could back the car uphill onto the tarmac. But turning around would be easier, if there was room. Shivering as the cold leached into her fashionable boots, she squinted ahead, checking to make sure that she had room enough. The whirl of snow was slowing. She had trouble judging the distance. The beams of her headlights were swallowed up by a stand of conifers dead ahead, but there was plenty of room. Except, when she looked again, the trees were a forest, and miles away, on the other side of a steep gorge. Her toes skirted the edge. She shuffled backward. Had she tried to turn around instead of backing up, she would likely have gone over.

There in a nutshell was life since Jericho: backing up and backing up, never taking chances. One plunge over the cliff was enough for any life.

Beck stood at the edge and peered into the yawning darkness. High up on the opposite slope, she could pick out what had to be the lights of Jericho's vast house. His family wealth had purchased the property, and the scandal of their relationship had sentenced him to life imprisonment within. She had dropped out of college. He had dropped out of much more. She did the arithmetic, all the presidential ears into which he had whispered his devious advice. She remembered the year they met, the start of his indefinite sabbatical from public life, spent among the lawns of Princeton, the hushed and reverent tones in which the faculty murmured Jericho's name. She remembered how his seminars were interrupted almost weekly by protesters branding him a war criminal; and the relish with which he had baited his young accusers, demanding that they explain which of the regimes he was alleged to have overthrown they would have preferred to preserve, and why.

Since leaving government service, Jericho had published half a dozen books on international politics, but nobody cared any more. Hardly anyone remembered who he was, or had been. Not two months ago, she had found his recent nine-hundred-page tome on the achievement of peace in the Middle East remaindered at Barnes & Noble, going for three dollars and ninety-nine cents.

Her cell phone vibrated on her hip. Beck was surprised. Usually there was no service up here, but every now and then one found a patch of mountain digitally linked to the rest of the world. She fished the phone from her jacket. The screen said the number was unknown. When she answered, she got a blast of static in her ear, followed by a whine like a fax signal. Annoyed, she cut off the call. The phone immediately rang again, another unknown number, the same screech in her ear. No third ring. She decided to test her momentary connectedness by checking her messages, but when she tried she had no bars.

So how had whoever it was called her? She walked back and forth in the clearing, but found no service anywhere.

Never mind. Time to get moving. Rain was falling again, big freezing drops, and she managed a smile at the absurdity. Rain, fog, snow, rain again—all she needed was a flood to complete a biblical weather cycle, because, in her current mood, she was ready to believe in anything.

The *whup-whup* of an approaching engine caught her ear. Another car, she thought, but then an inky form shot across her vision, and she crouched protectively until she realized that her perspective was still playing tricks: it was a helicopter, flying low but still hundreds of feet in the air. She had not realized they built them so quiet. The helicopter passed directly over her, then swooped down the valley, joining other shadows. It climbed again, reaching Jericho's house, where the pilot seemed to hesitate, circling, cutting back for another look. Was she too late? Could this be the medevac chopper, preparing to rush the patient down to Denver? Or was it perhaps carrying a VIP, come to say farewell, the trip too secret for daylight?

The answer was neither. The helicopter never landed. For a long moment the pilot hovered. Another false departure, another circle. Then, evidently satisfied, the craft rose once more, returning the way it had come, and Beck found herself shutting off the headlights. An unnamable instinct warned Beck not to let whoever was aboard see her.

The media, she told herself firmly, climbing back into the car as the craft vanished over the hills. Television networks, compiling footage for the obituary. No question, that's who it was.

And yet—

And yet, why risk a flight through the Rockies to shoot the house in the dead of night? Atmosphere, she decided, starting the engine. They wanted to convey the sense of dread.

There was plenty to go around.

CHAPTER 2

The Redoubt

(1)

For another ninety minutes, the mountain owned her, hiding the small car against its immensity the way mountains do after nightfall. She popped in and out of forest and descended into the valley, then climbed the other side, winding upward until she reached the plateau that she remembered. The helicopter had it easier. The passage of time had altered the landmarks along the road. The storm-split tree that used to mark the way was gone, and the little culvert had disappeared. By hit or miss, she eventually found the turnoff, an unmarked gravel lane that fifteen years ago had rated an unmarked security car. A bumpy mile farther along was the empty guardhouse, its roof caved in, and a pair of wrought-iron gates, wide open. A faded sign announced STONE HEIGHTS, Jericho's pretentious name for his mountain redoubt. In the spill of her headlamps as she passed, she could see the mounds of snow-speckled brush and debris that had collected along their hidden base. It occurred to her that the gates had not been closed in years, and now might never be closed again. She felt bad for Jericho, who had been proud of the security even as he had pretended to hate it, back in the days when he wandered his stronghold with a head chock-full of Cold War secrets, sleeping with a gun near at hand because, as he whispered to her in bed, sooner or later the Russians or the Chinese or somebody worse would be coming for him.

The driveway climbed farther up the mountain, still in the trees, and, finally, she glimpsed the black Suburban she had been looking for, complete with polarized windows. The driver was a pallid smear in the darkness. Beck slowed down automatically, but he did not even lift his head. As the house loomed into view, boxlike and stolid, trees and brush cut back fifty yards on every side to provide clear lines of fire, Rebecca almost smiled. Just one guard nowadays, but at least they were watching. State Department, Secret Service, state trooper, whoever it was, the dying man still rated security. Rebecca felt a warm wash of relief, for Jericho's sake.

Cars were scattered in the forecourt, dusted with varying amounts of snow. The silver Prius probably meant that Pamela was here, the younger of Jericho's daughters, although both were older than Beck, a distinction that had put the fat in the fire from the first. The battered brown van would likely be Audrey's, borrowed from the abbey where she was cloistered, or whatever they called it. Rebecca, who despite her churchgoing mostly kept a careful distance from the overly religious, was none too sure of such details. Outside the garage stood a shiny pickup truck, and pickup trucks were what Jericho liked, although it was difficult to imagine that he did much driving these days.

Jericho had an unforgiving son named Sean, who helped run an environmental foundation in New York, but Sean would no more attend his father's final days than he would fund a coal mine. Besides, Sean would not be caught dead in a pickup. Jericho used to have friends spread over his mountain, quiet, self-reliant men who attached themselves to the land and sported National Rifle Association decals on their bumpers. Maybe the truck belonged to an old acquaintance. But the snow lay thick on the hood, and the same instinct that had counseled Beck to hide from the helicopter proposed that the pickup truck had another significance entirely, one she had not fathomed. It was Jericho's, and there was a reason it was not in the garage.

Never mind. Not her business.

Rebecca parked her modest rental next to Audrey's decrepit van. Climbing out, she was struck by the silence. In the old days, Jericho would have bounded from the house to sweep her, literally, off her feet, and pepper her with ribald jokes in four languages about her mode of transport. The house had always been boisterous, the forecourt thick with the cars of visitors who wanted his wisdom or his money or his liquor or his connections, or just to shake his hand. He would have dragged her inside and forced her into whatever party he had going, even if the party consisted of two or three cold-eyed men from the clandestine services division of the Central Intelligence Agency, discussing a project in Malaysia or Peru or Iran. That was what Jericho called them, projects, even after the men stopped coming to the house.

Her good humor began to fade. She wanted an excuse not to go inside. If Jericho was not partying, he was not Jericho. The bounding, energetic, globe-straddling man she had loved, if love was what they had shared, was upstairs suffering in a bed from which he would never rise. The house was lonely now, merely the residence of a rich but no-longer-important man, whose encroaching demise rated not even a television truck at the bottom of the hill. The attendants of his last days were few, and, although Jericho had been the epitome of the man's man, all were female: a pair of daughters who were distant from him, and, mounting the steps, the woman who had wrecked his career.

Except that another observer was present.

As Rebecca stepped onto the gravel, noisily dragging her suitcase, her friends in the helicopter whup-whupped overhead once more, then circled back, dipping the dark nose briefly as if in salute.

(11)

The woman who opened the heavy door was tall and slim and so pale that one might have been forgiven for thinking her the patient. She wore aged jeans and an ageless sweater, neither bearing a designer label, and pearls that didn't need one. Her feet were bare. Her dark hair was comfortably awry. Her clear eyes were appraising. She had achieved that ethereal beauty that attaches to certain coolly distant women from their late thirties onward after having eluded them most of their lives.

"I see you made it," she said, in the sullen voice of one already seeking out your faults.

"Sorry I'm late. Hello, Pamela."

"The drive from Denver's only two and a half hours. It's almost midnight."

"My flight was delayed," said Beck, already on the defensive; but, with Pamela, she always was. The two women had spoken on the phone twice over the past twenty-four hours, and, so far, Pamela had yet to concede the possibility that Rebecca might do anything right. "The storm."

"You should have called."

"I couldn't get through."

Pamela said nothing to indicate what she thought of this pitiful excuse. She had inherited from her father the effortless assurance of a person with more important things to do, and when she stepped aside her body language said she was doing Rebecca a favor.

Beck crossed the threshold. She had to hold her breath to do it. The vast space was as empty as she remembered, and as sad. The wide plank floors were ancient, and devoid of rugs, creaking with every step, because Jericho, as he used to say, wanted to hear them coming. This was what Jericho called the great room. A central fireplace dominated the space, but although logs were heaped in the grate, no fire had been lighted. The ceilings were two stories high, bordered by colorful clerestory windows salvaged from a burnt church. At human height, attractive seating arrangements stood near picture windows, but near the stairs, a handful of stout wooden chairs were scattered haphazardly, obstacles over which invaders might stumble. They looked like the same chairs from fifteen years ago, when Jericho had fired the maid for moving them.

"How is he?" said Beck, not daring to meet Pamela's eye.

"Dying."

"Are they sure?"

A snicker of disdain from the prim mouth. "You're here, aren't you? That means you're sure."

Rebecca moved toward the wide windows that, during the day, provided dizzying views down into the valley, but at night were bright with the wash from the floodlights Jericho required. Where there were no windows, bookshelves covered the walls, crammed with thousands of volumes, most of them hardcover and dog-eared. Jericho used to point his young lover to a shelf and command her to pull a book at random, and give him a report by the end of the week. He had loved these little games. But tonight the room pulsed with animosity. Pamela had been twenty-two and about to graduate college when her father announced that he was leaving her mother for a nineteen-year-old.

"Audrey said he was asking for me," Rebecca said.

"He's been asking for you for years," said Pamela from behind her. "That never got you up here before."

Beck said nothing. She looked up at the balustrade. She heard a door slam. She assumed that Jericho was in his old suite, commanding the magnificent views suitable to a man of his station. In the Rockies, if you angled your windows just right, the mountains went on forever, and his windows were angled right. Her own, smaller suite had been next door, but she spent most nights in his.

"Rebecca?" said Pamela. "Hello?"

Still Beck did not speak. She stood very still. She did not want to go up there. She wanted to be back home in Alexandria with Nina and their cat, Tom Terrific. She wanted to be back at the office, listening to Pfister's rants while pretending not to be as smart as he. At this moment, she would even rather be down in Florida, sitting across the living room from her poisonous mother, soaking up the gospel according to Nancy Grace. Anything to avoid seeing Jericho again. Not because he had wrecked her life: after all, she had wrecked his, too.

No.

Beck was beset by the same emotion that had flattened her yesterday, when she got the call. Jericho was supposed to be immortal. His distant presence, not just in her memory but here in his mountain fastness, had formed the background of her adult life. They might never again be lovers, but a world where he did not exist seemed unimaginable.

Now, standing beside the cold fireplace, Rebecca began to tremble. She remembered stepping into this house for the first time, squealing delightedly as she ran across the floor—*You bought this for us?—Not for us, my dear. For you*—pressing her face against the sparkling windows like the child she had so recently been, then turning into his bearish hug. She remembered the times she had danced for him in front of the lovely fire, slowly removing her clothes and his own, and the way the flames playing over their bodies had heightened their intimacy. She remembered, too, the night their fun was interrupted by a trio of hard-faced men from the CIA's Office of Security, who had led them to separate rooms and interrogated her for an hour and a half, growing particularly angry when she had trouble remembering the name of her fifth-grade Spanish teacher. Afterward, Beck complained to Jericho that the men had refused to let her dress and made her spend the whole session wrapped in a blanket. He confessed that he had co-authored the manual that suggested precisely that form of humiliation for getting answers out of reluctant women.

But what do they want? she had asked. *Why did they come?*

Until last year, I was Director of Central Intelligence, he had answered calmly. *Before that, I was Secretary of Defense. Before that, White House National Security Adviser. You're in my life now, my dear. You'll be in their files forever.* Making this sound like an honor. *To most people, sex is just sex. In my profession, unless we see proof to the contrary, we have to assume that an affair is a cover for something else.*

He had wanted to resume their conjugality, but Rebecca marched upstairs to her suite, locked the door, and showered for what felt like a week, then put on about three layers of pajamas. That night they slept apart.

And Jericho had been right about their files. Five or six times over the years, always without warning, another couple of visitors from Security had dropped by her home or office, never calling first, although occasionally they apologized. Once, they surprised her during lunch on a Caribbean cruise. Another time they had showed up at a pub in Edinburgh. Beck had trouble believing that every ex-girlfriend of every ex-Director was treated this way, and now and then she asked them what made her special.

Their pitying smiles were the only answer she ever received.

"Yes," said Pamela, still behind her. "He's been asking for you."

"I should go see him."

"It's late."

Beck turned her head, trying to make peace. Pamela was halfway to the kitchen. "Still. I should see if he's awake. I won't keep him long, I promise."

"Fine." Her voice was crisp, in charge, even satisfied, as if she had cinched a deal: for Pamela, who used to make indie films, now coproduced disaster movies with her husband, and lived in Beverly Hills. She pointed toward the balustrade. "Dad's in the master suite. I'm sure you remember where it is. Audrey and I are on the main floor. I've put you in the back."

What Jericho used to call the grandchildren's suite. Coincidence or insult? With Pamela you could never tell.

"Thank you."

"I hate this place," said Pamela, arms crossed over her sweater, rubbing her own biceps. "I never lived here. It was never my house, Rebecca. Never Audrey's, never my mom's. We grew up in Virginia. This place—well, this place was his." A pause. *And yours,* Pamela was saying, wordlessly. "Dad should have sold it long ago."

Again memory teased her. "Does he still booby-trap the doors after dark?"

"Not that I know of."

They shared a laugh, tinny and forced.

Pamela cocked her head, the two women listening to the same sound. "Damn helicopter," she muttered. "It's been buzzing us all night."

"The press—"

"Like hell. It's just a troublemaker. We've had all these people up here, the ones who used to do the protests everywhere Dad spoke? They're ready to dance on his grave."

Rebecca glanced at the window, the floodlit grounds. "In a helicopter?"

"Any way they can. You should see what's on the Internet."

"I probably shouldn't."

Beck was climbing the curving uncarpeted stairs, hand on the rail, when she heard Pamela's voice behind her, unexpectedly sad. "Rebecca, look." She never used the nickname. "My father doesn't have much time."

"I understand."

"I'm not sure you do, Rebecca. It's just the three of us. Audrey and Dad and me. Sean's not coming. There's no nurse. Dad keeps firing them. He thinks they're spying on him. Besides"—again she seemed to wrestle—"well, there's not much a nurse can do at this point."

"I see," said Beck, over her shoulder.

"Dad knows he doesn't have much time left. Aunt Maggie's been here and gone. She's not coming back. Dad's office in Denver is closed. Mrs. Blumen died last year." Jericho's longtime assistant. "There's nobody else."

"I said I understand, Pamela."

"What I'm saying is, I don't know how he'll react to your being here, Rebecca. Please try not to disrupt things again."

This, finally, was too much. But when Beck rounded on her old adversary, ready to tussle, Pamela had vanished into the kitchen. She seemed to be the only one who knew how to walk Jericho's creaky floors without making a sound. As Beck climbed the stairs, her phone rang again. Unknown number, and a digital whine. But by this time she was no longer surprised: when she checked the bars, she had no service.

CHAPTER 3

The Sickroom

(1)

Like the rest of the house, the second floor was brightly lighted, so that Jericho could see the bad guys when they came. Beck stood at the top of the stairs. The balcony ran along the three main bedchambers, including the master suite and her own old room, now occupied by Pamela. The hallway ran to Jericho's study in the back of the house, then made a right turn to the remaining suite, tucked away in a corner, because Jericho wanted to keep future grandchildren as far from him as possible. *I've put you in the back.*

As Beck approached the double doors to the master suite, they swung open and out stepped a smiling Audrey—Saint Audrey, as Jericho liked to sneer, always so sweet, and therefore, in Beck's tortured mind, even less trustworthy than her younger sister. Audrey enfolded Rebecca in thick arms, drawing her against ample breasts. She was a large woman, more squarish than round, with a plump, somehow grandmotherly face. Her dark hair, frosted at the edges with gray, was more organized than styled. In green pajamas and brown robe, she could have been part of the mountain.

"You look great," said Audrey, exhausted eyes less delighted than the fulsome greeting. She was a nun, Beck reminded herself, marveling. An Episcopal nun. Until Audrey joined her order ten or twelve years ago, Beck had been unaware that the Episcopal Church had nuns. "How do you stay so thin?"

Rebecca offered her standard answer: "I'm too busy to eat during the day, and too tired when I get home."

"You work too hard."

"So my mother says."

A momentary hiatus, both women perhaps thinking about Audrey's late mother, eight years dead. Audrey's mother, Jericho's ex-wife. The one he had left for a college student.

"And how's that darling little girl?" said Audrey brightly, who had never met Nina in her life.

"She's wonderful. She's perfect."

"Sean says she's as gorgeous as her mother."

Were those eyes mocking her? Rebecca could not be sure. She looked away. "Thank you," she muttered.

"You're so blessed," said Audrey, hands still clutching Beck's shoulders. "You have so much to be thankful for."

"I'm thankful, Aud. Believe me." Beck bit her lip, hoping Audrey would not start babbling about God, as she often did; although another part of her longed for any distraction that would postpone the moment when she had to walk into the sickroom. "I'm content with my life," she added, as if to bat away weightier emotions.

But the nun was hardly listening. Keeping a heavy arm locked around Beck's shoulders, Audrey drew her away from the master suite. "He isn't the Jericho you remember, Beck. Try to keep that in mind."

"I will."

"I'm not talking about the illness." Audrey was brisk, even impatient. And no matter how welcoming the words, the eyes were watchful and withholding, as if she worried her guest might steal the silver. "He's been waiting for you, Beck. He's too happy about the fact that you're here. He has the look that always used to mean he was up to something. Be very careful. He'll fool you. He'll seem to be himself. He'll be brilliant and funny and sarcastic. He'll taunt you and argue with you and play with your words for hours. He'll charm you, Beck, and then he'll scare you, and then he'll charm you some more. Same as in the old days. You'll think, other than the cancer, nothing's the matter. But don't fall for it. The cancer's moved into his brain. Even before it got there, my dad wasn't right. Now he's worse. Everything he says is going to seem logical. It isn't. Bear that in mind. It isn't logical, and it isn't necessarily true." She kissed Beck's cheek. "I guess you should go on in. He's waiting for you. Just try to remember that he's a madman."

(11)

At first glance and even second, Jericho Ainsley looked the picture of rosy-cheeked health. Oh, there was an oxygen tank beside the bed, but the rest of what Rebecca had expected was not there. No tube in his nose, no monitors bleeping forth their useless data, no hospital-style bed, none of the cloying odor of sickness and death that she had imagined must attach to the departure of even the very rich, and the very secret.

Beck advanced upon the bed cautiously, the way she had in the last days of their relationship, when neither of them quite knew whether the next touch would ignite the fires of passion or the explosion of warfare. The furnishings were as lush as ever. More bookshelves, new since her day, had been built into the walls. A desk near the bay window was cluttered with files. In the background, the first movement of Mendelssohn's *Italian* Symphony—one of his favorites—played softly. Moving closer, she expected to find Jericho ravaged by the cancer. But he looked as powerful and handsome as ever, the curiously golden eyes open and alive, flicking from face to hands and back, alert to her every move. Only the viselike grip on the bedclothes, and the line of sweat on his lip betrayed his battle against the pain.

"How are you?" she said, once she trusted herself to speak. She stood beside the bed, hands fighting each other nervously, wondering if she should be offering water from the plastic cup with its little straw. The question, she knew, was absurd, but nobody had ever worked out the proper protocol to greet the openly dying. Perhaps that is why we tend to be so quiet in the company of those who will not be long with us: we are waiting for them to tell us what to say.

Jericho frowned—that is, the lines of his face flexed and tautened, more a memory of emotion than the genuine article. He whispered a few words in return. She could not hear, and leaned close. His breath was hot, and damp, and rich with pain and fear.

"You shouldn't have come," he croaked.

Beck kept her face near his. On the table beside the bed was a thick volume by a Nobel laureate, which tried to explain the collapse of the financial system. "Don't be silly. Of course I'd be here."

"Why?"

She hesitated. If she said she was here because he called for her, she might offend him. "I miss you," she said, wondering if it was true.

Again he whispered something she did not catch. She discovered that she was holding his hand, or, rather, he was holding hers, the fingers strong as talons.

"You should go," he said.

"Go where?"

"Home." He coughed and squirmed and could not get comfortable. "You can't be here, Beck. This is insane."

Remembering Audrey's caution, she wondered whether he might be reliving their arguments back when she first began spending her nights with him. She said, covering both possibilities, "I'm here because I want to be. No other reason."

He lifted his head and shoulders, trembling from the effort. "They'll kill you," he said, distinctly.

She blinked. "What did you say?"

"Have you gone deaf? I said, they're going to kill you. You watch. Not now. But as soon as I'm out of the way, they'll kill you."

"I don't—"

"Will you listen to me? For once in your life just listen?" His cheeks reddened further, and, if only for an instant, his old strength returned. He jerked his hand free, waved toward the closed door. "They're going to kill you. The girls, too. Idiots. Sentimental idiots. Take them with you, Beck. Don't be a fool. Take them and get out of the house."

Everything he says is going to seem logical, Audrey had warned. *It isn't. It isn't logical, and it isn't necessarily true.*

"Who's going to kill me?" she asked softly.

"What difference does it make? Is there somebody by whom you'd particularly like to be killed?" He tilted his chin. "Get my PDA. I have a whole list of killers for hire. I'll arrange one for you if you want."

"That's not funny."

"They're very good, Beck. The killers on my list. Short and sweet. A quick bullet to the head and you're pleading your case to Saint Peter. It's better than the alternatives, believe me."

She kissed his forehead, gentled him to the pillow. It occurred to her that he was talking about what he wanted for himself. "You need to rest."

"You don't believe me. Silly girl. You should pay attention to what I tell you."

"Please, honey." The endearment came automatically to her lips. "Try to conserve your energy."

The clever eyes held hers. Again the apparent health of his face challenged her perceptions of death. "Why? Will I live longer?"

"It's late. It's past midnight."

"Especially for me."

Beck needed a second. She made eye contact with the signed photographs of Johnson and Nixon, twinned devotedly above the bed, but neither President offered her any help. Three more Presidents graced other walls, but the men who had presided over Vietnam were his favorites. "Jericho—"

"You're a fool," he said, waggling a finger at her. "You never were much good at doing what I told you, were you? That was always your problem, Beck. If you'd spent more time listening to me and less time totting up my shortcomings, you'd have wound up with something better to do with your life than being a glorified cashier."

Rebecca wiped her eyes.

"Stop it, Jericho. Please. Is this how you want to be remembered?"

He was suddenly fierce. "I don't want to be remembered at all. That's the point. I want to be the one sitting around after the funeral doing the remembering. I want to be the one who gets drunk and tells stories about the poor bastard we just buried. Do you have any idea how it feels to know you won't be?"

She shook her head but did not rise. Jericho subsided. His breathing grew harsh. She chanced a look at his face. His eyes were open, and pained, staring at the ceiling.

"Audrey said you were waiting for me," she finally said. "That you're happy I'm here. Why? Because you finally have the chance to get back at me?"

He tried to grin but wound up coughing. "Isn't that reason enough? The deathbed confers many advantages, my dear, and one of them is that you can say whatever you like to whomever you please, and there's nothing they can do about it. I recommend that you try it sometime. Dying." A ragged, gargling laugh. "Well, pretty soon, you'll see what I mean."

"Tell me," Beck persisted.

The eyes mellowed. "Thank you for coming, my dear. That was classy." He squeezed her hand. "And as to the why"—suddenly as didactic as he used to be in the classroom—"well, you're here to help me."

"Help you do what?"

"I'll tell you tomorrow. I'm tired. Where's Saint Audrey?"

The swift change of topic slowed her. "Taking a break."

"Why'd she do that?"

"She's tired, too."

"No. I mean, why'd she quit her job? Become a nun? Brilliant. Brilliant psychologist. Almost as brilliant as you could have been if you hadn't decided to waste your life. Then, one day, she ups and quits the family business, leaves her husband, turns into a nun. Problem, that. Ask her."

"Ask her what?"

"Why she became a nun. Why she quit the family business. And her husband. Ask her about her husband." A grunt of pain, followed by a gruesome grin. "Did she jump you?"

"What?"

"Saint Audrey. She didn't jump you? She likes girls now. Didn't you know?"

Beck shook her head. "That isn't any of my business."

"It is if she jumps you." He coughed. His watery eyes fluttered, then focused. "I'm cold."

"I'll get another blanket."

An unexpected wink. For a delicious instant, the Jericho she had loved. "I can think of better ways to get warm." Tapping the sheets. "Come on, my dear. I'm not too sick for a little playtime. Dying man's prerogative. You can even be on top this time. Just lock the door first." He laughed, then coughed, then laughed harder, then coughed harder, and then his head was back on the pillow, eyes as empty as before. "It's too cold. Tell them."

"I'll tell them," she said, and, weeping, held his hand until he slept.

The next day, she found the headless dog.

MONDAY

CHAPTER 4

The Protest

(1)

Rebecca DeForde was an early riser. This was the first Monday in months when she had not had to worry about getting Nina ready for school or rushing to the office or visiting a store, and a part of her wanted to snuggle into the thick down comforter in the back guest room, and shut her eyes for hours. But her mother had trained her otherwise, and by half past six, as the rest of the household slumbered, she was in her running shoes, striding across the sprawling grounds, letting the chill wake her. She was no runner, but she was an enthusiastic walker. During her time up here with Jericho, she had come to love the unsettling clarity of the brisk mountain air. In those days, Rebecca would spend hours rambling alone through the woods, planning escape strategies she would never implement, for Jericho always seemed to anticipate her: the instant she crossed the threshold, prepped to explain why she had to go, he would be ready with flowers or some more expensive gift. Sometimes, in bed, she would ask Jericho what drew him to her—not merely why he had chased her in the first place—goodness knows, Beck had been *chased* before—but also why he insisted on staying with her, and keeping her with him, and why they spent almost all of their time on his mountaintop, mostly alone. He would never answer, but now and then, when she pressed too hard, he would vanish into his study, only to pop out an hour later with everything arranged: a private jet to a private villa, on Tenerife, say, or in New Zealand—someplace where they could travel, and yet be alone. Best of all, he would have a driver take her into Aspen or Vail, where she would spend the Ainsley money at the finest boutiques, acquiring a wardrobe suitable to her station as what Jericho merrily labeled his accompaniment, and what her mother called his concubine.

She had loved him. There was no question in her mind. She had been only nineteen, and had loved him with a passion she had not lavished on a man since. He had been dashing. She had heard the word but never understood before how a man, in his maturity, could combine a smooth affection with a gentle villainy. Jericho had been smart, and funny, and in most ways kind. He had a temper, true, but it flashed rarely, at least at her. He had introduced her to a world of such privilege she still could not fathom it. And he had given up his career for her.

That was the other reason Rebecca had finally returned to Stone Heights after avoiding it for so many years. Because she owed him. Jericho Ainsley had sacrificed his remarkable career in order to be with her, and although a part of her was grateful, in her introspective moments she admitted that another part of her felt guilty.

Even the vast property itself symbolized the scandal of their involvement. Jericho had purchased it fifteen years ago, when at last forced to acknowledge that their relationship made normal life impossible for either. *Bought us a place in Colorado, Becky-Bear. Lots of privacy. Just for the two of us. You'll love it.*

She had expressed her doubts.

Eight hundred acres, Jericho told her. *Great views, the middle of nowhere. Nearest town is thirty miles away.*

At the time, Rebecca had been thrilled to think that he would create a secret world for the two of them. The house was halfway up the mountain, and Jericho owned land most of the way to the top. Sometimes the two of them would climb the rocky path and stand at the summit, gazing down on a view that went on for miles, first crisp, then vague, then vanishing amidst higher peaks.

Which was, in a sense, the arc of Jericho's career.

This morning Beck headed down toward the gate, not up toward the peak. She wandered the woods, staying near the gravel road so as not to lose her way, wondering why Jericho had asked for her, or if he even remembered. The sun was just clearing the peak. In the valley to the east of Jericho's mountain, the high trees cast sharply etched shadows toward her like daggers. She heard animals snuffling by, spotted their tracks in the wet earth and light snow, but never quite saw them except for darting flashes of brown or gray farther down the path. The hike down to the gate was ten minutes. The Chevy Suburban from last night had vanished, and nothing had yet replaced it. Maybe Jericho rated security only after dark. Maybe the security was hidden. Maybe her true feelings were hidden, even from herself. Maybe this had been an act of madness, coming up to Stone Heights to be tortured by Jericho's madness, Pamela's hostility, and Audrey's sweetly repressive tolerance. In three days she had to be on that plane from Denver to Chicago. She wondered if the four of them could stand one another until then.

A mile past the gate, huffing and stretching in the thin air, Rebecca reached the main road. She turned west, away from town. The road climbed higher up the peak. She knew that her mother would have Nina up early, and tried the cell phone, but, as usual on this side of the mountain, there was no signal. A panel truck rumbled past her, two heads turning to ogle as it hurried downhill. A bright-red Explorer with tinted windows overtook her and curved upward out of sight. The angle into the valley was sharper now. Houses scattered thinly below her, and, in the distance, sunlight glistened on the pleasures of Vail. After a mile or so, Rebecca reached the next entrance, the getaway of some software baron many times richer than Jericho. The house was shuttered for the season, but the gate was spanking new and seemed to work just fine. Depressed and not sure why, she turned and started back down the road, and the red Explorer passed her again, heading the other way. She wondered what dawn expedition had led the driver to visit the peak so briefly, or whether he was just lost, and she remembered how Jericho had warned her long ago to keep track of cars that kept turning up.

Then she heard the gunshot.

Beck knew guns, of course. Jericho had required her to learn to shoot, and even now, single woman that she was, she kept a loaded revolver in her house, in a locked box under her bed. She lifted her head. There was no second shot. A rifle of some sort. Probably a hunter. At altitude, sounds carried a long way, but she could not escape the impression that the shot had been relatively nearby.

Short and sweet. A quick bullet to the head . . . It's better than the alternatives, believe me.

No. No. Not possible. Not so soon, and not like this.

Nevertheless, she headed back toward Stone Heights, fast. Hiking down the peak was easier than hiking up. Rebecca reached the property in mere minutes, hurried along the dirt road to the frozen gates, and then had to climb again. She encountered the dog halfway up the drive.

She stood very still.

The dog was black and sleek and must once have been beautiful, but somebody had blown its skull all over the gravel. There was blood, there were bits of white that were brains or bone, there was vomit nearby but that was all hers.

When she had passed this spot forty minutes ago, the driveway had been clear. She was sure of it.

The panel truck. The red Explorer. Beck was still babbling about the two vehicles while Audrey made her tea in the kitchen and Pamela went off to phone Jimmy Lobb, the caretaker, to do something about the mess.

"We should call the police," Rebecca shouted after her.

Audrey's grin as she rubbed Beck's shoulders was sheepish. "We get vandalism every couple of days. Somebody's idea of a joke. The sheriff will just tell us to scrape it up, and then they'll stick the report at the bottom of the pile."

"A joke?"

"Everybody knows Jericho Ainsley hates dogs. Cats. Animals generally."

Beck was not so sure about the *everybody*; and she wondered why, if Jericho hated animals so much, anybody would think that killing one would upset him.

Pamela was back. "No answer at Lobb's." She shrugged. "Well, maybe he's already on the way. And it's about time."

"About time?" said Beck, sitting up.

"Mr. Lobb usually drops by at least once every morning," said Audrey. "But he hasn't been here in a couple of days. Isn't answering the phone, either." She tilted her round chin toward the stairs. "As far as I know, Dad hasn't fired him yet."

"He wouldn't fire Jimmy Lobb," Pamela objected. "How would he keep the place clean?"

Audrey supplied the explanation. "Dad doesn't like strangers in the house. Mr. Lobb brings women up from town to do the cleaning, and follows them around from room to room. Mr. Lobb is the only one Dad trusts to supervise them."

"He's worried about stealing?"

The sisters looked at each other. "Bugging," said the nun, softly.

A silence, broken by Beck. "What about the guard? Maybe he saw something."

"What guard?"

"The guard at the bottom of the hill. In the Suburban. Why's he just there at night, anyway?"

Again the sisters looked at each other. "There aren't any guards," said Audrey. "Dad got rid of them years ago. He thought they were spying on him."

(11)

Jericho rang. He had a buzzer that could be heard throughout the house, and although he was hardly bedridden, he liked to keep the three women hopping. They took turns answering, although in truth Audrey seemed to shoulder most of the burden. She never complained.

Meanwhile, using the house phone, Rebecca finally reached her mother, who lectured her for not having called to report her safe arrival, then grudgingly put Nina on, with a grim warning to keep it short, because they were going to the aquarium.

"I have a surprise for you, Mommy," said her daughter.

"What is it?"

Childish giggles, then a recitation of one of Beck's own mantras: "If I tell you, it won't be a surprise."

"When do I get the surprise, sweetie?"

"When you come home."

"I'll see you this weekend. I have to go to Chicago first. I'll be back on Sunday."

Nina's tone grew censorious. "That's six *days*."

"I know, sweetie."

"Grandma says when you were little she *never* left you alone this long."

Beck closed her eyes and clenched a fist, wishing she had someone to strangle. "It's just a few more days, sweetie."

They loved each other and missed each other, but Nina had to go. Beck asked her to put Grandma back on, but the little girl, presumably by accident, hung up instead.

(III)

Meanwhile, they had called the sheriff after all. It was Audrey who had joined in wearing Pamela down, although another part of Rebecca wondered why the nun would not make the call without her younger sister's say-so. The deputy was a gangling man named Mundy. He arrived in his patrol car, siren off but lights flashing. Mundy had a boyish shyness that on another occasion Beck might have found endearing. He wore glasses and looked like an earnest accountant. He evidently knew the family well, because he teased Audrey and flirted with Pamela. But to Beck he was coldness itself, as if he suspected her of doing the deed, which perhaps he did.

"There's no bullet," Deputy Mundy told them after a three-minute inspection. "No bullet, no shell casing, no nothing. You should scrape it up like you did the other."

Beck looked at the sisters. "A cat, day before yesterday," Pamela conceded reluctantly, eyes downcast.

"And that's it?" said Beck.

"Yes, ma'am. That's it. Unless you want us to put out a bulletin for everybody in rural Colorado who owns a dog and a gun."

"What about the man I saw at the bottom of the hill last night?"

"Anybody else see him?" The sisters shook their heads. "Well, then," he said, as if that was the end of the matter.

Rebecca was not the sort to give up without a fight. "So what do you think we should do, Deputy? We're up here alone."

"Maybe you should get a gun," said Mundy. He inclined his head toward the stairs. "From what I hear, Mr. Ainsley's got plenty of 'em."

"Why do we need a gun?" she persisted. "Are we supposed to shoot the next stranger who comes on the property?"

"Better him than another dog," said the deputy.

"Isn't it your job to protect people?"

"Up here, ma'am, people pretty much take care of themselves."

Sometimes one-upmanship requires a politic lie. "Back where I come from, we take care of each other."

Mundy was fiddling with his belt. "Look. Here's my card. If you have any more trouble, call me, okay?" Pointing. "That's my cell on the back."

They stood at the window, watching the deputy turn the cruiser around. "He likes you," said Audrey.

Beck looked at her. "What?"

"Deputy Mundy. He likes you." She surprised her sister with an unwanted poke in the ribs. "He never told us to get a gun. He just told you." She touched Beck's pocket. "And he never gave us his card, either. 'Call me if you have any more trouble, cell's on the back.' He likes you."

"Cell phones don't even work here," growled Rebecca. She handed the card to Pamela and stalked up to her room.

(IV)

The grandchildren's suite was located above the kitchen, and connected through a bathroom to Jericho's disordered study next door. Had Jericho been more ambulatory, this inconvenience might have bothered her. Under the circumstances, however, Beck in effect had two rooms to herself, except when Pamela wanted to use the computer. The house possessed no wireless modem: Jericho was too worried about someone listening in. The only way to get connected, therefore, was to log on to the clunky desktop machine, at least a decade old, and wait. As she was waiting now, sitting in Jericho's comfortably cracked leather chair, checking her e-mail. Most of it was either spam or business, and neither kind excited her more than the other. She assured Pfister that she would meet him in Chicago as promised. Her flight left Denver around noon on Thursday, and she would arrive just in time for dinner, when she would brief him yet again for Friday's meetings. Scrolling through the rest of her e-mails, she decided she did not need to meet any horny housewives in her area, and chose not to lend assistance to an exiled African prince who would transfer ten million dollars to her if she would first provide her bank-account information. She logged off.

When she got back to her room, her cell was vibrating. Annoyed, she snatched it up and, sure enough, heard static and the fax tone. She ended the call, then tried the phone, but again had no bars.

She stretched out on the window seat and dragged her leather briefcase over, because she wanted to finish the new Danticat, which she had been reading on the plane. She reached into the side pocket, where she always kept her fiction, and she pulled out not the novel but a printout of a memo she had left Pfister. She sat up again, delved into the middle, where she usually kept her work, and found the magazines she had bought in the airport. Confused now, she peeked into the outside pocket, where she always stuffed magazines, and there was the Danticat.

"A senior moment," she muttered to the air, although she was only thirty-four. "Either that or I'm losing my mind."

Because the other possibility was that, while Beck was out walking, somebody had rifled her briefcase, and stuffed the contents back all wrong.

And that was ridiculous.

(v)

Downstairs, the women took turns dealing with the trickle of visitors who came to the front door. Jericho's sensors told them when a car entered the driveway, and the monitors in the security room behind the kitchen let them watch the forecourt, so they always knew in advance what sort of visitor was approaching. They kept hoping for Jimmy Lobb, the caretaker, but it always turned out to be a wily reporter or a nervous former associate or a sycophantish newcomer hoping for an endorsement for a book about what really happened on 9/11. Perhaps Jericho was less forgotten than Rebecca had thought. Thundershowers were promised for later in the day, and she hoped the rain would hold the visitors at bay.

When one o'clock came and Mr. Lobb still had not appeared, Pamela took Beck into the mudroom, grabbed a large garbage bag and a pair of shovels, and led her on a forced march down the hill, where, together, they removed the dog's remains—made worse now by the tires of cars unable to swerve in time. As they tossed the squishy bag into the back of Jericho's pickup, for later delivery to the county landfill, Beck noticed the padlocks on the garage.

"What are those for?"

"Ask Jericho."

"How long have they been on there?"

The inquiry was evidently beneath Pamela's dignity. She turned her back and strode imperiously up to the house.

Beck dawdled. The sky was darkening. All four garage bays were padlocked. The locks were shining new. She tugged, but they never budged. She tried the side door, but it was bolted. The first freezing droplets spattered. She peered in the windows, but they had been covered with fabric on the inside.

Weird. Not a clever way to keep people out: a good set of bolt-cutters and a little stealth would have the doors open in no time.

Maybe he's keeping something in.

"Not your problem," she announced, and ran up the hill as the droplets became a downpour.

An hour later, Rebecca brought Jericho his lunch. He was sitting in the chair, studying a thick brown file. "My will," he said, setting it aside. "The lawyers are driving up from Denver to collect my revisions." He chuckled. He seemed fairly bursting with energy. In the background, a soprano sang a challenging aria. The second act of *Don Giovanni,* Beck vaguely recalled: an opera Jericho dearly loved, and had twice taken her to see, including once at La Scala. "Don't worry, my dear. You and the little girl are quite well provided for."

She did not dignify this with a response.

"I want to apologize for my behavior last night," said Jericho, cautiously slicing into some sort of soy patty. "I wasn't myself."

"I understand," she murmured.

"You'll have read the literature, I expect. You never go anywhere without prepping first, do you, my dear?" He coughed. "Yes. I imagine you've read up on dying, haven't you? I seem to be suffering from rather a classic case of *timor mortis,* wouldn't you say? Paranoid delusions involving the death of loved ones are not exactly uncommon, I believe. There's this psychiatrist, Eisenstadt, who describes them as the brain's frantic effort to reassure the dying individual that he'll have his friends and family along on his journey."

"You're making that up."

"The paranoid delusions?" He sipped his juice. "I have them, I assure you."

"The literature."

"Oh?"

"Eisenstadt, as I'm sure you know perfectly well, is the name of my therapist."

Jericho pouted. "I had no idea you were consulting an expert on *timor mortis*. Tell me, my dear, are you ill? Anything I should be aware of?" A dreadful wink. "Planning to throw yourself over the cliff and keep me company when I'm gone?"

"Stop it."

He nodded, and drank his juice. "Dak is coming today."

She remembered Dak, of course. Philip Agadakos had been Jericho's friend, protégé, and aide-de-camp in the White House, at Defense, and at the Central Intelligence Agency—his tool, people said, in the dirtier jobs, although a few revisionist histories suggested that Dak had tried to restrain his boss from the worst of his potential excesses: suggestions, she suspected, planted by Dak and his supporters club. They had trained together at the Agency in the sixties, before Jericho had departed for his stint in the overt world, then begun his climb to the top. Bob Woodward's book about their tangled careers had been titled *The A & A Boys,* a nickname from their early years. Jericho had very publicly hated it.

"That's nice," she said after a moment.

Jericho grinned nastily. "Yes. Nice. Very nice, the way old friends come to watch you die."

"I thought the two of you were in regular touch."

"You'll have heard that from Sean, I expect. Oh, don't look at me that way. I know about the two of you. Anno Domini, to be sure, but one is still not entirely without one's contacts. Do you really think my son can have an extramarital affair without my learning of it?"

She was on her feet. "I am *not* having an affair with Sean!"

Hand on withered chest, clotted voice all wounded virtue: "Did I say you were?"

"You implied it!"

"Oh, sit down." Back at his soy patty. "You look ridiculous, pretending you're going to walk out on me. Sit."

"No."

But she did not bolt from the room. She stood there, watching him eat. Jericho had always had this ability to get under her skin with his clever pinpricks, teasing and teasing until she exploded. Sean was the same way. Rebecca saw him from time to time when she was in New York or he was in Washington; he was her principal source of news about the family. But whatever Jericho might think, the two of them were friends, nothing more; and if Sean, married and a father, occasionally hinted at a willingness to transform their friendship into something more intimate, Beck did her best to ignore his signals.

If Jericho was aware of her uneasiness, he offered no sign. He flipped the pages of his will, occasionally making a note with a red marker. There were hundreds of pages. She had never heard of a will that long, but she had never been that kind of rich.

"Sean thinks I'm a monster. Did you know that?" Another bite. "So does Cousin Maggie, for that matter." The junior Senator from Vermont. "The two of them think people who do what I do—what I did—are the death of our nation. They think we'd be better off without our spies. Fancy that. The American idea destroyed by Jericho Ainsley." He peered at her over the rim of his glasses, putting on the donnishness she had once adored. "How do you stand on that one, actually? Am I a monster?"

"No," she said, too shortly, not liking herself in this mood, and glad it was he who had broken the brief silence. She remembered that *Don Giovanni* was a tale of passion, betrayal, and murder.

"I am, though. A monster." He seemed inordinately pleased. "I lived a monster, I'll die a monster. America needs monsters. We're the Morlocks. We stay underground, but we keep the machinery working. The rest of you get to pretend we don't exist." He coughed. "I'm a monster, and proud of it. Whereas you, my dear—"

She never found out whether an insult or a compliment was coming—he could do either in the same donnish tone—because, at that moment, the lights flickered, came back, went out. Both of them waited, staring at the ceiling.

The lights came on again.

"They're just testing the system," said Jericho. "No need to worry yet."

"It's the storm."

He nodded vaguely. "Or an assault team getting ready." He took up his papers again. "If they cut the mains, there's a backup generator, but I suppose a proper team would shut that off, too, wouldn't they?"

"Jericho—"

"Cousin Maggie was here last week, the bitch." The golden eyes flashed with anger. Rebecca remembered how years ago, when his cousin was lieutenant governor of Vermont instead of a United States Senator, the mention of Margaret Ainsley's name had moved him to near-violent furies. "Did the girls tell you? Only stayed a couple of hours. Probably wanted to make sure I'm really dying. Staff came along. By now I'm sure she has a poll in the field on whether to attend the funeral of a monster like me. Whether to eulogize me or just send flowers. See what the voters have to say. Dear Cousin Maggie's running for the big chair next time. Her people will probably hit you up for money."

Beck raised her hands in surrender. "I'm not going to get in the middle of your family quarrels, Jericho. You know that."

"Of course I know. That's not why you're here." A clever grin. "I need your help, my dear. I want to tell you where the guns are."

"The guns?"

"I keep them in the basement. We'll need a couple today. You, me, Pamela, I suppose. I don't think Saint Audrey would take one. But the rest of us, I fear, must arm ourselves." Beck was sitting again. She did not remember precisely when the hand had grabbed her wrist. His tone was conversational. "You see, my dear, Dak is coming to the house to make me tell him certain things. After that, he plans to kill me."

CHAPTER 5

The Aide-de-Camp

(1)

Phil Agadakos arrived on the dot of four, just after a raggedy genius who, for a million dollars in small bills, was prepared to keep to himself his discovery of the secret code hidden in Jericho's books, and a pair of furious activists in an indistinct cause who sprayed red paint on the side of the abbey van and tried to do the same to Pamela when she opened the door but wound up flat on their backs, angry faces full of Mace. Gibbering on the gravel, rubbing their eyes, they threatened to call the police. Pamela had Deputy Mundy's card in the pocket of her fraying sweater. She handed the card to one of the writhing protesters.

No, said Audrey as the couple drove off down the drive. She did not want them arrested. The crumbling van looked better this way, defaced by a human hand rather than the random workings of road salt and acid rain.

"There isn't any acid rain in Colorado," said Pamela, sourly.

The next time the doorbell rang, she refused to answer, and so it was Audrey who actually admitted Dak.

He stepped into the great room with no more ceremony than a plumber, for Phil Agadakos remained, as Jericho had once called him, a man of no presence. His face was so plain as to defy description. Although not fat, he seemed somehow more wide than tall, and bald into the bargain, resembling at first glance the tired headwaiter at a restaurant on a side street into which you stumble on a rainy night, finding it empty, and with good reason. All he needed was the discolored smock and peeling plastic menus. Rebecca, rising from the sofa near the window where she had been reading her Danticat, was surprised at how little he had changed. He glanced sadly around, drooping a bit, then waved a shyly endearing hello, and she had to remind herself that he was a master spy with blood aplenty on his conscience.

If he had a conscience.

"Rebecca," he said, taking her hands in his, when he was done greeting and commiserating with the sisters. Like Pamela, Dak never used her nickname. Audrey had already vanished into the kitchen, as if that was her proper place. "You're here. I thought you might be. I didn't know for sure. I didn't dare hope."

"Hope?" she answered, very surprised.

The old spy nodded. "He's missed you, Rebecca. You have no idea how he's missed you. He talks about you all the time."

"He does not."

"But he does. We're the A & A boys, remember? He tells me everything, Rebecca, and, believe me, the year and a half with you was the happiest time of Jericho's life. So to find you here now—well, your lovely presence is sure to ease his passing."

She blushed, and went on blushing. "I'll do whatever I can."

Dak still had not released her hands. His long fingers were warm and strong and loose and confident, the fingers of a man on good terms with tools of all kinds. If half the stories were true, these fingers had committed astonishing violence. *Dak is coming to the house to make me tell him certain things. After that, he plans to kill me.*

"Do you really mean that?" he asked, pale eyes holding her.

Beck hesitated, sensing that more was at stake than a pleasantry. "I don't want him to suffer," she said carefully.

"Jericho hasn't lived an ordinary life, Rebecca. He isn't likely to have an ordinary death." He paused, perhaps waiting for her to challenge this, but she was listening keenly now, for, in her secret self, ever since her uncertain childhood, listening had always been what she did best. "He might ask you to do things that are . . . unusual." Another pause. "Maybe he already has."

A weak stab at lightening the mood: "Other than hop into bed with him, you mean?"

Dak was not a smiler. He did not smile now. "Be alert, Rebecca. Be alert to every nuance. He asked you here for a reason. Not to say good-bye. The Jericho Ainsleys of this world don't bother with goodbyes. He's a great man, Rebecca, and it is in the nature of great men to want their great works to continue once they are gone." Another pause, as if waiting for her to write this down for posterity. "It may be that Jericho will seek to enlist you."

She laughed uneasily. "In what? You make it sound like he's at war."

A tight nod. "Jericho Ainsley has always been at war, Rebecca. Jericho will be at war until the day he dies."

"Which could be tomorrow."

"Yes." Serious as the grave. "And that's why I think, whatever he wants to enlist you in, he's likely to ask you soon."

As they parted, Beck put a hand on his arm. "Mr. Agadakos—"

"Dak."

"Yes. Dak. You should know—he's been talking about you."

"Has he?"

"He's not himself. He thinks you're going to kill him."

The old man gazed up at the balustrade. "I suppose he does," he said, entirely serious. "But I'm afraid it's too late for that." And, releasing his arm from her grasp, he headed for the stairs.

(11)

"I don't know," said Pamela. "He's been acting crazy the last few months. Ever since Dak started coming."

They were eating an early supper in the kitchen, salad and mountain trout. All three were exhausted. As a blessing, the driveway monitors were silent for once.

"How often has Dak come?" Beck asked. The two men had been closeted together in the master suite for over an hour now. She longed to interrupt, if only to check on Jericho's safety, but the daughters had seemed unperturbed when she shared their father's fears.

"Every two or three days," said Audrey. She ate very fast. She had forced them, unwillingly, to pray before the meal. Now she was energetically dabbing up olive oil with crusty bread, making a marvelous mess. Pamela and Rebecca avoided carbohydrates like the plague, but plump Audrey could hardly live without them. "That's just in the three weeks I've been here. Before that, I don't know."

"Crazy how?"

Pamela had recently quit smoking. She had little interest in eating. She chewed furiously on nicotine gum, and, like a B-actress doing hauteur, addressed herself to a point a foot above Beck's head. "Fixing things that aren't broken. Changing crap around for no reason. The alarm people were here three times in two weeks, and then he fired them anyway and hired a new contractor to rewire the place. They just finished. He had the roof replaced, right down to the last shingle, even though he just had it done last winter. The driveway. The storm doors. The well-water people were out twice in a week. New softening system. New pump. He switched satellite providers. Junked his old pickup, bought a fresh one right off the showroom floor, no waiting, charged it to his American Express Black Card."

"He was afraid of bugs," said Audrey.

"He was always afraid of bugs," said Beck, dubious. "He never tore up his house before."

"He was never dying before."

"And then there was the business of the garage," said Rebecca. The sisters turned her way. "I saw the padlocks. The fabric over the windows. The cars all parked outside, even in the snow." They were still waiting for her to finish. "He's hiding something in there."

Pamela snorted. "Something that takes up four garage bays? What do you think's in there, an airplane? Or maybe a crate full of zombies?"

"The locks were already on when I got here," said Audrey. "But there were these rumors about a delivery. Big wooden crates." Pamela glared, and her sister dropped her eyes. "I heard them in town."

"What rumors?" said Beck.

"Nothing," said the others, simultaneously.

"His mind is going," said Pamela. "We have to accept that." She got up from the table. "Nothing he does has to make any sense."

But after half a day of tending to Jericho's needs, Beck was already unsatisfied with the tempting simplicity of that answer. Maybe Jericho was mad, maybe he was sane. Either way, he remained the same schemer he had always been, seeing the world as a series of conspiracies, to be defeated by counterconspiracies. Pamela and Audrey might think they knew him, but Beck had known him better. She could tell when he was conspiring, and he was conspiring now. The question that troubled Beck was not precisely what Jericho might be up to: that was a very moot point. No, what she worried about was whether Phil Agadakos was right, that Jericho planned to make her a co-conspirator. And she remembered the tag line of a dreadfully biased but alarmingly penetrating documentary on Jericho's career produced by a popular leftish filmmaker who had won about twelve awards for it: *Whenever Jericho Ainsley had an idea, people died.*

"I think we should try to find out," she said.

"Find out what?" said Audrey.

"What's in the garage."

Pamela laughed. "You're not the mistress of this house any more, Rebecca. You're leaving on Thursday. We're here for the long haul. Nobody's breaking down any doors."

Beck was about to say something sharp in response when the *beep-beep-buzz* told them that a car had entered the forecourt.

The screen showed a red Ford Explorer, exactly like the one that had passed her on the road just before the dog was shot.

(III)

When the doorbell rang, Beck and Pamela were looking at the monitor. They saw a very tall man, skinny, almost scrawny, with a mop of fiery hair and a short beard to match. He was staring directly into the camera, features calm, letting them know that he was aware of their scrutiny. "Come on," said Pamela. "I'll show you how it's done."

"How what's done?" said Beck, hurrying after her.

"How we get rid of these nuisances. Like the couple I Maced today. I'm so sick of these people. Even in Hollywood, people don't pull this shit." She hesitated, licked her lips. Audrey was in the kitchen, washing up. "Tell you what, Rebecca. You do this one. Just be mean, and he'll go away. You remember how to do that, right? Be mean? That's when you hurt other people for no good reason."

Before Beck could answer, Pamela had the door open.

"May I help you?" Beck said, once she realized that everybody was waiting for her.

"Rebecca! What a pleasure to see you again. Remember me? Clark. Lewiston Clark." The redheaded visitor unveiled a brilliant smile, and held out a slender hand for a shake before Beck quite needed it. Then held on. His grasp was confiding, like an invitation to intimacy. She had no memory of ever meeting him before, so she supposed he was the type who greeted everyone that way, just in case. "Don't worry. I'm not crazy, and I'm not a reporter. Well, I am, but that's not why I'm here. I'm here to pick up my notes."

"What notes?" said Beck, having finally wrested her hand free.

Lewiston Clark had a smooth voice, mellifluous, made for television. His sentences were short, to accommodate commercial breaks. "I should apologize. For being away so long. The research took longer than we planned." He noticed Beck's confusion. "I'm sorry. I thought you knew. We've been working together. The Ambassador and I. I assume he's mentioned me?" Evidently he had not, because Pamela was squaring to start throwing things. "On his biography. That's what we're working on. I'm his authorized biographer." He seemed to be waiting for applause. "I have a contract. I have a letter—"

"I just bet he does," whispered Pamela, from behind.

"And, anyway, he was going to put together some notes for me. Scribblings, really. On those yellow pads he likes. I just came to pick them up."

Beck realized that the moment had arrived to do her job. "I'm sorry, Mr. Clark," she began. "This really isn't a good time."

"Of course. Of course. I do understand. But I think he'd be rather upset if you turned me away—"

"I'm afraid we'll just have to take that chance," said Pamela, edging Rebecca out of the way. "You'll have to come back."

The smile broadened. "Pamela. You're Pamela."

"That's right. And it's not good to see me again, because I've never met you in my life."

Lewiston Clark toyed with his beard. "He would have left something for me. Notes for the biography. Or he might have written 'auto-biography' on it, but he means me."

"Another time, Mr. Clark," said Pamela, starting to swing the door. "I'll be sure to tell him you came by."

"I was his student," the writer persisted. "This was years ago. I was his student, and then we worked together. I know the Ambassador's memory is slipping, but I can't believe he hasn't told you about me." Actually Jericho had never been a real ambassador. As Director of Central Intelligence, he had held the rank as a courtesy when traveling abroad, but nobody used the title except for people who wanted to pretend to be in the know. "I should say, by the way, that it's an honor to work with him, and—"

As Pamela went through her chilly explanations again, the visitor's eyes lifted, and widened, and Beck turned to see what had caught his attention. Up on the landing, Phil Agadakos had emerged from the sickroom. Jericho used to say that Dak had the best poker face he had ever seen; even so, a shock of recognition passed over his tired features before he suppressed it; and when Rebecca turned back to look at Lewiston Clark, she spotted the smiling wariness with which she herself had learned to soldier through unexpected encounters with creditors, or ex-lovers, or old adversaries.

They knew each other.

CHAPTER 6

The Interrogation

She left Pamela to deal with the pushy visitor, and crossed the creaky foyer to greet Dak as he descended the stairs. "How's he doing?" she asked.

Phil Agadakos was not looking at her. He continued to stare at the bearded man being refused entrance by an adamant Pamela.

"Mr. Agadakos?"

"Yes?" Eyes still on the door, now successfully shut.

"Does he want me?"

"Hmmm?"

"What did he say? Is he awake?"

"He's fine," the old spy said, and Beck knew he was hardly listening. The blue eyes had lost their grandfatherly quality, regaining a shadow of the chill that she remembered from another age. "Fine," he said again.

Pamela joined them. She had at last managed to get Lewiston Clark off the doorstep. "Are you staying for dinner, Dak?" she asked sweetly. "We have a freezer full of trout."

He conjured a small pucker that was almost a smile. "Alas, duty calls."

"Duty?"

"Work."

"I thought you were retired," teased Pamela, who could be warm and welcoming as spring, or chilly and forbidding as mountain snow.

"Retired from a particular job, yes. Retired from my line of work—well, one never really retires, does one?"

Pamela laughed, although nothing seemed funny, and headed off to the kitchen to join Audrey, who, in the continued absence of Jimmy Lobb, had taken on the household chores.

Dak waited until the kitchen door was firmly shut. His smile vanished. He turned back to Beck.

"Who was that man at the door? The redhead?"

"A writer. Clark, Lewiston Clark. He's working on Jericho's biography. Used to be his student."

Mr. Agadakos tugged at his vague clouds of hair. "Are you sure?" he finally said.

"Of what?"

"That he's who he says he is."

Beck looked at the closed door. From the kitchen came quarreling voices: the two sisters, not quite getting along. It occurred to her that Audrey had barely said hello to her father's oldest friend, and had not come out to say goodbye. Maybe nuns, like other people, held grudges. Maybe Dak was the reason for the fight. She wondered what the grudge could be.

"All I know is what he told me," Beck said. "I didn't ask him for ID."

"In the future, maybe you should." He puffed out a lot of air, then unlimbered himself. He tufted his hair some more, and the deep-blue eyes grew warm again, so suddenly that Rebecca knew it was an act.

"You know him. I saw it in your face."

"I met him a few years ago. He wanted to interview me for a book on the Agency. I said no. And, so far, no book. He's nobody, Rebecca. A hack writer. Forget him."

"He said he's working with Jericho."

"Once upon a time, I'd have said that Jericho wouldn't give the time of day to a twerp like that. Now? Who knows?"

He opened the door. Chilly wind snapped in. She felt his alertness tauten, and stretch outward, farther even than his eyes could see. He was like an animal, scenting the air for predators; or prey. Evidently satisfied, he drew her onto the front step. He was concerned about microphones, she decided. Just like Jericho.

"What's going on, Dak? Is there something we should know?"

But Phil Agadakos had Jericho's trick of answering the question he wanted to rather than the one you asked. "Tell you what." He pulled a notebook from his pocket. "If you're worried, I'll have somebody give the state police a call. See if they can't put a car down at the end of the driveway. How does that—"

He stopped. His head jerked upward. Her gaze followed his. The cold rain had taken a hiatus. In the glowering sky, the helicopter was passing overhead. Dak had heard the engine before she had; and the expression on his tired face was one of such utter contempt that if he'd had a gun, he'd have been trying to shoot it down.

"This is not a good moment," he said, "to know what Jericho knows."

(11)

Very gently, Dak took her hand and led her down the steps, until she was standing beside him. "I need you to do something for me," he said.

"Something like what?"

"Keep an eye on him."

"That's why I'm here."

He shook his head impatiently. "That's not what I mean, Rebecca." He glanced at the house. "Jericho hasn't been entirely right for a long time. In the head, I mean. He hasn't been right for a good fifteen years." He read her dark thoughts on her face. "No, honey, no. It's not your fault. It's not. Okay? If anything, what happened with you was a symptom, not a cause. Okay? I'm not saying what he felt for you wasn't genuine—isn't still—only that the Jericho I used to know would never have yielded to his passions, no matter how powerful, or pure."

Beck turned her gaze aside. She said nothing. They were standing beside his car.

"I don't mean he would never have cheated on Lana. He would. He did. You must know that. Before you, yes, he had his flings. In our business, well, when you have a fling, you report it. There's even jargon for it. Unveiling, we call it. That's what you do, you unveil your relationships to a security officer. We say, it's better to unveil than to be unveiled. And Jericho, well, Jericho did a fair amount of unveiling. But he never left Lana. He never wanted to hurt her or the kids. Okay?"

"Okay."

"He had his flings, he unveiled them, and life went on. That's the key. Life went on."

"I said—okay."

Maybe it was the rising wind that made Dak's voice seem harsher. Or maybe, old spy that he was, he had sensed her shrinking, and was in pursuit. "Now, Rebecca, let's do the hard part. Flash back to fifteen years ago. He left the Agency and went to Princeton because he had to. He was being pushed out. He could call it a sabbatical, but it was intended all along to be permanent. That isn't in his official bio, and it hasn't shown up in any of the unofficial ones, either, but it's a fact. Whatever is wrong in his head was going wrong that last year or eighteen months of his term as Director. Okay? Now. This is what happened. We didn't tell anybody. How could we? Washington still remembers Angleton."

Beck, as it happened, did not, but she was not about to break the spell.

"So, we kept it in-house," Dak continued. "Some people went to see him. Maybe I was one of them. The delegation told him what had to happen. Told him why. Jericho was no fool. He left the Agency. Told the President it was time to give the academy a chance, at least for a while. He went to Princeton, the Institute for Advanced Study. He didn't take his family with him. He left them down in Virginia. He fell in love with you. He left them, brought you up here. You remember those days."

"Faintly," Beck said, wiping her eyes. Still, she remained alert. Dak might be doing the talking, but she was the one under interrogation.

Philip Agadakos was not a man one could tease. At least, he was not a man who teased back. "I remember them, too. But for a different reason. You can't imagine it, Rebecca. The storm he left behind. The Director of Central Intelligence seems to be losing his bearings. Then he takes up with—I'm sorry—with a sexy teenaged seductress. That's what we thought. Once I met you, yes, you were very sweet, but, from Langley, it looked like a setup. As if our enemies, say, had wind of Jericho's mental problems, and had put you in his path. You can imagine the panic. The former DCI, former SecDef, former everything, sleeping with a nineteen-year-old. Not just a fling. Leaving his wife. Buying a house so she could move in with him. What secrets was he whispering to you in bed? What was your motive? Who were you, really? You were under a microscope, Rebecca. Every second of your life was studied. And, I'm sorry to say, when the two of you were together—every time you were together—we were listening in. It wasn't legal, and it wasn't the behavior of gentlemen, but we had to know. I'm sorry, Rebecca. You asked."

She would cry later, she decided. Cry, throw things, slit her wrists, whatever came to mind. Right now, however, at this crucial moment, she would be—well, what Jericho would have been. Rock solid. Even disdainful. She was close. Everything was about to pivot. She could feel it.

"That's not all," she said. When Dak waited, she fed him the next piece of the story. "You got down in the gutter, you listened to us in bed for a year and a half. Well, if you were listening, you heard Jericho tell me you were listening. Two, three times a day, he would remind me. First I thought he was playing games, then I decided he was nuts after all. But he wasn't. You were listening. And if you listened, you know he didn't betray any secrets. The only thing you heard in bed was Jericho telling me which way he wanted it tonight. So—that isn't why you're worried. There's more."

"You were always smart."

"Tell me the rest."

Again he looked down the road, then off at the woods, cut back the regulation fifty yards on every side. Nothing stirred in the cold mountain afternoon; or nothing to rouse an old spy's suspicions.

"There isn't any more," Agadakos said after a moment. His smile was kind, and a little sad. "He's an old man, Rebecca. He's dying. He's not sure what his life meant, so he wants to make sure his death means something." He laughed. "And he sure has a lot of people paying attention, doesn't he?"

Beck refused to be deflected. "But what is it? What does he want his death to mean? He's plotting something, Dak. Maybe the two of you together. And we"—waving toward the house—"we're caught in the middle."

"There's no danger, Rebecca, if that's what you're wondering. It's nothing like that."

"That isn't what I asked."

"The truth is, Jericho's malady isn't that unusual. The work we do, especially the people at what we call the hard end—there have been a few serious problems over the years. Not just from post-traumatic stress. The tension in general." A look of pain flitted over his face, then was gone. "And even at the soft end, well, we don't put it on our Web site, but there are people who survive our psychological screening but still can't take the pressure."

"Including Jericho?"

"Nobody knows what triggered his illness. But we have to deal with the reality. So, please, Rebecca. Just keep an eye on him. He's lying there with a head full of secrets. I'd hate to think that—in his illness—he'd start to babble about some attempted coup from thirty years ago."

Rebecca's eyes, like Dak's, were on the gravel drive, where it wound into the trees, but her gaze was on the past. In their year and a half together, Jericho had never let a secret slip through his lips. Not once. "That's why you're here," she said flatly. "In case he tells what he shouldn't."

"Something like that."

"So I suppose the helicopter is keeping an eye on him, too, huh?" No answer. Emboldened, she crossed the line. "And what if Jericho does talk about some coup from thirty years ago? What are you going to do? Euthanize him?" Still Agadakos said nothing. "There's something else going on, Dak. Why don't you tell me?"

He had the car door open. An experienced interrogator, like a good stage magician, knew when to leave them wanting more. "Because you haven't earned it."

"How do I do that?"

"You have my numbers," he said, face toward the distant craggy peaks. "I'm at the Red Roof Inn in Bethel, but it's better to use my cell, because I'm constantly up and down these mountains. Call me if anything changes."

"Cell phones don't work up here."

The ghost of a smile. He had the door of his rental car open. "Mine does." Dak climbed in and started the engine. Beck stood in the forecourt, watching as he vanished down the drive, wondering if a single word of his story was true.

MONDAY NIGHT

CHAPTER 7

The Summons

(1)

Audrey was explaining how to prepare Jericho's macrobiotic meals. Beck made careful notes about the shoyu soup and raw vegetables, and even kept a straight face when they reached the hemp milk, but was forced to stifle a giggle when, working through the various whole grains, the nun showed her something called psyllium husk, which sounded less like a cancer-killing food than the name of a radio superhero from the old days. They were going over the rules for brewing Jericho's tea when Pamela walked in.

"Sean's definitely not coming," she said, crossly, marching past them to hang up the portable phone. She did not excuse herself. She did not ask if this was a bad time. She launched herself immediately onto the subject she wanted to discuss. It was a bit past six, and the sun had long since dipped behind the peaks. "I talked to him three times today. Do you know what he said? 'That old bastard lived fine without me. He can die without me, too.' I said, 'This is our father, Sean.' And Sean said, 'He was never my father. He only ever wanted daughters.' "

"That's not true," said Audrey, pleasantly. She was still munching on pieces of the bread from supper. She had shopped in town this morning. A huge pot was simmering, a soup, she promised, that they could all four eat tomorrow: meaning it would be suitably unseasoned, and tasteless. "He loved all of us the same."

"They never got along," her sister persisted. "Even when Sean was a baby, he never let Dad hold him if he was crying—remember, Aud? Mom had to hold him, or even you or me, but never Dad. You wouldn't know this, Rebecca—not unless Dad told you—but when Sean was a boy, they had this terrible fight, I forget over what, and Sean told Dad he hated him for the way he'd treated Mom—you weren't his first little fling, Rebecca, not by a long shot, but I guess you know that—and, well, anyway, Dad hit him—"

"Not all that hard," cautioned Audrey.

"Three stitches. That's what they put in his forehead. His own son. If it had been anybody but the President's Deputy National Security Advisor"—she frowned, perhaps not sure precisely which title Jericho had held at that particular moment—"well, they would have had him up on charges."

"He was repentant," said Audrey. "He got down on his knees and asked Mom to forgive him."

"Mom wasn't the one he hit."

"He stopped using his hands after that," Audrey persisted. "He was a changed man." She was fixing herself a sandwich. "And he never laid a finger on Mom."

"He hit Rebecca, though," said Pamela, eyes glittering in malicious triumph. "Didn't he?"

Rebecca met her old adversary's gaze. She shook her head, but said nothing.

"He confessed to Mom. This was later, after he came to his senses and was trying to get her back. Dad told Mom, Mom told me."

"That's absurd," said Audrey, and looked to Beck for confirmation.

Beck took her time. Pamela had touched a nerve, but not the one she thought. Yes, Jericho had a temper. No, he had never laid a hand on Rebecca: not in anger. The DeForde household of her youth had been stormy. Beck had seen how her father treated her mother. She would not have spent five minutes with a man who behaved that way. "I'm sorry, Pamela. I'm afraid you've been misinformed."

Pamela nodded. With satisfaction. "You know what? You lie just like he does. The same words, the same intonation, the same every-thing."

An awkward silence, which the nun at last tried to break: "Nobody knows what's become of Mr. Lobb. I asked all over town. Everybody said they assumed he was up here. I even went to his house. No truck, no Jimmy Lobb, not even that mad dog of his. It's weird."

"Too weird," muttered Beck. The others barely reacted, perhaps thinking her comment intended to reinforce Audrey's. But she was thinking about how Dak had come but not stayed, how Sean was refus-ing to leave New York, how Jimmy Lobb, after years of faithful service, had vanished into thin air. It was almost as if somebody wanted the three women alone in the house with no male present but Jericho him-self.

The notion was absurd, and sexist to boot, but she could not get it out of her head. And Dak—it seemed to her that he had thought she knew something, or that Jericho was going to ask her something—

Why don't you tell me?

Because you haven't earned it.

"If Mr. Lobb doesn't turn up by tomorrow," Beck said, "we should get somebody else up here."

Pamela's chilly gaze challenged her. "For what? To do the chores? Fix the roof?"

"Clean up the next dead dog," said Audrey, in an ineffectual stab at defusing the mood.

"I'd feel better." Beck knew this sounded lame. "We should have another man around. Just to be on the safe side."

"The safe side? What are we supposed to be worried about?"

Beck was not sure how to frame her answer. She was the one with the misbehaving cell phone. She was the one being chased by a heli-copter. She was the one who should be home with her daughter, and would be, but Jericho needed her. Suddenly that fact emerged with crystal clarity. Jericho Ainsley needed her. He had not summoned her out of caprice, or malice, or even to say goodbye. He had called her for a purpose.

A serious purpose.

She did not know yet what Jericho would ask of her, and she certainly did not know what her answer would be. But she knew she had to give him the chance. She had loved him once, and he had loved her back. Even though Dak insisted that Jericho had been eased out of public life, in Beck's romantic image he nevertheless had tossed away his career for her, and, like it or not, her mother had raised her to a sense of obligation so powerful that few competing priorities could stand against it. Dr. Eisenstadt, her therapist, had tried to help her overcome her guilt about the end of Jericho's career.

So far, without noticeable effect.

"Trust me," said Beck.

"Trust *you*?" laughed Pamela.

"He's ringing," said Audrey, on her feet, but they all heard the same buzzer.

"I'll go this time," said her sister, and hurried off toward the stairs.

Audrey turned to Beck. "What was that about?"

"What was what about?"

"You're scared."

"That's ridiculous."

But Audrey for once refused to let go. "Did Dak say something to you? If he did, you should tell us. It's not right to keep it to yourself."

Rebecca looked at the round, worried face. Audrey's plump fingers were cradling the cross around her neck. "You sound pretty scared yourself."

"I don't like all these people coming to the house." She glanced at the archway to the foyer. "And Pamela—she's not usually like this. Really, Beck. She's not. I know the two of you don't get along, but—well, she's worried. Maybe it's just Dad dying. Maybe it's something else. I don't know. She hasn't been herself since she arrived."

"Since *she* arrived, or since *I* arrived?"

Audrey took a ferocious bite of her sandwich. "What is it with you two? My dad is upstairs dying, and you guys won't even try to—"

She stopped. Beck's cell was ringing. Audrey looked impressed, presumably because they didn't work up here. Beck lifted it slowly to her ear, knowing what to expect. And was not disappointed. A blast of static. The fax whine. With a shudder, she pressed the red button.

"Wrong number?" said a voice behind her. Pamela stood in the doorway. "He wants you, Beck." Her tone was listless. "He's agitated. He gets this way sometimes. Please don't upset him."

(11)

Tonight was different. Tonight she was afraid. Not of Jericho. For Jericho. She climbed the wide stairs to the second floor while the sisters chattered in the kitchen, and she might have been back at Princeton, in the echoing stairwell at the Institute for Advanced Study, shivering as she made her way to Professor Ainsley's drafty office. When she reached the landing, she almost expected to see the bookshelves and portraits that had lined the halls of the dingy but prestigious building. She stood outside the double doors to the master suite, hesitating with her hand on the knob, much the way she used to hesitate before slipping into Professor Ainsley's office suite, and trying, with mixed success, to wheedle her way past Mrs. Blumen, the professor's intimidating secretary, who had come up to Princeton with the great man when he left the Agency.

Then he takes up with a sexy teenaged seductress. That's what we thought.

That's what Mrs. Blumen thought, too. Rebecca would hear it in the acid tone every time she called for an appointment; she would read it in the furious protective glare every time she showed up; she would sense it from the set of the broad back when she tiptoed out again, now and then slightly disheveled, and Mrs. Blumen was hunched over her typewriter, pounding away in anger until the nasty little harlot left. Of course it had never occurred to Mrs. Blumen, any more than it had to Phil Agadakos and his crowd, that Jericho might have been the seducer; that he might have taken advantage of a starry-eyed nineteen-year-old who had bluffed and begged her way into his seminar, braving the boycotts and protests from those who wanted him kicked off campus for his crimes; that Beck herself might have been the wronged party.

The possibility of Jericho's fault had never occurred to them because they were trying to protect him, and when we love someone enough to offer protection, we prefer to imagine that the object of our affections is always in the right. Mrs. Blumen had taken care of Jericho Ainsley for most of his professional career; and now she was gone, as were most of his friends, and there was nobody left to protect him.

Nobody but three women who could not manage to get along.

(III)

His eyes were closed when she took the chair beside the bed. A different book was on the night table now, a collection of classic chess problems. Jericho's hand was chilly, but she kept squeezing it, wanting to gift him her warmth. She called his name, then again, louder, and he seemed to smile. He looked so healthy still. She wondered what kind of God would create a world where people had to die, and why Audrey worshiped Him. She wondered what Pamela was worried about, and whether Dak was as crazy as Jericho. She remembered Jericho in the old days. He had struck her as eccentric, but in possession of his senses: brilliant, and handsome, and commanding. She thought about their first night together, and how he had guessed that she was a virgin. *I know things,* he had told her, eyes fiery and delighted. *I just know things.*

And she remembered, too, the afternoon Jericho's cousin Maggie, in those days lieutenant governor of Vermont, had come to talk to the seminar, back when they were still trying to hide their relationship. There were thirty-two students, and Beck's seat was toward the back, but she felt Margaret Ainsley's judgmental gaze on her for the entire two hours. The next day, she met Jericho in his office.

She knows, Beck had told him. *Your cousin knows.*

She's like me, he said. *She just knows things.*

"Did you ask her?" he said suddenly, jolting Beck back to the present. She saw that his eyes were open. Maybe they had been open for a while. She realized that she had no idea, because she had been dozing.

"I'm sorry." Rubbing her eyes. "The mountain air. Uh. Ask who?"

"Audrey. You were supposed to ask her why she quit the family business. Why she left her husband." He gestured. "Pain pills. Give me lots. Don't look at me like that. I can't sleep without them, not for more than an hour. Maybe I'm addicted, but I don't actually think it matters. Do you?"

She got the pills, poured water from the carafe. "Did you and Dak have a nice visit?"

"Help me turn on my side."

She did that, too. His body felt warm and vigorous. It was difficult to accept that he might only have weeks. She remembered how her mother had shaved her father near the end, so that he would not have to go to the mortuary looking ragged. She wondered if anybody would bother shaving Jericho.

"Yes," he said.

"Yes, what?"

"Yes, we had a lovely visit. Simply lovely. Poor man. It's driving him crazy. I bet by now he's recruited you to keep an eye on me, hasn't he?"

Beck was back in the chair, holding his hand. "What's driving him crazy?"

"I won't tell him, and he doesn't know if I'm bluffing."

"Won't tell him what?"

A wolfish grin. "See? He's recruited you. He would."

"Nobody recruited me to do anything, Jericho."

"Not yet, maybe." He yawned. "But once you start working with me, you're going to become very popular."

"What exactly am I working with you on?"

He flashed the roguish grin she had once adored and pointed at the stack of pages from this afternoon.

"Your will?"

"It's not a will. Ask Audrey. She'll tell you what it is. I don't have time to finish it. I want you to finish it."

Because Audrey turned you down, she decided suddenly. This was what Dak was asking about, whatever was in the folder, and Audrey wanted nothing to do with it.

"What is it? In the folder?"

"Beck, listen," he said, dying mind already on to another subject. But she was listening already. "Any unusual visitors? Anybody who seemed suspicious?"

About to dismiss the question, Beck had a thought. "There was one. A writer. Lewiston Clark. Red beard. He said he's working with you on your autobiography."

"Working with me. That's a hoot. Acts like he wants to be my Boswell, but what he really wants is to be my Iago. My evil genius," he translated unnecessarily. "He's a fool, Beck. A pushy little fool. Called a couple of times. He wants me to tell him secrets. But I don't tell secrets. I keep secrets."

"He said you had something for him. Notes. Papers, maybe." She eyed the thick document.

"Then he's a lying little fool." A crafty look came over the tired face. "You remember him, Beck, don't you? Young Mr. Clark?"

"No. But he acted like he remembered me."

"I'm quite sure he did. You were rather a memorable undergraduate my dear."

She was surprised. "Was he at Princeton?"

"Practically led the protests. Against me. Invaded my classroom. Figured he must have hit on you, the way you got around."

Beck let this thrust slip past her. She was recalling the incursions, the ragtag group of angry students who would barge into the seminar every other week or so, chanting their slogans, waving their signs. And she remembered, hazily, a scrawny kid with red hair—

"That was him?"

A nod. "G. Lewiston Clark himself. 'G' is for 'Gordon,' and that was what he called himself in those days. Gordon Clark. Arrogant little prick then, arrogant little prick now. Lewiston Clark. Get it? That's the problem with journalism today, isn't it? Lot more interested in being clever than being wise. Gordon Clark. Think he wound up with a *summa*, didn't he? A *magna*, anyway."

She shrugged. She had no idea. Those who drop out of college rarely keep close track of the achievements of those who finish.

The hand came up and seized her wrist. "Don't let him have it. My notes. Promise me."

"I promise." She patted his hand. "What's he up to? He said you're working together. Why would he tell an obvious lie like that?"

"I wouldn't know, my dear. But Mr. Clark is the mercenary sort of writer. He writes only books that can get him on television. Scandals. Lies. If you want to know what he's up to, find out who's paying him."

While she considered this, he grinned again. "Now, don't worry, Beck. My papers aren't what Dak is looking for. Not sophisticated enough." Whether he meant his old friend or the papers was unclear. "Don't worry," he said again, subsiding.

"I won't worry."

"Good girl." The fire was gone again. "And ask Audrey. Don't forget."

"I'll ask her."

"It's not your fault," he whispered. "Don't let Dak make you feel guilty. You don't owe him anything. Neither do I." His eyes were closed. All at once the words were an effort. "They forced me out, Beck. They shouldn't have done that. They all got together. They forced me out, and now it's my turn."

"Your turn to do what?"

No answer.

Rebecca waited a bit, whispered his name, stroked his hand. When he seemed to be sleeping peacefully, she bade him good night, kissed his forehead, stood up, headed for the door.

"Becky."

The voice froze her. He had not called her Becky since—well, since. "Yes, Jer-Bear?" she said, the nickname slipping out before she thought about it.

"It's not my will."

She moved back toward the bed. He was trying to sit up, eyes alive with a desperate energy. "You told me, honey. Please rest."

He smiled, and slept.

Or pretended to.

(IV)

She was tempted. She knew he wanted her to be. She had held his hand for a while, just like last night, but now was on her way to the door, and there it was, the very folder he wanted her to protect and also to finish, a couple of hundred pages, sitting there unguarded. She turned toward the bed. He was on his side, back turned toward her. He would never know.

And yet he would. Of course he would. Jericho just knew things, and whether or not he was awake, he had left the folder as some kind of trap. That was how his mind worked, sick or well. All the world was conspiracies, and counterconspiracies, and whether one was plotting the overthrow of another government, a corporate takeover, or just your everyday seduction of a wide-eyed student, all Jericho cared about was coming out on top.

Dak, she was thinking. Dak would find the papers useless. Jericho had said so. But Phil Agadakos knew what was going on, and he had promised her information, as soon as she had something to trade. And he had no way to know that the papers were not what he was looking for.

Beck slipped into the hall, leaving the papers undisturbed as she shut the door behind her.

CHAPTER 8

The Deputy

(1)

The town of Bethel was thirty-two miles from Stone Heights, most of the road downhill, and pointed away from civilization. The first white settlers had been members of a separatist religious sect, and a mossy plaque in Veterans Park commemorated the founders with noble lies about their brave battles against the local Indian tribes. Jericho, she remembered from the old days, was a great admirer of the plaque. *You tell a lie long enough and loud enough,* he used to say, *and it's the man who knows the truth who sounds like the idiot.*

She parked the car on Main Street and made her way to a café called Corinda's Corner. Corinda was a thousand-year-old country singer waiting to be discovered. At night, she sat on the low stage, crooning her own compositions, amid the smoke and alcohol. Rebecca took a booth in the front, near the window, so that she could watch the parking lot. A robust waitress whose name tag christened her Zeelie brought a light beer. The place was half empty—Beck supposed due to the lateness of the hour, although another possible cause was the music. Or maybe it was never full. She had never been here before. She had used her cell to call Phil Agadakos as soon as she was far enough down the mountain to have service, and this was the place he had named. Ten sharp, Dak had insisted, and it was five minutes past. The drive had been longer than she remembered. She hoped he had not left because she was late. Beck sat and sipped and wondered if she might be on a fool's errand.

Jericho had already been crazy when they met. That was the sum of the message Dak had delivered this afternoon. She had been in love with a madman. All those memories, the fantasy life he had bestowed on her, the money, the gifts, the flowers, the places: the entire romance had been the product of a diseased mind.

All these years, in her secret self, Rebecca had looked back at her time with Jericho with the knowledge that she had, just once in her life, snared the storybook prince. Whatever else might have happened in the course of her existence—so Beck would whisper to herself in the long chilly nights—a rich and powerful man had once been madly in love with her. The former Secretary of Defense, former Director of Central Intelligence—*former everything*, as Dak put it—wealthy and powerful and dashing on top of it, madly in love with her.

Madly is right.

"What's that, honey?" said Zeelie, back with a fresh bottle, and Rebecca realized she must have spoken aloud.

"I didn't order another," Beck protested, for she wanted to keep a clear head.

"You've got an admirer," said the waitress, nodding toward a dark corner near the stage, where a couple of men had their heads together.

"Who?"

"Name's Pete. He's in here most nights. He's a cop."

"His last name wouldn't be Mundy, would it?"

"Oh, so you guys know each other. How cool is that?"

A moment later, Deputy Mundy and the other man were standing beside her booth. "Good to see you again," he said, eyes taking her in with a good deal more enthusiasm than he had shown earlier today. He introduced the darker man beside him, his fellow deputy and occasional partner, Tony Frias, "who was just on his way out."

"I was?" said Tony. He grinned. "Oh, right. I was." He winked at Beck. "Be careful. He's a married man."

Frias made his exit, flirting with Zeelie and any other woman in earshot. Rebecca watched him go. She felt Mundy watching her.

"I looked you up," said the deputy, sliding into the booth.

Beck turned toward him. He sipped his own beer. Behind the glasses, his eyes were warmer than this morning, but still appraising. "Looked me up?"

He nodded. "You were the only stranger in the house. You could have done the dog, and lots of the other shit that's been going on. Excuse my French. Anyway, I looked you up." He had carried the ugly remains of a roast-beef sandwich from his own booth. He bit into it now, chewed slowly. "I didn't realize. You're the one he had the affair with, aren't you?"

She colored. "I guess you could put it that way."

"I thought you'd be older. That was a long time ago."

"I am older."

The deputy almost smiled. Not quite, but almost, and the florid cheeks grew round and friendly. "You don't look older. You look—nice."

Not sure how to take this, Rebecca just nodded and sipped her beer. She looked around. The small crowd was mostly strangers hunting desperately for one another as they fought to stay young. There was country music, disconsolate dancing, and the sad barroom smell of rancid beer and ancient sweat.

"There's a lot of strangers in town lately, Ms. DeForde," said Mundy after a moment. "We're not sure what they're all doing here—"

"Please, call me Beck."

"I'm Pete." A pause, each feeling the other out. "Just this week, six or seven people we've never seen before are here. You're just one of them. A town like this, that many strangers—you get my meaning."

"I'm not sure I do." She hesitated. "Pete."

"Makes people nervous. That's all I'm saying. One or two reporters. Fine. They interview the fella who picks up Dr. Ainsley's trash. Talk to the gardener. No story, so they leave town. Then somebody does the dog up there on Dr. Ainsley's property, and last week there was the break-in at the public library—I mean, who breaks into a library?—but the librarian's desk gets rifled, all kinds of books get thrown on the floor. Miss Kelly—she's the librarian—she gets a bunch of the ladies together, they clean up the place, and then Miss Kelly tells us nothing's missing. Not one book, not one file. The sheriff, well, he thinks it's kids, having fun. I think it's the strangers."

Beck thought about what Jericho had said, that there were things Dak wanted him to tell. Pamela and Audrey had described his crazy behavior since the cancer reached his brain. She wondered if somebody—Phil Agadakos, say, or Lewiston Clark—thought Jericho had hidden something in the library. She glanced at the clock on the wall. Almost half past ten. Where was Dak?

"You're meeting somebody," said Pete, tracking her eyes.

"Yes. Sorry."

He shrugged. "Nothing to be sorry for. I just thought you and I might have another drink." He downed his beer. The wedding band glistened in the spill of light from outside. "Talk about what's been going on in town."

"What makes you think I know anything about it?"

"I want you to do something for me." The gaze had turned earnest, the voice cold sober. "Very slowly. Raise your eyes, look over my shoulder, at the table in the back, under the fake boar's head. See the couple?"

She did. A man and a woman, early thirties, heads together, smoking and drinking and giggling. Both wore black.

"Yes."

"Now look at me, not at them." She did that, too. "Notice how they picked the one booth in the bar that lets you see the whole room?" She had not noticed, but was willing to take his word for it. When Pete Mundy put on his serious cap, he had that quality that the best teachers possessed, the sort of authoritative voice that creates a pleasant buzz in the back of your head. She was gaining a fresh appreciation of this man. "They got here twenty minutes before you did. Now, they're pretending to be so into each other they don't notice a thing. Really, they watched the door till you came in, and since then they've been watching you."

"Me?"

"You." Hunching forward. "They're two of the strangers. Staying at the Motel 6, got here a week ago, all they do every day is go off on long drives, come back at nightfall."

"Long drives."

"Up the peak," he said, and waited.

Strangers. Long drives. A week ago. "What kind of car—"

He was ahead of her. "Not a van. Not an Explorer. A Chevy Impala, blue. Rented in Denver, like yours."

"I haven't seen a car like that."

"It's not a car people notice. That's my point, Beck. Now, I don't know exactly what's going on here, but, the way those two are watching you, I have a hunch you might be in the middle of it. Anything you want to tell me?"

She shook her head in confusion. All of a sudden everybody wanted to protect her. First Jericho, then Dak, now Pete Mundy. And she did not even know what she was being protected from.

"I have a lot of respect for Dr. Ainsley," said the deputy, signaling for the check. "A lot of people don't like him, but he's a nice guy. He did good things for this country. We could use more like him. I'm sorry he's dying."

Dying. He had spoken the word. She looked down, trying to remember when the third beer had arrived.

"That's life," she said, inanely.

Meanwhile, Pete was passing another business card over the table. "Keep it this time," he said. "Call me if you need help."

"Cell phones—"

"Don't work up there. I know. But they work in town."

"Town is thirty miles—"

"All you have to do is turn right out of the gate and drive eight, nine miles downhill, and your cell should work just fine. Okay?"

"Okay." But she dropped her eyes, oppressed now by his intensity.

"If you need help, if you just want to talk—"

"I will."

"Good. I'll look forward to hearing from you." Lifting his gaze. "I think your friend is here."

She turned, but saw only the couple beneath the moose head. "I don't see him."

"In the front window. He was peeking in. I caught his face in the mirror. I've seen him around town. He's always going up there. To Stone Heights." He saw her expression. "I told you. It's my town. I keep an eye out. I know who he is. Used to be in the CIA, right? Deputy Director?" Behind the glasses he winked. "And he was looking for you, Beck. Definitely. He's pretty cautious. I'd guess he's waiting outside." He put a hand on her arm. "Listen. You go. Don't worry about these two."

"I wasn't worried about them," she lied, wondering whether the couple was watching her at all, or whether Pete was just trying to impress.

"Good. I've got this." Pointing to the drinks. "See you around."

She smiled back, nervously. "Yes. Thank you, Pete."

"You're welcome. Now go."

Beck walked to the door as calmly as she could. This was absurd. Outside, she glanced through the window in time to see the couple beneath the moose head slipping from their booth. The man threw some bills on the table. The woman in black was already threading her way past the tables. Then Pete Mundy was blocking her way, first serious, then laughing. The woman dropped her head and tried to shove past. Pete never budged. Her friend joined the argument. Tony Frias, Pete's scowling partner, materialized. There was some bumping and grabbing. Somebody threw a punch, and the whole bar went into an uproar, but by that time Beck was around the corner, because Phil Agadakos had taken her by the arm and was hurrying her toward the car.

(11)

"That was smoothly done," said Phil Agadakos. "Who's your new friend?"

They were sitting in her rental, and she was driving toward Route 24 and the commercial strip outside town. Dak wanted them moving, and warned her to keep the conversation going, because people riding in cars and not talking strike bystanders as angry, and angry people leave impressions.

"Pete Mundy. Deputy sheriff."

"What did he want?"

"Why were you late?" Her chin indicated the dashboard clock. "It's twenty of eleven."

But Dak would not be deflected. "What were the two of you talking about?"

"He wanted me to go somewhere with him. Have a drink."

"You could have had a drink right there."

She gave him a faux-sultry look. "I think he wanted to have a drink in more intimate circumstances," she drawled.

Dak did not believe her. She was sure of it. For a moment, she saw in his eyes the fierce skepticism with which the A & A boys had once confronted a dangerous world, and the fierce energy with which they had marched off to fix it. But he only reached out and turned down the radio. "You have to be careful who you're seen with," he said.

"I thought spies always turned the volume *up*."

"Only in the movies. In real life, any engineer worth his salt can separate loud sounds from soft ones in about ten seconds. If you want to hide your words, use sound around the same volume."

"And what words are we hiding, exactly?"

"I don't know, Rebecca. You're the one who called." He nodded. "Something's changed up there, or you wouldn't be down here."

"You said if I wanted more information, I had to earn it. That implies you'll trade with me."

"Depending on what you can tell me." The eyes grew chilly again. "Now, Rebecca. The ball's in your court. Tell me why I'm not asleep in my nice warm hotel room."

And so she did: mostly truth, but a little bit of lie, because she had learned already, or perhaps remembered from the old days, when Jericho would wax eloquent about the plaque in the town park, that in the world of men like the A & A boys, good facts mattered less than good stories.

(III)

"I told you what Lewiston Clark said," she began. "That he was helping Jericho write his autobiography." They were sitting in the parking lot at Dunkin' Donuts, drinking coffee from the drive-through. "I don't know exactly what contacts the two of them have had. I do think part of his story was true. He's interested in Jericho's autobiography. He just isn't the one writing it. Jericho is writing it himself."

If Beck had hoped to surprise him, or perhaps to hear grateful hallelujahs, she was disappointed. Dak's voice was calm. "How do you know?"

"I saw the manuscript. It's in his bedroom."

"Do you know *exactly* where it is?"

So she had been right. Whatever Jericho was writing, Phil Agadakos craved it every bit as much as Lewiston Clark did. She wondered why Dak had not noticed it on one of his visits. "Earlier tonight it was on a table near the bed. I couldn't swear to where it is at the moment."

"Have you read it?"

"No." She swallowed. "Dak, he's dying. He doesn't think he'll finish. He wants me to help him." She left out the fact that Audrey had turned him down. "That's why he asked me to come out here in the first place. To help him finish."

The old spymaster looked alarmed. "I hope you told him no."

"I haven't told him anything."

"That's not good enough, Rebecca." He sipped his coffee. "This is for your own good. You can't go anywhere near his autobiography. And you have to tell him that as loudly and clearly as you can. Jericho is very good at going deaf when he wants to, so keep telling him till he accepts it." The calmness of his voice made the plea all the more chilling. "I'm not joking, Rebecca. You have to tell him no. Don't hint, don't delay, don't beat around the bush. Say it loud and clear."

Beck looked at him. The other half of the A & A boys. "Because you're listening. You, or somebody else. You want it on tape that I said no."

"I'm not saying you're right. I'm not saying you're wrong."

"Are you taping me now?"

"No."

"If you were, would you tell me?"

"No."

She considered. "All right. Your turn. What's going on?"

"Will you tell him no?"

"What's going on, Dak? I did my part. Now you do yours."

He gave her a long look, and, for a moment, she wondered whether he had penetrated her lie, if perhaps the experienced interrogator realized that she was only guessing that the folder held Jericho's autobiography. Then it occurred to her that she would never know. In the old days, when Dak would visit Stone Heights, the three of them used to sit in front of the fire in the great room playing hearts for pennies. Phil Agadakos usually won. Jericho was too aggressive, Beck was too easily intimidated. But Dak was the kind of careful, conservative player who always saved his trumps for last.

(IV)

"You remember our conversation from this afternoon?"

"Vividly."

"Good. I told you, when Jericho left the Agency, we thought he was cracking up. Now let's do the math, shall we? You and Jericho got together in 1994. You split up in 1995. Things calmed down. Jericho calmed down. He wasn't crazy after all, we decided. Life went on. Oh, there were other women, of course. Not many. Nobody else he invited to move in. There was only one of you, apparently. As for Jericho, his life went on. He did some lecturing, he taught for a while at the University of Colorado. He sat on a couple of corporate boards. Joined a private equity fund, settled down to a long retirement of counting his money. He wrote his books, but he submitted them for vetting, just like he was supposed to. They always passed. Jericho was scrupulous. He never even walked to the edge of telling what we needed him to keep secret. After another year, maybe two, we backed off on the surveillance."

She saw it. "And that was a mistake."

He nodded. "That was a mistake. We kind of forgot about him. Our mad ex-Director. The way you think, if you don't open an envelope, the bill isn't due. We got on to other things. It's a busy world, and surveillance is expensive—a fortune to maintain, a bigger fortune to review and analyze. Resources are limited. Despite what our friends in the press seem to think, we're usually looking for targets to shut down, not new ones to add. So, yes, we turned off the mikes. Oh, we looked in on him now and then, but even that became desultory. Then, five years later, six, Washington went into a brand-new panic. Not only Washington. Some other capitals, too. Including the capitals of some rather unofficial nations. Because Jericho began to send out signals. He knew the back channels. He knew how to get his messages to the right people. And the signals he was sending out told the nastiest people in the world—and some of the best, too—that he had their secrets marked down, that he had provided against any threat to himself. If he were to die, natural causes or not, if any member of his family came to harm? He had so arranged matters that the secrets would come out. He was warning those still in the trade to leave him alone."

"He never mentioned anything like that."

Agadakos took a moment to answer, as if waiting for her to correct her testimony. "No. He wouldn't have. But, Rebecca, you have to understand the uproar that followed. Suddenly everybody had a motive to get rid of him. And at the same time, everybody had a motive to protect him. In those days, the Agency believed in psychologists. We had a dozen on the payroll. We told them the story. They said he was delusional. Well, we knew that part already. Nobody was trying to kill him. Nobody ever would. Nobody has ever murdered a Director of Intelligence, retired or not. It would be insane. I came up here, Rebecca. To Stone Heights. I told him. 'Jericho,' I said, 'it would never happen. Never. Nobody wants you dead.' Know what he said? He said, 'Look at Colby.' Do you know who Colby was?"

She did not.

"One of Jericho's predecessors. Director of Central Intelligence in the last years of Vietnam, right into Watergate. Retired. Went canoeing one night in 1996, had a heart attack. The canoe overturned, and he drowned. The rumor mills went wild. You know how people can be. The media, but insiders, too. Everybody had a theory. But most of us—the professionals, Rebecca, the people in the trade—we knew. It wasn't an assassination. It was just a heart attack. Some things happen the way they look. William Colby probably had the most complete autopsy in American history. Natural causes. No question. But you couldn't tell that to Jericho. He was obsessed with Colby. Whoever got Colby would be getting him next. This was his only protection: threatening the world. We had this conversation around 2002. But it was plain that Jericho had been worrying for five or six years. Most likely since Colby died, although the shrinks said he was probably deteriorating already."

Dak let the dates sink in. Beck chose silence.

"Anyway, I went back to Langley. We talked it over. Hands off, we decided. Give him some protection, but get word to everybody else. He's nuts, but don't take any chances. Let's all cooperate, and keep him alive. And we did. Not that he was ever under threat. That was all in his head, Rebecca. Nevertheless, in his head or not, we had to believe him when he said he'd arranged for the secrets to come out. He even had a cute little code for his project. JERICHO FALLS. Get it? He'd say, if Jericho ever falls, everybody's walls will come tumbling down. Meaning, no more secrets, anywhere."

Rebecca's gaze, like Dak's, was focused in the distant past. She remembered walking with Jericho in his woods, the only place he seemed to feel safe from surveillance, and how he used to assure her that if anything ever happened to him, if Jericho ever fell, the bastards would pay. "And Clark?" she said, as, in her mind's ear, a mountain wind teased through the branches. "Is that why he's here? Is he working for somebody who's also worried about what happens if Jericho falls?"

"I don't know why he's here, Rebecca. I don't know why anybody's here. He writes books about famous families. The Kennedys sued the hell out of him. Maybe he's doing the Ainsleys now."

"But you think he's on the track of JERICHO FALLS, don't you? That's what worries you. Lewiston Clark, whoever killed the dog." She waved a hand toward the street. "You think somebody might be out there. They've heard that Jericho is dying. They're wondering if the threat still stands. Even if he dies of natural causes, everybody's worried what secrets his death is going to spread. And they might have sent people to—to what?" Like a patient tutor, Agadakos did not help. He waited for her to work the answer out for herself. "They can't hurt him. They don't dare. All they can do is—is try to find whatever he's hidden. Just in case. They want Jericho to make it not happen. To promise to keep their secrets."

"I'm not saying it's anything like that—"

"It could be, though. That's what you're warning me about." Again the kindness in his eyes seemed forced. "But maybe there isn't anything." She had spotted a way out. "Maybe he never hid anything. No contingencies in case Jericho falls. Maybe he only thinks he did. Maybe he was looking for attention. He was always"—for a moment words failed her, and the one she chose did not entirely satisfy—"proud."

Dak's tone was mournful. "I tried to sell them that line, Rebecca. I tried ten years ago. I tried—well, more recently. Nobody will believe it. They can't take the chance." Lifting his chin. "No, honey. They think he's made provisions about what happens when he dies, and they're not happy about it."

"Who's *they*?" she demanded.

The old spymaster ignored her.

"We've done what we can to check, of course. But Jericho was once the best, and he's still very good. Every time we think we've found his footprints, they turn out to be a wisp." He saw her puzzlement. "A term from the old days of the Agency. It means a false trail, planted to fool investigators. Jericho was always very good at planting wisps, Rebecca. He once arranged to have Soviet Intelligence send operatives to London to assassinate one of their own best men, who they thought had turned. To this day, they're still fooled."

"I don't believe it."

"The London story? Good." He sipped his coffee. "It's better if you don't. I wouldn't want you spreading it around."

"What I mean is, I don't believe you can't find whatever it is he's hidden. You're the Central Intelligence Agency. You were. You're the CIA, and you have a whole alphabet soup to help you, right? FBI, NSA, DOD, I don't know who else. You have secret prisons, right? Mental hospitals, interrogation centers. Undisclosed locations. Why don't you just swoop down in your helicopters, gather him up, take him to one of your undisclosed locations, and make him tell you? Are you trying to tell me that the combined resources of the United States government can't find what one little old man has hidden somewhere?"

At last the surface calm faded. Dak's anger was swift and stormy, even though Beck suspected it was not directed at her. "You're naïve, Rebecca. You have the press-eye-view of what we do. Let me tell you the facts of life. Number one, even if we possessed the facilities you mention, we can't just sweep up the former Director of Central Intelligence and Secretary of Defense and lock him away somewhere. As the consultants would say, it creates all the wrong incentives. Your people start to wonder which one of them is going to be next, and all of a sudden they're not as loyal to you as they were yesterday. Number two, suppose we did. Suppose we put him in a hospital somewhere and pumped him full of drugs. Interrogated him till he vomited his knowledge onto the floor. He's sick, Rebecca. He's sick and he's sixty-six years old. We'd be more likely to kill him than get information. And number three—"

He hesitated. *Say it,* Beck urged silently, wanting Dak to be the man she had always taken him for. *Say he's your friend. Say friends don't do that sort of thing to each other. Say you've been holding off the dogs.*

"Number three," he resumed, "if Jericho Ainsley were to disappear, well, for all we know, that would set off whatever chain of events he's arranged. No, Rebecca. Jericho is untouchable. He knows it, and they know it." The calmness settled on him once more. "I know what you're thinking. You're thinking the autobiography is what everybody's looking for. I'm sure it isn't. Jericho is too canny. You've been at the house all of twenty-four hours. He won't be ready to trust you. He asked you to help him so you'd come running to me. He was testing you, that's all."

"And I failed," she said. Then she saw the real point. "But if it doesn't mean anything, then why did you tell me the rest of the story?"

"I told you this afternoon, Rebecca. You need to keep your eyes open. And not just that." He leaned forward, folding large hands around his cup. "You see, Rebecca, the trouble is, there are lots and lots of interested parties. We've figured out that somebody up here is helping him, and that's about it. You're the most recent arrival. You're his one true love. The one he's kept tabs on all these years. It won't be easy persuading people that you're not a part of whatever he's up to. You're about to become very popular." He saw her face and, finally, smiled. "Oh, don't worry. Don't worry. Jericho would hardly spread his umbrella of protection over his family and leave you out."

Sometimes Beck's mind surprised her with its speed. "All those years. The security officers from the Agency who kept visiting me. This is why, isn't it? Jericho had me on his list of people who couldn't be touched, and they wanted to know if I might be part of whatever he's up to." Her knuckles whitened as she gripped the wheel. She imagined Jericho, alone in his mountaintop redoubt, brooding as his years of glory slipped further into the past, scheming and conspiring, but with himself as lone co-conspirator. All at once she ached for him.

Dak was not finished. "There's one more thing, Rebecca. You may be the last person on the face of the earth Jericho loves. If anybody can talk him out of this madness, it's you." His cool eyes measured the effect of his words. "There's nobody else, Rebecca. You have to do it. For the good of your country. And because—"

She waited him out. "Because?"

"Because, sooner or later—unless Jericho changes his mind—somebody might decide to take the chance. Your dear Jer-Bear could wind up in one of those secret hospitals after all."

The smile had gone ice cold.

CHAPTER 9

The Message

(1)

The drive from town was forty-five minutes in daylight and good weather, but that night she made it in twenty-five flat through a freezing rain. She practically hydroplaned through part of the woods, but barely slowed. Nobody ran her off the road. No black helicopter buzzed her. She felt foolish and small, caught up in battles too large for her abilities, but another part of her wondered whether Phil Agadakos was as crazy as Jericho; or whether, even, the two of them were in it together—whatever *it* was—the A & A boys, fulfilling one last project before the end.

This is for your own good. You can't go anywhere near his autobiography. And you have to tell him that as loudly and clearly as you can.

She wanted to believe that Dak was exaggerating, that nobody would care about secrets well over a decade old. But she reminded herself that this was a world in which cartoons could spark deadly riots. All points of the ideological compass were rife with hatred and fanaticism, searching for outlets. There were reasons other than avoiding embarrassment for keeping Jericho alive, and appeased. Philip Agadakos, in short, could be acting from honorable motives.

Or maybe not. Ever since Dak's top-secret history lesson, Beck had been trying to avoid the obvious. William Colby had died in 1996, and Jericho Ainsley had started his steep slide soon after. That was what

Agadakos wanted her to understand: a year after Rebecca left him, Jericho had slipped from unbalanced to unhinged. Dak, no fool, was trying to feed the very guilt that Dr. Eisenstadt was trying to help her overcome. The more responsible Beck felt for whatever Jericho was up to, the better the chance that she would help stop him.

And if that was Dak's plan, it was working.

She turned in at the immobile gate, and there was no Chevy Suburban and no dead dog. But there were two new cars up at the top of the hill, and one of them was Deputy Mundy's cruiser. Beck flew up the steps and, lacking a key, leaned on the bell. But Pamela already had the door open. Pete Mundy had his hat in his hand. An older man in an ill-fitting suit was barking orders. Two unsmiling strangers, a man and a woman, sat talking to the family. The atmosphere was grim.

Audrey forced upon her an unwanted hug, and, holding Beck within all that motherly softness, tried to explain what was going on. Rebecca hardly heard. She was staring at the settee, where Jericho himself sat—in slacks, not pajamas—oxygen bottle on a little trolley in case it was needed, looking sad but somehow tough, momentarily fit.

Then she tuned in the news that had forced Jericho from his bed. The older man was the sheriff, Pete's boss. The two suits were detectives from the state police. Jimmy Lobb's truck had turned up at the bottom of a gorge on the far side of the mountain. Mr. Lobb's remains were in the cab. There was only one set of skid marks, the detectives were explaining. Nobody was chasing him. Nobody had forced him over the side. He had simply lost control of the truck.

His dog was missing.

"Probably drunk as a skunk," rumbled the sheriff, who in Colorado was elected. His name was Garvey.

"We'll know when we get the lab reports," said one of the detectives.

"Coordinate with my man," Sheriff Garvey snapped, pointing to Pete. Heading for the door, the sheriff looked Rebecca up and down. "Where was this one?" he said to the air. "Take her statement."

He left.

Beck went and sat next to Jericho, who was shaking his head, whispering to himself. She tried to listen.

"Bastards killed my friend," he whispered, clutching her wrist. Tears ran freely down his face. He put his mouth close to her ear. "You just remember who fired the first shot."

(11)

Later.

Beck was dreaming fitfully, something about the old days, not her time at Stone Heights with Jericho but a year or so afterward, back when she was learning the secrets of life from middle-aged hippies in Thailand, working in an American bar, half the time stoned out of her mind, but always looking blearily over her shoulder, because she knew that they were after her, Jericho had said they would never let her go, that she would be in their files forever, and in her dream she could sense their wraithlike presence, feel their bone-cold fingers on her neck, but when she turned there was never anybody there, nobody except—except—

Except her cell phone was ringing.

Beck sat up, head pounding the way it used to when she was hungover. But surely the beers she had consumed at Corinda's—

Still ringing.

She told herself not to answer. She was sick of the weird high-pitched whine. She shut her eyes in the gray darkness, waiting for the voice mail to cut in, but it never did. The ringing continued. With an angry sweep, she grabbed the phone to shut it off, and that was when she saw the number on the screen.

Her mother's condo in Sarasota.

In the middle of the night.

She fumbled twice before she was able to push the green button. "Mom?"

"Hi, Mommy," said Nina.

"Sweetie-pie!"

"Mommy, I've been trying and trying to reach you, but you won't call me back, and so—"

"I'm sorry, baby. Mommy's phone hasn't been working—"

But Nina was still talking, nonstop, the way she did.

"—and so Grandma said I should stop leaving messages, but I'm leaving one more, just in case, okay? Because I really wanna tell you about the surprise we have for you—"

Voice mail. Somehow she was listening to the voice mail.

"—because I love you and I'm so excited and I just want to tell you, okay? So, call me, okay? And—and—*I'll be there in a minute!*—I have to go, because Grandma is calling me, and I didn't tell her I'm calling you—*Just a minute!*—I'm in the bathroom and I guess I better go, but call me, Mommy, okay? Call me soon, so I can tell you about the d—"

The message stopped.

She stared at the screen. The call had been lost. She tried to call her voice mail, but she had no bars. She felt a wave of vertigo. Her brain was slushy, as if she had just opened her eyes, and she wondered if she had dreamed it all. Her hand was sweaty as she slipped out of bed. Not bothering with a bathrobe, she hurried through the bathroom to Jericho's office and picked up the phone. She heard Pamela's voice. She was doing business. Two in the morning, and she was doing business. Something about cutting out one of the chase scenes, at a savings of a million and a half.

The d—

The dog?

No, no, no, Beck, no, your imagination is working overtime—

I dreamed it.

It was real.

She picked up the phone again. Pamela chattered away. She stepped into the hallway, peered around the corner toward the master suite. Dak wanted her to talk to Jericho, she remembered. To reason with him. But whatever part of Jericho's mind remained was readying for war.

Beck tiptoed down the back stairs to the kitchen and poured herself a glass of water. She heard a faint rumble, possibly her friends in the helicopter, but when she peered out the window, the night sky was innocent. Still breathing hard, she went to the fridge, got a beer. Pamela strode in the door, still in her jeans, eyeing Rebecca's nightie with disapproval.

"What are you doing up?" Now eyeing the beer bottle.

"Are you done?"

Pamela looked at the phone in her hand. "With this?"

"Yes. I need it."

"Why?"

Beck was ready to fight somebody, and Pamela would do fine. "I just do."

"I'm waiting for a call—"

"I'll only be a minute," said Rebecca, and took the handset without waiting to be told she couldn't. Pamela gave her a foul look, muttered something about letting her know when she was done, and stomped from the room.

Rebecca, relieved, at once tapped out her mother's number. Busy. At this time of night. She tried again. Busy. She tried Nina's cell phone. Voice mail. Her mother's phone again. Still busy.

She was about to give up when the busy signal stopped. A wave of static washed over the line, just like the one she kept hearing on her cell. Then, distant and fuzzy, what might have been laughter. Yes. A man, laughing, on a phone line not at that moment connected to a call.

"Hello?" she said.

More laughter, louder. Then, surrounded by static, a familiar voice. Jericho's voice, on the line. The Former Everything. Scratchy but intelligible. "Bought us a place in Colorado, Becky-Bear. Lots of privacy. Just for the two of us. You'll love it."

"That's not funny!" she shouted. "You bastard!"

"Eight hundred acres, great views, the middle of nowhere."

"You fucking—"

"The middle of nowhere," Jericho repeated. "The middle of

nowhere." The static rose. His voice seemed to fade. "The middle of nowhere. The middle of nowhere."

"What are you—"

"The middle of nowhere. Of nowhere. Nowhere. Nowhere."

The static drowned the words.

Beck slammed down the phone and charged up to the master suite. Audrey, in pajamas and robe, was just about to go in.

"Hey, honey, what's wrong?"

"He's a monster," Beck snarled.

"I know that, but what's wrong right now?"

Quaking too much to explain, Rebecca smashed the door open and rushed the bed, Audrey on her heels. All the old insults were pouring out of her mouth, some of them not only obscene but tongue-twistingly long, while the nun tried frantically to quiet her.

Beck stopped.

Jericho was fast asleep. The nose tube was in.

"He's had a rough couple of hours," said Audrey, brushing past her, lifting the arm to check the pulse. "I gave him an extra pain pill."

"I just—I just talked to him—"

Audrey's eyes were gentle. "No, honey. You didn't."

There was no telephone in the room. Beck had forgotten. Audrey unplugged it at night, so that her father could rest.

CHAPTER 10

The Nun

(1)

"That's very"—Audrey searched for the word—"unusual," she finally said, busying herself with the kettle. Tea seemed to be her solution to everything.

"You don't believe me," said Beck, still trembling.

"I didn't say that," said Audrey, too quickly, and Rebecca remembered that she used to be a psychologist. The heavy shoulders moved. "I'm sorry I wasn't there."

"The house phone works fine," said Pamela, as though this was the point. "I tried it twice. No ghosts."

"I didn't say it was a ghost."

"Excuse me." Pamela leaned against the aging counter, arms folded, malice in her eyes as she smiled down at her father's ex-lover. "No inexplicable recordings of Dad's voice from fifteen years ago."

"I know it sounds crazy."

"That's exactly how it sounds."

Audrey was serving the tea. "Leave her alone," she said tiredly. "She's had a fright." One of her father's phrases.

Pamela's face was hard. She was wearing the same faded jeans. She never seemed to sleep. "Maybe she did, maybe she didn't."

Beck's temper boiled. "I didn't make it up."

"I don't know. You were always the drama queen."

"Meaning what, exactly?" She looked from one daughter to the other, the spooky phone call forgotten. "Is there something I should know?"

Pamela folded her arms. "You always seem to wind up the center of attention, don't you, Rebecca? There's always an emergency with you. You'd fit in nicely in Hollywood."

"Now, look—"

"I'd love to stay and chat," Pamela said, "but some of us have actual work to do." She stalked out.

"You have to understand my sister," said Audrey, mopping up the counter as Beck stared after her longtime adversary. Nothing had spilled. The granite gleamed. But cleaning was what Audrey did. "She's not usually this way."

"Only around me."

A wan smile. "Pretty much."

"She blames me because Jericho left your mother. Doesn't she get that I was a kid?" Rubbing her temples. Sipping the tea. Herbal and calming. "And your father—he was the one who—"

Again she hesitated, the memories rosier than she wanted them to be, the brilliant and overpowering Dr. Ainsley charming the inexperienced sophomore in his office at the Institute for Advanced Study, teasing her, flattering her, one week after another, undressing her with his eyes, and Beck herself drifting out of the room in a fog, passing Mrs. Blumen, who glared as if Rebecca were Hester Prynne. And then, at last, the night he maneuvered her to his house, the party for his graduate students and a few selected undergraduates, lying through his teeth—but, then, she had guessed that he was—

Belatedly, she found her place. "He said the marriage was already over."

Audrey grew thoughtful. "It was, in a way. My folks were pretty much living separately by then. Still, it was a shock when he actually left. A shock for the kids especially. Not so much for my mother. Dad had been enough trouble to Mom, and, frankly, Mom had been enough trouble to Dad, too." She was cupping the cross on its chain around her neck. "I'm supposed to believe that marriages are made in heaven. Believe it or not, the official position of the Episcopal Church remains that divorce is not a part of God's plan. But some marriages, Beck—well, some of them are doomed from the start, despite the best intentions of the parties. And my folks didn't always have the best intentions."

"Then why does your sister hate me?"

"She doesn't hate you. Not really. She hates the same thing I do, that the people who brought us into being weren't willing to stick it out. You're a symbol for her, Beck—sorry, this is the psychologist in me coming out—but you are. You're a symbol for what she hates, the two-facedness of the Ainsley marriage. And of course you're the only one he ever moved in with. She hates that, too."

And that Jericho outlived his ex-wife. Beck was willing to bet that her father's relative longevity was something else Pamela unknowingly hated.

"And what do you think?" she asked after a moment.

"I think life is complicated."

"Meaning what?"

Scrubbing, scrubbing. "You know what my father says? People are like countries. They never really understand each other. Your enemies have virtues you might have to count on one day. And your best friends can let you down."

While Beck turned this over in her mind, the cell phone rang.

(11)

It had been sitting there on the granite countertop, the forgotten exhibit during the conversation. Beck stared at it in mute horror. Before she could force herself to answer, Audrey had swept it up.

"Don't," Rebecca said, making a futile grab.

Audrey shushed her, pressed green, listened.

"Is it Nina?"

"No."

"Who is it?"

The nun made a face and pressed the disconnect button. "I see what you mean," she said, turning the phone over and over in her hands.

"You heard her, didn't you?"

"I heard the static. I heard the whine. I didn't hear any voices."

"But—"

"Sorry, honey." She passed the phone back across the table. "It's random scatter. Electronic noise. It happens up here with mobile phones sometimes." She was at the sink again, washing cutlery. She picked up a fork, pointed at the window. "Especially in bad weather."

"I've never heard of that."

"It's a mountain thing. Reflections of distant signals, distortions—"

"What about the static on the house phone?"

"Up here? Phone calls that travel over miles and miles of old copper wires? Happens all the time."

Something in Audrey's tone bothered her. "Why are you trying so hard?"

"Trying to do what?"

"To persuade me that there's nothing to worry about."

The angelic smile, the eyes as always withheld. "Because I don't want you to worry."

"Why not?" Tapping the phone. "I'd say I have plenty to worry about."

Audrey hesitated. "I was a psychologist, Beck. That's how I was trained. And, well, I think you're worrying too much."

"You think I dreamed it. Or I'm making it up."

"I think you're worrying too much."

Exhaustion and frustration fought an inconclusive battle. Beck's voice was brittle. "Let's say you're right about the random scatter. That explains the snippets of voice mail. It doesn't explain Jericho's voice."

"Or what you thought was his voice."

"I know what I heard."

Audrey shook her head. "No, Beck. You don't. You can never know what you heard. You can only know what your mind tells you that you heard." She waved down the rising objection. "Listen for a minute. Please, honey. When I was a psychologist, my field was cognition. The tricks the mind plays to make sense of the world. One of the classic cognition experiments involves playing static for people but telling them that there are voices hidden in the noise. In fact, there's nothing but static, but if the subjects think there are words, they'll find them. They'll sit and strain and shut their eyes, and then, when the sounds are done, they'll tell you they heard somebody reading Bible verses, the President giving a speech, their grandmother's dying advice. It happens all the time. There's even a name for it—"

"We can skip the details, thanks."

"It doesn't mean you're crazy, honey. That you heard Jericho's voice. It means you're normal."

Another awkward hiatus. Audrey was back at her scrubbing. Rebecca sipped the tea, then tried the phone again, but there was no service. She cocked an ear toward the window. "Listen," she said.

"It's raining."

"No. Not just the rain. Hear that? It's a helicopter."

The nun dutifully shut off the water. She shook her head. "I don't hear it."

"It's very faint. But, Aud, the thing is, Dak said people might be watching me. Let's say you're right. I'm making things up based on the static. Well, every time I get the static, the helicopter is around. I don't know how they do it, but whoever's up there has been sending static to my phone. Messages, too. Even Nina's voice mail—"

Rebecca stopped. Audrey's eyes had that kindly look again. Beck realized how she must sound.

"Forget it," she said, not wanting to hear another lecture from the former psychologist about how the mind plays tricks. Beck tried to remember exactly how many beers it had actually been. Angry, bitter, exhausted, a little tipsy: oh, Audrey could cite a million symptoms if she tried.

But the nun was washing dishes again. "I'm sorry," she said. "Whatever you heard, I'm sorry you have to go through it."

"Thank you," said Beck, and meant it. A beat. She listened, but could no longer hear the helicopter. *You're about to become very popular.* "Can I ask you something else?"

"Sure, honey."

"Jericho said—well, he seemed pretty adamant that I should ask you why you quit your job. Why you left your husband. Why you became a nun."

Audrey smiled. "I bet he told you I like girls, too."

"That's not my business."

"It's not even true. Well, maybe it is a little. But that's not why I left my husband. Dad just likes to get under people's skin. He's desperate to get under mine." She had moved on to the pots now. "My husband was a very sweet man named Teddy Gould. I left Teddy because he wanted children and I didn't. He was a nice guy, ergo, in Jericho's mind, I was gay. But, the truth is the reason I didn't want children had nothing to do with sex. It had to do with children."

"You don't like children?"

"I love children, Beck." Scrubbing harder. "I just didn't particularly want to bring any into the world my father made. The world I helped him make."

"You?"

"Didn't he tell you? We used to work together."

Beck shook her head, but already the pieces were falling into place. Jericho was angry at his elder daughter for quitting the family business. And what was the family business? Beck had assumed he meant the academy, but Jericho was a professor for all of two years. Dak had told her that the Agency sometimes employed psychologists. Her father had specialized in—

"Interrogation. You worked with him on interrogation techniques."

"Only the painless ones," she said, then laughed at her own glib self-justification. "Yes, Beck. That's what I did. This was the nineties, the early days of what everybody wound up calling the War on Terror. I don't want to go into details." She put one pot on the drying rack, took up the other. "This was when I was a professor. My dissertation was about containing certain cognitive deficits by controlling the environment in which the patient functioned—never mind. The point is, when my father saw it, he realized there were applications to—well, to his work."

"Brainwashing. You're talking about brainwashing."

"Not exactly. No. But interrogation, yes. Getting the subject to the point where he wants to cooperate. Oh, no, not like you're thinking. Not like in the movies. Drugs. Torture. Not like that. Just slowly breaking down the world your subject knows, and replacing it with a world of your own devising. You never touch him physically. You control his environment. You keep him guessing, keep him off balance, keep changing the rules, until, after a while, he doesn't know what's real and what isn't. That's when he'll cling to any anchor. And you give him a new reality. A better one."

"Sounds awful."

The nun was unfazed. "You're right. It was awful. Only I didn't know it. I had consulting contracts with the Agency. I made a good living, dispensing advice. And sometimes I got to help put my own theories into practice. Pretty exciting for a social scientist."

Rebecca felt slightly ill. "Are you saying you actually participated in—"

Audrey held up a hand. "Yes." She dropped her eyes.

"But you stopped."

"Let's just say I got disgusted with myself. I became a psychologist to help people, not to—"

A roll of thunder, loud as a car bomb, distracted them both.

"I stayed at the Agency after Dad left," Audrey resumed. "I was there until shortly after 9/11. I had charge of an interrogation of one of the suspects in—well, never mind what he was a suspect in. We always did these interrogations abroad. No lawyers, no courts, no journalists. We were the Morlocks. That's what we told ourselves. The Morlocks, protecting the country in ways you could never explain in the sunshine." She saw Beck's face. "Yes. I see he's told you that line. Pretty pitiful, isn't it? But that's what we were. The Morlocks. Anyway, this particular interrogation—well, things got a little out of hand. We followed the rules, we applied my theories, we didn't do any physical harm, but the results—oh, Beck. We had a man who had done—well, something really terrible—and we used my techniques, and they all worked perfectly, and he wound up regressing so far that he—he just couldn't—" She stopped. The broad shoulders slumped. "Anyway, when I got back to the States, I realized things were getting out of hand more and more often. I won't say extreme measures are never necessary. I will say, well—once you admit they're necessary in certain rare cases?—you wind up deciding that all the cases are rare ones." She returned to her scrubbing, although everything glistened. "Anyway, my marriage was going to pieces. I was traveling all the time, Teddy was getting adamant about kids, and—well, I came up here to see my dad, and he was his usual crazy self. 'You can be a torturer *and* a mother,' he said. 'It's pretty much the same job.'"

"He could be nasty," Beck breathed, but her mind was on something else.

"Still can. Anyway, we argued for a couple of days, Dad and I, and then I just left. I had no idea where I was going. I just got in the car and drove around. For two, three days, staying in motels. I was near Colorado Springs when I saw the sign. A convent. An Episcopal convent. The nuttiest thing—but I was curious. I've never been a shrinking violet. I rang the bell and had a bite to eat. Had a little tour, saw the work they did, and"—she looked up, an unexpected defiance in her glare—"and it was like God had hit me over the head. I knew what I had to do. I left my job, I left my husband, and I gave away what money I had. The rest—I wrote instructions for the lawyers to get rid of that, too, once I inherited it." The anger melted into peace. "We're not like the Catholics, Beck. We don't require a vow of poverty. Celibacy, either. But I took both. It made things—better."

Beck sipped her tea. "And that's what Jericho wanted me to know?"

"I have no idea what he wanted you to know." Scrubbing the gleaming refrigerator now, still refusing to let her guest lift a finger. "But that's why I left the family business."

"It doesn't make sense. None of this makes any sense."

"What's going on, honey? Why are you so spooked?"

"I'm not spooked," she said, too fast. "I was just wondering."

Audrey did not turn from the sink, but her gaze lifted. She was looking out at the brightly lighted grounds. "I don't know exactly what's going on here, Beck. It's obvious that Dak told you something that you haven't told us. Ever since you met him in town, you've been on the lookout for—oh, I don't know. But it's obvious that you're on the lookout." She put the sponge aside. "If you need any help, you only have to ask."

Rebecca stared. Why was everyone so determined to know what was going on in her head? Then she talked herself down. Jericho used to say that only paranoids thought everybody was in on the conspiracy. In real life, he would preach, it's usually two or three idiots, a mascot, and a dog.

A dog?

Sure. Because you need somebody to kick when the plan doesn't work.

(III)

Up in her room, Rebecca perched on the window seat, looking out on the storm. Floodlit trees snapped angrily in the wind. The clatter shook the panes. Why had Jericho wanted her to hear Audrey's story? Was there a message, or was Jericho just having his mad fun?

She thought about Audrey, so strong and self-certain, her stolidity itself somehow proclaiming an eternal faith. Colorado Springs was three hours away. Three and a half at the most. Dak had said someone out here was helping Jericho with—well, with whatever madness he was up to. Audrey was his daughter, she lived nearby, she had been, as he quaintly put it, in the family business. And yet, even on her first night back under Jericho's roof, Beck had detected his sizzling anger at the woman he derided as *Saint.* Had Audrey been helping and then quit? Was that the point? Or was the message in the story itself?

Lightning flashed. Beck jumped.

Ask her, Jericho had said.

Ask her what?

Why she became a nun. Why she quit the family business.

The story. What did the story boil down to? Audrey used to be a consultant to the Agency. A specialist in interrogations. The painless kind, just in case anybody might be up there keeping track. Something had gone wrong, Audrey had quit, she had left her husband, given away her share of the money, become a nun. Maudlin, yes, but a message? Beck could not find one. What was she missing?

She yawned. Too much for a single day. Or a single night.

She stood up, moved to the bed, slid at last between the sheets.

But not before turning her cell phone off.

Still, in the night, she dreamed that it rang, and whined its whine at her; and when she woke on Tuesday morning, the phone was on.

TUESDAY

CHAPTER 11

The Deputation

(1)

On Tuesday, the sheriff returned, with Deputy Frias rather than Deputy Mundy in tow. The weather was clear and cold. On her early morning ramble, Beck had encountered no dead dogs and heard no gunshots. Back at the house, she had just settled down to review the memoranda for the weekend meeting when the *beep-beep-buzz* of the sensor said that a car had entered the forecourt. Audrey was busy with Jericho, and Pamela was on the telephone, so it was Rebecca herself who admitted the officers.

Sheriff Garvey demanded to speak to Dr. Ainsley. Beck said he could not be disturbed. The sheriff said it was important.

"Then maybe you should tell me."

Garvey sized her up, much as he had the night before: the way a policeman appraises a potential suspect. "You had a drink with my deputy, Pete Mundy," he said. Beck noted the possessive pronoun, but said nothing. "He says he interviewed you about what's been going on in town." Still she kept silent. "Deputy Mundy is a good man, but he gets a little wild sometimes. He has these crazy ideas." The hard eyes were awaiting her confession. "There's nothing going on in town. Is that clear?"

Rebecca had not liked condescension even when she was a teenager. She was not going to put up with it now. "Is that the message?"

The sheriff flushed, and she knew at once that he was not a man to cross. "That's for you personally. Pete Mundy arrested a couple of folks in Corinda's last night. Private investigators. Licensed. Did you know that?"

"No."

"Well, he did. Said one of them threw a punch at him. My Deputy Frias here backed him up." She glanced at Tony, but he was examining Jericho's bookshelf. "I don't put up with anybody assaulting one of my deputies, but I had to turn them loose this morning."

"Why?"

"I just did. Never mind why." His irritation at her was growing. Well, she had always had a talent for rubbing men the wrong way. "Now, look, Miss DeForde. My Deputy Mundy is a good man, but lately he's been asking a lot of silly questions, and causing a lot of silly trouble. I would like you to please keep out of his way. Is that too much to ask?"

She folded her arms. By now Audrey had crept down the stairs. "It's good of you to come all the way up here, Sheriff Garvey, to tell me who I should and should not spend my time with. But I've been making up my own mind on that subject for about twenty years, and I don't think I'm ready to stop."

"I'm telling you for your own good, Miss DeForde. I wouldn't want you to get in any trouble." The words were conciliatory. The tone was not. "I have a lot of respect for Dr. Ainsley. Ask him. He's been good for this community. He'll tell you I only want what's best for everyone."

Still she refused to back down. "Excuse me, Sheriff. Exactly what kind of silly questions is Deputy Mundy asking?"

Garvey ignored her. He turned to Audrey. "How is your father, Miss Ainsley?"

"He's having a good day. Thank you, Sheriff." She looked at Beck. "Is there some kind of trouble?"

"Not at all. Miss DeForde and I are just shooting the breeze. Oh, but listen. I have a message for your father."

"I'll see that he gets it."

"Please tell him"—a wary glance at Rebecca—"please tell him that I spoke to my friend, and he is aware of the, ah, problem. He's going to take every precaution."

Audrey nodded as though this made perfect sense, which, to her anyway, perhaps it did. "I'll tell him. Thank you, Sheriff Garvey."

He turned to Beck. "Remember what we said."

The nun walked the sheriff to the door. Tony Frias followed. He winked at Rebecca as he sauntered out.

When the door was closed, an anxious Audrey turned to Beck. "What was that all about?"

"Nothing. I think I got on his nerves."

"His nerves are easy to get on." Her tone was somber.

"And the message for your father?" said Beck. "What was that all about?"

"I wish I knew," said the nun, turning away and heading for the kitchen. Beck watched her go, puzzling. She had known Audrey almost as long as she had known Jericho.

The woman had always been a poor liar.

(11)

Fifteen minutes later, by a mercy, Pamela relinquished the house phone. Beck immediately called Sarasota, where her mother denied having been on the telephone in the middle of the night, but wanted to know why Beck had called so late in the first place. "You might not need your sleep, but you should think about the rest of us now and then. I've never known a girl as willful as you."

"Thanks, Mom."

"Oh, come on. Don't sulk. I'm just saying, you should try to be a little more thoughtful of others. That's all." A pause. "And how is your gentleman doing?" she asked politely: *your gentleman* being what Jacqueline had called him back when she was busy calling her daughter his concubine.

"He's hanging in there."

"You hang in there, too." A small laugh. "I can tell when my little girl's upset about something. But don't you worry, Rebecca. You'll come out fine. You were always the kind who wouldn't let anybody stop you from landing on your feet."

Not sure whether she had been complimented or insulted, Rebecca chose to sidestep. "Speaking of little girls—"

"I'll get her."

From Nina, Beck learned that Grandma had indeed bought her a gift, and it did indeed start with the letter "d," but, bubbling over with delight that her mother had not heard the whole message, Nina refused absolutely to say whether the "d" stood for "dog" or "dominoes" or "dinosaur." She asked the child to put Grandma back on the phone, who hemmed and hawed and finally confessed to having bought her granddaughter a doll: the latest in the American Girl series, priced at something north of one hundred dollars.

A doll. Not a dog.

"I know you don't approve of spending that kind of money on toys, but it's my money, dear, and, frankly, if a woman my age can't spoil her grandchild now and then, what's the money for? She can leave the doll down here, if that'll make you feel better, and maybe that way you'll let her visit more often—"

"Mom."

"—and—who knows?—my own daughter might grace an old lady's doorway every now and then—"

"Mom!"

"—and, besides, it's just a doll. You don't have to get all bent out of shape. Just because a girl plays with a pretty little doll doesn't mean she won't grow up to be a good feminist, or whatever you people call your-selves these days—"

"Mom, I love you," she blurted.

Silence from Sarasota. For a mad moment Beck expected Jericho's chuckling voice to intercede.

"You be careful out there," her mother finally said. "Sorry, dear. Have to go. We're taking a ride on a glass-bottom boat."

Me, too.

That was what it felt like: a glass-bottom boat, because when she looked down she would see the occasional darting creature, but mostly just inky depths she could not seem to fathom.

(III)

Around mid-morning, the sensors announced that another car had entered the forecourt. Beck was in the kitchen, drinking coffee and reading, and went to look at the monitor in the security room next door. She saw a dark late-model Mercedes—a bit muddy, as if from a long drive. A man of some years and a woman who could have been his daughter climbed out. Both were wearing business suits, and it occurred to her that they could be something federal, but over the past thirty-six hours she had learned not to trust what people appeared to be. She stepped into the foyer in time to see Pamela admitting them without any fuss, and was grabbed by Audrey, who was heading upstairs.

"You can help me," the nun said.

"Help do what?" Hide the evidence? Establish an alibi?

"With Dad. He wants to meet them in the study. We have to get him ready."

The visitors were lawyers, said Audrey. From one of the big Denver firms. They had driven up at Jericho's request. The two women were on the landing. Rebecca peered down at the lawyers. Their four eyes watched her with calm calculation. Dak had a gaze like that.

"What are they doing here?" she asked, automatically.

"He's their client. They came to pick up that big document he's been working on." The two women stood on the landing. "It's his will."

(IV)

Once more, Jericho had lied to her: another hard-earned medal for the private wall where she kept the grief he caused her. She remembered the time, a bit more than a year into their mad relationship, when he went to town to play poker with his cronies and returned reeking of a perfume considerably less expensive than the scents he made her wear. He insisted that it was just from hugging a waitress, and Beck never doubted him for a moment. She simply disbelieved his denial that the hug took place while they were prone. She threw a few things and broke a few things, and he accused her of jealousy and delusion and ordered her roughly to clean up the mess. She suggested that he get his girlfriend to do it, then stomped upstairs and locked herself in her suite for half a day. Upon emerging the following afternoon, Beck told him that she was leaving for good this time, but Jericho had already pulled one of his magic acts. A messenger arrived from Denver that very moment, and the diamond earrings in the beautiful box must have cost considerably more than the median family income.

She never wore them, but she owned them still.

For investment purposes, she always told herself.

The story that the pages constituted his autobiography had been, as she suspected last night, a test: as Phil Agadakos would have put it, a wisp. She supposed that she had half betrayed her onetime lover, by telling Dak of the manuscript's existence; but she hoped she had held the middle ground by never actually opening it to look; or maybe even won the latest round with Jericho by not allowing him to badger her into saying she would help.

Especially when there turned out to be nothing to help with.

His will.

And yet another part of her was persuaded that matters were never as simple as they appeared, not where Jericho was concerned. In Jericho's world, every word had about sixteen motives, as did every action. The papers in the folder might not be his autobiography, but the Former Everything had not gone to all the trouble of lying simply to test her devotion. There was a deeper meaning to it all. Not just one of Jericho's games. Something more.

Today was Tuesday. She was leaving on Thursday. That left her forty-eight hours to figure it out.

(v)

The lawyers were nervous, perhaps because they were attending the death of a madman. Jericho insisted on meeting them in his study, not in the sickroom. He proposed to seem strong. Audrey propped him up to keep him from slouching, while Beck slid the oxygen tank out of the way beneath the desk. She noticed a holster fastened to the bottom of the drawer and supposed that Jericho had hidden a gun here. She wondered what had become of it.

"I think we're ready," said Jericho.

The folder was sitting on the blotter. The will peeked out, complete with Jericho's blood-red emendations.

"Are you sure?" said Rebecca. "Do you need anything else?"

"I want to give you one last chance," he said, not looking up.

"Chance to do what?"

"I'm quite annoyed at you," he said, tone as affectionately correcting as she remembered from the old days. "Sneaking out in the middle of the night to see other men. If I were five years younger, I'd tan your lovely hide."

She tried to work out who could possibly have peached that fast, how word could have climbed the mountain. But Jericho, she reminded herself, just knew things.

"I was getting cabin fever."

"After twenty-four hours. Imagine." He adjusted his spectacles. "Audrey tells me Sheriff Garvey was giving you a lecture. He does that."

"Yes, well—"

"Don't worry. Garvey's all bark and no bite. He can't lay a finger on you, whatever he thinks you've done. I pretty much paid for both of his election campaigns." A hard stare. "Remember, Beck. Garvey's not your friend. Got it? That deputy of his isn't your friend. And neither is Dak. This is my mountain. I know these people. You don't. I love you, and I'm telling you. The only people up here you can trust are the people in this house. Got it?" He turned to his daughter. "Let's do this." He coughed. "But let's keep it short."

The lawyers were waiting downstairs, watched over by Pamela. Audrey wanted to stay for the meeting, but Jericho said he would be fine. So she pulled Beck aside, and proposed to listen in from the guest room next door.

"Why?"

"Just in case."

"In case what?"

The nun gave that eerie, floating smile. "He can be funny."

"I'll wait with you," Beck proposed.

"You can't. You're meeting Pamela."

"Meeting her?"

Quick nod. "After Jimmy Lobb's accident, Dad is sure they're after him. So he told my sister to show you the basement."

"What about the basement?"

"Just go," said Audrey, and actually gave her a shove, only half playful. Beck could not remember when she had seen Audrey so assertive; she wondered what the Ainsleys did not want her to overhear.

CHAPTER 12

The Basement

(1)

"I was thinking I might leave early," said Rebecca, who found herself missing her daughter more than ever. "I was thinking I might go to Florida."

"Don't let me stop you." Pamela was flicking on the lights to illuminate the basement. One by one, additional sections opened up. Beck was surprised. The space went on and on. She remembered the basement as smaller, and unfinished, just concrete blocks and the heating system and a few garden tools. Now there was a bright playroom, complete with pool table, bar, and the only television set in the house. According to Sean, Jericho watched little other than *24* and DVDs of *The Sopranos*. Farther along, a hallway led to a phalanx of other rooms. "If you need to go, go."

"I don't need to," said Beck, arguing the other side because she found it impossible to agree with Pamela. "I was just thinking about it." She realized that she was whining. "So—we're here. What did Jericho want you to show me? He's not kicking me out of the grandchildren's suite, is he? I hope he doesn't expect me to move down here."

"Only in an emergency," said Pamela, with her just-so smile. She fondled a pool cue, and seemed ready to challenge her nemesis to a quick game of nine-ball. "And then we'd all be moving down here."

"What kind of emergency? Rockslides?"

"Breach of the house security."

"Breach of *what*?"

Pamela was still playing with the cue. "Why are you here, Rebecca? You don't like us. You don't like me. You don't like Dad. You pretend to like Audrey, but I don't think you like her, either. You don't like us, you think you're better than we are, smarter, too, but here you are, dropping in for a few days to join the deathwatch. Before we go any further, I'd like to know why."

"I told you—"

"That he asked for you. I remember. But the two of you haven't spent much time together, have you? Half an hour here and there." She used the cue as a pointer, aimed it at Beck's chest. "Still. You can't leave. Dad wants you here. I'm not sure why. Has he told you?"

Beck shook her head. "I haven't talked to him today," she said.

"I know. He said he's getting a proposal ready for you. He'll see you when it's done." A sardonic smile. "Not a marriage proposal, I trust."

"Afraid I'm out to steal his money?"

"Doesn't matter. There's hardly enough of it to go around."

"Come on, Pamela. Even Jericho couldn't have gone through the entire Ainsley fortune."

That hooting laugh that Beck hated. "See? He fooled you, just like he fools everybody. There isn't any Ainsley fortune. Never was. My grandmother—Dad's stepmother—was a Hilliman. There's the Hilliman fortune, but Dad doesn't get to touch much of that."

"But his father was an investment banker—"

"His father was a nobody. A political hack. He became Secretary of Commerce after the war and then went into banking. And, yes, he made some money. And he married my grandmother after his wife died. But the Hilliman trusts aren't open to people who marry into the family, and they're not open to stepchildren. Only to blood relations. The money Grandpa made, well, it was enough to keep him comfortable, but that's all. And, yes, after he left government, Dad went into private equity. But, the truth is, he blew a lot of his money on Stone Heights and the land around it." Pamela let this sink in. "And, yes, the property is valuable, but it's also heavily mortgaged. Most of the rest

Dad lost when Scondell Bloom collapsed. I'm sure he has five million salted away. Ten maybe, fifteen at most. But after inheritance taxes and the meltdown—the point is, it's money, but it's not a grand fortune." The golden eyes, so like her father's, became hard again, as if Pamela feared that her tone of sad reminiscence was drawing the two women together. "So. Happy now? Or are you angry, because he misled you?"

"I think I understand him better." A pause. "I think I understand all of you better."

And the odd part was, she really did. She saw Jericho for the first time not as a superstar but as a striver, determined to make his mark in the world in order to prove his mettle to a family that had all but disowned him. The children, all so very different, shared this quality, too: that hardheaded determination to move forward, lest the world think they were living off their family after all. Beck had seen Pamela glittering on television at the Academy Awards. Sean jetted around the world, much as his father had done, even if he was handing out grants to build green factories. And Audrey—well, Audrey was special, wasn't she? But she, too, after a stint at following in her father's footsteps, had quit the Agency, left the husband who wanted children, and divested herself of any connection to the family money, doing everything she could to be the opposite of the woman she had been—

Beck went very still. For a moment she almost had it. What Jericho had wanted her to know. Why Audrey left the family business. It was so close, near the surface of her mind, scratching to get through—

"Are you there?" said Pamela. She had put down the cue and was playing with her pearls. "Hello? Are you catatonic, or just remembering the good old days with my dad?"

"Sorry." Fighting through the cobwebs. She had been so close. "I'm sorry, Pamela. For everything. I mean that."

"Good for you."

As Beck bit back a retort, her cell phone rang.

Pamela pointed. "What carrier is that? Verizon or something? I'd love to have a network that can reach up here. Mine isn't even on."

Rebecca did not take the phone off her belt. "There's something wrong with it."

"You're not answering? How can you not answer? It might be important." Truth dawned in the pale eyes. "You're still hearing ghosts, aren't you? You're scared to answer the phone."

"I don't want to talk about it."

Pamela laughed, but awkwardly. "Well, maybe it's not so bad to be scared."

"Why would you say that?"

"Can't you feel it?" She was hugging herself. "Something's getting ready to happen."

"Something like what?"

"I don't know." The golden eyes seared her. "But it's nothing good. I'll tell you that."

(11)

"My father's not all there," said Pamela. "Well, that's obvious. He sits up in that room all day, plotting and plotting. I wish he'd get out of the house." She looked at Beck. "Oh, he can. He's ambulatory. The doctors think getting out a bit would be good for him. I've tried to take him to Bethel, or even Vail, but he won't go. Maybe you can persuade him. He—likes you." She nibbled her lip, wrestling with a fugitive emotion. "He likes you," she said again.

More than me. A child could have read the body language.

"I'll try," said Beck.

Pamela's shoulders drooped. She shook her head, contriving to convey by these signs that she disapproved of what she was about to do. "Dad has made changes in the house since you . . . lived here. He worries a lot. You know that. Upstairs, there's all kinds of security devices. You haven't seen them all. Well, down here, we have more. This is where Dad always says we're supposed to make our last stand—when the bad guys come. You know. When Jericho falls."

Beck's attention tautened. "Jericho falls?"

"It's an expression he uses sometimes. You must have heard it. Anyway, that's what this—this tour is all about. What to do when Jericho falls. So. Look around, Rebecca. Other people build panic rooms. Dad builds traps. Seriously. That fits his personality, doesn't it? He's not a hider, he's a counterpuncher. You come after him, he comes after you. The idea is, you get the bad guys to chase you down here, and then you spring these traps on them, and— Oh, shit, Rebecca, I can't believe I'm telling you this. It's all so silly." Nevertheless, good soldier that she was, Pamela marched across the basement. "Here. Under the bar. You push these buttons—see?—all three at the same time. And—watch."

Pamela pressed.

A gate came clattering out of the wall, splitting the basement in two. The pool table was on the far side of the new barrier. Beck felt a familiar itch around her shoulders, the same sensation that plagued her in elevators, for she suffered, ever so slightly, from claustrophobia.

"Aren't we shutting ourselves in?"

"If you were in the kitchen, you'd see there's another gate there. So the bad guys are trapped. If you get trapped by accident, there's a set of buttons, just like this one, over by the television. You press them in order—three, four, nine, one—easy to remember, the year Dad was born, but in reverse—like that. And the gate opens again. Okay?"

She had known Jericho was mad; until this moment, she had not appreciated how mad. No wonder there was no money left. "Yes, Pamela, I get it, but don't you think—"

"Good. Follow me." Striding down the hall away from the play-room, into the section of basement obviously built since Beck's residency. She pointed. "Utility room. Furnace, water heater, water-softening system, pump system for the well." Another room. "Storage. Three rooms. They're all full of boxes." Opening each door in turn to show her. "But in this one"—the second one along—"there's three more buttons. See? We press them all at once, and—"

And another gate clattered, this time down from the ceiling, sealing the hallway. Only this time the mesh was between Pamela and Beck.

The lecture continued. "Again, there's another gate on the other side. If you turn around, you'll see it. The idea is, if somebody chases you down here, you run into this storeroom and press the buttons, and the bad guys wind up caught in the hall."

"Which button releases the poison gas?"

A wicked grin. "Nervous?"

"What?"

"You're kind of caged in, aren't you?"

Beck drew in a breath. "Let me out, Pamela."

"Why?"

"Because this is silly."

But Pamela seemed to think it was fun. She walked back and forth on her side of the bars. "Unnerving, isn't it? Being caged up like that?" She laughed. "I should leave you here. Teach you a lesson."

Beck said nothing. She twisted around, searching for another exit, saw none. Of course not. Jericho would be thorough in his madness.

"That's your problem, Rebecca. You're spoiled. You don't have people setting limits on you. Well, I just set one."

"You bitch—"

"Hey, don't be like that. I'm just giving you a taste of your own medicine."

"My own medicine? What did I ever do to you, Pamela?"

"Not to me. To Dad." Waving a hand. "Look around, Rebecca. Look where he's living. This was a great man. Presidents listened to him. Prime Ministers. Everybody. He ended civil wars. He caught terrorists. And look where he ended up. Look who he threw it all away for."

Beck had her hands on the bars. To her annoyance, her palms were sweating. She hated confinement of any kind. If she was ever imprisoned, she thought she might last an hour before hanging herself. "Let me out of here, Pamela. Come on."

"I wanted you to see what it's like for him." Her eyes were moist. "Living in prison, when the whole world was his playground."

But she punched in the code anyway, and the gate rattled open.

"I think we need a boxing ring," said Rebecca, much relieved.

"Follow me." At first Beck thought Pamela meant to take this seriously. Instead, she led her to the back of the storeroom, and pointed to a metal door, with a digital combination lock. "Stairs."

"Don't you ever do that again."

"Will you please pay attention? The stairs lead to the garage."

"The garage that's all sealed off with padlocks and so on."

"That's right. That's the escape hatch, so to speak. You close the gates to stop the bad guys, and you run for the garage."

"What do you do when you get there and the bad guys are waiting outside?"

Pamela pressed a series of numbers and then pulled the door open. "Let's go."

They did. The stairs were narrow, merely functional. They were also, like so much of Jericho's world, unlighted and shadowy. At the top was another reinforced door. Pamela punched in the same combination.

Nothing happened. The door would not budge.

She tried again, with no better result.

"Dad must have changed the combination," she said.

"We should ask him."

"You ask him." Pamela had already brushed past her, heading down to the basement again. "He likes you."

"But what if we need to go up there?" Beck demanded, hurrying to catch up. "What if somebody breaks in?"

Pamela refused to dignify this with a response. "Last part of the tour." They were back in the storeroom. She opened a metal cabinet. It was empty, but its purpose was obvious. "Jericho had guns in here, Rebecca. Lots of them. All kinds, with enough ammunition to fight a war."

"What happened to them?"

"Audrey took them."

"Audrey?"

Pamela seemed amused. Her sister, she explained, had collected all of Jericho's guns, from all over the house, shortly after her arrival, and disposed of them in town. "She's against all forms of violence. She says guns are immoral and un-Christian."

Beck glanced at the gate across the hallway and marveled at the ease with which the mad old man's cleverness had been subverted. "Well, let's hope all forms of violence feel the same way."

CHAPTER 13

The Request

(1)

This time, lunch was pasta, drenched with sauce and cheese. Colorado was the healthiest state in the Union, but Audrey seemed determined to fatten them up. Jacqueline, firmly unslim, was the same way, admonishing her daughter constantly that men preferred women with a little meat on their bones. At home, Beck fed Nina a steady diet of fish, chicken, tofu, and salad. Nina liked visiting Grandma because she got hot dogs. Or so she told her mother in a breathless summary of the morning's trip to the beach.

"How did things go with the lawyers?" asked Beck.

Audrey's mouth was full. "Great," said Pamela, who was in the basement distracting Rebecca throughout the meeting. "It was really important to Dad that he finish getting the will rewritten." Before he died, she meant. "Well, he did, and it's on the way to Denver."

"Great," said Beck, still puzzled by Jericho's weird deception.

"It's good for Dad," said Audrey. "Talking to people." She swigged heavily at her Coca-Cola. "Until a week or so ago—two weeks, maybe—he was out walking every morning. And when he was getting all that crazy work done on the house? The roof, the alarm, the well, everything? He'd always be talking to the men, even if he had to trundle his oxygen cart around. It's hard for him, being stuck in that room."

"He came downstairs last night," Beck pointed out.

"And look how it wore him out," said Pamela, contradicting her own earlier advice. She turned to her sister, in effect shutting Rebecca out. "I forgot to tell you. I talked to Sean again last night. No way he's changing his decision. I don't understand how his mind works." Another Jericho-ism. "I really don't. His own father lying on his deathbed, and he can't be bothered."

Audrey leaped to her brother's defense. "He has to go to Guinea. They're opening that demonstration project on clean bauxite mining—"

"There are fifty program officers at the foundation. One of them can go."

"I don't know what you're so upset about. Aunt Maggie isn't coming, either, and you're not mad at her."

"She was here last week."

"For all of two hours."

The sisters argued back and forth. Tuning them out, Beck wondered at Audrey's story. Jericho, walking the grounds, talking to the men who came to fix the roof and the alarm and whatever else, and then, suddenly, taking this turn for the worse. Was Audrey exaggerating? Would her father really have spent the last measure of his strength on—

Well, on whatever it was he was doing when he had his house practically rebuilt over a period of three or four months. Was it just his paranoia manifesting itself in an inflexible certainty that there were bugs beneath the shingles, and that even the alarm company must be spying on him? Or was there, as so often, a secret subtlety to Jericho's words and actions? She remembered the obsessive care with which he plotted her initial seduction fifteen years ago, right down to the caterer's van parked craftily in the driveway, even though Beck turned out to be the only guest. His madness had not stripped away his ability to weave conspiracies. Audrey had told her when she arrived Sunday night that her father was plotting, and Rebecca believed it, especially after the business with the will. Phil Agadakos had told her last night exactly what Jericho was plotting, but the more she thought about Dak's story, the more it seemed to her full of holes.

She perked up, and turned to Audrey. "What did you just say?"

"I said I found an overdue library book." Swirling butter over her bread. "Dad was supposed to take it back months ago."

"Why would he go to the library?" Beck wondered aloud.

Pamela's voice was silkily derisive. "Maybe he likes to read. You might have noticed a book or two around the place."

"That's my point," said Beck, quite undeflected. "Your Dad's a millionaire. He can buy any book he wants and get it delivered tomorrow. Why go to the library?"

"Maybe he's just frugal," Pamela began, and then stopped, confusion on her face, because the man she had been describing down in the basement was anything but. "Maybe it was an excuse to get out," she said, rallying. "Not everybody sits home all day long if they don't have to."

"I'll take it back," said Beck.

"You'll what?"

"The library book. I'd love to see the town library. I'll drive down after lunch and return it."

"That's great," said Audrey. "I have to run over to the Wal-Mart on Route 24. I'll drop you."

While Beck tried to think of a way out of this trap, Pamela resumed her assault. "What are you up to, Rebecca?"

"Up to?"

"I told you. You have all the same mannerisms as Dad does. I can tell when he's plotting something; I can tell when you are. The only question is if you're plotting with him or against him." She waggled a finger. "I don't know what it is with you. You're acting like Dad's whole illness is some mystery you should be solving. You should be tiptoeing around and showing some respect. But you just keep running off and having secret meetings. There's nothing going on, Rebecca. Dad's just dying. Shit happens."

"What about Jimmy Lobb?"

"What about him? He had an accident."

"And you don't think it's a little strange? Just as your father gets sick, his best friend up here goes over a cliff? A man who's been driving on these roads for who-knows-how-many years?"

Pamela put her fork down. She looked like a predator spoiling for a fight, but her voice remained calm. "I'm sorry Mr. Lobb is dead, Rebecca. But actual accidents happen sometimes. Real crashes, with real cars, and real people." She lifted her chin toward her sister. "Otherwise, Audrey and her friends wouldn't have anybody to pray for."

The nun blushed, rather prettily. "Oh, don't worry about us. If God decided tomorrow never to allow another auto accident, we'd still have enough of the dearly departed to keep us busy." She crossed the kitchen to get the book. "Here it is."

A brand-new novel by a writer of whom Beck had never heard. She turned it over in her hands. The binding was fresh and uncracked. Nobody had read this book. She was certain of it. She checked the due dates in the back, and found to her delight that the town library still used the old-fashioned system of stamps. And, just as she guessed, Jericho had been the first one to check it out.

He had checked the book out but had not read it. The press of other business? The effect of his illness? Or—

The telephone rang. Audrey scooped it up, said hello, and for once did not smile. "Hi, Sean," she said, in a voice calculated to be heard at the table. Pamela almost sneered in derision, and gave Beck a disgusted look. Beck dropped her eyes and broke off a piece of the delicious but forbidden bread.

"Yes," said Audrey. "Uh-huh. Sure. Yes. You know we will. Yes. How's Hayley? Is that right? Wow. And the— Oh. Sure. Well, tell her happy birthday from us. We'll pray for her. Uh-huh. Oh, she is? And I guess Kara is ten. Eleven? That's such a blessing."

Pamela leaned toward Rebecca, her tone conspiratorial. "She doesn't believe that for a second."

"Believe what?"

"That children are a blessing. That's why she left dear Teddy Gould—"

"That's not what happened. She doesn't hate children."

"Oh, right. You've been here two days, and you know my sister better than I do." She let this sink in. "Audrey hates them, believe me. She thinks they're nothing but trouble. And let me tell you something.

She's right. My Madeira? She's an absolute pistol." Another of Jericho's expressions. It took Beck a moment to realize that Pamela meant her daughter, not a fortified wine. "Madeira's fourteen, right? So she comes home one night with a double pierce in her lip. In her lip! Can you imagine?"

Beck could not. She tried to think of Nina that way, saw only her sweet little smile.

But Pamela's question was rhetorical. "So I say to her, I said, 'What the fuck is wrong with you?' She says, 'It's my fucking body, and it's my fucking freedom of expression.' I say, 'You know what? You're an idiot. You think any boy's gonna want to kiss you like that? Not to mention, you could get a nasty infection.' She says, 'All the boys want to kiss me.' Then she marches up to her suite and slams the door. Well, fine. So I don't know how to talk to kids. My husband took care of it, though. Hank's very good with her. He says, 'If those things aren't out of your lips in five minutes, or if they ever go back in, you don't get the BMW convertible.' "

Beck was a second catching up.

"I thought you said Madeira's fourteen."

"She gets it on her sixteenth birthday. We promised it to her last year, to get her to stop going out with this college guy." She shook her head. "I love her to death, but, believe me, kids aren't a blessing. That girl is going to be the death of me." A grimace. "So—how's yours?"

Beck was spared having to answer by Audrey's intervention. She was holding the portable phone. "He wants to talk to you."

Beck reached for it.

"Not Sean. Jericho."

(11)

"So—what did Dak tell you?" said Jericho. They were on the deck, enjoying the afternoon sun. He wore a thick parka and a scarf that hid half his face. Audrey had insisted. "Last night, when you got together.

What did he want? Did he tell you I was paranoid? Threatening the nation's security? Something like that?"

"Something like that," said Beck, sipping her cocoa. The trip down the mountain with Audrey had been postponed by Jericho's summons. Another part of her was brooding over Sean's snub of her on the telephone, and wondering what the sisters thought.

"Did he happen to say what my threats were?"

Clouds scudded across an eggshell sky. The peak was brilliant and crisp in the mountain brightness. "Not really. Just that you had information you were planning to reveal—"

"Disclose."

She looked at him. "Sorry?"

"I'm disclosing it. Not revealing it. Humans disclose. Only God can reveal. Typical of the way the language has deteriorated in this era of— Never mind." But his brief descent into wordplay heartened her: another sliver of the old Professor Ainsley peeking through. Whatever Audrey might think, Jericho's mind seemed to be working fine. "And Dak is right. I have secrets. And I'm going to let them out if any harm comes to me. To you. To any of my family." There was a bowl of shoyu soup beside him. He had yet to touch it. "You don't mind, do you? That I think of you as one of the family?"

"Of course not."

He seemed pleased. "You loved it up here, Becky-Bear. Remember how you loved it?"

"I was lonely."

"Lonely? You had me."

"Not really. You were always on the phone, or playing cards, or you had people in, working on one of your projects—"

He cut her off. Gently. "And we used to walk. Remember our walks? We walked all the time, Beck. In the woods." He pointed. "Even up the peak now and then. Remember? And down there. The valley."

She turned to him in surprise. She was the one who had walked all the time. Jericho had only rarely joined her, and although they had once climbed the peak, they had never hiked down into the valley behind the house. Was his mind slipping away after all, or was he trying to tell her something? She was about to correct the record when he put a finger to his lips.

"I remember," she said. "Of course I do."

"We were quite the couple in those days," he continued. A guffaw, then a cough. Maybe twenty minutes of fresh air were enough. "Aspen. Vail. The parties. The glitter. Admit it, Becky-Bear. I could be hell on earth, but sometimes we had fun."

"We did." Except there had been no glittering parties in Aspen or Vail, or anywhere else. They had tried, once, the New Year's Eve festivities of a venture capitalist in Snowmass. But even in that sophisticated crowd, people had stared and whispered, until Jericho, to shield them both from embarrassment, made his excuses. The ride back to Stone Heights in the stretch limo was three hours. On the way, pressing her head into his strong shoulder, she cried herself to sleep.

"And your birthday. Remember how we celebrated your birthday? The time I led you into the garage and there was the Ferrari?"

Beck was ready to cry again. For a life never lived. The world Jericho was describing sounded so much more delightful than their actual days. "Yes, Jer-Bear. Sure. I remember."

"Still, these times were the best," he said, still gazing up at the mountain. "Sitting out here at the end of the day, just the two of us. We always took the time to relax like this. We were all we needed in those days—remember?"

"I remember." No. I don't.

"But it didn't last. It never does. We had all these hopes and dreams, but they melted away, didn't they? Dreams are like the snow. They have their season, and then they're gone." He was holding her hand. "I'm sorry, Becky-Bear. Sorry I didn't do better for you." Jericho coughed. "I want you to see Dak for me. I want you to tell him"—a pause, and she could almost hear the gears whirling—"tell him it's not his fault. Tell him I have to do what's best. He'll understand."

Beck reached out, took his chin in her hand, made him turn to look at her. "It won't work, Jericho. You know it won't."

"What won't work?"

"They won't let you get away with it. Come on, Jericho. These are the nation's secrets. Maybe the secrets of other nations, too." The golden eyes just watched her. She grabbed his shoulder, shook him. "Don't you understand? They won't all wait around to see what you do. Somebody's going to kill you. Can you get that through your head? They'll kill you, Jer-Bear. Do you want that to happen?"

She thought for a moment that she had reached him. Those hunter's eyes widened, and he flushed. Then his expression hardened, and she knew that she had only sparked his anger.

"I see." He lifted a hand, removed hers from his shoulder. "You're saying you won't help me."

"Help you! You haven't even told me what you want me to do!"

Another station break while he thought this over. When he spoke, his tone was again one of reminiscence. "I always adored your mind, Beck. From the very first. Back at Princeton, in the seminar. I loved your mind before I loved the rest of you. Boundless potential. Ambitious as any politician." That small laugh. He stood up, shakily, but on his own. He kissed her cheek, and whispered. "What I'm saying is, you'll figure it out." He straightened again. "I hear you're leaving us."

"Day after tomorrow. I have to go to Chicago—"

"I'll take care of it."

"Excuse me?"

"I want you to stay longer, Beck. I miss you."

"But—"

"At least one more day. Stay till Friday."

But another day in the madhouse sounded like a prison sentence. "I can't, Jericho," she said kindly. "I have a meeting. It's my job."

A dismissive gesture. "Not to worry. Your boss—not that fool Pfister, but his boss's boss's boss?—he worked for me at Defense. I covered up a scandal for him. He owes me. If I tell him he can spare you another day, he can spare you another day."

"Please don't do me any more favors."

A chuckle, then a cough. "I'm not doing it for you, my dear. I'm doing it for me."

And that was that.

(III)

When Beck went upstairs to get her jacket and her wallet for the ride to town, she took a moment to stand by the window, looking down past the stone deck where she had sat with Jericho. It was nearing two. The sun was still almost precisely overhead. Every feature of the lawn should have been bright. Yet she imagined shadows. The view seemed somehow gauzy and insubstantial. She felt as if she were looking into a dream.

Movement.

The play of gray against green and brown, winking into her vision, then vanishing as soon as she shifted her gaze.

An animal, she told herself, pulling on her jacket as Audrey called from downstairs. A bear, maybe. The season was right. Up here, one even saw the odd elk, or, now and then, a mountain lion. So that was what she had seen out there: an animal, surely, and not a man.

Nevertheless, as she crossed the forecourt beside the happily chattering nun, Beck felt a fresh surge of loyalty to the man whose warm yet powerful arms had been, for a while, her entire world.

Maybe. Maybe not.

Their affair began in the spring of her sophomore year. By the following fall, they were living in Colorado. But first came the seduction. Beck, fascinated by her professor and well aware of the significance of his sneaking glances, had little experience of men. She had done more fighting off than giving in. She took to dropping by Dr. Ainsley's office at the Institute for Advanced Study. Each time, she would prepare a list of thoughtful questions, but she discovered, to her chagrin, that she was merely enhancing her reputation as a hardworking, perhaps overzealous student. She decided to flirt a bit, but, alas, she was not quite sure how it was done. At nineteen, she had little practice, because her mother had taught her that boys chased girls. In Jacqueline's universe, the only girls who chased boys were the bad girls.

Which was what Beck longed to be: a bad girl.

Then the opportunity arose. During one of her visits to Dr. Ainsley's office, watching his face for evidence of interest, she mumbled some nonsense about wanting to know him better, and the distinguished professor, after thinking it over, told her he was having some of his graduate students to dinner at his house. Would Miss DeForde, as his star undergraduate, care to join them?

Miss DeForde would.

Miss DeForde consulted her wealthy roommate, Tish, without telling her just why. A gleeful Tish, who got around, took her to a boutique in Philadelphia and helped her pick out a budget-busting but terrifically slinky dress. Beck spent the rest of the week rehearsing lines she suspected she would be too shy to use, and moves she knew she would be too intimidated to make. Tish schooled her with care, pretending all along to be in the dark about the object of Beck's affection.

She arrived at five minutes past eight, very nervous, and Professor Ainsley told her she was the first. He gave her a glass of wine, sat beside her on the sofa, and asked about her dreams. He was very smooth about the whole thing. By the time it occurred to Rebecca that she was the only guest, he had her half undressed. None of her plans turned out to matter, because Jericho did all the seducing.

It sounds like he took advantage of you, said Dr. Eisenstadt, some years after. *He was older and experienced, you were younger and you had a crush. He took advantage.*

He did, Beck agreed. *But I absolutely wanted him to.*

Your desire has nothing to do with it, said the doctor, with unexpected firmness. *Jericho Ainsley abused his position, and he abused your trust. You shouldn't be too quick to forgive him.*

After the first time, they agreed there could not be a second. After the second, they were adamant that there must never be a third. After the third, they began plotting to keep it secret. As the secret slipped out—in part because of their carelessness, in part thanks to the delighted Tish—they decided to hold their heads high. Even when the Institute informed the Ambassador that they would be needing his office next year for some little-known behavioral ecologist from Europe who was taking a year to write a book about how humans were a cancer on the planet.

Beck cried. She felt horrible. She had wrecked his life.

He sat her down and told her she had two choices. She could return to Princeton next year and have everybody stare and point, or she could travel with him.

Travel where?

Wherever we want.

For how long?

For as long as we want.

Tough choice.

They had done a great deal together, Jericho and Rebecca. They had shopped, they had traveled, they had quarreled vehemently about big things and little ones, and gone back to bed to make everything fine again. She had learned a lot from him, and she liked to believe that he had learned a bit from her, too. Their life up on the mountain had been passionate and full.

But he had never surprised her with a new Ferrari in the garage. They had never partied in Aspen or Vail, and hardly ever took long walks, or sat together on the deck as the evening drew in the day.

Jericho was sending her a message.

CHAPTER 14

The Library

(1)

They clattered down the mountain in the battered abbey van, complete with the graffiti the protesters had spray-painted on the sides, and Audrey talked about her childhood in Virginia with her father never home, and about how to this day she wondered whether she should have stayed with Teddy Gould and had children, and how Beck should study Luke's Gospel, so much of which is about finding that which is lost. She talked about pretty much everything, except what had happened upstairs with the lawyers while Beck was stuck in the funhouse basement with Pamela. Because, by the time she had made it back upstairs, the Mercedes was gone and Jericho was in bed.

"But have you ever actually read Luke? Really sat down and read it, start to finish?"

Beck admitted she had never had the pleasure.

"Well, it's full of stories of the lost and found. The lost sheep. The lost coin. The prodigal son. One story after another of God calling home that which has gone astray."

"You know, Aud, just because somebody doesn't share your view doesn't make them lost."

"It doesn't make them found, either," said the nun, with punch, and for a while they rode in silence.

But Audrey was not the sort who could long bear animosity, and so she hunted for another subject. "So—what exactly are you doing in town?"

"Returning the library book, remember?"

The nun laughed. "Come on, Beck. You jumped at the chance. Tell me who you're meeting this time."

"Nobody," she muttered, feeling adolescent and hot. It was plain that Audrey was the source of her father's information about Beck's drink with Pete Mundy. The former intelligence consultant had evidently built her own network of informants in the town of Bethel.

"Such a woman of mystery," said the nun, trying to tease. "Such a busy social whirl."

"Audrey, come on."

"My brother says he sees a lot of you."

Beck, watching thick forest roll past, decided that the double entendre must be coincidence. Audrey was a nun. "I don't know what your father told you, but—"

"Never mind. None of my business."

Rebecca was unmollified. "You should know as well as anybody that your father makes things up, just to have fun. To see people's reactions."

The nun's smile faded. "I'll say he does."

They reached Main Street a few minutes before three. Audrey's errands would take her out to the commercial strip where Route 24 brushed the far edge of town. She would be back, she said, in two hours—that is, about five. They would meet at Corinda's. Rebecca waited until the van was out of sight before crossing the street toward the public library.

Remembering the pain of Stone Heights in the old days, she had forgotten the beauty of Bethel itself. Neither the encroaching of chain stores nor the closing of local businesses had yet managed to dull the luster of the town. The rows of aging Victorians seemed to glisten in the brilliant afternoon sun. In whatever direction she turned, distant mountains watched over Bethel like wise elders.

Walking along Main Street, she let memory catch her. A woman who waved from the bakery turned out to be one of Rebecca's few friends from when she had lived here. Old Man Kruger still ran the pharmacy with an iron hand. It occurred to Beck that her months up here had not all been pain; much of it had been wonderful.

Then a cloud passed in front of the sun, and the screen of memory went gray. She had not come to town to reminisce. All business again, she checked voice mail on her cell, but Nina's message about the surprise was not there. Presumably the same magical burst of static that had delivered it had also deleted it. She looked up, but no helicopter dogged her.

Last week there was the break-in at the public library. Miss Kelly tells us nothing's missing. The sheriff thinks it's kids, having fun. I think it's the strangers.

You know what, Pete? So do I.

One last call to make.

She reached her cell-phone provider, fought through the automated menu, and explained to a human being about the fax tones and the unexpected voice mail. She had to wait on hold, was transferred to someone else, who was no help, and finally reached a personable young man, probably in Bangalore, who took her through a list of useless options and then suggested that she bring the phone in for service.

Beck glanced up and down Main Street. "There's not really a store in this area."

Then she could mail it, he said, and, if it could not be repaired, they would send her a new one, free of charge. "Here's what I am thinking, ma'am," said the personable young man, once she had further detailed her limitations. "A cell phone is simply a small computer. There are people, these days, who write viruses for cell phones. Yours could be infected."

(11)

The library turned out to be not, as Rebecca had expected, an aging relic of the town's better years, but a sleek new building, of contemporary design, with lots of glass and unusual angles to catch the mountain sun. Smallish, yes, befitting the size of the town, but the plaque near the door named a famous architect, and an infamous donor: the public library was a gift to the people of the town from Jericho Ainsley, in honor of his parents.

Beck tracked down the librarian in the children's corner. Story time had ended an hour ago, and Miss Kelly was busy reshelving books and brushing up crumbs. Beck pitched in without being asked.

"They're not supposed to eat or drink in here," the librarian explained in apology. She was a black woman, tall, and smart, and nearly without humor. She wore fifties-style dresses, and glasses on a chain, and evidently lacked a first name, because even the plate on her desk called her only Miss Kelly. "But their mothers don't bother to ask, and the children—well, they're just so cute."

"I know," said Beck, stooping to help.

"We don't get as many as we used to for story time. It's been every Tuesday afternoon for the toddlers and Saturday morning for the older kids since the memory of man runneth not to the contrary. The old-timers keep telling me the place used to be packed back in the old days, but they also seem to think the snow was deeper and the winters were colder and—well, maybe they're right," she concluded, mopping spilled juice from the table as Beck relieved her of the broom and dustpan.

"I don't suppose Dr. Ainsley came for story time."

Miss Kelly straightened. Her gaze was ever on the roam, so that half the time she seemed to be speaking not to Beck but to the walls, or the ceiling, or the floor. "That's right. You're Beck, aren't you?"

"Yes."

"I wondered what you'd be like."

"You did?"

The librarian nodded. Beck felt herself blushing. Everywhere she went in Bethel, it seemed, her story preceded her. But Miss Kelly's smile neither judged her nor mocked her, and Beck relaxed. The librarian brushed her hair aside, then took her visitor by the upper arm and led her to the side of the room. Colorful bulletin boards proclaimed the magic of reading. Posters touting books by Stephanie Meyer and J. K. Rowling were prominently displayed.

They sat side by side on low desks. "Everybody in town's been talking about you." A grin, half hidden behind all that hair. "Especially after last night."

"Last night?"

"Your drink with Pete Mundy. It's a small town, Rebecca."

"It was just a drink." She tried a smile. "I brought the book back. I don't think Jericho's had a chance to read it, but it's overdue."

"What book? Oh. Thanks." Miss Kelly did not even check the due date. She set the tome aside and waited, eyes once more focused on the middle distance.

"Is there a fine?" said Beck.

"I think you should tell me why you're here."

"The book—"

"Come on, Miss DeForde. I'm willing to believe that you're a very fine person. I'm not willing to believe that you would leave the sickbed of a dying man you once loved to return a library book."

Beck took a minute. "You know Jericho hasn't been well. I'm out here—well, to visit him. To help out a little. You understand." The librarian was not saying whether she understood or not. Her gaze continued to roam the room. "To be honest, there have been some strange things going on. I'm leaving the day after tomorrow. Going back east. I just want to make sure that"—she hesitated, searching for the word— "that all he has to worry about is getting better."

Miss Kelly nodded. She was swinging her long legs like an impatient little girl.

"You had a break-in here," said Beck. "I was hoping I could ask you a couple of questions about it."

The ghost of a smile. "You're here to nurse a dying man, but you take a couple of precious hours to drive into town because you're curious about an act of vandalism at the public library?" She shook her head. "You're going to have to do better than that, Miss DeForde."

The librarian's elaborately quaint formality was beginning to throw her, as was perhaps the intention. Beck realized that in this case, at least, she would be able to buy truth only by paying truth. "I don't think it was vandalism, Miss Kelly. I don't think it was local kids or the town drunk. I think it was somebody who's interested in what Jericho has been up to. I'm thinking that maybe Jericho spent some time here. Reading. Doing research. I'm not sure exactly what, but I'm betting he was in here a lot. I think that's why there was a break-in. Somebody else was betting the same thing."

Miss Kelly was on her feet. She had an unusually firm bearing for a woman so tall. "I had a reporter in here the other day. Some kind of writer, anyway." She was strolling toward her desk. Beck followed. "He asked me the same thing."

"Lewiston Clark?"

"Sounds right. Big guy, red beard."

"That's him." Although, in Miss Kelly's austere presence, she felt as if she should have said, *That's he.* "So—what did you tell him?"

"The same thing I'm going to tell you. Mr. Ainsley has been very good to me. All this"—waving her hand again—"didn't have to happen. My degree isn't in library science, Miss DeForde. I was a literature major. But I needed a job. Mr. Ainsley is a power in this town. He got them to hire me."

"Where were you before this?"

"A foundation back east. I lost my job last year. I had trouble finding another one. Then a friend of a friend called Mr. Ainsley, we met, he thought I was smart—and, well, here I am. A librarian in Nowheresville."

Rebecca looked at Miss Kelly: tall and competent and hiding something. An accomplished, professional woman, retreating to a little Colorado town. Owing Jericho. Just the sort he would choose to—well, to help him.

Naturally.

Miss Kelly owed him, and Miss Kelly was an outsider. Beck had not seen many African Americans since arriving Sunday night, and her considered prejudices insisted that it was strange for a black woman to move to a Colorado mountain town.

Jericho builds the library, and the library hires an outsider as librarian: no wonder they burglarized the building.

Whoever they were.

Meanwhile, Miss Kelly was still talking.

"There isn't much to tell. It was—let's see—the Monday. Eight days ago. I usually get here about seven-thirty on weekdays. We open at eight-thirty. I was a little late that morning. When I arrived, that whole section over there"—she swept a hand—"was a mess. Books on the floor, some of them damaged. We keep DVDs over there, too. A lot of them were out of their cases. A couple were missing." Another shrug. "I called some of the women from town. We cleaned it up as best we could."

Beck was on her feet. "Do you mind?"

"Not at all." That quick, shy grin. "If you see anything out of place, let me know."

The corner of the library Miss Kelly had indicated contained books on literature and history. At first Beck was not sure why they would be shelved together. Then she realized that the collection was organized according to the old Dewey decimal system, rather than the Library of Congress system so many major libraries used today. Literature was the 800s, history was the 900s. She roamed the shelves. She could not see why this area would be chosen for—well, whatever it was chosen for. She saw no obvious link to whatever Jericho was hiding.

If he was hiding anything, she cautioned herself.

On the wall just past those shelves were reference books, everything from home-improvement manuals to wildlife guides filled with photographs of flowering plants. Had one of these, she wondered, struck Jericho's fancy? Was it possible that he had checked out the novel as an act of misdirection? That he had never read it because he had never planned to read it? That he had snatched it off the literature shelf to explain his visits to this corner of the library?

Then something else occurred to her.

Miss Kelly had said this was the only section where there had been vandalism. Perhaps it was just that—vandalism—in which case there was no reason to worry. If, however, the break-in was related to Jericho, then there had to be a reason the damage was limited to this section.

Whoever the people were who broke in, they knew what they were looking for, which meant they knew which part of the library Jericho used.

Which meant somebody had told them.

(III)

Back at the desk, Miss Kelly was filling out requisition forms. Reading upside down, Beck realized that she was asking the selectmen for money to buy more books. In the current climate, she suspected, the selectmen would have other priorities.

"May I ask you something else?"

"Of course," said the librarian, not looking up.

"Did Jericho—did Mr. Ainsley check out any other books? You would have records, right?"

The librarian was already shaking her head. Not in denial. In refusal. "You know, Miss DeForde, after 9/11, the government adopted all these rules about libraries keeping track of their readers. The library association has been adamant in opposing the rules. We're not supposed to cooperate with inquiries like—well, like yours."

"I'm not the government."

"The principle isn't anti-government. It's pro-privacy." She crossed her arms, prepared to do battle.

"The difference is, I'm trying to help him."

"A principle isn't a principle if it respects such differences as that." Miss Kelly waited, perhaps to see if her visitor would write this down. "I don't doubt your sincerity, but you are asking questions that it would be unethical for me to answer."

"I don't think he'd mind if you talked to me."

Miss Kelly nodded toward her desk. "There's the phone, Miss DeForde. Why don't you call Stone Heights and we'll ask?" Beck was growing annoyed, but the librarian turned out not to be finished. "I appreciate what you're saying. I do. But you have to understand my position. There are lots of ways for a librarian to get in trouble these days. I have a good job here. A job I'd like to keep. I had lots of trouble being accepted here. And Mr. Ainsley—well, he's sick, but he helped. He was on my side when other people weren't."

Beck could hardly mistake the message: without Jericho's patronage, Miss Kelly's thin supporting ledge might crumble. So she hunted around for a question the librarian might answer without getting tangled in her ethics.

And found one. She was thinking about Jericho's games with the folder, and wondered whether the library, too, might be a false trail—what Dak called a wisp. Perhaps Miss Kelly herself was neither his helper nor the witness who had told the strangers where to look. Perhaps she was but a diversion from a deeper truth.

"I'm sorry. I don't mean to ask you to divulge any confidences." Miss Kelly smiled her disbelief. "Let me ask something that has to be public knowledge. The times that Jericho came in here, did he ever speak to anyone? Someone else from town?" She considered how to frame the idea. "Maybe someone who was here as often as he was?"

Miss Kelly was no fool. Dark eyes narrowed as she got the point. But if Beck had imagined that the librarian would again take refuge in the rules of her trade, she was mistaken.

"You're thinking that Mr. Ainsley used my library"—Beck noticed the pronoun—"for some kind of meetings."

"It's possible."

Miss Kelly pondered. "Is this related to—well, the work he did before? The national security? All that?" A puzzled frown. "Forgive me, Miss DeForde. I respected the man, but not his politics. I never really approved of the kind of positions he took." She pointed. "We have all six of his books, of course. Several copies. I've read them. I have to be honest: they frighten me. With all the troubles we have in the world, I think things would be worse if he'd been whispering all these ideas into the ears of the last couple of Presidents. I hope you're not offended."

At last, a chink in the armor. "I'm not offended, Miss Kelly. I don't like his ideas, either."

"Mr. Ainsley likes to talk about Richard Nixon. Maybe you know that. He says Nixon was a scoundrel, but he pulled off the greatest intelligence coup of the twentieth century."

"China," said Beck, who had forgotten how Jericho would go on about the subject. Not only that Nixon went to China, but that he managed to fool the world. Nobody knew the old Cold Warrior was heading to China. All the negotiations were conducted in secret. And then, suddenly, the Soviet Union faced an unexpected alliance of its two greatest ideological enemies. Secrecy plus reordering the world: Jericho's twin passions. Nixon obstructed justice and was driven from office, but Jericho Ainsley, who at the time of Watergate had been a young Agency case officer, remained devoted to him.

"I would argue with him," the librarian was saying. "I didn't understand how he could admire a man of Nixon's—views. And he would tell me how FDR lied about whether he planned to send American boys to fight in Europe, and Lincoln lied in the run-up to the Civil War—he seemed to think that lying in the national interest was something to be proud of. The bigger the lie, the more successfully the wool was pulled over the eyes of the American public, the greater Mr. Ainsley's admiration for the liar."

Beck remembered this, too, how Jericho would teach, even in the classroom, that lying was neither right nor wrong; that truth was not a virtue; that all that mattered about words was what they accomplished.

"Don't get me wrong, Miss DeForde. I'm not saying we don't have real enemies in the world. I just don't happen to think lying for your country or blowing up every bad guy to Kingdom Come creates new friends. I think it creates new enemies." She was getting wound up. "Are you saying he was using my library for secret meetings? Is that what you mean? *Here?* This is a citadel of knowledge. A sacred space. Books are the repository of ideas. They represent reason, argument, the interplay of—" She saw the visitor's eyebrows arch and made herself stop. "I'm sorry, Miss DeForde. I'm afraid my passions on this subject run high."

Again Beck knew not to press. "I'm not saying he was up to no good in your library, Miss Kelly. I honestly don't know what he was up to. I'm trying to find out."

"And that's why you want to know if he met anyone regularly?"

"Yes."

A slow nod. "Well, I suppose there might have been one."

"May I ask who?"

"You may." That ghostly smile again. "A man named Brian Navarro."

"Where would I find him?"

"He's a lawyer. There are only two in town. His office is on Main Street."

Miss Kelly walked Beck to the door and, unexpectedly, hugged her. "I should clarify what I said before. About why I needed this job. About why I'm indebted to Mr. Ainsley."

"You don't have to—"

"But I do. Because we have more in common than you might think. I told you that I lost my job at a foundation. I didn't tell you why." The girlish look was back as the librarian stared at her feet. "The head of the foundation resigned. Very quietly handled. The foundation was reimbursing him for a New York apartment. Turned out that he was overbilling for it, and using it as a kind of love nest besides. He used it for trysts with one of his co-workers, and—well, he resigned, and I got fired."

"I had no idea."

A grim smile. "In a scandal involving a great man's marriage, nobody ever asks what happened to the other woman. But there's one thing you know as well as I do. After the dust settles, she discovers that there's a scarlet letter on her résumé. And it can't ever be erased."

Beck nodded and mumbled something indistinct, uncomfortable with the librarian's assertion of a commonality between them. Then she realized that there was a question Miss Kelly had not addressed.

"How long have you been the librarian?"

"I moved up here about six months ago."

From what Dak had said, Jericho's madness—and his threats—began well before that. "Did Jericho use the library before you arrived?"

Miss Kelly nodded. "That's what I'm given to understand. He was in and out of here all the time, just like now."

"Where's the old librarian? Your predecessor. Can I talk to her?"

"Oh, I'm sorry. That wouldn't be possible. Miss Waller died last year. That's why there was an opening."

"Died?"

"A traffic accident. She went off the road into one of these gorges." A pained expression. "Very tragic."

CHAPTER 15

The Classmate

(1)

Brian Navarro's office was in a stucco townhouse on Main Street. He had the entire second floor, but the receptionist said he was out for the day. Rebecca made an appointment for the following morning. She gave a false name and a false story, but only, she told herself, because she did not want word spreading around town; or back to Jericho.

Although why she cared what he knew, she could not precisely say.

With half an hour to kill before Audrey would return to pick her up at Corinda's, Beck decided to have a cup of coffee and a sandwich. In the late afternoon, the place was nearly empty, so she was able to grab a booth by the front window. Zeelie, the talkative waitress of the night before, was not on duty, and Beck immediately forgot the name of whoever was.

The coffee was cold.

Rebecca sat there, puzzling, as she watched what there was of life passing by. When she had lived out here with Jericho, the town had possessed a thriving factory that manufactured machine tools, and another that specialized in printer's inks. Now both were shuttered. There were still jobs, mostly in light industry, an hour or more away. Closer to home, there was retail, but not much tourism. Efforts to build a ski resort had come a cropper. But the town hung on, and had recently been discovered by some among the smart set, who were building their *Schlösser* on the nearby mountainsides. She wondered what would be left when the smart set moved on.

The point was, as Miss Kelly had indicated, Jericho Ainsley's presence in town was a big deal.

A town like this, that many strangers—you get my meaning.

Beck, pondering, stirred her coffee, and engaged in what Jericho used to call doing her sums.

Fact: Jericho had something he had threatened to disclose, and, whatever it was, people were frightened.

Fact: at the same time, nobody dared harm him, or any of his family, a protective umbrella that evidently covered even Rebecca herself.

Fact: Dak said Jericho had to be working with someone in town.

Fact: it was Jericho who had established the library, and then brought in Miss Kelly as librarian.

Conclusion: Jericho was working with Miss Kelly.

Supposition: if so, then Miss Kelly was in terrible danger. After all, she could not plausibly be considered a member of Jericho's family.

Yet, having worked her way to this point, Beck could almost see his face, not as it was now but as she remembered from the seminar room at Princeton, and, later, the bedroom, the mocking smile proposing that she had done her sums wrong.

Fine. What had she messed up? Well, for one thing, Miss Kelly was a little obvious. She was practically the only person in town who was neither white nor Latin, and therefore stood out like a sore thumb. Hiding in plain sight was one thing; but imagining Jericho meeting secretly with the librarian bordered on the absurd. Besides, according to Miss Kelly, she and Jericho had not met until last year. Hardly the best qualification for a trusted assistant.

Fine again. Suppose, therefore, that Miss Kelly was telling the truth about everything. Suppose Jericho had met her last year, then brought her up the mountain only because he felt sorry for her, and also because he wanted to strike a blow for—well, for whatever cause he had in mind that week. Miss Kelly said the only person she remembered spending much time with Jericho as he hunted through the library was Brian Navarro, but what if—

"Now, this is a lucky break."

Rebecca looked up in surprise, but she knew the voice even before she spotted the red mop of hair and fiery matching beard.

"Mr. Clark."

"Please. Call me Lewiston." Without being invited, he slid into the booth across from her. "I was hoping to get the chance to talk to you—"

"I have no interest in talking to you, Mr. Clark."

"Why not? I'm a nice guy." An infectious smile. "Besides, we're classmates."

"I never graduated, as I'm sure you know perfectly well."

"I do know. Still, I thought it would be nice to catch up."

"Catch up? We didn't even know each other."

"Not sober." He saw her consternation. The waitress brought Beck her grilled-chicken sandwich and, without asking, put a burger in front of Lewiston Clark. He waited until she had gone. "We got drunk together on Newman's Day freshman year. There were five or six of us. You don't remember?"

"No." But she did. Hazily. Her big breakout from Jacqueline, Miss Goody Two-Shoes allowing her wicked roommates to tempt her into joining the Princeton tradition of downing twenty-four beers in twenty-four hours on the twenty-fourth of April. Before then, she had never attempted more than the occasional glass of wine with dinner.

"Don't worry," he said, grinning. He took a largish bite, chewed while she blushed. "You weren't one of the girls who wound up— Well, never mind what they did. You were so sweet and innocent. You weren't a sloppy drunk. You didn't start swearing or kissing strangers or dancing on the tables. You just got quiet and a little sad. I don't think you made it past eight beers. You fell asleep. You were really cute." He stopped laughing. "And if anybody had told us that night that mousy little Becky DeForde was the one who would smash Jericho Ainsley's marriage to bits a year later—"

"I think I get the picture."

"Not that you weren't good-looking. As a matter of fact, some of the guys had these little bets going—"

"I said I get it, Mr. Clark. Please, leave me alone."

But some men are encouraged rather than deterred by firmness. "I can see you're not that helpless little nobody any more, but I don't think Jericho is any less obsessed with you now than he was then. I think he wanted you *because* you were sweet. He wanted you *because* you were innocent." Clark's next bite seemed almost angry: a man with scores to settle. "He's a corrupter, Beck. That's what he does. He messes with people the way he used to mess with countries. If he drew you back in after all these years, it's because he wants one last shot at corrupting you. So, the way I see it, if I keep an eye on you, I'll figure out what he's up to."

"Believe me, I'm corrupt enough already."

"Maybe not in Jericho's eyes." He had lifted the bread to examine the burger. Severely underdone. "So—what did Agadakos want?"

The sudden change in subject threw her, as it was intended to. "I'm sorry?"

He had a notebook open on the Formica. "Philip Bartholomew Agadakos," the writer said. "Sixty-eight years old. Former chief of staff for the National Security Council, former Deputy Director of Operations at Langley. Jericho's favorite hatchet man. Long talk the two of you had last night in your car. Mind telling me what it was all about?"

"Yes." She turned her attention to her food. The mention of Dak had reminded her of the stakes. "I do mind. Please leave me alone."

"Which side is he on? That's all I want to know. Agadakos. Is he on Jericho's side?" She continued eating. "Because, you know, Beck—"

"Ms. DeForde."

"Whatever." He sipped his water. "Here's the thing. I've picked up these wild stories about what Jericho is cooking up. I hear some pretty prominent people might wind up in prison if he doesn't get what he wants. The part I don't know is what he wants."

This was new to her. Dak had said nothing about prison, or even prosecution. "Which prominent people?" she asked.

"Presumably, the ones who are paying Phil Agadakos."

She remembered what Dak had said about the man now sitting across from her. "Or the ones who are paying Lewiston Clark," she suggested.

"Could be," he agreed, quite unbothered. He turned a page. "So—what did Miss Kelly tell you? Does she know who did the break-in?"

"I would imagine it was you."

He was unfazed. "Wish I'd thought of it. They won't let him get away with it. Jericho. You have to know that."

"I don't have any idea what you're talking about."

"Come on. I bet he has the papers lying around the house somewhere, doesn't he? Maybe he showed you where. He didn't invite you all the way out here for nothing." Another bite. Maybe he liked underdone meat. "Look. If you could maybe find a way to let me have a peek, there might be some money in it for you. A lot."

Again the money. Everyone she met seemed obsessed with it. "Are you going to leave," she asked softly, "or do I have to call the manager?"

"You could call your friend. The deputy. People tell me the two of you were pretty cozy last night. Caused him trouble at home, from what I hear."

Rebecca was impressed. Not with Lewiston Clark, who seemed to her a particularly pernicious dope. With herself. With something that had changed inside her—if not over the past few days, then perhaps over the past few years. Pamela had been largely right this morning. Once upon a time, Beck had possessed a fierce temper, and when she had lived with Jericho, their arguments had been explosive. She could no longer recall the other half, whether the sex had been sufficiently fiery to compensate for the fury. That side of life with Jericho seemed oddly hazy in her memory.

What she did know, however, was that there was a time when she would have been trying to gouge Lewiston Clark's eyes out. Now she simply shook her head and took another bite of chicken.

"Was there something you actually wanted?" she asked, calmly. "Or are you like a cable host who doesn't care what he says as long as he gets a rise out of his guest?"

The writer stroked his beard. "Hey, I'm just doing what I do."

"Spreading rumors?"

"Tracking down the story."

"And what story are you tracking this time?" She tilted her head toward the window, the mountain, Jericho's shrinking world. "I doubt there's fifty people in America who remember him. And I doubt that there's ten who care."

Her cell phone rang.

(11)

They both stared.

"Aren't you going to answer that?"

She had taken it from her belt. The screen said UNKNOWN NUM-BER. "No."

"You don't even know who it is."

"It's fine."

"Is it Jericho? Is that why you won't answer?" He grabbed for the phone, but Beck had learned her lesson from Audrey's success with the same move. She swept it off the table and into her handbag. "You can't protect him forever."

The phone was still ringing. She had pressed the button to kill the call, and it was still ringing. People were beginning to stare.

Lewiston Clark was grinning. "Well?"

With a furious snarl, she pressed the green button and put it to her ear, and, yes, sure enough, the familiar fax whine. Random scatter, my ass.

"Leave me alone," she hissed, and ended the call.

"It was Jericho, wasn't it?"

"No."

"You're shaking like a leaf."

Her eyes hardened. "You were about to tell me what story you're tracking this time."

The writer sat back. "Jericho isn't the story. The story is money. Lots of money. Where it all went."

"What money is that, Mr. Clark?"

He seemed amused. "Know what your problem is? You have Jericho frozen in time. The national-security stuff. CIA. DOD. All of that. It's what he did after that's interesting. When he was a partner at—"

"Scondell Bloom," she said tiredly. "The private equity firm. Jericho was cleared of any wrongdoing—"

"I'm not saying he committed a crime. I'm not saying he breached any kind of fiduciary duty. I am interested, though, in how he got involved with a bunch of people who did both of those things." He took another bite. "Here's the thing, Beck. Jericho's an old man. He's dying. He wants to go out in a blaze of glory."

About the same thing Dak told her. "So?"

"So I'm saying, whatever happened to Scondell Bloom, there's more to it than meets the eye. That's all." Another sloppy bite. "Beck, look. Here's the thing. Scondell Bloom Notting was the most powerful private equity shop in the world, and then, just like that, it vanished into thin air. How? Billions of dollars gone. Where?"

"Congress investigated. Grand juries. Jericho didn't do anything—"

"Anything wrong. I know. You told me. But I'm not writing about Jericho. I'm writing about the firm." His eyes were glowing with the intensity she now remembered from their college days. The cause did not matter. The intensity itself was his motive. "I think Jericho knows what took the firm down. Where the money went. And I think there are people who are afraid he'll tell."

The cell phone rang again. Beck did not even glance at it. The reporter paused in his tale, waiting for her to answer, because the bizarre modern conceit was that it was rude *not* to interrupt whomever you happened to be with to talk to whoever happened to call.

"Go on," she said.

"I have sources, Beck. One of them says the firm was washing mob money."

"Come on."

"I'm not saying it's true." The phone was still ringing. Clark spoke slowly, in measured cadences, as if expecting her to correct her faux pas.

The ringing stopped.

"The mob," she said, with patent disbelief.

"These days, the mob doesn't have that much money. Not the American mob, anyway. But overseas? Crime syndicates are big. And Jericho—well, overseas was his specialty, wasn't it?"

"You're out of your mind if you think a man like Jericho Ainsley would—"

"Would what, Beck? Lie? Cheat? Manipulate people?" His fury was sudden, like a mountain storm. "You think all his contacts were nice congressionally vetted spies who go to Georgetown cocktail parties?"

Audrey stepped brightly into the restaurant, saving her from the necessity to answer. Lewiston Clark immediately turned his charm on her, but her tolerant smile said she knew his kind of old.

"I'll get this," said the reporter, still smiling, reaching for the bill.

"No," said the nun, snatching it. "If you let him pay," she told Beck, calmly, "you'll feel beholden. The next time, it's easier to get you to talk. That's how these people work."

People like reporters. Or interrogation specialists.

(III)

Deputy Mundy and his partner pulled up outside just as Audrey and Beck were stalking out. Tony winked and walked on past. Pete lingered. "I was hoping to run into you. I heard you were in town."

She eyed the van. "Hi, Pete. Look. I'm sorry. I have to get going."

He looked appropriately crestfallen, the boyish earnestness hopeful behind the glasses. She had known that kind at Princeton, too: keep sweet, keep teasing, and sooner or later she'll come around. "Oh. Too bad. And here I am on my break."

Beck could not help smiling. "Goodbye, Pete," she said.

He tipped his cap and started to turn away, the gesture reminding her that he was official. An idea struck her. She touched his hand.

"Actually," she said, "it might be good if we had a talk."

"Now?"

"No. Not now. I have my ride waiting." She hesitated, remembering Garvey's warning. But she was a big girl, and Pete was a big boy. "I'll meet you here at eight-thirty."

She walked over to the van and climbed in.

The nun grinned as they pulled away. "I told you he likes you."

"Stop it."

"Pete Mundy, Lewiston Clark. I wonder who'll be next?" She laughed. "You know what Dad says about you, Beck? He says you're the kind of woman who when she's seventy and she's been married five times will still have all these guys lined up. He says you can snare a guy by raising your eyebrow—"

Rebecca slapped the shoddy dashboard with the flat of her hand, startling them both with her vehemence.

"Enough, okay? Enough! I want Jericho to stop. I want all of you to stop. I came here to say goodbye. That's all. I came here to say goodbye, and I'm sick of being treated like it's my fault Jericho's dying."

"I didn't mean—"

"Look at me, Aud. No, look at me. I'm nobody. I don't even have a degree. I dropped out of Princeton, remember? Moved in with your father, moved out a year or so later, spent the next year working hard to pick which drug to get high on every night. Jericho even dropped by to see me, ordered me to clean myself up. Very paternal. Got myself a new boyfriend, another druggie, wandered around Europe and Asia. Read palms in Edinburgh, waited tables in Greece, tended bar in Bangkok, did the Kathmandu trail, what was left of it. Came back, worked at McDonald's, and nearly gave my mother a stroke. Worked in retail, moved up, and now I've reached my level of incompetence." Audrey, alarmed at what her teasing had unleashed, was making ineffectual shushing noises. "Do you know what I do for a living, Aud? What I really do?"

"You're an executive at—"

"Right. Some executive. I advise the folks who own my company whether to put the perfumes to the right or the left of the jewelry counter as you walk into the store. That's what I've been doing for six years, and I'm not moving any higher on the letterhead. Along the way I married a total shit who turned out to have another couple of children with another couple of wives he never got around to mentioning. The only thing I care about in this world is my little girl. I don't have any ambitions, and I don't have any hopes. So get off my case, okay? I'll be gone the day after tomorrow. I'll be out of your hair."

"I didn't mean anything. I'm sorry."

"I'm sorry, too."

Except she wasn't. Not really. Audrey was a psychologist who specialized in interrogation. And she was no fool. If she had goaded Beck into an explosion, it would not have been by accident. The nun wanted Rebecca angry. She wanted the engine stoked, fiery hot.

In the chilly silence as they climbed the mountain, Beck wondered why.

(I V)

Back at Stone Heights, she put in a call to Tish Kirschbaum, her college roommate and one of her few close friends. If anybody knew the inside story of the collapse of Scondell Bloom, it would be Tish, who had spent years defending accused white-collar criminals, and now taught eager law students to do the same. No answer at home, office, or mobile. Tish already had Beck's cell number. She left Jericho's number on all three of the voice mails. She did not say why she was calling.

Waiting for a callback, she took herself off for another ramble, this time behind the house, where the land sloped toward a creek, then rose again. Jericho owned a good chunk of the mountain itself, and it was toward his private mountain that he had pointed earlier, sitting on the deck and lying his head off for the benefit of the microphones.

We walked all the time, Beck. In the woods. Even up the peak now and then. Remember? And down there. The valley.

But the valley was simply the border, separating well-tended lawn and sparse trees from the heavier forest beyond. Climbing the trail, she mulled the tiff with Audrey. The nun had baited her, and Beck still was not sure why. Maybe messing with other people's heads was how all the Ainsleys had their fun. For the first time she saw Pamela and Audrey not as her rivals but as Jericho's daughters, and wondered what a little girl's life would have been like with Jericho as father. Was he overbearing and sarcastic, criticizing every tiny error? Did he like them to dress up and be ladylike? Or did he, as in his weirdly paternal relationship to Rebecca, demand both? No wonder they—

Wait.

There on the trail before her were human footprints, preserved in the frozen soil and sprinkled with snow, but whether they were two days or two months old she had no way to tell.

Besides, maybe they were just random impressions in the ground, onto which she was projecting a structure. As Audrey said, the mind plays tricks.

Eight hundred acres. The middle of nowhere.

The sun had slipped behind the peak, but daylight would not flee the mountain for a while yet. Beck kept walking. She had looked up Scondell Bloom on the Internet, but the thousands of stories explained little that was helpful. The firm had been a giant, and the founders were regarded on Wall Street as buyout geniuses. Its full name was Scondell * Bloom * Notting, complete with asterisks. For over a decade, the geniuses at Scondell Bloom had left lesser titans trembling with envy. Then, suddenly, the firm had imploded. Billions were lost. Now Rufus Scondell was awaiting trial, Doolie Bloom had committed suicide, and Jack Notting had vanished. On the run, said some. In witness protection, said others.

Washing mob money, Lewiston Clark had suggested, a possibility that would provide a somewhat different explanation for Jack Notting's disappearance.

Rebecca shivered, and kept walking.

At an elevation of two hundred feet or so above the house, the path opened onto a small plateau, where she used to sit and sulk when she thought Jericho was being mean. She sat there now, on the same boulder, but hastily stood up, because the rock was icy cold. Down below she could see the house. Because the trees had been cut back fifty yards in every direction, the sight lines were unbroken. With binoculars she could have looked into half the rooms.

"Close your curtains tonight," she muttered.

She hugged herself, and was about to descend when she saw the footprints again, this time a whole line of them, leading past her boulder. Now Beck was sure. She followed the prints into a copse of trees, where they vanished. But from here, she realized, the sight lines were even better. And there was cover: you could hide in the trees and watch the house without anyone's noticing.

Something glittered.

Rebecca knelt down and picked it up.

A chewing-gum wrapper. It looked fresh.

TUESDAY NIGHT

CHAPTER 16

The Photographs

(1)

Rebecca finally reached her mother. Evidently, the trip to the beach had turned into a visit to Disney World, a two-hour drive each way. Yes, said Jacqueline. Of course she had heard her cell phone ringing. But she had not wanted to spend a single second more than necessary distracted from her beautiful grandchild.

"You should at least pick up when you know it's me."

"How would I know it's you if I don't even look at the screen?"

"Come on, Mom. What if it's important?"

"When you call, you always say it's important. Maybe if you'd call more often I'd believe you."

The logic of this riposte was so absurd that Beck was left sputtering. Only then did a thoroughly delighted Jacqueline put Nina on the phone.

"Grandma gave me another surprise today."

"The trip to Disney World. She told me."

"Not that. There's another one." Giggle. "I'll show you when you come."

Beck did her best to giggle back. "Is it another doll?"

"It's a *surprise.*"

"Sweetie-pie? Can you put Grandma back on for Mommy?"

Hiatus. "She says she has to call you back."

"Please put her on, honey."

Longer break. "She can't come to the phone. She's fixing up the surprise."

"Nina—"

Dead air.

Beck was sitting in the living room with the portable phone. Nina sounded so happy, yet Rebecca felt depressed. She stood up and pulled a book at random from the shelf, playing Jericho's old game. *The American Commonwealth,* by somebody named Bryce, an aging leatherbound edition. Flipping the pages, not really reading, she tried to figure out why the conversation with her daughter had worried her so. Maybe she was still thinking about Lewiston Clark's dark insinuations from this afternoon.

The cell phone rang. Reluctantly, she pressed the green button. Static. She pressed red, and then, because she was methodical, scrolled through the missed calls, just in case the one she had not answered at Corinda's this afternoon was from somebody she knew. To her surprise, the screen did not say UNKNOWN. Instead, there was a number, with a northern Virginia area code. Beck glanced at her watch. A little past seven. Just past nine back east.

She picked up the house phone, punched the number.

"Hello?" A woman's voice, cultured and smooth, bursting with confidence.

"I'm returning a call. My name is Rebecca DeForde—"

"Rebecca!" The voice was suddenly joyful. "It's Margaret Ainsley. How've you been?"

Jericho's cousin. Pamela and Audrey's Aunt Maggie.

"I'm fine, Senator," said Beck, mystified. "And yourself? Oh, and I hope I'm not calling too late."

"No, not at all, it's fine." She noticed that the politician did not ask to be called Maggie. "But you're doing well? And Nina?"

"Yes. She is. Thank you." Beck's interest was piqued. This could not be a social call: she and Maggie Ainsley had not exchanged a word in over a decade.

"I'm so glad. I hear wonderful things about her. It's a shame we don't see more of each other, you and I. I'm in McLean, and you're right there in Alexandria, near Old Town, isn't it?" Showing off her resources. Beck wondered who was left that was not keeping tabs on her. "We'll do a date for dinner. Can we do that? I'll have my people set something up. And bring the little girl, or the deal's off." A practiced political chuckle.

"It would be my pleasure."

"Great. I'm so glad. Rebecca, look. Let me tell you why I called. I'm hoping you can help my cousin out of a rather serious jam."

She pulled the phone away from her ear, stared at it, put it back. "I'll do my best, ma'am."

"Good. Good. Listen. Here's the thing. It's a funny problem to discuss on an open line, but I don't think we have any choice, unless you have an encrypted phone on you." The chuckle was beginning to grate. "Look. My cousin, well, he values your counsel, of course. That's very smart of him. You're a smart woman, Rebecca. You might be able to help him." Her cadence picked up. "I spent an hour yesterday with the Attorney General. We've spoken three or four times over the past few weeks. He told me that Jericho is holding on to copies of documents that have classifications of 'Secret' and above. That's a serious offense, Rebecca, as I'm sure you know. They've tried and failed to get them back. Nobody wants a fuss. My cousin is sick, after all, and, well, whatever might have happened in the past, we Ainsleys tend to avoid public scandal whenever we can."

Whatever might have happened in the past. Cute.

"So I told him I'd see what I can do. I talked to Jericho when I was there, and of course he said it was a pack of lies. Well, he would say that, wouldn't he? And maybe it is. But if you should happen to come across anything—"

"You'll be the first to know," said Beck, somehow unsurprised.

"Great. Just great. Listen. You have my cell. You can call me directly. And don't forget our dinner. You'll be hearing from my people."

Beck was about to answer, but she was talking to dead air. The Senator was too important to bother with goodbye.

Furious, she stepped into the kitchen to put the phone back in the cradle. Audrey was mopping the floor.

"How's the little one?"

"Oh, she's great. Just great."

The nun looked up at her. "Are you okay?"

"Yes. I have to go out, Aud."

The searching look gave way to a grin. "Remember he's married," she said, and went back to her mopping.

(III)

"Your boss said I should stay away from you."

"Garvey?" Pete Mundy made a face. "Don't take him seriously. Besides, he's only technically my boss."

"Technically?"

"In Colorado, the sheriff is elected. The deputies are permanent. Joe Garvey knows as much about the job as I know about brain surgery."

She grinned. "I'm in kind of the same situation. My boss can't take two steps without me. I have to do his job and my job both." Serious again. "But, Pete, that doesn't change anything. He's still my boss. And Garvey is still your boss. You don't want to cross him."

"If I didn't want to cross the sheriff," said the deputy, with punch, "I wouldn't be sitting here—now, would I?"

Beck looked away. The conversation was supposed to be on her terms, not his. But Pete Mundy had landed with both feet where she did not want him to go. "I know," she said softly.

"I like you, Beck. You're interesting."

"I like you, too." She nodded toward his ring. "But you're married."

Pete Mundy tilted his bottle, clinking hers, although it was not clear what he was celebrating. Corinda's was crowded tonight. In his pullover, the deputy looked boyish and charming. He said, "Separated."

Beck squirmed. He was not going to make this easy. "How long?"

"Two months."

"That's practically still married. That's you and your wife telling people you're trying to work things out."

He looked away, said what men always say, even the boyish ones. "It's complicated."

"No, it isn't. You're married or you're not."

"There's all kinds of marriages, Beck."

Making up her mind for her. "I've done it both ways, Pete. I've been the other woman with a married man, and I've been the married woman whose husband left her for the other woman. You're very sweet, but it's not going to happen."

A slow, sad nod. Behind the glasses he again had a teenager's earnestness. "Then why are we here?"

"Because I'd like to ask a favor."

"For which I get nothing in return."

"For which you get my undying gratitude."

He laughed, signaling that they were friends. Zeelie came over with new beers for them both. She winked at Rebecca.

"What's the favor?" Pete asked when she was gone.

"I was just wondering," she said. "This is hypothetical. But say the federal government was conducting some kind of operation here. Would they notify you?"

He sat back, amused. "The federal government?"

"Yes."

"An operation? Here?"

"Yes."

The deputy shook his head. "I don't know what you think is going on, Beck. We're a small town. This isn't New York or Chicago or Denver or"—he seemed unable to come up with another city—"one of those places. You couldn't hide two FBI agents in this county without somebody noticing." He took a long swallow of beer. "What I'm saying is, it wouldn't matter if they notified us or not. Probably they wouldn't, they're such supercilious assholes. But—even if they didn't? We'd notice."

Beck looked past him, toward the table beneath the moose head. Last night he had insisted that the couple there was watching her. Now it was occupied by a trio of sixtyish women drinking gin. Maggie Ainsley had suggested that the Justice Department was after Jericho now.

"What about the strangers?" she said. "You said there are all these strangers in town. Couldn't they be federal?"

He gave her that lovely boyish grin. "I thought you said this was hypothetical." He waved away her objections. "Never mind. Look. Anything's possible, okay? But I've dealt with the feds, even the undercover kind. These guys—they're too cocky, Beck. Cocky and clumsy at the same time. Full of themselves. No. The ones we arrested? They're not federal. They're private."

"So the sheriff told me." She toyed with her napkin. "He said he had to turn them loose."

"Somebody called him. Somebody powerful."

"Jericho said he paid for the sheriff's election."

"That he did." He sipped. "And Sheriff Garvey is not a man who forgets a favor. He also has the spine of a caterpillar. He would do whatever Mr. Ainsley said. But why would Mr. Ainsley want them turned loose?"

"You're saying somebody else made the call."

"All I know is, when I called the sheriff after the arrests, he practically slapped me on the back over the phone for keeping the peace. Two hours later, he's tearing me a new one. In the middle of the night, Beck."

"Any idea who hired them?"

He took a long swallow, wiped his mouth. "Somebody who doesn't much like the Ambassador, I'm guessing."

She thought about it. "Is Jericho popular in this town? Do people like him?"

"You could say that."

"He doesn't have enemies, say?"

"If he does, I don't know about them."

She hesitated before her final question. "The sheriff also told me something else about you."

"That I'm a wild man, right?" Pete never cracked a smile. "That I have these crazy ideas about what's going on in this town?"

"Something like that," she said, with a trace of déjà vu.

He tossed some money on the table. "Come with me."

"Where?" They were on their feet.

"We're going for a drive."

"I told you, I can't—"

"It's not that kind of drive," he said, taking her arm. "Well, not unless you want it to be."

They were outside. He had the pickup tonight, and held the door gallantly. Light snow was twinkling down. "We'll come back for your car," he promised.

"Where are we going?"

"I want to show you something."

She hesitated. "Pete, ah, the thing is—"

He touched her, with surprising gentleness, on her cheek. "This has nothing to do with you and me, okay? It only has to do with you."

"With me?"

"Get in the truck."

(I V)

They drove for several minutes—not along Main Street, but through the town's residential area. She noticed a photograph on the sun visor, a snapshot of a freckled boy about Nina's age. No mother in sight.

The boy looked forlorn, but Beck supposed she could be projecting.

Pete pulled over on a street of pretty Victorians. He pointed to one, with lace curtains in the window and a warm homey glow from within. The shingles needed paint. "The house is owned by a widow, Mrs.

Rennie. Lived her all her life. She takes in boarders. Mostly transients, migrant workers, and so on." He paused. "We can go talk to her if you want, or you can take my word for it."

"What would we be talking to her about?"

"She called the police about one of her boarders. He'd rented a room for the past week, and today he checked out. A certain Mr. Clark. I believe you've made his acquaintance."

Beck sat a little straighter. "What about him?"

"This is why she called the police. Another man came looking for him around dinnertime, and they left together in a big hurry. He left so fast he didn't take everything from his room." The deputy slid an envelope from beneath the dash. "Here's part of what he left."

She opened the envelope, slid out grainy photographs. For a moment she was confused. "What am I looking at?"

"These are photocopies. The originals are in the sheriff's vault. But those two are overhead views of Mr. Ainsley's property, probably taken from higher up the mountain. And that one is a side view, probably taken from the woods behind the house, meaning the photographer had to be *on* the property."

Rebecca continued to stare. Her mind besieged her with so many questions she hardly knew which one to raise first.

"And then there's this one. I thought you'd find it especially interesting."

She looked.

It was a photograph of a woman, on her knees, vomiting.

Beside her was a dog, its brains blown onto the gravel.

"When he took that one," said Pete Mundy, "he was no more than twenty feet away from you."

(v)

Rebecca felt her gorge rise afresh, had to cover her mouth. He handed her a Diet Coke. She drank greedily, then sat beside him, waiting for the explanation she knew was coming. The rooming house was quiet and dark. She wondered how it must feel to live your whole life in one place, if not happy, at least content.

"Sheriff Garvey is right," said the deputy, soft and boyish once more. "I do have some pretty wild theories about what's going on in Bethel. I told you I don't like all these strangers in my town. I don't like all those visitors to Stone Heights. I don't like trespassers, or people who shoot dogs to send messages. I don't like people who can make a phone call and get out of jail free. I don't like reporters, I don't like spies, and I don't like that you're mixed up in this." She glanced at him. He was gazing, sadly, at the photo of his son. "It's surveillance, Beck. That's what I told the sheriff. Stone Heights is under surveillance. You asked about federal. I figure these guys are private, like their licenses say, but who the fuck can tell? Pardon my French. The point is, people are waiting for something to happen. I don't know what they're waiting for. I don't know when it's happening. But, whatever it is, I kind of doubt it's going to be good for Bethel."

Pete waited for her to fill the gaps in his knowledge. She did not.

"The thing is, whatever's going on, since you arrived it's . . . intensified, I guess is the word. It's like, you came to town and this whole wave came with you. All these strangers. All waiting. And Sheriff Garvey—well, whenever I try to look into this, he tells me to leave it alone. *Orders* me. Gets all furious. He's protecting somebody, Beck. I'd kind of like to know who. I'd like to know who's giving the sheriff *his* orders. I have a hunch it's not Mr. Ainsley."

Beck shut her eyes. She was exhausted and lonely and angry at the world. In this mood, she was prone to life-changing mistakes. "I can't help you," she said. "I'm as much in the dark as you are. Anyway, I'm leaving the day after tomorrow."

"Leaving the rest of us to cope."

"I'm sorry, Pete. I am. But it's not my mystery. I have a job. I have my daughter to look after. I'm afraid the town—"

"That's not what I meant," he interrupted. "I meant, I'm sorry we won't get the chance to know each other. Because, you know, what you said before—about me being married—"

Her head was resting against the leather seat. Her eyes remained closed. Her hands were in her lap, but her fists were clenched. "I don't want to hear this," she murmured, possibly just to herself.

"The separation is for real," said Pete, doggedly. He was very near. "We're not getting back together. Laurel and I are just working out the details."

There, in the closeness of the cab, Beck felt it. Felt the tug of human weakness. She had yielded before, and not only with Jericho. There were moments when sheer bone-wearying loneliness made it easy to believe whatever nonsense a married man whispered—or at least to pretend to believe it, when what you really believed was your own need for ordinary human warmth, a need so strong you would do harm to another woman to get it.

Eyes still closed, she shook her head. "No."

"Beck—"

"I saw how you looked at that photo, Pete. The photo of your boy." Clenching tighter. "I don't know anything about your marriage. I don't want to know. But you would never harm that boy, and if that means going back to his mother, then you'll go back. Whether you love her or not."

She did not need to see his face to know she had struck home. She felt the sudden stillness in the truck, like the last moment before the avalanche, and waited for him to say what too many men had said to her over the years, that he would have thought she would be the last woman to worry about another woman's marriage. Men were boys, mostly, and even the sweetest boy, upon failing to get what he wanted, could throw a tantrum.

"You're a good woman," he said, starting the engine. He backed out into the road.

They rode back to town in silence. Beck kept her eyes shut. She was hoping to doze, so that she could forget the ache, and the doubt, and the desperate urge to change her mind. Her several selves were at war, independent versus needy, suspicious versus trusting, the new Beck versus the old. The drive up the mountain tonight would be the longest of her life. The thought of returning to the cold insanity of Stone Heights suddenly appalled her. When they were a block from Corinda's, she turned to him and said, "Pete, look. I might not be as good as you think—"

He covered her mouth. "You were right the first time. I do love my boy. I'd never hurt him."

"I know, but—"

"There's nothing I wouldn't do to protect him." He walked her to her car, and even ventured a chaste hug. Behind the glasses, his eyes were grim. "I bet you feel the same way about your little girl."

"Oh, yes, I do." His fervor surprised her. "I do."

"Then I guess we pretty much understand each other," he said, and turned away.

Rebecca stood in the sprinkly snow, watching the taillights of his pickup until they were out of sight. Part of her wished he would turn around and give her another chance, but most of her wanted to be quit of Bethel forever.

CHAPTER 17

The Folder

(1)

"Okay, fine," said Pamela. "So your new boyfriend showed you a bunch of photographs. So what?"

"Somebody took them on the property. And Deputy Mundy is not my boyfriend."

"You're saying we've had a trespasser."

Beck nodded. They were in the great room, on one of the sofas near the window. Outside, the floodlights pounded their unnatural yellowy brightness into the night. "Exactly. And on more than one occasion."

Pamela's smile never touched her eyes. "We've had trespassers every day, Rebecca. I'm sure some of them have cameras." She waved at the photos. "If it makes you happier, call your boyfriend and tell him to arrest the photographer."

"He's not my—"

"So you keep saying. But that's not what Audrey hears in town."

Beck decided to let this go. "They can't arrest him. Pete says he checked out of the rooming house today, and nobody's seen him since."

"So it's *Pete* now." A sneer.

"He's just a friend."

"Oh, is that what they're calling it these days?"

"Pamela—"

"What is it with you and married men?"

"I didn't wreck your parents' marriage," she said.

"My late mother was of a different opinion."

"I was a kid—"

"And he gave you presents, didn't he? That's what he did. That was always his style when he wanted a woman." She stood up, began to pace barefoot across the floorboards. "He'd shower her with expensive gifts. Jewelry. Fragrances. Whatever it took. You weren't the only sweet young thing he went after, Rebecca. No matter what you might think, you weren't special." She laughed. "My father's a piece of work. Did you know he keeps records? I'm serious. All the gifts to all the ladies. He has folders and folders of them. It must come from being in the intelligence business. Nothing's official until it's on the record."

Beck said nothing.

"Your folder's very thick," said Pamela. "I haven't finished working my way through it yet."

"You don't have any right—"

"Makes fascinating reading. You can have it when I'm done."

Rebecca kept her temper, but only by furrowing her palms with her fingernails. "We have to talk about these photographs, Pamela. We have to decide what to do."

"You're not interested in reading your file?"

"I'm interested in the present and the future, Pamela. If you want to wallow in the past, that's your problem, not mine."

A thin smile. "Interesting response. I wonder what could be in the folder that you're afraid I'll find."

"Come on, Pamela. When exactly do you plan to stop this shit and grow up? I don't care what you spend your time doing. There are things going on that we have to deal with, but you just can't get over yourself, can you? You're worse than Jericho. My Nina is more mature than you are, and she's just seven."

"You—how dare you—"

"I'm going to bed," said Rebecca, with bitter satisfaction. She headed for the stairs. For the first time since walking in the door Sunday night, she had gotten the better of her adversary. But she knew that such advantages were transitory.

(II)

Upstairs, she brushed her teeth and brushed her hair and wondered how the face in the mirror had aged five years in just two days. She rubbed her eyes. She should have talked to Pete Mundy. Shared her suspicions and fears. Told him Dak's story about national security, told him Lewiston Clark's story about Scondell Bloom, and let him help her choose between the two.

God knew, she needed the help.

Back in the bedroom, she lay down with a sheaf of printouts about the financial firm, and woke an hour later because her cell phone was ringing. She let it ring. She stood up and opened the window, letting in the night sounds, but heard no helicopter. So maybe her thesis had been wrong.

The ringing continued.

She decided to answer. Maybe she would get voice mail again.

She did, but it was the same message as before: "I have to go, because Grandma is calling me, and I didn't tell her I'm calling you— *Just a minute!*—I'm in the bathroom and I guess I better go, but call me, Mommy, okay? Call me soon, so I can tell you about the d—"

And again it ended.

Audrey must be right: it was some weird effect of the mountains. What she could not understand was why, when she'd accessed her voice mail in town earlier, the message wasn't—

She froze.

In the floodlights, a human figure was moving furtively across the snow-whitened lawn.

He was heading for the house.

(III)

Pamela didn't believe her, but Audrey, who admitted to having not seen a thing, wanted to make peace, and so they dutifully trooped to the security room behind the kitchen and flipped through the monitors. An animal or two, trees swaying in the night breezes, but no people.

"There was somebody," said Beck.

"Look for yourself," said Pamela.

The images from the cameras were digitally stored, Beck pointed out. Pamela, the filmmaker, and the only one who knew how to work the equipment, replied that she was not about to waste her time tracking down Beck's nightmares.

"I was awake."

"Daydreams, then."

"I know what I saw."

Pamela straightened. Like many tall women, she often carried herself slightly hunched, as if her height was a burden. But when she wanted to, she could look down on most people, and right now she wanted to.

"Has it occurred to you"—addressing Audrey, even though her glare was directed at Rebecca—"that all of these little problems seem to have started when she arrived?"

Beck muttered an expletive. Pamela advanced on her like a boxer cutting the ring to size. "Think about it, Aud. The dead dog. The helicopter that keeps buzzing us. Now the phantom visitors in the night. What is it going to be next, Beck? A power outage? A home invasion?"

About to reply in kind, Beck found her mouth covered by a soft, pale hand. "Come on, you guys. Stop. This isn't why we're here." A nervous chuckle. "How about a little Christian charity?" To their general surprise, she covered Pamela's mouth, too. "Now, come on. I was baking oatmeal cookies. They're ready to come out of the oven, and they're *very* good."

Beck forced herself to reply in kind. "I bet it's not real oatmeal. It's some kind of macrobiotic oat husk—"

"Don't encourage her," muttered Pamela, changing sides for the moment, or perhaps just targets.

But they all marched into the kitchen anyway. Audrey slid the tray out. The cookies neither looked nor smelled like any oatmeal Rebecca could remember. "They need time to cool," said the nun.

"I'll be upstairs on the computer," Pamela began.

Then they all heard the thump.

Audrey said it was her father falling, and headed for the stairs. Pamela said it was a branch tumbling from a storm-blasted tree, hitting the house. Beck said it was a man on the roof.

Pamela had already started in on her, and Beck was starting in right back, when Audrey shouted.

They followed her pointing finger upward.

A shadow passed over the skylight.

"An animal," said Pamela.

"It's a man," said Audrey, very tense. "I saw his face. He was looking right at us."

CHAPTER 18

The Accident

(1)

In the security room, Pamela lifted a panel and turned a key, and all around the house, a security mesh began closing, thick metal grates covering the doors and the first-floor windows. She pressed a button and an alarm klaxon sounded. The volume made everybody jump. On the monitor, a shadow shot past one of the cameras, hitting the ground hard.

"What was that?" said Audrey.

"With any luck," said her sister, very complacent, "that was our friend from the roof."

She pointed to another monitor. Sure enough, a man lay on the frozen ground, writhing and clutching his leg. They could not see his face.

"We have to help him," said Audrey.

Pamela snickered. "We don't owe him any help. He's a trespasser. We wait for the police." She pointed. "When you sound the alarm, they come automatically."

"We can't just leave him," said Audrey. "He's hurt."

"Maybe we shouldn't go out there," said Beck. "Pamela's right."

The phone rang in the kitchen. The sisters, still arguing, made no move to answer, so Beck picked it up.

The alarm company.

She started to explain what had happened, but the woman at the other end cut her off and asked for the security code.

Beck asked her to hold on, called Pamela. Pamela listened, then turned away, cupping her hand over the mouthpiece, to repeat the code, even at this moment showcasing her lack of trust in her father's ex-lover.

"Come on," said Audrey, grabbing Beck's arm. "We're going out there."

(11)

Pamela insisted on a backup plan.

Audrey went to tend to the injured man, while her sister stood nearby with a Beretta she had obtained from somewhere. Beck was assigned to stand in the doorway, in case the others had to make a run for the house, ready to press the button to slam the gates closed again as soon as they were safely inside. Beck was surprised that Pamela trusted her this far; as for Audrey, she tried and failed to talk her sister into giving up the gun.

"He's can't hurt us," said Audrey.

"He could have friends," said Beck—and Pamela agreed.

The man who had fallen from the roof seemed vaguely familiar. He wanted them nowhere near him. He clenched his fist, holding his leg and warning them to stay away as he called them inventively misogynistic names, and promised to sue various parts, mostly private, off their bodies. Audrey kept assuring him, calmly, that she was trained in first aid, and the man told her in detail what she could do with her first aid. Pamela waved the gun in his face and screamed back at him, a move that evidently scared everybody, because the man finally calmed down and let Audrey go to work splinting his leg.

Beck, meanwhile, was remembering where she had seen him before.

The wind picked up again. Dry leaves tumbled across the lawn as Pamela, gun in hand, crouched beside the stranger in the snow. She whispered something. Audrey argued, and Pamela shouldered her aside. The man shook his head. The gun came up. He started shouting. The gun pointed between his legs. He went very quiet. Pamela whispered. He nodded. She whispered again, the gun closer. Trembling, he whispered back. She stood up, his wallet in her hand.

Audrey went back to work, and Pamela strode over to Beck. "His ID says he's a private investigator. He says some magazine hired him to get a couple of shots of Dad on his deathbed. Fifty thousand, cash on the nail." She was trembling with fury. She held up a camera. "No way he's getting this back. Not for fifty thousand, not for a hundred. On his *deathbed*."

Beck was trying to come up with a suitable response when the gendarmes arrived, two cruisers and an ambulance.

Two deputies guarded the prisoner while the paramedics tended to him. Another talked to the sisters. Emboldened now that Pamela could do him no harm, the man was once more thundering threats of litigation. Sheriff Garvey lumbered over to Rebecca.

"Quite a character," he said.

"Pamela says he's a private investigator."

He nodded. "Name of Pesky. One of the punks my deputy arrested last night. This morning I kicked his ass over the county line, and here he is back for another round."

Beck remembered now, Pesky and his partner under the moose head. "What's he going to be charged with?"

A shrug. "That's not up to me. That's up to the State's Attorney. But I'm betting he stays in jail this time, no matter how many honchos call." His face betrayed no emotion. She knew there was something else the sheriff wanted to discuss. She was peering over his shoulder, eyes alert for Pamela's gun, but it had vanished: into Audrey's black medical bag, she suspected. Pamela would never see it again. "This Pesky says he was taking photos through the skylight. I don't see a camera anywhere. I suspect that one of you has it, but I don't suppose you'll admit that, will you?" He watched her face. "You don't believe that story about the magazine any more than I do. Any idea what might be inside the house that he'd want to get pictures of?"

The manuscript. Pesky had been hoping to get a shot of the manuscript, not realizing that the papers were just Jericho's will, and no longer on the premises. "Sorry. No idea." She bore his scrutiny, wondering what those honchos had whispered in the sheriff's ear, and whether he was asking his questions or theirs.

"I hear you were at the library," he finally said. "You talked to Miss Kelly."

"I was there," Beck said, carefully.

"Miss Kelly says you asked her what Mr. Ainsley had been up to. She says you wouldn't leave her alone until she told you."

"Our conversation was confidential."

Sheriff Garvey nodded, one hand on his belt. Behind him, they had Pesky up on the gurney and were rolling him toward the ambulance. "Is that why you were at Mr. Navarro's office this afternoon?"

"That was another confidential matter."

"And what about having another drink with my deputy? Which I distinctly told you not to do? Was that confidential, too?"

She spread her hands. "I really can't help you, Sheriff."

"May I give you a word of advice? Stay away from him."

"Because of his—theories?"

"Because Pete Mundy is a married man and it's a small town." He spoke softly, the way the executioner does when he knows you have nowhere to hide. "A woman like you can wreck a man's career."

She stifled about sixteen different retorts. "Thank you for the advice," she said coldly.

"Just doing my job," he said, unsmiling. "I understand you're leaving us day after tomorrow."

"Probably."

"I think that's a very good idea." Garvey turned away, but before he did, Beck caught his glance. He was looking up above her head, toward the house. She swung around. The windows of Jericho's suite. Although in the darkness the sight could easily have been her imagination, Rebecca thought for an instant that she saw his rigid face, glowering down at the mess on his lawn, before receding into the shadows.

(1 1 1)

Beck crouched on the window seat of her bedroom, curtains wide open, staring up at the plateau from which she had, just hours ago, looked down at the house. Pesky had been up there, taking photographs. Pamela had downloaded the images from his digital camera. The investigator had been all over the property, unseen, snapping photos of everything in sight. Pete Mundy had arrested him. Sheriff Garvey had let him out again because some honcho had called.

And he had returned to the scene to snap more pictures.

All this for a magazine, and fifty thousand dollars?

Some of the images were the same as the ones Lewiston Clark had left behind when he left Mrs. Rennie's boarding house in a hurry. It did not take a genius to see that the two men had been working together; or that Pesky had to be the man who had visited Clark, causing him to leave in such a rush.

After his release. After the call from the honcho.

Doing her sums, she put the events in the proper order. Pesky and Clark, working together, Pesky as outside man, Clark as inside man. When Clark could not talk his way in, Pesky doubled his efforts with the camera. When Pesky got arrested, somebody had him sprung, and that somebody obviously lit a fire under them both. So Pesky returned to the house, and even climbed on the roof in his desperation.

As for Clark, she had no idea where he was. If he had any sense, he had fled. It occurred to her that there was a Keystone Kops quality to the episode. If these two were the best that Pete Mundy's strangers could muster, then Jericho had nothing to worry about.

And yet she wondered.

Dak's presence suggested another, more malevolent force at work. The old spy was concerned, and the likes of Pesky and Clark would not concern him.

She wondered whether Jericho has reached her boss's boss's boss, to extend her stay at Stone Heights. She hoped not. In any event, this time, Beck decided, she would not allow Jericho to dictate events. She had promised him only that she would be here until Thursday, and so Thursday it would be. To leave any later would be to allow her ex-lover to manipulate her. But to leave earlier would be a breach of her promise, and a sign of panic besides.

Dak had assured her she was not in any danger, and Jericho had told her the same thing. She assumed they knew what they were talking about. Nevertheless, sitting there on the window seat, gazing out into the darkness, Rebecca experienced a sharp surge of gratitude for the unexpected gift she had found on Sunday night under a false bottom in the bamboo basket that held extra towels in her bathroom. Searching in odd places had become second nature to her during her time with Jericho—whenever they would check into a hotel, she would join him in peeking under furniture and behind cabinets for hidden bugs—and even after fifteen years, now that Beck was back at Stone Heights she had reverted automatically to old habits.

A good thing Audrey was less suspicious, because what Beck discovered, courtesy of Jericho's paranoia, was a Glock 9mm, Model 19, complete with extended magazine—the compact version of the gun he had once taught her to shoot, up in these sad, brooding mountains.

Not that she would need it, of course. In two days, she would be gone from Stone Heights, presumably forever. Nevertheless, she locked both doors to the suite, then sneaked the Glock from its new hiding place beneath the mattress. She stood in front of the mirror, practicing her grip, and remembering her second-biggest fight with Jericho, after he marched her into the woods one afternoon and made her fire off an entire magazine at a family of squirrels.

She killed one.

When they come, he had murmured, leading his weeping lover back to the house, *your aim will have to be better than that.*

She could hardly fire a gun in the guest room, but she could work on her grip and her draw. And so, silently acknowledging Jericho's long-ago instruction, she practiced and practiced, on into the wee hours.

WEDNESDAY

CHAPTER 19

The Lawyer

(1)

On Wednesday morning, everything was fine. Pamela was monopolizing the computer, and Audrey prepared a huge breakfast too healthy for anybody to eat. Swallowing the slithery remains of whatever is left of an egg after you take the good stuff out, Rebecca found herself longing for those carb-heavy meals of pasta and bread. The nun said excitedly that she had a line on a handyman to take Mr. Lobb's place, and also that she was making headway in persuading Jericho that the house needed a full-time nurse.

Beck sat in the kitchen and picked at her food, then turned the conversation where Audrey obviously did not want to go: toward the events of the previous night. And Audrey, after initially resisting, yielded, and joined her at the table.

"He wasn't trying to break in," the nun pointed out. "He was taking pictures."

Beck swirled the egg whites with her fork. She watched Audrey's cautious eyes. "And that doesn't seem strange to you, Aud? That a man would climb on top of your father's house with a camera to take pictures?"

Audrey crinkled her nose. "Of course it's strange. That's why I'm glad they arrested him. I'm sorry about his leg, though. I hope he heals soon."

Beck choked back a wave of sympathy. "I'm sorry, too. But he shouldn't have been on the roof."

The house phone rang, but neither of them moved, because they knew it would be for Pamela, who would pick up the extension in the study.

The nun shook her head. "Everybody who gets hurt by somebody else, there's always a reason. A lot of them are good reasons. But the people are still hurt." She was fingering the cross around her neck, and Beck knew she was remembering the work she had fled. "Sometimes I think that's the main grudge Sean holds against Dad. He thinks Dad made the world worse."

"And what do you think?"

"I think he made mistakes, and some of them were costly. But we all do that. He did the best he could, same as we all do when we—"

"Didn't you hear me calling you?" snapped Pamela from the doorway. "It's for you. Not you. For Rebecca."

(I I)

"I'm not calling too early, am I?" said Tish Kirschbaum. "I figure you guys get up early out west."

Beck took the portable phone out onto the deck, enjoying the mountain chill. For three or four minutes, the old friends exchanged pleasantries. Tish was every bit as divorced as Beck, and was raising a son alone, but seemed to suffer less.

"Scondell Bloom," said Tish, when Rebecca finally got around to the reason for her call. "Wow. I totally forgot your guy was there."

"He's not my guy."

"Used to be, though."

"What can you tell me?"

"Not much. I assume you know how the firm collapsed— Wait. Do you know how private equity works? They raise money to buy companies—not stocks, whole companies—and then they make the companies more efficient, stripping them of a lot of valuable assets on the way, and restructure them, and sell them back to the public, usually at a profit. And the partners, well, they make out like fat rats. The guys who founded Scondell Bloom paid themselves hundreds of millions of dollars each."

"What went wrong?"

"Nobody really knows. I have a friend at the United States Attorney's office in Manhattan, and from what he says, I would guess that the firm did a lot of investing overseas, and a lot of that money just vanished. What has them puzzled is that these weren't dicey Third World investments. This money was in countries with serious financial regulation, transparency, whatever you want. It still vanished. It's as if the foreign regulators were all looking the wrong way. But a lot of them are upstanding citizens, wealthy in their own right. Not the sort to commit crimes, and not the sort to take bribes. The prosecutors don't know what happened. That's why they just indicted Bloom and Scondell for wire fraud and mail fraud. They can't prove what happened to the money, so they accused them of continuing to raise funds when they knew the money was gone." A laugh over the line—Tish loved to find the flaws in capitalism. These days, she had a lot of company. "A billion dollars might be missing. Maybe more. We're not talking losses. We're talking money that just disappeared."

Beck was sitting where she had sat with Jericho yesterday, looking up at the peak. She could not figure out what Lewiston Clark thought he knew. Jericho had not been indicted and was not the subject of an investigation. It was absurd to think that he had a billion dollars squirreled away somewhere.

"Doolie Bloom killed himself after he was indicted," said Rebecca, half to herself.

"That's right," said Tish. "Only Scondell is facing trial."

"What about Jack Notting? He didn't get indicted."

"True. And nobody knows where he is, although the smart betting is that he's on the lam. He'll turn up someplace with no extradition treaty, and spend his life counting his money."

"Who is he? Where did he come from? I hear he was in the Foreign Service."

Tish hooted. "Come on, Beck. Don't be naïve. I bet when your guy was in Vietnam, in the sixties or whenever, his résumé said 'Foreign Service,' too. As a matter of fact, I'd bet it still does."

"Are you saying—"

"Jack Notting was CIA. I thought everybody knew that."

Tish made her promise to come for a long weekend when she got back. "Oh, and bring Nina. Maybe we'll matchmake them one day."

Rebecca hardly heard herself agreeing. She was remembering how Jericho had described his work for Scondell Bloom, and, just like that, she knew part of what he was hiding. Now all she had to figure out was where he had put it.

(III)

Her appointment with Brian Navarro, the lawyer, was at ten. She would have preferred to talk to Jericho before she left for town, but Audrey said her father was resting and could not be disturbed. Beck was upstairs putting on her good shoes when her cell phone rang. The screen said UNKNOWN NUMBER.

Not again.

She considered not answering, but the phone went on ringing. She went to the window but saw no helicopter. She picked up the phone and turned it off.

The ringing stopped.

"Okay, then."

She decided to take her briefcase so that she would look professional. She was checking her face in the mirror when the phone rang again.

It had switched itself back on.

There are people, these days, who write viruses for cell phones. Yours could be infected.

She answered. The fax tone, and the whine.

She hung up and turned the phone off. The screen went blank, then recycled, brightening again. The phone began to ring. She hesitated. If the phone was malfunctioning, the problem was getting worse. If not, somebody somewhere was feeling rather . . . urgent.

Beck reminded herself that she was leaving tomorrow. She was just opening the back to take the battery out when she was startled by a knock, hard and peremptory, on the door connecting to the bathroom and the study.

Pamela's voice: "Will you please stop playing with the damn phone? Some of us have actual work to do."

Out on the landing, Beck ran into Audrey.

"He's awake," the nun said. "He's asking for you."

(IV)

"They tell me you're running off again," said Jericho with a frown. He was lying down. The body seemed strong but the energy was fading. "They tell me you're collecting men like—oh, I don't know." He pushed himself up on his shoulders. "I'm the one who's dying, Becky-Bear. When is there time in that busy schedule of yours for me?"

"Whenever you want," she said, very surprised.

"Good. Let's go out."

She blinked. "Out?"

"You know. A date."

"Jericho—"

"I'm told you're heading for town. You told the girls you'd be back at noon. Fine. I have some calls to make anyway. I'll be ready to go at one, and we'll go for a little drive. How does that sound?"

Rebecca was, for a moment, wordstruck. She had promised Pamela that she would try to get Jericho out of the house, but, deep down, she wondered whether he was healthy enough. Then it occurred to her that this might be her only chance to get him alone, and away from the house—

"Jer-Bear?"

"Yes?"

"You mean, just the two of us?" Squeezing his hand. He squeezed back. "No Pamela? No Audrey?"

"Just the two of us." He flopped back onto the bed. "I have to get away from them."

She smiled. "I'd be honored."

"That's right," said Jericho. "You would."

Halfway to the door, she had a thought. "Jer-Bear?"

"Hmmm?"

"Do you know anything about—about people planting viruses in cell phones?"

One eye opened. "Are you planning to plant one?"

"Just tell me how it works."

"It happens," he said. The other eye opened, and Jericho was all professional again. "If you just want to wreck a phone, it's easy as pie. If you want to cut a phone off from the network, so it can't make calls? That's even easier. On the other hand, if you want to hack it—use it as a GPS, say, to follow somebody with—or a listening device? Technically possible, but a lot harder. The phone companies take lots of precautions against that kind of thing. The equipment you would need you can't just buy on the street." He laughed, then coughed. "The good thing about living up here is, you don't have to worry about them bugging your cell phone. There's no service."

Down in the kitchen, she announced the plan to the sisters. She would pick up Jericho at one, and they would go driving. Audrey was adamant: the risk was too great. Pamela was *dubitante:* after all, she was the one who had asked Rebecca to get her father out of the house. As the sisters quarreled, it dawned on Beck that the outcome didn't matter.

"You know what?" she said. "It's not up to you."

The sisters were startled. "Try to keep it to an hour," said Audrey.

"It'll take as long as it takes."

And, very pleased with herself, Beck left for town.

(v)

Brian Navarro was broad and sixty and brown and voluble, a man delighted to be a power in his town, and not particularly concerned about what others thought. His gestures were wide. He filled a lot of space. He dressed beautifully. He insisted on showing her his ego wall, the scattering of poses with the state and congressional representatives from the district, then toured her through his wife and five children, delightedly following their photographs as they grew, and wedded, and brought forth children of their own. She oohed and aahed at the right moments, and, probably, meant it. Then he sat her in the conference room adjoining his office, and chose the side of the table with the sun at his back. He asked if she minded his smoking, and lit a cigar like a gas bomb. Then he waited while Beck, sufficiently softened up, and squinting and occasionally coughing into the bargain, explained what she wanted, all the while thinking that Brian Navarro was more clever than she had thought.

Yes, he said. Sure, he hung around with Jericho. He was Jericho's friend, he said proudly, as well as Jericho's lawyer. She noticed that no receptionist was present. She wondered how large a practice an attorney could maintain in a town like this. She didn't have the heart to tell him about the duo who had driven up from Denver to take possession of the will.

"He talks about you all the time, Miss DeForde. You're very important to him. I hope you know that, because that old coot isn't much on showing he cares."

"Beck," she said.

"Fine. Beck. I'm Brian." He blew smoke rings. "Jericho came to me a few years ago with a tax question. I hope I'm not giving anything away. He said he'd given you a gift, and that you gave it to charity. He wanted to know if he could get a deduction. I told him no. I hope you took one, though. For the full value. Doesn't matter if the cost basis was zero."

Beck dropped her gaze, momentarily embarrassed. "I never thought about it," she confessed.

"Well, it doesn't matter. You can file an amended return. Just talk to your accountant."

"That would be H&R Block."

They shared a laugh, slightly strained. Each was waiting for the other.

"The two of you spend a lot of time together," she said at last.

"Some. Not as much as we used to, of course. He's been sick, and even before that, he hadn't been coming to town quite so much. He used to play in the mayor's poker game, but I don't think he's been there in a year or so."

"But I understand he spends a lot of time at the library."

"I know I've run into him there a time or two. I'm in and out a lot. My wife teaches history at the regional high school down in the valley. We're writing a little history of the native people on this mountain, and the town doesn't have a historical society. Bethel has some archives—not a lot, but some—and they're kept at the library."

"Is that what Jericho was looking at? The archives?"

He shook his head. "Not that I know of. But the archives are in a little room behind the librarian's desk. Same room where they keep the photocopier and the printer. Jericho did lots of photocopying, and he printed stuff off the Internet. We'd chat while the machines were running."

"Do you remember what he printed?"

"Not really. Well, once. Schematic for some kind of motor or something. I couldn't really tell."

Beck was frustrated. For all of the lawyer's evident openness, she felt as if she had less information than when she started. The meetings in the library were casual and unplanned. That part had to be true. If Jericho had wanted to meet Brian Navarro in private, he could have done so right in this room, protected by attorney-client privilege.

"Does he have other friends in town?"

"Jericho Ainsley isn't the kind of man who has a lot of friends."

"Still."

The lawyer was tapping his fingers on the table, a device that annoyed her until she realized that he was making a decision. She had the wit to stay silent.

"You have to understand something," he finally said. "Jericho and I are friends, after a fashion, but we aren't particularly close. We enjoy each other's company, but he doesn't confide in me, except in the course of my representation. So, whatever I tell you, I'm only surmising. These aren't things I know. And the only reason I'm telling you anything at all is that I do think he's having some trouble, and I do think that knowing some of the background might help. And—well, you're who you are. You're his Beck."

"I understand," said Beck, controlling her eagerness.

"Before he got sick, Jericho used to come into town once or twice a week, in the evenings. He'd have a couple of drinks at Corinda's. If he arrived early, maybe dinner. I joined him a couple of times, and he was with strangers from out of town a couple of times, or maybe one of his daughters, but mostly he would sit there alone, looking at the room. He didn't read anything, he didn't watch television, he just sat there and stared into space." He continued the drumming. "The only one allowed to wait on him was Corinda herself. Have you met her? Jericho liked her a lot. She was the only one who could ever get his drink order right, or even his dinner, which was always the same. That's what he said, anyway. If Corinda was away somewhere, he wouldn't even come into town."

"I see," she said again, feeling her face grow warm, knowing where this was leading.

"One night, very late, I saw them together. This was, oh, three or four years ago. They were in the cab of Jericho's pickup. They were arguing, Rebecca. Pretty passionately, too." He had the grace to blush. "Naturally, I thought—well, you know—a lovers' quarrel."

"I see."

"I'm not saying they *were*. I'm saying it *looked* that way."

And Beck nodded, thinking it was odd indeed, if Brian Navarro was Jericho Ainsley's friend, to say nothing of his lawyer, that he was confiding so freely these more personal aspects of his client's business.

She wondered why.

All at once, in a great flurry, yet without being rude, he was shepherding her toward the door. He had another client coming in, a bankruptcy, a local store owner, very sad case, big family, first-generation immigrant, good people, he explained, not letting her get a word in.

In the anteroom, the lawyer asked if she was headed back up to Stone Heights.

She nodded. "Uh-huh."

"Good. Then you can save me a trip." He handed her a manila envelope with Jericho's name typed on an address sticker for Brian's firm. The envelope was marked *Personal and Confidential*.

"What is it?" she asked.

"Well, I guess I can tell you, because you're practically family." He put a finger to his lips, playfully, and it occurred to her that he just liked to tell secrets; and that he had managed nevertheless, through all his artful bonhomie and gossip, to keep the important ones. Her esteem for him grew. "It's his will," said the lawyer. "He asked me to make some changes."

She looked at the envelope. "His will."

"That's right."

"How long have you been Jericho's lawyer?"

"About ten years. Twelve."

"And how often has he redrawn his will?"

"A lot." The smile faded. "I'm afraid I can't say more than that."

Driving back up the mountain, Rebecca kept the envelope on the seat beside her, shaking her head in admiration. Once more Jericho was five steps ahead of everyone else. The document he had sent to Denver had not been his will, and the people who picked it up might not even have been lawyers. Whatever he was hiding, he had slipped a copy down the mountain under everyone's nose, by being so obvious about the whole thing that even the great Philip Agadakos had been fooled.

CHAPTER 20

The Break

(1)

"Thank you for getting me out of there," grumbled Jericho. He did not sound particularly grateful. She noticed that he was watching the outside mirror. The Former Everything, even in his last months, was never off his guard. "Those harridans are driving me crazy."

"They're not harridans," she said. She searched for more, probably missed the mark. "They love you."

"Love. Let me tell you something about love." Beck had heard it from him before, but did not interrupt. "People who love make bad decisions. It's a rule. Love isn't rational, ergo, people who love aren't rational. They can't be trusted."

"You don't trust your own children?"

"Are you joking? I have one daughter whose only goal in life is to make sure every movie grosses nine figures, and another who can't cross the street without asking Mother Superior for permission. And my son—well, that's a wasted life if ever I saw one." Every life was wasted, it seemed, if not lived according to Jericho's advice. "But you, Becky-Bear. You I trust."

"Me? We haven't even laid eyes on each other in years."

"That's why I trust you."

They descended another mile or two in silence. "Jericho?"

"Yes, my dear?"

"What exactly are you trusting me with?"

A lovely laugh—rich and mellifluous, as in the old days, without a hint of rattle or cough. "At the moment, given how you drive? My life."

More silence. The wheels slithered here and there, but with Jericho beside her, Beck was not about to start talking to the car. Trees crowded the road for a while, then fell back like a retreating army. She pondered the competing stories. If Dak was right, Jericho was a madman, threatening the security of the United States, and some unofficial nations as well. If Lewiston Clark was right, he was threatening only the interests of a handful of financiers; and Tish's intelligence made that explanation seem more likely.

"Tell me about Jack Notting."

Jericho stirred. He had been dozing. "What?"

"You worked with him at Scondell Bloom."

"I worked *for* him. I didn't work *with* him."

Beck thought this over. It was difficult to imagine Jericho as anybody's subordinate. Serving at the pleasure of the President was honorable and, in a family like the Ainsleys, expected. Serving at the pleasure of a financier—well, that was something else.

"I was just wondering—how did he recruit you?"

A guffaw became a cough. She glanced his way, but he seemed to be peering out at the mountain rain. "Recruit me. That's one way to put it. Jack came to me, Becky-Bear. He asked how I'd like to make five or ten million dollars a year. I said that sounded like a nice idea. End of recruitment." Another cough. "Earned every penny, too. Flew around the world, shook hands with oil sheikhs and Chinese billionaires—a Russian tycoon or two—so Jack and his friends could swoop in and collect a little more business. I knew some of them from the old days."

"You knew Jack's friends."

"Incorrect." His tone was perfectly pleasant. "Some of the sheikhs. The tycoons. A lot of them used to be in intelligence. Maybe they owed me a favor or three. See why Jack wanted me?"

But Beck suspected that, even now, Jericho was indulging his habit of dissembling. There had to be more to the story. Sure, he would have known some of the billionaires and tycoons. She doubted, however, that this was his principal value to Notting. If the scheme was anything like what Tish had described, what was vital was to be owed favors not by the investors but by the regulators. Jack Notting could dig up billionaires on his own. What he needed was a way to persuade the people charged with overseeing the financial markets of other countries to look the other way. And Beck, without even asking, was willing to bet that a lot of the foreign regulators were formerly with their nations' intelligence services—and that they, too, likely owed favors to the Former Everything.

Which could explain how the money had disappeared; and what people might think Jericho knew.

She wondered which was the cover story. Was Jericho hiding financial secrets, letting others think he was threatening national security? Or the other way around?

"Drive faster," said Jericho.

She glanced at the mirror. "What is it? What's wrong?"

"Trust me."

"But why—"

"Faster."

And so she did. She lifted her foot from the brake, and on sloping, twisting Rocky Mountain roads, nothing else is necessary. The little car took off. She kept her hands firmly on the wheel, steering around the bends long before she got there, just the way Jericho had taught her years ago.

"Not fast enough." His eyes were locked on the mirror. "Hurry, Becky-Bear. Faster!"

"Is there somebody behind us?" She thought she caught a distant glimmer in the rearview, but it was gone before she could be sure.

"Just go. Go!"

She went. The car flew. Trees zipped past, then distant valleys. A sudden mist rose toward them, but Jericho commanded her to drive straight through it, and she did. They hit a bump, swerved, kept going.

"We're far enough down to use a cell—"

"Just hurry. Hurry!"

The mist cleared. Bethel was a brown smear on the horizon, and then it was upon them, the ramshackle town where Jericho had decided to make his home when the world decided it could get along without him. They passed the Arby's that marked the city limits. All at once they were on the town streets, and the speed limit was twenty-five. Nothing was behind them. Beck pulled into a service station.

"What was that back there?" she demanded, shivering now. "What were we running from?"

"Not what," said Jericho. "Who." A finger to his lips. "I'm afraid I can't tell you."

Was he truly so paranoid, or only playing paranoid? She had never fathomed the layers of that remarkable mind, even when they were sleeping together.

"Come on, Jericho. My car's not bugged." He said nothing. "It's not even the car I originally reserved. That one was dirty, so I got this one instead. Nobody could know which car I'd pick. And the car's been at your house—"

"And in town," he said, watching the wing mirror.

"Even so—"

"It doesn't matter." He reached up and flipped down the mirror, then pulled out a comb and worked it through his smooth gray hair. He looked the portrait of good health, but his weakness was apparent. "Let them listen, Beck. It doesn't matter. You want to know why you're here. I'll tell you. Because you're going to help me, whether you want to or not."

Typical Jericho: *whether you want to or not.* He could be gentle or demanding, furious or delighted, but, in the end, his every emotion was in bondage to the larger project of getting his way.

"Help you do what?" she asked after a moment.

"Buy me lunch."

"What?"

"Buy me lunch, and I'll tell you."

"You're not supposed to—"

"Becky. Listen. That offal that Saint Audrey feeds me? It's not going to cure my cancer. That's to make her feel better, not me. If I'm going to die in the next couple of months, I'd like to have at least one decent meal first." The old booming laugh. "If Saint Audrey gives you a hard time? Tell her I forced you at gunpoint."

"Audrey threw the guns away," said Beck, sourly.

"Not all of them," said Jericho, patting his jacket. He seemed inordinately pleased with himself.

(11)

There was no place in Bethel where Jericho could get his decent meal, and Beck absolutely refused to drive him into Vail, as he demanded, which was an hour and a half from Stone Heights—in the opposite direction. Teasing, she suggested Arby's. They settled on Corinda's.

His reception was royal.

Rebecca was astonished. Pete Mundy had told her Jericho was beloved in the town, but only now did she see what he meant. People of all ages came over to the table to shake his hand and clap him on the back and say how glad they were that he was feeling better. Corinda herself, who generally slept during the day, roused herself from her upstairs apartment to enfold him in her strong arms, and nibble proprietorially on his ear. Beck remembered Brian Navarro's story.

Corinda waited on them personally, and Jericho managed to flirt with both women at once. Beck remembered the old days, how when he turned his charm in your direction, you felt like you ruled his world, but when his magic settled elsewhere, it was like being overthrown in a coup d'etat. The highs had been higher than the lows were low, but not by much. In the end, Beck had left him because of another woman, and his fevered denials rang in her head even today: painfully but not quite believably.

Beck ordered poached salmon and a salad. Jericho ordered a steak sandwich with a double layer of melted Swiss cheese, and an extra order of fries. And, for an appetizer, fried onion rings. "Don't forget the dessert menus," he called after the departing Corinda, who favored him with a fond but weary smile.

"Come on, Jer-Bear," said Beck as soon as they were alone. "You can't eat that."

"Why not?"

"Because it's not part of your diet—"

He waved her silent. "You're being silly, Beck. And romantic. I told you in the car. No special diet is going to save me. You know that. So does Saint Audrey, no matter how much she pretends otherwise." He coughed. "As you see."

"Jericho—"

"I told you, Becky-Bear. I have a month. Maybe two or three if I get lucky. Is it really so terrible, wanting to have a little fun before I shuffle off this mortal coil?"

She let it drop. Waiting for the food, he chattered. He made jokes. He was jovial. She had not seen him this way since her arrival. He asked after Nina, and in detail, laughing to hear about her award for the most imaginative story in the second grade, but pressing Beck with questions when she said that the school was doing a unit on diversity around the world, wanting to know if the teachers were the sort who indoctrinated seven-year-olds with the mantra that America had no enemies in the world but the ones we created for ourselves.

Beck hastily changed the subject.

The first courses arrived: Beck's salad, Jericho's onion rings. When he took a bite, he groaned ecstatically and shut his eyes.

"Now, *this* is the way to die," he said, munching.

"I'm glad you're enjoying it."

"Have one."

"No, thanks."

"You know you want one." His old teasing self. "Come on. You can afford it."

She patted her hips. "I don't think so." But she took one anyway, because he was Jericho, and because he was right: she really did want one. She took another.

"That's the way," he said. He pushed his water glass aside, told Corinda to bring him whatever beer she had on tap, held up a warning finger to restrain Beck's objection. "We already had the argument." A roguish grin. "Besides. Alcohol is medicinal. Helps with the pain. Some people like marijuana, I like alcohol." A long swallow. He smacked his lips. "By the way, I talked to Beltran."

"Who?"

"Beltran. My ex-employee. Your boss's boss's boss. You're all set, Beck. You can stay as long as you want."

For a moment she could not form the words. "You have no right to interfere with my life," she began.

Hands over his heart. Wounded virtue. "Are you saying you want to go? We might not ever see each other again."

"You can stop with the manipulation. You already made your call."

"Should I call him back? Tell him you'll be in Chicago tomorrow night after all?"

She shook her head. She felt trapped and angry and crowded and hot, the other side of the life she and Jericho had led in these mountains. "Don't bother." She drew in a breath. "Friday. I'll stay one more day, Jericho. That's all I can spare. Number one, my daughter needs me. I'm picking her up on Sunday. Number two, I have an actual job. I work for a living. Please don't interfere again."

The main courses arrived. Jericho dug into his sandwich with delight. "Whatever you say, my dear."

"I'm serious."

"Fine." Chewing hard. "Tell you what. If you don't like me interfering, I'll call Beltran back, tell him not to promote you after all."

She sat straighter. "Not to what?"

"We chatted about your career. Beltran saw the light. He's going to kick you a few rungs higher on the ladder. An extra sixty, seventy grand a year. And, best of all, you get to look down on Pfister, Becky-Bear."

Rebecca was on her feet. Swaying. Furious. "Don't you—don't you dare—"

The hand went over the heart again, but his act was very old.

"I'm sorry. I thought this was what you wanted. A parting gift, you might say."

She could not speak. She stormed through the restaurant, heading for the ladies' room. She washed her face, and then, staring at her reflection, let loose the stream of invective she wished she could direct at Jericho. Then added a little more for herself.

When she felt calm enough to face him, she returned to the dining room. No sign of Jericho. Presumably, he was in the men's room, but when she sat down, there were bills on the table, and a copy of the check. She stood up, went over to a married couple, asked if the husband would mind checking the men's room.

"Not a problem," he said. "But if you're looking for Mr. Ainsley, you just missed him."

"Missed him?"

"He left maybe two minutes ago."

Beck flew to the door.

The space where she had left her rental car was empty. She checked the purse she had left in the booth. The keys were gone.

CHAPTER 21

The Flight

(1)

"We'll find him," said Pete Mundy, steering his cruiser toward the commercial strip. Rebecca was in the passenger seat. Tony Frias was reconnoitering the other end of town. Another deputy was checking the road to Stone Heights. "He can't have gotten far."

But she was thinking about Jimmy Lobb's truck at the bottom of a mountain gorge, and said nothing.

"I didn't even know he was up and about," Pete continued. "Pretty impressive for a man with his . . . problems."

"He always had a strong will," she whispered, aching.

"I said we'll find him. It's a small town."

"I hope so." She had not found the energy to call the house and tell the sisters she had lost track of their father.

They nosed through the parking lot of the strip mall, then the Wal-Mart. They checked the pharmacy and the grocery store and the gas stations, but saw no sign. They passed the turn for Route 24. There was no point in checking. If Jericho had taken Route 24, he could be on his way to another state.

"Pesky made bail," said the deputy. "I thought you'd want to know."

She was miles away. "What?"

"The man who was arrested last night. He made bail. A hundred thousand, cash."

Another silence as they drove past a row of abandoned warehouses. A photograph of Pete's son adorned the visor of the cruiser, just as it did the pickup. Beck wondered where her ex-husband kept the snapshots of Nina.

"By the way," said the deputy. "Thanks for calling me."

She looked at him. Men. "This is about Jericho."

"You could have called 911. But you called my cell."

"Even so—"

The radio beneath the dash crackled to life.

Pete spoke a few words, then listened. The car had been found. There was nobody inside.

It was in the parking lot next to the town clinic.

(11)

The town of Bethel did not possess a real hospital. A small clinic behind the elementary school had eight beds and provided some emergency services—mainly setting broken bones for skiers. Difficult cases went by ambulance or helicopter to the Vail Valley Medical Center.

Jericho Ainsley was not a difficult case.

As a matter of fact, he was not any kind of case.

The fidgety receptionist in the small waiting room insisted that nobody of that name was a patient. She checked twice. She was nervous. Sheriff Garvey had appeared briefly, and his expression said he blamed Beck for what had happened, maybe with reason. Then he had gone off to continue the search.

Pete Mundy asked sweetly if she would mind checking all the admissions this morning. She looked at her screen. A boy this morning with the sniffles. A woman delivering a baby.

"Other than that, nobody since this guy last night."

"What guy last night?" said Beck.

"Well, I wasn't on duty, but Wendy—she does nights?—Wendy says there was this guy who fell off a roof up on the mountain—"

Pete Mundy was already pelting for the stairs. Beck was on his heels.

"I thought you said Pesky made bail," she said as they climbed. The beds were on the second floor.

"His injuries mean he can't be moved. All making bail changed is that the trooper's gone from his door and he's not cuffed to the bed any more."

Eight beds, five rooms, two private. One nurse, two nurse's aides.

Pete grabbed one of the aides. "Did an old man come up here?"

She was chewing gum. Her pink uniform was stained. Medical care on a budget. "A what?"

"A man, about sixty-six, white, broad shoulders? Within the past hour?"

She was still for a few seconds, eyes rolling upward as if consulting memory storage. "The doctor," she finally announced.

"He's not a doctor," Beck began.

"Yes," said the deputy, waving her silent. "The doctor. Where did he go?"

"Mr. Pesky's room."

She pointed the way.

The door was locked.

"Hospital doors don't lock," said Beck.

"There's a thing you can do with a piece of wire—never mind." Pete hammered on the door. "Mr. Ainsley? Are you in there?"

The head nurse came around the corner and tried to shush him, and Beck drew her away. From inside the room came a crash. Then another.

"Move away," said the deputy.

He drew his service revolver, held it in two hands, pointing at the floor, and kicked the door. It failed to give. He kicked a second time, and the knob assembly burst from the jamb.

Inside, Marvin Pesky, licensed private investigator, was on the floor, groaning. Jericho Ainsley, the Former Everything, dying of cancer, was sitting on his back, holding a gun to Pesky's head and twisting the bones in his broken leg.

He looked up.

"We're done here," he said. "You can have him back."

Pete never flinched. "Put the gun down, Mr. Ainsley. Good. Now stand up. Step away."

Jericho, on his feet, looked over at Beck, and smiled. "Oh, good. My ride is here."

Then his eyes rolled up in his head and he collapsed.

WEDNESDAY NIGHT

CHAPTER 22

The Flag Code

(1)

They wanted to keep him overnight for observation, but Jericho insisted that he was fine, and the doctor could not prove otherwise. Pamela was all for forcing him to stay in the clinic, but Audrey wanted him back inside Stone Heights, the sooner the better. Corinda, who had arrived moments ago, said the ride was too long, and he should stay at her apartment. Beck sat this one out. Both sisters blamed her for what had happened, and she could hardly fault them.

Pete Mundy had slapped the cuffs on Jericho as soon as he woke after his fall, but Sheriff Garvey arrived and made him take them off.

The two men argued right next to Jericho's bed. "If the State's Attorney wants to charge him, we'll arrest him. Right now, though, we don't have anything. Pesky isn't pressing charges."

Pete fought back. "This isn't Hollywood. Pressing charges doesn't matter. I observed Mr. Ainsley in the commission of multiple crimes." Ticking them off on his fingers. "Assault. Aggravated assault. Illegal use of a firearm. Illegal possession of a firearm. Use of a firearm in further-ance of a felony—"

"He has a license," said the sheriff, lamely.

"Not for this gun."

Audrey stepped forward. "My father has been suffering from delu-sions," she said. "The cancer's moved to his brain."

"Well, then," said Garvey, as though that ended the matter.

"Delusions, my ass," said Jericho from the bed, where one of the nurses was checking his blood pressure. "Ask that fool of an investigator what he told me."

"Don't you dare," said the sheriff, because Pete Mundy looked ready. Angrily ready.

"Please don't say anything else, Dad," said Audrey, holding her father's hand.

"Ask him," Jericho repeated.

Corinda kissed his hand and told him to hush.

He subsided.

Sheriff Garvey turned to Rebecca. Even in front of his patron, his tone as he addressed her was gruff. "I understand you're leaving us."

"Soon," she said, testily, adrenaline still pumping.

"I think that's a good idea." He glanced at Jericho in the hospital bed. "You've caused enough trouble in Bethel." He took her silence for defiance, and he was not a man to defy. "Was there something you wanted to say to me, Miss DeForde? Were you getting ready to say, 'Yes, Sheriff, thank you, that's a good idea'? Something like that?"

"I'd like you to stop harassing me," she said evenly.

His color grew splotchier. His hand came up, and for a moment she thought the sheriff was going to strike her, right here in the middle of the hospital. But he only beckoned to Pete.

"Deputy Mundy. Would you be so kind as to escort Miss DeForde off the hospital grounds?"

The sisters took Jericho home in Pamela's Prius. Beck said she would be along shortly.

Outside the clinic, she lingered with the deputy. They watched as the sheriff drove off in one direction, Corinda in another.

"I think we've seen the end of Mr. Clark," said Pete, with rough humor. "He strikes me as a pretty smart guy, but he's not that big where guts are concerned."

"Guts?"

A shrug. "Tony and I pulled him over and made him see that maybe he shouldn't be bothering you folks up at Stone Heights. Maybe we were a little rough. Anyway, he took off, and another deputy saw his car heading for the Interstate. He's gone."

Maybe, she thought. Maybe not. And even if Pete was right—even if they had indeed seen the end of Lewiston Clark himself—the reporter's theory about what was going on had, so far, survived every test. The more Beck thought about it, the more sense Clark's story made. Jericho was not at war with his government. He was at war with Jack Notting. The only fly in the ointment was Maggie Ainsley's call. The Senator had implied that the interest was federal. Unless she was lying about the Justice Department—

"The State's Attorney will have to charge him," Pete continued. It took her a moment to realize that he had switched topics and was talking about Jericho. "I'm sorry, Beck. She won't have any choice. Even a man like Jericho Ainsley, acting that way in front of all these witnesses—"

"I understand."

"Why did he do it?"

She hesitated, knowing that her pause was itself information to a man as clever as Pete Mundy was turning out to be. "What Audrey said. He's not all there. He gets this way sometimes. He thinks everybody's conspiring against him."

Together they watched the sun dropping over the mountains. Snowcaps glistened brilliantly. Colorado was possibly the most beautiful state in the Union. But it never failed to break her heart.

"Why did he do it?" the deputy said again.

"I told you—"

"He wanted information, Beck. Ainsley didn't do this for the fun of it. The sheriff might buy that delusion story, but I don't." Pete was all cop now. She noticed that Jericho, now a suspect, had lost his *Mr.* "Do the math. Ainsley persuaded you to take him to town. He had this all planned. He waited for you to go to the ladies' room, he stole your car, he knew exactly where to go. He pretended to be a doctor. He'd lived here long enough to know that nobody at the clinic would ask any questions. For my money, that's a little too clever for a paranoid fantasy. He brought the gun along. He locked the door. A lot of preparation went into this afternoon's events, Beck. And then there was the risk."

"The risk?"

"He's a sick man. This kind of activity could make things worse. Evidently, it almost did. And he had to know he was going to get caught. What was worth taking a chance like that?"

Rebecca shook her head. "It all makes perfect sense, but only if you assume that Jericho knew that Pesky had been bailed out and the state trooper was gone."

"Oh, he knew. He absolutely knew. This is the best part of the story. Want to know who bailed Pesky out? Brian Navarro, Esquire, that's who. Jericho Ainsley's own lawyer. Maybe Navarro posted the bail and then told Ainsley about it. Maybe he posted the bail because Ainsley told him to do it. Either way, it shows premeditation." Her silence was starting to anger him. "Come on, Beck. This isn't just your problem any more. This isn't an old man sitting up on his mountaintop while the strangers come to town. This is a guy waving a gun around a hospital room to get information. I think you should tell me what's going on."

Rebecca had a nice way with anger herself. "I wasn't there, Pete. I'm the one he fooled, remember? I don't have the slightest idea what Jericho wanted. Why don't you ask Mr. Pesky?"

"He won't talk to me. I think he's afraid."

"Afraid of what? Never mind." She saw Dak lingering near the school across the street. She put a hand on the deputy's arm. "Pete, look. I'm sorry. You're right. Well, half right. There are things going on up there that I can't talk about. Don't give me that look. It has nothing to do with Bethel. I promise."

"What does it have to do with?" He took her hand. "Beck, look. Are you in some kind of trouble?"

"We're pretty well protected up there. You know how Jericho is."

"Not you, plural. You. Rebecca DeForde. Because it seems to me that you're getting in over your head."

She smiled. Gently. He was a kind man, but she sensed the strain in him, a helpless concern about events beyond his control. Beck felt warmed by his worry, but also knew that she could never draw him into what was happening.

Especially not with Sheriff Garvey watching his every move.

"I told you," she said. "It's nothing to do with Bethel. It's all about the past. Jericho's past. The people you've seen around town—the strangers you keep asking about—they have secrets. They want them kept. That's all."

"And what means are they willing to use to keep their secrets secret?" She shook her head. He spread his arms. "Beck, look. I'm not up there on the mountain, okay? So I don't know what's going on in that man's head, or in that house. Now, you can tell me that it's nothing. You can tell me to mind my own business. You tell me either one, I'll leave you alone. I promise. I won't ask again." Behind the glasses, the dark eyes waited. "On the other hand, if you need some help? Maybe there's something I can do."

An idea struck her.

"You know what? Maybe there is."

She whispered for a moment. Pete shook his head, then nodded. "I'll have the answer by tomorrow," he said. Beck crossed the street.

(I I)

"How is he?" said Dak. "I heard about what happened."

Beck was not through being furious. "Whatever he was doing, I bet you could have avoided it. I'm sure you already know who Pesky was working for."

"Is that what this was about?"

"I don't have the slightest doubt. What else would have been worth the risk? Jericho can't help himself. He's still an intelligence officer at heart. He still wants information."

"I can't blame him."

"He tortured that man."

Dak nodded. "I can imagine. He's very good at extracting information. He always was. He had a theory. Interrogation should be fast, not slow. You don't mess around. You go for the subject's weakest point and stick with it."

"You know what? You're a couple of coldhearted bastards."

"I should hope so." He patted the roof of her car. "Let's go for a ride, Rebecca."

He refused to talk in the car, except to give directions. They drove down Main Street, past the public library, finally stopping at a little park, complete with bandshell, dedicated to the town's veterans. They climbed out. The flag was flying but unlighted, whipping darkly in the rising mountain wind.

"You're wrong," said Dak when they had walked a bit. "I don't know who Mr. Pesky is working for. Despite what you seem to think, I'm not as plugged in as I used to be. I came up here for one reason: to persuade Jericho not to go forward. That's my only motive, Rebecca."

"You're here for the good of the country. Out of patriotism."

"And friendship," he said, quite unfazed by her sarcasm. "I care about him, Rebecca. I love that crazy old man. I don't want to see him hurt."

The words hung in the air between them. Beck finally broke the silence. "I've been doing some digging," she said.

"Good. Did you find whatever Jericho's hiding? Because your nation is depending on—"

"No. But I have a theory about what's been going on. I'd like to share it, if I could, and get your reaction."

"Please."

"My theory begins with Jericho's activities in recent years. His time at Scondell Bloom." When Dak said nothing, she continued. "The scandals never touched him. Not a single breath."

"Lucky him. But what does this have to do with the threat to national security that's represented by his—"

"Stop it." The sharpness of Beck's tone evidently surprised them both, because Phil Agadakos shut up at once, and looked at her with a fresh respect. "Please, Dak. Just listen, okay? Scondell Bloom was basically a leveraged buyout shop. A lot of private money, sure, but they also borrowed heavily in the financial markets. So if, say, they bought a pipeline company for ten billion dollars—which, as a matter of fact, they did—only about two billion was money from Scondell Bloom and their investors. Another billion or two would be from other shops like theirs; the rest they'd borrow. Then they'd strip off the valuable assets, load the debt onto the company they'd bought, cut its costs, fire a bunch of people, and sell the shares back to the public."

"I know how the system works, Rebecca."

"But Scondell Bloom wasn't like other private equity shops. It was remarkably successful abroad. They even penetrated markets in certain Asian and Gulf states where everyone knows foreign capital isn't welcome. The prosecutors have a theory about why. They can't prove it, which is why Jack Notting hasn't been indicted. Rufus Scondell and Doolie Bloom were indicted. Jack Notting wasn't. May I share the theory as to why not?"

"Please."

"The theory is that, in stripping valuable assets from the companies before reselling them, the first thing Scondell Bloom did was remove all the cash, or sell all the liquid assets. Most of the cash flowed into the operating budget and the investment pool, meaning that a big chunk was returned to the partners as income. The rest of the cash was invested around the world in a variety of foreign companies, where a lot of it vanished. Some of the companies were thriving, some of them were shells. Either way, the money flowed into them, and then out again, untraceable. On the books, the money had been reinvested, and then those reinvestments had taken huge losses. In real life, with the compliance of a few foreign nationals, it had been siphoned into offshore accounts controlled by the partners—"

"That sounds terribly illegal, Rebecca. Somebody should do something about it."

"The puzzle for the prosecutors—the reason they're not sure they can prove any of this—is how on earth the firm built this network of willing helpers around the world. Why would the directors of foreign corporations, or the currency regulators of foreign countries, put their livelihoods on the line to help a handful of American businessmen steal a fortune? And then lie to investigators about it? On Wall Street, they're shaking their heads. Nobody knows. All they keep saying is, somebody must have owed somebody else some huge favors."

"I see."

"But you and I know what the answer is, don't we? Jack Notting was CIA. Jericho Ainsley was CIA. I bet, if we went down the masthead, we'd find a few others, from managing directors to bit players, who were CIA. I think the whole bunch of them called in favors around the world. I think people owed them, and made up for it by looking the other way. I think Scondell Bloom was their retirement account."

"I see."

"And I think that's what Jericho's threatening to disclose. I think you cooked up the rest of it—the national-security angle—just to get me to cooperate."

"That's quite a story." They were back at the car. "Can you prove any of it?"

"No. It's a theory." It was nearly dark. "Like I said, I was wondering what you thought of it."

"Well, for one thing, to make it work, you'd have to assume that only Jack Notting was CIA. Not Rufus Scondell and Doolie Bloom. These were smart men. You'd have to assume that Notting pulled the wool over their eyes. They had no idea what he was up to."

"Or that this was the deal. They'd get their share, but if anything happened, they'd take the fall."

"Yes. I see. I see. And they'd be too frightened to talk."

"That's right."

"But a friend of mine overheard Lewiston Clark telling you that Scondell Bloom was washing mob money. I don't think the Agency and the mob get in bed together these days."

A friend of mine. An unsubtle confirmation that Dak's people were watching. "That would be a good cover story, wouldn't it?" Beck said. "It would explain perfectly any acts of violence or intimidation that might occur. The perfect rumor to cover whatever is really going on."

"Fascinating." He leaned against a bench, crossed his arms. "And what do you plan to do with this theory of yours, Rebecca? Write a book? Call your Congressman? What did you have in mind?"

"Nothing. I'm not doing a thing. That's what I wanted to tell you. I'm getting on that plane tomorrow—no, Friday—and forgetting any of you ever existed."

Dak nodded. They left the park, crossing back toward the clinic, where Beck had left her rental. "I think that's a very good idea."

"Still, there's one thing I don't understand." He did not warn her off, so she plunged. "These men who did this thing—whoever they were—they'd spent their careers serving their country. They were patriots. Why would they turn around and spit in their country's face?"

"Maybe that's not how they saw it, Rebecca. Maybe they looked at the size of their pensions after decades of risking their lives, seeing things too terrible to think about and sometimes doing them, all so the pigs-in-clover crowd could sip champagne in their private jets and party with movie stars who give speeches about how terrible these people were, the people working to protect them. Maybe they got sick of it. Maybe they wanted their fair share."

"By theft? By fraud?"

"By whatever means necessary, Rebecca. Just the way they'd been trained."

"But they were patriots," she objected again, the last safe harbor of her secret romantic view of her country. "They loved America." A pause. "Didn't they?"

Dak's tone was kindly. "I suppose, in their way, they did."

"In their way?"

He pointed. "See the flag, Rebecca? It's flying at night, but it's not lighted. That violates a federal law. Did you know that? There's a federal statute called the Flag Code. It was adopted by Congress during World War II. It's still on the books, but nobody enforces it. Nobody cares. People call themselves patriots, and then they violate the rules for flying the American flag. Because patriotism—left, right, or center—means whatever people need it to mean."

They drove back to town in silence.

The were at the Red Roof Inn, standing beside the car.

"I'm leaving," he said.

"Leaving? Leaving where?"

"Going home. I'm retired." He had his hands in his pockets. "This isn't my fight. I wanted to help him, but he doesn't want to be helped."

She rubbed her eyes. "And this wouldn't have anything to do with the story I just told you."

"My arrangements are already made, Rebecca. You can call the airline if you don't believe me."

Beck was not sure why she wanted so badly for him to stay. Maybe the same reason children wanted so badly for Santa Claus to be real. "What if I were to agree?" she said. "What if I helped you find whatever he's hidden?"

For an instant, the chilly eyes warmed with interest. Then he shook his head. "I'm sorry," he said. "It's too late. My work is done. I tried to change his mind. I couldn't. So I'm going home."

"Just tell me first, Dak. Tell me if I'm right. That this has nothing to do with national security and everything to do with the stolen money—"

He shrugged. "Most of your story makes perfect sense to me. But it's not my province. I'm not a rich man. I didn't get into the intelligence business to protect rich men. If Jack Notting stole money, I hope he rots. If Jericho helped him—well, I love him, but he'll have to take his chances with the rest of the crooks. No, Rebecca. I'm here for my country. What I told you the other night isn't some cover story. It's the truth."

"Then why—"

"I'm not finished. I said most of the story makes sense. The part about Jack Notting being a thief? I'm willing to believe it. But the notion that Jericho has the goods on him? I'm skeptical, Rebecca."

"Why? If Jericho is willing to blackmail the government of the United States, why would he stop at doing the same to a rogue billionaire?"

"With what? His word against Notting's?"

"Evidence. Records. Whatever there is. He could have collected it, and hidden it somewhere." She grew eager. "My theory connects all the dots. Jericho has the records of Jack Notting's illegal transactions—"

Dak waved this away. "Say you're right. It's a big assumption, that anybody would organize all of this over money, but say you're right. Fine. Jack Notting stole money, he hid it abroad, Jericho helped him. But you have to understand something about a man like Jack Notting. There wouldn't be records."

"There would have to be. They could be hidden. Fine. But nobody could remember so many details. Someplace, somewhere—"

"No, Rebecca. No. Listen. A couple of years ago, there was this movie. The bad guys were CIA agents running a secret assassination squad, right? Killing American citizens, all that. And how did they get caught? Because the bad guys kept these files, on official CIA stationery, in a safe in New York City. The files said who got killed and who did the killing. Right? Now, that's the Hollywood version. Let's talk real life. I was Director of Operations for six years. Suppose—hypothetically—that we really did decide to get rid of somebody. I'm not saying we did. I'm saying, suppose we did. Number one, nobody would be crazy enough to put it on paper. Number two, if we did put it on paper? There was a little trick we pulled, whenever we had to keep records that we might not want people to see. We never put them on stationery, only on blank pages. And there were always typos. Lots and lots of typos. Typos, cross-outs, pieces taped together from different typewriters or fonts. Now, why would we do that, Rebecca?"

She saw it. So obvious, once you thought about it. "So if the records ever got out they would look fake."

"Exactly. That's exactly right. And a lot of government secrets are kept just that way, Rebecca. On cheap paper with no letterhead and lots of errors. So if the *Times* or CBS or some blogger ever gets hold of them they won't even bother to run with the story. That's Jack Notting's background. I don't believe he'd keep records. But if he did? They'd be in a form that couldn't possibly incriminate him. No, Rebecca. I know you don't believe my story. You don't think Jericho is threatening national security. You think either I'm lying to you or people are lying to me. But my story makes the most sense."

"But what about—"

His cell phone rang.

He glanced at the screen, and something much like pain flared in his eyes. He walked several paces away to answer, and spoke in a whisper. But Rebecca's ears were excellent. "Yes. What? Who? Max? Max is coming here? Who sent— I see. I see. No, I'm leaving anyway. What? No. With Max around, it doesn't make sense, does it? Yes. Okay."

Agadakos hung up and swung back. "It doesn't matter what's true and what isn't," he resumed, as if the other conversation had never taken place. "Because you're flying to Chicago on Friday anyway, right?"

"Right," she said.

Wrong.

(I V)

Margaret Ainsley called while Beck was driving back to Stone Heights. She had heard about what happened, she said. She was so sorry. She asked Beck to pass on her best wishes. She would call Stone Heights tomorrow.

"You could call tonight," said Beck. "I'm sure everybody's up."

"Oh, no, no, I would just be a bother."

"It would be fine—"

A pause. "And as to the rest of what we talked about, there's been another development."

"Which is what?"

"Well, according to my sources, it seems that—"

The static rose suddenly, and the call was lost. The screen said Beck still had bars, and when she called the house to say she was on the way, she had no trouble. But, try as she might, she could not get through to the Senator.

THURSDAY

CHAPTER 23

The *Réseau*

(I)

On the last day, heavy thundershowers arrived, like heralds of coming tragedy. Jericho, exhausted, slept late. The three women tiptoed around one another like partners in a bad marriage. Beck, for a change, was the one hogging the single telephone. She left multiple messages for Senator Ainsley, both on her cell and at her office, and logged a series of conversations with an increasingly frantic Pfister, who seemed terrified at the idea of attending the regional sales conference alone. She assured him that everything he needed was in the memos she had left behind, and reminded him that she would be arriving only a day later than planned.

"What are you doing out there, anyway?" Pfister demanded, his nervousness making him shrill. "What's the big meeting?"

"It's hard to explain," she answered, realizing that Jericho had never briefed her on the details of the excuse that would keep her here another day. She wondered whether the big promotion was on or off, or a figment of Jericho's fevered imagination.

When she said goodbye to Pfister for the third time, the phone immediately rang again. She wished somebody else would answer, but she was sitting right at the desk.

"Hi, Beck," said Tish Kirschbaum. "Have you been stepping on somebody's toes?"

Rebecca, very surprised, asked what she meant.

"I had a call from my friend in the U.S. Attorney's office. He said all the assistants got this confidential e-mail, wanting to know which of them had been talking to you." She laughed. Nothing had scared Tish in college, and nothing scared her now. "Nothing stays confidential long these days, huh?"

"What exactly did the e-mail say?"

"No idea. He didn't send me a copy. He made it sound all bureaucratic. You know. That they should report any and all contacts with you to a supervisor, et cetera, et cetera, and a reminder that the work of the office is not a subject for public discussion."

"Tish, you could get in trouble!"

Another hooting laugh. "Why? I'm not bound by their secrecy rules. I'm legally free to repeat anything I hear, and so are you."

"Legally," Beck muttered.

"Say again?"

"Nothing." How do you tell your best friend that your phone is tapped? Especially when you're talking on it. "Tish, I have to go. I'll call you when I'm home. Please don't discuss this with anybody else."

"Now you sound like the memo my friend got."

"Every now and then," said Beck, borrowing from Jericho, "the government of the United States is actually right."

(11)

Sheriff Garvey stopped by. He was very somber. He wanted to see Jericho, but Jericho was not available, so he settled for the sisters. Rebecca tried to make herself scarce, on the theory that this was family business and she was leaving tomorrow, but the sheriff said she might as well hear this, too. So they sat in the great room, over near the window with the spectacular mountain view, and listened quietly as the man the Former Everything had elected explained that Jericho would soon be arrested.

"Mr. Pesky took a turn for the worse during the night. He already had a couple of broken bones after his fall from the roof. What your father did to him—well, that made it a whole lot worse. There's some internal injuries."

"The injuries could be from the fall," Audrey objected.

"The doctors say they *are* from the fall. They've been aggravated, is all. He's being airlifted to Denver"—a melodramatic glance at his watch—"even as we speak."

The women looked at one another. The atmosphere in the room was ugly, and Beck knew that as soon as Garvey was gone it would get a lot uglier.

"Now, everybody knows Mr. Ainsley is sick," the sheriff continued, "and, well, he is who he is. Nobody's in a hurry. He's not going anywhere. The State's Attorney will convene a grand jury, and that'll take time. Maybe the grand jury will decide he's delusional, Miss Ainsley, just like you said last night. But the State's Attorney, well, she's gonna push hard. She's made that clear. A prosecutor doesn't get all that many shots at a rich white guy. Sending the former head of the CIA to prison for assault is the kind of thing that can get you your own talk show on CNN or Fox. And—well, he did do it, after all."

"Yes," said Pamela, jaw jutting grimly. "He did."

"The only thing is—nobody seems to know why."

"I told you," Audrey began.

"Right. That he's delusional. My Deputy Pete Mundy doesn't happen to agree. My deputy thinks Mr. Ainsley wanted actual information, and right now the State's Attorney is listening to him, not to me. The only way I can help is if you tell me what his real motive was. What he's been up to. Why so much craziness is happening up here. What he wanted from Mr. Pesky."

"No idea," said Audrey.

"None," said Beck.

"He wanted to know who Pesky was working for," said Pamela. The other women turned on her in dismay, but she was not done. "And, no, he didn't tell us whatever he found out. If he found out anything. I doubt that he did. From what Rebecca says, he wasn't in the room very long."

The sheriff looked more dismayed than ever. "My deputy reports that when he arrived on the scene and broke down the door, Mr. Ainsley said, 'We're done here.' Now, my deputy has the State's Attorney believing that meant he already had, uh, extracted whatever information he was looking for." He opened his jacket. "Look. I'm not wearing a wire. I'm not taking notes. But I need something to take back to the State's Attorney. Something to persuade her that Mr. Ainsley was acting"—he squinted at the ceiling, searching for the phrase—"out of some rational fear. Isn't there anything you can tell me? About what he's been doing?"

Audrey and Beck exchanged glances of growing kinship, and growing suspicion, but once again Pamela marched into the breach.

"We don't know what he's been doing, but we do know he's been worrying a lot. He thinks people are out to get him. Maybe they are. But he just sits up in that room all day and broods and broods." Where had she summoned those tears from? Pamela was no crier. "He might not be delusional, Sheriff, but he's not well. It's not just the cancer. It's more than that. My father spent his career sniffing out other people's conspiracies and planning his own. It's how he sees the world. He never believed Pesky was taking those pictures on behalf of a magazine. None of us did." Drawing the others, unwilling, into what Beck thought of already as her treachery. "You say the State's Attorney wants an arrest. Fine. We can't stop her. But we've been complaining for weeks about trespassers, and your department has done squat to protect us. If my father has gone off the deep end, I think you and your deputies have to shoulder some of the blame."

"What are you—"

Her voice was now coldness itself. Pamela could do all the moods at once, a talent that gave her far too many weapons for ordinary mortals to take on in conversation. "As soon as you walk out that door, Sheriff—and I would like that to be momentarily—I am getting on the phone to everybody I know in the media. And believe me, Sheriff, I know everybody. I am giving them all the same story. That the former Director of Central Intelligence, the former Secretary of Defense, has been endlessly harassed during his dying months, and the county sheriff has done nothing to protect him. Finally, he snapped, and, yes, what happened to Mr. Pesky is unforgivable, but the truth is, if the county sheriff had done his job—"

Everybody was standing. Somehow Pamela had maneuvered the group halfway to the door.

"—well, then, Mr. Pesky would never have been on the property, to say nothing of the roof. Oh, and another thing. This is Colorado. Mr. Pesky was a home invader. My father had the right to use deadly force against him."

"Not once he was off the property!"

Her smile was silky. "I suspect that the media will obscure that particular detail. You know how they are."

When the sheriff had gone, Pamela lit into the other two women. "Help me out next time. Don't just sit there like bumps on a log." She was breathing very hard. "Listen to me. Dad might be a bastard, but they are not arresting him. No chance. We are not going to let that happen. Is that clear?"

Astonished, they watched her stalk up the stairs. And it occurred to Rebecca that Pamela's anger this time was not at the other women. It was Jericho himself who was the object of her fury. Perhaps for the past; perhaps for the present; perhaps it made no difference. Fathers whose frustrations marked their wives could hardly be expected to be honored by their daughters. She remembered, again, how her mother had shaved her husband before his death. Beck, watching, had thought her mother a fool.

(111)

The storms had passed. They were out on the deck again, Jericho and Rebecca, enjoying the thin afternoon sun on her final day at Stone

Heights. The temperature was dropping, and the forecast for tonight called for sleet or perhaps more snow. Jericho was wrapped in, if anything, more layers than yesterday. He was coughing a lot, too, and she kept urging him to go inside. He refused, and it occurred to her that he was showing signs of the petulance with which he often masked unhappiness.

"So Dak's leaving us," he said, when he heard about last night. "Well, well. I guess I scared him off, didn't I?" Jericho's eyes followed a small animal skittering along the edge of the woods. He laughed. "It's driving them nuts, isn't it? That they can't figure it out."

"You're having fun."

"I hope so."

"I talked to your cousin," she said quietly.

His bonhomie vanished. "What did the bitch want? The same thing as Dak, right? Talk the madman out of wrecking the nation's security?"

"Something like that." She discovered that she was holding his hand. "She's worried about you."

"The only thing my cousin is worried about is whether to run for President this next time around or the time after."

Rebecca felt herself bristling, and was not even sure why. She snatched her hand away. "There is such a thing as love in the world, Jericho. Not everybody acts out of base motives."

"Just me? Is that what you're saying? Everybody else is noble, I suppose."

"I just want to know if it's worth it. If you really want to tell the secrets." She returned to her question from Sunday. "Is this how you want to be remembered?"

His voice was oddly soft, a sign, she knew, of anger. "Is it my turn, Becky-Bear?"

"Yes," she said, feeling sullen and hot, already expecting him to out-argue her.

"Fine. Number one"—he took a finger—"I told you already, I don't particularly give a crap how I'm remembered. Two"—another finger—"if Mr. Philip Agadakos or Senator Margaret Bitch Ainsley think I'm damaging the nation's security, then they're welcome to call the gendarmes and have me thrown into Leavenworth. Notice they haven't done that. Remember not to overlook the obvious, darling." He tried to bare his teeth in defiance, but coughed again instead. He took another finger. "Three. If nobody's planning to hurt me, then nobody has anything to worry about, do they?"

"Are you saying that the secrets in question have nothing to do with national security?"

"Is Dak still saying they do?"

"Yes."

"Do you believe him?"

"I don't know what to believe, Jericho. That reporter—your old student Lewiston Clark—he seemed to think the secrets had to do with Scondell Bloom."

Another derisive hoot. "Now, that was one of my stupider ideas."

"Is that what you're hiding? How the money went . . . wherever it went?"

"Maybe."

"Dak said it was impossible. There wouldn't be written records."

"Not written. No."

"So what is it? Audiotape? Videotape? What?" She could not hold back. "And if you have records like that, why don't you give them to the FBI or somebody? Why keep them for your own personal pleasure?"

"Maybe it's not pleasure," he snapped. "Did you ever think of that? Maybe it's justice."

So Beck fired the only arrow left in her quiver. "The man I used to love," she said, forcefully, "would not be doing this."

She had reached him. She could tell. The eyes widened and he leaned away from her, his response somewhere between fear and admiration. For a moment, she almost believed he was ready to give up the whole thing.

Then the animal cunning closed down once more, and he chuckled. "The man you loved died when you left him, Becky-Bear." Wounding her despite the pleasant tone. He touched his chest. "The man who took his place is going to be dead in a couple of months."

"That's not fair!"

Jericho coughed again, then propped himself on an elbow. "Let me tell you a story, Becky-Bear. Back when I was a case officer—the sixties—I had charge of an operation that went bad. Never mind where. Eastern Europe—that's all I can say. I was running what old Agency hands used to call a *réseau*. What you'd call a network. I had diplomatic cover, but the spies I was running didn't. They could be arrested and tortured until they gave up the names of the rest of the members of the *réseau*."

He coughed, and for a moment had trouble sitting up, but when Beck moved close to help, he waved her away.

"Well, a couple of the members got blown. Doesn't matter how. I met one of them. He was on the run. We met in a public park. Lots of people around. Poor man knew it was only a matter of time before the secret police got him and he wound up chained to a wall with his jaw broken and his balls wired up to the house current. He wanted to escape. Demanded money, a passport, everything. I told him none of that was possible. I was going to be expelled any day now for activities inconsistent with my diplomatic status. Then I let the other shoe drop. I told him that we couldn't let him be taken. That we couldn't let him blow the rest of the *réseau*. He looked around. I'd brought a couple of minor goons with me. He knew where this was going. He said, 'But I've done my job! You can't do this to me!' All the things you'd expect. I said I was sorry, I had no choice. He tried to make a break for it. My goons got him. The last thing he said was 'This isn't fair!' And it wasn't, Becky-Bear. He was innocent. Even a hero. He had served our country and his movement, and we had to get rid of him." His energy gave out at last, and he slid to the pillow. "It wasn't fair, but it was real life."

"Did that really happen?" she asked, reeling at this casual lifting of the curtain shrouding the least savory aspects of his work.

The golden eyes were hooded, unreadable. "I was in a grubby trade, Becky-Bear. Dak knows that. And you, my dear—well, don't let yourself forget. Sometimes your own friends will kill you for the crime of doing what they ask." He stood up. "It's late. We should go in."

He was plainly exhausted. Before he crossed the threshold, she put a hand on his arm. "Jericho, wait."

"Yes, my dear?"

"Mr. Pesky. What did you find out? Did he tell you who he works for?"

"Whom. It's the object of the preposition."

"Did he tell you?"

"Yes," he said, and went into the house.

But at that last moment, just before they parted, his mask had slipped for a fraction of a second. Beck had read the abject suffering in that familiar face. Maybe the cancer cells were emerging for the last battle. Maybe Jericho was still worn out from his foolish exertions of last night. Yet the romantic in her preferred a third explanation:

That Pesky had indeed told Jericho the identity of his employer; and that it was the knowledge of who had hired him that made life suddenly not worth fighting for.

CHAPTER 24

The Pin Lights

(1)

Back inside the house, the sisters were both busy. Beck had finished reading the Danticat and, although she had a briefcase full of memos for tomorrow's meeting in Chicago, was in no mood to work. Although it was not yet dinnertime, Jericho had turned in for the night. Finally, she decided to go to the basement and shoot some pool, another joy of their time together. He used to drag her to a now vanished pool hall in town, where he would take on all comers in nine-ball as she rooted for him and, occasionally, played a rack or two. Since then, she had found that the clean clack of the balls helped her to think clearly. And that was what she needed now, a clear head.

Down in the basement, she racked the balls and considered turning on the television, but operating the remote control was as complicated as piloting the space shuttle. She chalked a cue, leaned over, made satisfying contact, watched the balls carom around the table as the worries caromed through her mind. From the moment she had walked through the door, the only bits of truth had been Pamela's animosity and Jericho's illness—and, but for that terrible cough and the need to have bribed a few dozen doctors and medical technicians, she might have decided that the cancer, too, was just another wisp. Still, their conversation this afternoon had confirmed, indirectly, the hypothesis she had proposed to Dak.

Whomever Jericho was blackmailing, it was not the federal government or some other interested country.

He was blackmailing the survivors of Scondell Bloom—in particular, the old friend who got him involved in the first place, Jack Notting, formerly of the Foreign Service, postings unlisted, meaning that he, too, had worked for the CIA. She was not sure which of the men had come up with the retirement plan. She had no idea what to do with her knowledge; but she was glad to be leaving tomorrow.

Maybe she should leave the whole mess on Pete Mundy's desk.

She made a tough combination shot and missed an easy bank shot, and asked herself why Jericho had wanted her here. The answer, she suspected, was hidden in the two conversations out on the deck, and in his repeated questions about why Audrey had quit job and family to become a nun. Dak had warned her to keep clear, and Beck had tried to preserve an emotional distance, but Jericho's tantalizing clues had enticed her and enticed her until it was Princeton all over again: the Former Everything manipulating Rebecca into doing what he wanted.

Beck realized that she had worked herself into a fury. She tossed the pool cue aside, then played with Jericho's mesh security gates for a while, making sure she knew how to open and close them. She accepted that Jericho was mad, and that she would never need this knowledge; all the same, she felt better possessing it.

Then she had a thought.

Shutting the gates behind her so that she would not be surprised, she followed the path Pamela had charted Tuesday, down the hallway, into the storeroom, through the reinforced door, up the stairs to the garage. Jericho, she suspected, wanted her to make this visit.

At the top of the stairs, she shoved the door—

It was still locked.

No matter. She knew the combination. Jericho had told her Tuesday with the silly story about giving her a Ferrari on her birthday, leaving it in the garage.

She entered her birthday, date, then month, then year—

And the door swung open, easily.

With a final glance behind, Rebecca stepped into the darkness.

(11)

At first she was confused. The gloom was too complete. She thought there would be light from the windows. Then she remembered that the windows were covered with fabric. She slid her hand along the wall, searching for a light switch, only to realize that she would have to step away from the door, and that it would close automatically behind her.

Another clever Jericho Ainsley touch: she should have brought a flashlight.

To step or not to step? She shut her eyes, reaching into the darkness with her ears. She heard a thrumming, but that was the furnace wafting up the stairwell. She listened harder. A scratch. A scuttle. Probably mice. Great. She was not afraid of many things, but mice were near the top of the list. She was not sure which was worse, seeing them or not seeing them. She heard something dripping, but could not tell whether it came from in front of her or behind her. She heard a footstep, and it was definitely in front of her, and, just like that, she was back inside the stairwell, holding the door shut with her weight.

"Don't be silly," she whispered. "There's nobody in there."

This was absurd. There was nothing to be afraid of. Jericho was hiding something in the garage, there was no doubt about that, but whatever was in there had been delivered by a truck from town: crates, Audrey had said. Just crates. And crates that arrive by truck do not usually contain

—*a crate full of zombies*—

anything capable of walking around on man-sized feet. The truck might have brought papers or electronic equipment or maybe more guns, enough to start a war with this time. The truck could have brought the secret evidence with which Jericho was blackmailing either his own government or the survivors of Scondell Bloom or something else altogether. But the truck could not possibly have brought

—*zombies*—

something alive that was being stored in the blacked-out garage. If she had really heard anything at all, it was surely the rain plinking on the garage roof, for the showers had returned.

She decided to open the door just a notch, to listen again, but it was a good two minutes before her fingers would play.

Then she shoved the door, very fast.

And listened.

No mice, no footfalls, no dripping. Breathing this time. Somebody was in there breathing hard, gulping down the air. No. No. Her fight-or-flight reflex was sizzling, but Rebecca stood her ground. This was imagination. Nothing more. This was her mind inventing voices out of static, just as Audrey had suggested.

She slipped off her sneakers and wedged them in the doorway. Now she had a way out.

Then she stepped all the way inside.

Unable to see, she walked slowly, her hands in front of her. The concrete floor was chilly beneath her wool socks. She moved with a shuffle, more sliding her feet than lifting them. She listened hard, but heard only the occasional skitter of mice.

Her hands struck something.

It took her a long moment to gather herself. She turned around and saw the faintest glow of light from the hallway. This was why there was no illumination on the final stairway up from the basement: Jericho did not want his enemies to have even the slightest ability to see.

She reached out again. Wood. A wood surface, about waist high.

A crate.

She felt the thrumming again, and supposed that the furnace had kicked on once more. She leaned forward and put her ear to the crate, but heard nothing. She had not expected to. Keeping one hand lightly on the wood, she walked around the crate. About two feet on a side, she estimated. She felt a hinge, then a handle.

The top could be pulled open, she realized.

But when she tried, the lid would not budge, and her searching fingers found a padlock. She tugged, hard, but the hasp was closed. A beep made her jump. Somewhere off to the side, some sort of digital equipment had turned on. She saw a pair of fiery-red eyes, but they were only pin lights. She shuffled toward the glow, but another crate blocked her access. She began working her way around the side.

Another beep in the darkness. A series of what might have been numbers appeared on an LED readout, but too far away for her to make them out.

Her cell phone rang.

She shrieked.

She swept it from her hip, and dropped it.

It continued to ring. She got down on her hands and knees and felt around for it, and her fingers encountered bits of trash and wire and wood before she came up with the telephone.

A trembling hand put the phone to her ear.

Static. Whine.

She was about to hang up when she heard that voice again, faintly, shrouded deep inside the cocoon of noise. "Eight hundred acres . . . Middle of nowhere."

Imagination.

The virus.

Something worse.

A click. The static ended, and then she heard the best voice in the world: "I have to go, because Grandma is calling me, and I didn't tell her I'm calling you—*Just a minute!*—I'm in the bathroom and I guess I better go, but call me, Mommy, okay? Call me soon, so I can tell you about the d—"

The message ended.

Another click. Not on the phone. In the garage. One of the pin lights had winked out.

She stared at the screen across the floor, waiting.

Another red light came on, and a roar of static drowned everything else, followed by a faxlike whine.

Hastily, she pressed the button to kill the call.

The static stopped.

The red pin lights clicked off.

"Not possible," she whispered. She scrambled for the door, bumping another crate in the process. Another red light blinked as she stooped to get her shoes. She waited, but her cell did not ring.

Shivering, she locked the door securely behind her. She had to talk to Pete Mundy.

THURSDAY NIGHT

CHAPTER 25

The Romantic

(1)

Some evils are nothing but coincidence, and some coincidences are nothing but evil. All the way down the mountain, Rebecca tried to figure out the category into which the pin lights fell. Either the device in the garage was somehow sending signals to her cell phone, or else it had another purpose altogether, and just happened to begin cycling when she approached. Whatever the right answer, she knew she could not tell the sisters. She no longer trusted them. Pamela would dismiss her, Audrey would comfort her, and Beck herself would stare at them and wonder.

The showers had slackened to a cold drizzle. The late-afternoon sky was flat, and too close. The road down to Bethel was, as usual, devoid of traffic. Sometimes the solitude consoled her. Today the mountain felt desolate, like emptiness after the battle. One more night in the nuthouse, she kept repeating as she descended. She only had to make it to tomorrow.

The sisters had been surprised when their guest came rushing upstairs from the basement, frightened and uncommunicative, and more surprised still when she told them she was going to town. *We need you here,* Pamela had said. *It's almost dark,* Audrey had added.

As if she should be worried about vampires.

The sisters. She remembered Pamela's first visit to Stone Heights, back when the Jericho-Beck show was running strong. It was just past Rebecca's twentieth birthday; Jericho had surprised her with a week in Cancún. Upon returning, she had traipsed happily about the house wearing various gifts, and Jericho had emerged from his study and ordered her to dress down tomorrow because his daughter would be coming. Dress down: jeans, in other words, rather than the expensive and often skimpy attire he liked her to model for him. It was near Christmas, eight months into their relationship, and she had yet to meet any of the children but the sullen Sean, then in high school.

At that time, Pamela had been a D-girl at Warner Bros.—Jericho sat on the board of the parent company—and she favored granny dresses and wore her hair in oddly colored whorls. The introductions were awkward, and Beck could feel the antagonism coming off the other woman in hot waves, but both tried to behave themselves. Pamela, it turned out, had come to ask Jericho's assistance in raising money for a film she wanted to make—in other words, she wanted him to loan her a hundred thousand dollars—and, in consequence, had to make nice to the lady of her father's house. At that time there was a housekeeper, too, and she summoned Mr. Jericho to the telephone, leaving the two young women sitting in the living room with nothing to say to each other. And the part of the story Beck had always remembered best was the pain on Jericho's dashing face when he stepped back in to find them sitting silently: he had so wanted, he told her in bed later, for them to be friends. But the part she remembered now, and had never paid attention to before, was the other thing Jericho had told her in bed.

All that girl does is take. I loaned her the money, but it's the same as a gift. She'll never pay me back, and I won't own a piece of the movie, either.

He would never have trusted Pamela with anything.

Audrey, on the other hand, whatever else she might have been, was a specialist in interrogation. Breaking down the subject's environment. Changing the rules the subject lived by. And in a world in which people were ruled by their cell phones, that was as good a place as any to start. Her mobile had started to play games, and now her imagination was all over the place. In the garage she had thought she heard footsteps, but she could no longer trust her own perceptions.

Which was no doubt somebody's plan.

Somebody's plan. Rebecca grimaced. She was thinking like Jericho. But there were moments when paranoia was the rational course.

On the outskirts of town, she slowed, preparing herself for the worst. She was not yet sure whether she could trust Pete Mundy, but she had no doubt that he had kept his part of the bargain. Beck was not the sort to use a man's attraction against him, but until tomorrow she was still living in Jericho's world, and the rules were different.

He was waiting for her, pacing impatiently, in the parking lot of Arby's. She pulled up next to him, and he hopped in. He had bought roast-beef sandwiches for the both of them.

Her favorite.

(11)

They parked at a strip mall near the entrance to Route 24, where, said Pete, the sheriff was less likely to notice them.

"I have what you asked for," he said.

"Good."

His eyes measured her. "We have a deal, right? You give, I give."

She nodded.

Pete handed her a piece of paper, listing all the East Coast telephone calls received by Sheriff Garvey on his cell phone or his office phone for the past month. "I can't get home calls without a subpoena," he explained. But she was busily staring at the one number that predominated.

Beck looked up. "Where's the other?"

Pete shook his head. "Your turn."

And so she told him, straight out, gaining fluency with the telling. Until this moment, Beck had not realized how desperately she needed to talk, only how fearful she was that she would not be believed. She left out some important details—for example, her precise conversations with Dak and Maggie Ainsley. But she laid out the bare bones of the tale.

"Are you done?" he asked, when she wound down.

Rebecca saw his slight smile, remembered Audrey, felt her blood boiling.

"You think I'm crazy."

"No."

"You think I'm exaggerating."

"No." He toyed with his root beer. "I wish you were crazy, Beck. Seriously. But what you're telling me—well, it jibes with a few other things I've observed." A hard glance. "Not that there aren't any problems with your story. There are. Those lights in the garage, for instance. Even if somebody had a device in there that called up your cell phone, why should some red light flash every time? It's too convenient. No, Beck. What you saw sounds a lot more like an electric eye. You probably tripped a silent alarm, maybe more than one."

"What about the footsteps?"

Pete took a bite of his sandwich. He shook his head. "Look. Mr. Ainsley was in bed. His daughters were in the house. I think your mind played a trick or two."

"Maybe." She watched the street for a bit. Nighttime traffic was light. She did not see how an intruder could have gotten in. Pete was right. She had simply been spooked. "Okay. Let's say you're right. I was alone in the garage, and I tripped an alarm. That means Jericho knows I was in the garage."

"Somebody presumably does."

Beck did not like this at all. She did not want to worry about a *somebody* out there. But Phil Agadakos and Lewiston Clark, in their different ways, had already warned her that somebody was. "Whatever's in those crates," she finally said, "it must be pretty important."

"Seems that way." His soft drink was nearly gone. He took off the plastic top, drained what was left. "Beck, look. The only reason you got into the garage in the first place is that Mr. Ainsley gave you the combination. He's not a man who makes mistakes. He wanted you to see whatever's in there."

"But why?"

"I don't know." Drumming his fingers on the dashboard. "Look. Let me tell you my side of the story, and maybe we can put them together."

"Please."

Behind the glasses, his eyes were no longer boyish. They were no longer amused. They were serious, but also—frightened. "About six months ago—say, October—some men came to see the sheriff. Dangerous men. Not dangerous in themselves, but men who could order other men to be dangerous. It's just a quality some men have. You can sense it. Their presence implies legions of hard men, at their beck and call. So, anyway, three of them took the sheriff to a very long lunch. Not here—over in Vail. When the sheriff got back, he was—I don't know—excited, I guess is the word. Like he was moving up in the world. He called in his top deputies and he said we had big work ahead of us. His number two used to be a woman named Lofton. Very by the book. Lofton asked if it was official, and when we would get the paperwork. And the sheriff, well, he got annoyed. He said he wasn't answering any questions, he just wanted our cooperation."

"Cooperation in what?"

Again the deputy hesitated, and Beck had the sense that she had run up against not so much a desire to keep a secret as the reluctance to break a confidence. He was a loyal man, about to be disloyal. "The sheriff told us there would be a whole lot of strangers coming through town the next few weeks. They would be going for drives, taking pictures, wandering the mountains. He wanted us to give them a wide berth. That was what he said, Beck. 'A wide berth.' A couple of us asked exactly what he meant by that. The sheriff said he meant what he said. No hassling, no harassment. That's what he said. And Lofton, well, she asked how we could tell which strangers we were allowed to harass and which ones we weren't. The sheriff got hot. I guess he hadn't thought of that. Then she asked when we were allowed to go back to doing our jobs and protecting our town. The sheriff said we would be doing our jobs, we'd just be doing them with a certain measured deliberation. That was what he said, Beck. 'Measured deliberation.' Couldn't possibly be his own phrase: Garvey doesn't talk like that. Probably got it out of some memo his visitors held under his nose."

"Memo?"

"They had government written all over them, Beck." Again his hesitation. "That's why I was so evasive when you asked before about if there was anything federal going on in town. After our briefing, the sheriff and Lofton got together, and then she read us the riot act in two languages. Told us not to discuss our orders with a soul, on pain of losing our jobs, and maybe worse." He took another bite, chewed. "Lofton quit a month later. Got a better offer from another town, she said. Moved to Leadville. But I looked her up. She's not working in law enforcement. She doesn't even work for the town. She sells gimcracks in a little tourist shop. She's making maybe one-third what she was making here. Whatever's happening, she knew more than we did, and she didn't want any part of it."

"And that's not all, is it?"

He shook his head. "That investigator. Pesky. I visited him in the clinic after Mr. Ainsley attacked him. A very informative conversation. Pesky wanted to know if we were going to charge Mr. Ainsley. I told him it wasn't up to me, it was up to the State's Attorney. And Pesky, well, he said in that case a lot of people were going to be calling the State's Attorney in the next few days. They wouldn't want Mr. Ainsley charged. They wouldn't want him locked up. They'd want him to stay right where he was, at Stone Heights. I assumed he meant Mr. Ainsley's political connections would be trying to protect him. Now I'm not so sure." He tried to sip his root beer, momentarily forgetting that it was empty. "And then—before I left?—Pesky offered me money. Not a bribe. Not exactly. Not for any dereliction of duty. He just said, if I should happen to find out what Mr. Ainsley was hiding, and where he was hiding it, my family and I would never have to worry about money again. I told him where to stuff his money." He nodded his head, glumly. "Anyway, that's why I believe your story. Because now every-thing makes sense."

Even in the darkness, the street seemed to brighten. Her breath came easier. The music from the radio was suddenly catchy and smooth. Not to be insane was a marvelous thing.

"So—what are we going to do about it?" she asked.

The faint smile returned. "*We?*"

"About this, Pete. About what's going on." She covered his hand with hers. "Not . . . the other."

"A guy can dream."

"Not about this."

The deputy nodded, and took his hand back. "You have to under-stand, Beck. There's only so much I can do." He looked away. "I have a good job in Bethel, and, well, the sheriff—"

"I understand."

"But I have an idea."

"Okay."

"First, let's figure something out. Your CIA friend told you that Mr. Ainsley's working with somebody in town, right? It's not you, and, believe me, it's not me. So who's left?"

Beck had been giving this a lot of thought. "Not Corinda. It's too obvious. Not Miss Kelly. She kind of stands out. It has to be somebody he can see all the time without anybody noticing."

He frowned. "That's a short list, Beck. Brian Navarro. Jimmy Lobb. That's it."

"I don't think it's Navarro. He was too free with Jericho's business."

"He bailed out Pesky. At Jericho's request."

"Too obvious. Too open."

"So it has to be Jimmy Lobb." He grimaced. "Or it was." He hunched forward. "His tox screen was negative. Did the sheriff happen to mention that? Mr. Lobb was not drunk. He was not on drugs. He ran off the road. I don't know, Beck. This is getting a little dangerous."

"I'm leaving tomorrow."

"I think that's good. Fifteen minutes ago, I was ready to try to get you to stick around a little longer. But now—well, look at it this way. Say Mr. Lobb was helping Mr. Ainsley. Mr. Lobb's dead. So who takes his place? You seem to be the only one he trusts, Beck."

"I told him no."

"Maybe not everybody got the news." Seeing her stricken look, the deputy gestured her closer. "Beck, look. I'm worried about you. This goes a little bit against my interest, but I won't be sure you're safe until you're on that plane tomorrow." He hesitated. "That is, if you're sure you're going."

"I have a whole other life, Pete."

"It's possible to raise good kids in Bethel"—he stopped, offered that boyish grin. "Sorry. Sorry. Look. Just promise me one thing. If you run into any trouble tonight—even the hint of trouble—you'll call me. Okay?"

She smiled. "Sure. But town's forty-five minutes away. If there's trouble—"

"I'll be at Stone Heights in half an hour."

Outside the car, they hugged for a while.

"You be careful," he said.

"You're doing the hard part."

Pete held her by the shoulders, watched her face. "I'm not so sure about that," he said.

This time it was Beck who drove off first, too distracted to think about romance. She was thinking, instead, of the East Coast number that occurred most frequently in the sheriff's phone records for the past month. A number that appeared in the list of recent calls on Rebecca's own cell phone.

The sheriff had been talking to Margaret Ainsley.

CHAPTER 26

The Hireling

(1)

Beck cruised along Main Street all the way to the elementary school, swept past the clinic, turned for the return trip. Twice, three times, she circled the town.

Aunt Maggie.

The junior Senator from Vermont had been in regular touch with Sheriff Garvey, including a call, according to the records, on the night Mr. Pesky was arrested. The game had just changed so dramatically that Beck could no longer follow the state of play. A United States Senator from one state did not call up the sheriff of a tiny county in another state: not unless he was facing a threat with the potential to shake the nation; or at least a political career.

Margaret Ainsley had asked Rebecca to be on the look out for classified documents in Jericho's possession, and Beck had assumed that the Senator was simply accommodating a request from the Attorney General. But now it seemed that Aunt Maggie was pursuing an agenda of her own. She was reaching into Bethel and commanding a man Jericho considered an ally.

All to get her hands on whatever her cousin was concealing.

At a stoplight, Rebecca heard a horn honk. She jumped, but it was only Corinda, owner of the café, who had pulled up beside her and was rolling down the window of her car. Beck did the same, smiled, and blew an unenthusiastic kiss and said yes, Jericho was doing fine, and, yes, certainly, she would let him know that Corinda had asked.

"Ask him to call me," said Corinda, as if the rules prohibited her from initiating contact. Perhaps they did.

The light changed. Corinda gave a saucy wave and sped away.

"Jericho and his women," Beck muttered, with her own mother's disapproval.

But, of course, she had been one herself. She remembered the terrible day when Jacqueline made the pilgrimage to Stone Heights, hoping to shame her only child into coming home to New Jersey. She stayed at a boarding house in town—she would not be caught dead sleeping under the roof of a man like Jericho Ainsley, whom she considered the next thing to a statutory rapist. Once Jericho realized that his charm was wasted on Beck's mother, he made himself scarce, for he never enjoyed the presence of women he could not dominate. Jacqueline begged and cajoled and bribed. She played every trump in her hand, from I'm-getting-old-and-I-need-you to you're-being-a-slutty-whore to no-man-will-marry-you-after-something-like-this. Nothing worked. Beck was enjoying her newfound freedom too much after the imprisonment of life with her strict parents, even if the freedom was, really, only another sort of prison—

Her cell phone rang.

She pulled over to the side, looked at the screen. An actual number came up—not one she recognized, to be sure, but at this point any port would do.

"Hello?"

"Beck, it's Lewiston Clark. Don't hang up."

(11)

Another night, Rebecca told herself grimly, another clandestine meeting with a man in the town of Bethel. Tonight, actually, this was her second. They met at McDonald's, not Arby's; and yet, sitting across from Lewiston Clark, she could not repress the sense of being caught in a temporal loop, repeating the same experience over and over.

"You're wrong about me," he said, eyes haunted now, the confidence shot. "I didn't lie. About Jericho, I mean. About working with him."

"He denied it."

"But you're taking his word over mine. Why would you do that? I know you loved him, but he's spent a lifetime lying. At least hear me out before you decide I'm the one who's at fault."

She shook her head. "I don't have all night, Mr. Clark. Before you tell me your story, maybe you should tell me why you want to."

He was trying to look in every direction at once. He had shaved his beard. He had ditched the gaudy red Explorer and was driving some sort of rent-a-wreck. She did not understand why he was still in town.

"They're after me," he finally said. "I need your help."

"My help?"

A tight nod, Adam's apple bobbing. "You can't be touched, but I can. I'm in serious trouble, Beck. But I think, if you'll just talk to Jericho, he can call off the dogs."

"Jericho!"

"He's the one who hired me in the first place. Now people are trying to kill me."

Beck opened her mouth to dismiss his words as melodrama, then shut it with a snap: she was in no fit state to accuse someone else of seeing monsters under the bed. And so she listened. The tale was part whine, part complaint, part cri de coeur. And it was quickly told. After he lost the lawsuit over his Kennedy book, Clark had found himself suddenly without a publisher. Nobody would touch him. Then Jericho came along. Not personally. An intermediary. With an offer. He was to dig up all the dirt he could about Scondell Bloom. Every fact, but also every rumor. Beat the bushes. Use whatever tools came to hand. Hire people if he needed them: there was a budget, said Clark, and not a modest one. His fee, too, would be handsome. He had to sign various undertakings not to disclose anything to anyone but the intermediary, but he had no trouble with that. When his research was done, when it was all turned over to the client, he was free to write his book, subject only to the client's editing.

He had no trouble with that, either.

What he did have trouble with was his sense that somebody was dogging his steps. Somebody was keeping up with his interviews, not merely tracking him, but talking to people after he did, and sometimes before. There were searches of his apartment, too, and bugs—"In my business, you get used to those things"—but none of this discouraged him. On the contrary. He took the rough tactics as evidence that he was making progress.

"And then something went wrong," she prompted.

The writer nodded. He was ordered to Stone Heights. At this point, he and Jericho had not met. But the intermediary told him to visit the house to pick up some notes. He had promptly done as requested, and of course had been tossed out on his ear. So he hung around town, waiting for a call from the intermediary, picking up whatever additional information he could.

"And where did Pesky come in?"

Well, that was the point, really. He had hired Pesky as part of the budgeted staff. But, very soon, Pesky began taking orders directly from Jericho.

Through the intermediary.

So the two men worked partly together, and partly at cross-purposes. "For instance, I didn't know he was sneaking around Stone Heights taking pictures until he told me. I asked him why he took a risk like that, and what he hoped to get out of it. He told me to mind my own business. And then he had that fall, and Jericho went after him with the gun—"

Clark stopped and looked around again, as if awaiting the appearance of the same mad specter, only this time torturing him instead of Pesky.

"If you didn't know Pesky was at Stone Heights," she asked coldly, "then why did I see your car the morning he shot the dog?"

"He borrowed it." Offered promptly, as if Clark had anticipated the question. "Sometimes he drove my rental instead of his. For security's sake, he said."

"Who's idea was shooting the dog in the first place?"

"Pesky's. I didn't know about it until after."

Beck found the writer's lies unimpressive. On Monday morning, when she found the dead dog, the red Explorer had passed her twice, first traveling uphill, away from Stone Heights, then heading down again, both times *before* the gunshot. Lewiston Clark had dropped Pesky off, then returned to pick him up, knowing precisely when the poor dog would be killed. Or maybe she was being too hard. A third person might have been behind the wheel. As Pete Mundy kept reminding her, Bethel was full of strangers these days.

"So why are you on the run? Who's after you?"

Well, he did not know exactly. But somebody was. He knew the signs. Hotel rooms ransacked. Credit cards mysteriously canceled. Cars trying to run him off the curving mountain roads.

"Sounds more like harassment," said Beck, but if she intended her words to reassure, she failed.

"Exactly. First they harass you to flush you out, and then they take you when you're on the run." A crash at a nearby table caused the writer to half rise, fists inexpertly balled. Then he sank into his seat again. Only a dropped tray. People were laughing. Clark shook his head. He had yet to touch his burger. Beck had limited herself to a small Diet Coke. "I have no place to stay," he said, resuming his lament. "That's when they get you."

She was already shaking her head. "If this is some roundabout way to wangle an invitation to Stone Heights—"

"No. No. I wouldn't go there." A theatrical hesitation, as if his next line had just now popped into his head. "On the other hand, given what's been going on, Stone Heights might be the safest place."

"Why's that?"

"Because of who's after me. It has to be Jack Notting's people."

"If it is, what makes you think Jericho can call them off?"

"Because they were in it together. That's what my sources tell me. Thick as thieves, so to speak."

"Tuesday you thought Jericho was blackmailing Jack Notting."

"Today I'm hoping he isn't."

She drummed her fingers on the table, mildly astonished that the writer had been so easily taken in. She did not know who had hired him. She was sure it was not Jericho Ainsley. And so she asked the obvious question.

"Who was the intermediary? Why did you trust him?"

But even before he pulled out the signed contract, she had guessed. Lewiston Clark might play the clumsy oaf, but he was a dogged investigator. He would not have been taken in easily. The only person who could have persuaded him that he was really working for Jericho Ainsley was—well, someone very close.

She didn't even need to turn the letter around to see that it was signed, with a great flourish, by Sean Ainsley.

CHAPTER 27

The Break-In

(1)

In her car once more, having promised to talk to Jericho and sent Lewiston Clark off into the darkness of his own making, Beck did her sums. Either Sean was working with his father, or Sean was working against him. Given the intensity of Jericho's reaction upon discovering who—whom!—Pesky was working for, she would bet on the latter.

Beck continued to dismiss the writer's claim that his life was at risk. Someone was trying to scare him off, the way Pete Mundy and his partner had, except that this time the tactic was working. Indeed, she was not sure how much of Clark's story to trust. The entire encounter with the writer might have been nothing more than another contrivance of whoever was trying to spook her.

"Take it down a notch," she muttered—another Jerichoism.

Driving slowly through town, Rebecca thought it over. Sean Ainsley had hired a marginally successful writer and a marginally competent investigator to dig up dirt on Scondell Bloom. And why would he need the dirt? She was not sure he did. After all, had he really had it in for his father, he could surely have hired someone—well, better. The obvious answer was that the writer had not been dealing with Sean at all, that Jericho's son continued to sit in his New York office, dispensing largesse for environmentally friendly manufacturing projects around the world, as ignorant of the latest manipulations as he was of everything else about his father. In short, the writer might have been duped by someone else, using Sean's name. Another possibility, she supposed, was that Sean was working on behalf of someone else: a Third World government, say, to whom he made grants, and who could not afford the best investigators.

But she was teasing herself with the likeliest answer. Sean might not have been close to his father, but he worshiped the woman he and his sisters called Aunt Maggie. Margaret Ainsley, worried about her political future if another scandal exploded around her cousin, had been in regular communication with Sheriff Garvey. Other than that, she could hardly let her own hand be seen, other than in a couple of carefully scripted conversations on phone lines she knew perfectly well were bugged. On the other hand, a quiet word to Sean could have set off a whole chain of events.

And not only because Sean loved his aunt. He would also be acting out of simple malice. Rebecca remembered his unearthly glee one night when, after years of trying, he nearly got her into bed; and how the only thing that had saved her from an act of absurdist tragedy was what she saw at the last moment as she gazed into the handsome, triumphant face. In that instant, she understood that Sean's true desire was for victory not over her weak and lonely flesh but over his own domineering father.

(11)

Wait.

Police cruiser in front of the library, flashers on. Ambulance beside it.

Beck practically flew out of the car. She was leaving for Chicago in the morning anyway, but if something had happened to Miss Kelly, whom she genuinely liked, then she was leaving tonight.

And something had.

Miss Kelly was inside, sitting on a desk, talking to Deputy Frias.

She was holding a compress on her forehead, and looked woozy. She had not yet noticed Rebecca. Miss Kelly's head was down, and she was explaining to the deputy what had happened. Beck caught just the tail end, but the tail end was enough. She had been working late because they were revamping the catalogue. A couple of men—the strangers, Miss Kelly called them, just as everybody else in town did—a couple of the strangers had knocked. There was little violent crime in Bethel, and Miss Kelly had thought nothing of opening the door. The strangers had bulled past her, shoving her to the floor, where she had bumped her head on a table. In one minute, out the next. They knew what they were looking for.

What was that? the deputy asked.

The computers. That's all. The library computers that connect to the Internet.

The paramedics wanted to take the librarian to the regional hospital, but she refused. They made her sign a form, and Beck, who by now had been noticed, read over her shoulder, but the first name was illegible.

After everyone else had left, the two of them sat there, drinking unreasonably weak coffee from the convenience store around the corner.

"Did they say anything?"

The librarian grimaced. "I believe their main contribution to the conversation consisted of telling me to get out of the way."

"Did you recognize them?"

"The police asked me. I thought I might have seen one of them in the supermarket last week, but I'm not that good with faces." A moment's embarrassment as she checked the compress. "I have a cut, don't I? I'm afraid to look."

"It'll heal. You won't have a scar."

The black woman sounded doubtful. "I hope you're right." She grinned. "I know I must sound vain."

"Not at all. But it's going to be fine."

She offered Miss Kelly a ride, but the librarian's apartment was right across the street. Beck asked if she was sure she wanted to skip the hospital, and Miss Kelly asked if Beck was sure there would be no permanent scar. Then Rebecca asked the question she cared about most:

Did Miss Kelly know what Jericho had been looking at on the Internet?

Beck steeled herself for another assertion of librarian's privilege. Instead, Miss Kelly plunged right in. Perhaps the bump on the head had changed her ethical views. "Mainly, the financial news. I think he checked his own portfolio, too, even though we have signs warning people not to do that on these machines. Oh, and he visited home-improvement sites."

"To buy appliances?" Beck asked.

"I don't think so," said the librarian. "I think he was mainly interested in how things work. How to nail on a shingle or tape up drywall. Things like that."

Driving away, Rebecca was kicking herself for missing what the strangers had obviously figured out. Brian Navarro had told her that Jericho used the Internet at the library. She had not paused to wonder why a man with a perfectly good computer and modem at home would go to the trouble of driving forty-five minutes to the library when he wanted something off the Internet. The only reason she could think of was that he thought his home computer, like his home phone, was tapped. Whatever he was searching for, he wanted to hide it. The strangers had the computers, and would no doubt try to track down what sites had been visited. But Beck knew that her onetime paramour was a paper-and-ink man. He would not have relied on the screen alone. What he needed, he would have printed.

The printouts had to be somewhere in the house.

CHAPTER 28

The Hero

(1)

Rebecca noticed the headlights when she was halfway up the peak. Something big, she decided from the height and angle of the beams— bigger than her rental, anyway, and clinging to her tail a couple of hundred feet back. Probably nothing to worry about, but after seeing Miss Kelly with her forehead gashed open, she was prepared to worry about whatever might come along, thank you very much.

She looked around. The road narrowed here, and the forest closed in on both sides, obscuring the view up the looming, shadowy mountain and, for minutes at a time, even the night sky. Jericho had told her one misty night that the forest was haunted by the ghosts of warriors who had perished when the warring tribes met in the surrounding fields, and then, when he had her shivering with fear, insisted on pulling over and scurrying into the trees for some unscheduled fun.

There was no mist tonight. The storm had moved off, and the air was crisp and clear.

The headlights were closer.

Her cell phone lay on the passenger seat, but with the curves coming up, she needed both hands to steer. Besides, the only person Beck could think of to call for help would be Pete Mundy, and she was starting to worry that she was spending too much time around him. The deputy, in his sweetly protective earnestness, set her competing sides to war with each other, and the tension generated by the battle was more than she needed just now.

Closer.

This was not like the drive up from Denver. This was not an over-reaction to the stress of the reunion. This was real. Whoever was behind was gaining as she sped along the narrow mountain road. The headlamps filled her car. She was heading uphill, so acceleration was out of the question. The truck was on her tail now—

And a Suburban pulled out in front of her, blocking the road.

She slammed on the brakes and skidded. With a nasty screech, her bumper slid against the fender of the Suburban, which was parked crosswise. A second pulled up close behind. There was nowhere to go. Rebecca fumbled for the door-locking button and grabbed for her cell, but men were already pulling her out of the car.

Lights and badges.

"Miss DeForde? Federal Bureau of Investigation. Would you mind coming with us?"

Into the back of one of the Suburbans. No cuffs, but an agent beside her. Somebody had her keys and drove her car. They made a lit-tle caravan. Not up the hill. Not down. Off along a side road, into the darkness of the mountain forest, leaving civilization far behind.

(11)

They parked the Suburban in the middle of a field. She could see stars and the moon and the headlights of two other vehicles, one of them hers. She could see no houses, not even a distant flicker of light. The driver got out. So did the man beside her, instructing Rebecca to wait. She asked if she was under arrest. The man said no. She asked if she was free to leave. The man said no.

The wait was not long.

A fourth car drove into the field, moving very fast.

Two men got out, one about her age, one closer to Jericho's. They climbed in, the older man beside her, the younger one in the front, and she guessed at once that the younger man was guarding the older.

The younger man flashed a different badge. "I'm Deputy Krukoff, United States Marshals Service. I am informing you officially that you are about to meet a protected witness. You may not repeat to any unauthorized person any information that you acquire as a result of this meeting. Do you understand?"

She sized up Krukoff in an instant: a lover of authority, but over women especially. Jericho without the dash and wit.

"I understand."

"You are here because certain of your activities may place the protected witness at risk. Do you understand?"

"I understand."

"The witness has chosen to talk to you alone. This is against my advice." Having laid out his bureaucratic position, the marshal slipped from the car, lingering near enough to save his protectee should Beck pull a knife from her slacks.

The older man spoke for the first time. "Rebecca. What a pleasure to meet you at last." He put out a hand. "Jack Notting."

(I I I)

"You're very persistent," said Jack Notting, and she knew at once that he was the sort of man who was interested in no one's views but his own. He was a small man, almost boyishly slender, but he emanated the stony confidence of a successful manipulator of destinies. He spoke in the clipped, overly simple phrases of the morale officer. "You and Jericho both. How is the old bastard anyway? Cancer won't beat him. Not the type. You watch. Back on his feet in no time. He'll be back to blowing up the world or making his fortune or whatever turns him on this week. You're leaving tomorrow?"

The question caught her off guard. "Yes."

"Probably best. Jericho was a fine man in his day, but he's wandered off the reservation. So have you."

"I didn't notice any boundaries."

Jack Notting might not have heard. "I'm worth a couple of billion dollars. Did you know that, Rebecca? Two billion dollars, and I'm in witness protection. Want to know why? Because I decided to be a hero. To tell the truth. My partners lied their asses off in front of the grand jury, and I told the truth. Got it?" He did not wait to hear whether she had it or not. "Now, look. You've been asking lots of questions about Scondell Bloom. Time to stop. Keep it up and there won't be a trial. Know why? Because there won't be a witness. I don't care how many marshals they put around me. I don't care if they stash me in Saskatchewan. Keep this up and I'll be dead."

"I don't understand," said Beck. "How am I putting you at risk?"

"I told you. Asking the wrong questions, in the wrong places. It's time to stop, Rebecca. Time to call a halt, go home, take care of your daughter."

Her bewilderment was genuine. She had done a little research about Scondell Bloom, and she had called Tish, but she had not been going around digging. Not like—

"Lewiston Clark," she said. "He was writing about your firm, wasn't he?"

"I'd rather not discuss Mr. Clark, if it's all the same to you. Whoever stops him will be doing all of us a big favor."

"Who's *us*?"

Again he ignored her. Billionaires could be like that. "Rebecca, look. This all comes down to something very simple. Jericho and I both served our country. He served it longer than I did. He got medals, books about him, a Wikipedia entry a mile long. I made money. A lot more money than Jericho did. He's upset about the way things ended up, so now he's threatening to make trouble. I've offered him a payoff—I don't need the aggravation—and he's turned it down. He's sitting up there in that house all day, nursing grievances against the world. And now he wants you to help him. Well, don't. Go home and let him die in peace. Stay away from this. If you can make him stop, that's bonus. But, even if you don't, my associates and I will take care of you." A pause. "And your daughter." Another. "I hear she and your mom had a great time at Disney World. Personally, though, I wouldn't have stopped for ice cream on the way back to Sarasota. There is such a thing as overkill."

The bottom fell out of her world. The rest of his words registered, but only in the distant fashion of somebody else's conversation. Her womb ached. There was no other way to put it. Pain sizzled where she had borne the child this man was threatening to harm.

"And you really need to teach your daughter not to lie, just because Grandma says it's okay. American Girl doll, my ass. She bought your Nina a dog. He'll stay in Sarasota with your mother, of course, but now your daughter will be begging you to take her down there all the time. See how mothers scheme? Glad I never had one."

A buzzing had joined the pain, not in her ear or even in her brain but everywhere in her body at once, as if a horde of mad bees were fighting a war inside her. So this, she thought to herself, is panic.

"You know what I think?" Jack Notting was saying. "I think your plans are fine just as they stand. I think you should stay put for now, and fly to Chicago tomorrow. There's no need to make a special detour to Sarasota. Nina will be fine without you being there." He let this sink in. "So—kiss Jericho goodbye in the morning, fly off to Chicago for your meetings, pick up your daughter Sunday as planned. By then it'll be over. And you, Rebecca, will be a million dollars richer. And don't worry. It'll all be legitimate and aboveboard." He pointed out the window. "I'm speaking on behalf of your government, of course."

He opened the door, beckoned imperiously to Marshal Krukoff.

"We're done here," he said.

They drove off. An FBI agent led her to her car.

CHAPTER 29

The Sister

(1)

Jack Notting had not said she couldn't call. He could have placed that restriction, and did not. As soon as she was free of the clearing, she tested her cell. Hooray, she had bars. She called her mother's condo. The answering machine kicked in, and then there was Jacqueline, groggy with sleep, angry at being disturbed at this hour: after all, midnight in Colorado was two in the morning back east.

"I'm sorry, Mom, it's just—"

"There is no way in the world I'm waking her up. Not at this hour. You should be ashamed of yourself, Rebecca."

"I didn't call to talk to her. I called to talk to you." A pause as they both digested this innovation.

"About what?" said Jacqueline, cautiously.

"Is Nina okay?"

"Nina's fine."

"And you—you're fine?"

"Yes, dear. What's wrong?"

Beck looked out the car window, whirling head tipped against the glass. Beyond the glow of the headlights, the trees faded into heavy darkness. "Mom, listen. Did you buy Nina a dog?"

Defensive. "Well, you had one when you were little, Rebecca. Every little girl should have one. It's not my fault your condo doesn't allow—"

"Wait. Mom, wait. Listen. The dog. What color is it?"

"What earthly difference—"

"Please, Mom. I don't mind about the dog. I swear I don't. Just tell me what color it is."

"It's black. A black Labrador."

"A Lab. You're sure."

"Of course I'm sure, dear. I may not know much, but I do know dogs. Besides, it says right on the pedigree—"

"When?"

"What?"

"When did you buy the dog, Mom?"

"Sunday. We went out and got it the day Nina arrived. She's just a child, Rebecca. She missed her mother, and I wanted to give her a nice present. To cheer her up. Remember, dear, you won't be coming back until the weekend. That can be hard on a child. I never left you alone this long when you were a—"

Beck was not listening. Sunday. Jacqueline bought the dog on Sunday, and an identical dog was killed in Jericho's driveway on Monday. Impossible. But so was a helicopter sending messages to her cell phone. Dak had said they would come after her, and she had figured the house was a fortress. Until tonight, she had not considered that they might come after the part of her that was in Florida.

"Mom, listen. Are you listening?"

"Of course, dear. I was just saying—"

"Have you seen any strangers around? Watching the house? Watching you?" She swallowed. "Watching Nina?"

"Of course not. I'd report that—"

While Jacqueline continued to explain, Beck made her calculations. She was talking on her cell, so about fifteen of Dak's interested parties were probably listening, but any phone would be as bad, because her mother's was surely tapped. Well, fine. Let them listen. She was doing what any mother would do, and if they chose to treat it as a violation of the deal, no force on earth would stop her from killing Jack Notting.

Slowly.

"Mom. Mom, wait. Listen. I want you to leave."

"I'm sorry?"

"Don't argue with me, Mom. Just do what I tell you. I want you to pack up the station wagon and take Nina to my cousin's. Not in the morning. Now."

"Brad? Why? His house is so cramped and messy, with all those kids running around—"

"Just do it, Mom. Please. I'm begging you. Stay with Brad and Cheryl. Trust me on this. Please. I'll be there Sunday. I'd come before then, but I—I can't."

"But I don't understand, baby. Why do we have to move?"

"Because Brad's a cop. He's married to a cop. They both carry guns."

(11)

She needed some while to knock down her mother's objections, but at last Jacqueline gave in. After hanging up, Rebecca tried Margaret Ainsley, despite the hour, but the Senator was not answering.

Beck would have to curse her out later.

She lifted her cell again, intending to call Sean. If anybody deserved to be awakened, it was he; and if she woke his wife, well, those were the breaks. But Beck remembered, in the nick of time, that Sean was off awarding a grant for a green bauxite plant in Africa.

Exquisite timing.

Sean was too busy to be at his father's bedside, but failed to tell his sisters the true reason: that his investigator was out in Bethel turning over rocks. And, in case the whole mess went south, Sean possessed a perfect alibi.

"Bastard," Beck muttered, remembering again that look of triumph when he thought he had snared her.

Sitting alone in her car in the darkness, fighting the tears, she felt like a prisoner serving an indeterminate sentence, the brooding mountains her walls. She was leaving Stone Heights in the morning, but a part of her would never escape. She would be looking over her shoulder for the rest of her life. She remembered Jericho telling her once how, up until the early nineteenth century, prisoners of war were routinely granted parole, meaning that they would be sent home, on their solemn promise not to return to the battlefield. She would happily have made the same deal, but she did not think Jack Notting was the sort of man who kept his word.

"Move," she commanded herself.

Hurrying up the mountain, keeping a closer eye this time on the rearview mirror, she tried to work out the one connection that still eluded her. If Sean had hired Lewiston Clark, and Lewiston Clark had hired Pesky, who had told Pesky to kill the dog? She could not imagine Sean giving the order to harm a fly. Only one answer suggested itself: Jack Notting had penetrated Sean Ainsley's ragtag team, and was dealing with Pesky directly. That was why the private investigator, ostensibly Clark's employee, took the photos at Stone Heights without asking the writer first. And when Notting learned that Jacqueline had bought Nina a dog, he immediately—he immediately—he—

She pulled to the side of the road and at last let the tears flow.

(111)

When Rebecca arrived back at Stone Heights, both daughters were awake, despite the hour. Evidently Jericho had taken a turn for the worse. His breathing was shallow, said Audrey, and his pulse was down a hair. There could be a lot of reasons, but they were thinking they might move him to the clinic tonight to get him stabilized, then on to Vail, or even Denver, in the morning.

Beck said she would go along with whatever they decided.

They looked at her in surprise. She knew she was listless, but she could not help it. She was scared out of her wits, and trapped. No doubt they were reading in her face that she was sorry she had ever come.

"Man trouble?" said Pamela, but Beck was too haunted to play her games. She excused herself and went up the bedroom. She made a start at packing, then went into the study to call her mother again, but put down the phone before she finished dialing, because what she wanted more than anything was to hop on the next plane to Sarasota—an act Jack Notting had specifically forbidden.

She thought about the FBI agents. And Marshal Krukoff. How could they be protecting a man who would casually threaten her child? Did they suspect what their protectee was up to, and just not care? Or had he somehow kept them in the dark?

She wondered what Jack Notting could possibly know that would make him so valuable an asset that they would take the risk that Beck would go blabbing about her meeting with him. Unless, of course, they knew she had nobody to blab to. All at once, she found herself missing Jericho: the father figure he had been a decade and a half ago. Fifteen years ago, of course, nobody would have dared bother her. If they had, she would have run to his strong arms, sheltered her head against his chest, and let him call in a couple of friends to fix whatever was wrong.

By the time she came up for air, everything would be fine.

But as Jericho himself had told her this afternoon, that man no longer existed. The new Jericho could not help her. She would have to do it herself.

The trouble was, she lacked a weapon. She could hardly call her Congressman or the *Times*, not least because her daughter would be dead before they called her back, and she herself an hour later. They were listening, she reminded herself. If they could listen in on the great Jericho Ainsley, Former Everything, despite his many precautions, keeping track of Rebecca Marie DeForde would be child's play.

Then she remembered.

The printouts.

Jericho's printouts from the library. His Internet research.

She had finally figured out the trick. Dak was telling the truth, but so was Lewiston Clark, and, in his way, Jack Notting. Jericho must have begun by squirreling away his national-security secrets, and then, as his breakdown accelerated, moved on to include the collapse of

Scondell Bloom. This was, indeed, his revenge on the world that had tossed him aside at the height of his powers. He might be dying, but he would make them all watch—and pay for the privilege.

Whatever information Jericho had gathered—whatever form it took—it had proved sufficient to keep at bay the forces of governments and billionaires alike. Here, then, was the best protection, for herself and her daughter. If Beck could only possess whatever Jericho had hidden, she could hold them off as effectively as he had. And so, methodically, she got to work, searching through the office file cabinets, then moving into the sickroom, where Jericho snored heavily from the bed. She could not get over how strong he looked. She wondered how a disease could so thoroughly ravage one's insides while leaving the outside untouched. But as she made her away along the shelves, she remembered a girlfriend who had died, very young, of breast cancer, and had shown few overt symptoms even when they told her she had only six months to live.

And here were the printouts. They were in two accordion files on the windowsill, hidden in plain sight if they were hidden at all. She leafed through them, and, sure enough, found instructions about rebuilding virtually every system in the house.

Perfectly sensible, she realized.

Jericho would have researched the systems before tearing up the house. He would have hidden his secrets in only one, leaving the others as wisps.

She carried the files back to her bedroom, figuring that neither Pamela nor Audrey would miss them. And if they did, too bad. Rebecca had between now and midmorning tomorrow, when she had to leave for the airport, to outguess the former head of the Central Intelligence Agency, to find what neither a scheming billionaire nor an ambitious Senator nor the government of the United States had been able to uncover.

For her daughter's sake, she dared not fail.

(IV)

The clue was in the madness. By tracking the ravages of the disease through his brain, she could track his successive hiding places for what Lewiston Clark had called names, dates, and figures.

And what had he done, in his madness? What was the single concrete act of insanity to which both sisters could point?

He had rebuilt his house.

And so Rebecca sat in her suite, surrounded not only by the printouts, but by whatever she could cull from Jericho's files: the original architectural plans for Stone Heights, the survey showing plot lines and elevations, the receipts for the new roof and the alarm system and the electric wiring and the well pump and the new plumbing and the new windows and half a dozen other systems she had not thought of until now. She puzzled over wiring diagrams and instruction pamphlets and correspondence with contractors.

He always went to talk to the workers, Audrey had said. Whoever was replacing or rebuilding or restructuring, Jericho chatted with them while they worked. And to at least one of them—Beck was really rolling now—to at least one, Jericho had said, *Oh, by the way, I wonder if you could do me a favor.* No doubt cash had made an appearance, and then Jericho's documents or computer disks or whatever wound up sealed behind drywall or stuffed beneath a shingle.

But which? She could hardly tear down the whole house. She lacked the basic tools even to pry up a single floorboard.

She was deep into her reading when, half an hour later, Audrey knocked on her door. She was serving cookies and milk in the kitchen, she said. From a bakery this time, she promised, leading Beck out into the hall despite her objections: for Rebecca had been deep inside the owner's manual for Jericho's new Asko dishwasher, looking for hidden spots that remained dry, and hated to have her concentration broken.

But she went, and not to be polite. If she was to solve this puzzle, she might need help. She dared not tell the sisters what she was looking for, not with Jack Notting and his friends listening in. She could, however, ask questions about their father.

And so she did.

No, said Audrey. She did not remember whether Jericho's obsession extended to hiring a different contractor for every job, or whether he tended to use the same ones.

Yes, said Pamela. Jericho paid the people who repaired things very well, often throwing in an extra couple of hundred, because "times are so tough out there." This habit of overpayment had won him affection throughout the valley. The affection, in turn, led to a protectiveness among the people of Bethel, and their vigilance provided Jericho an effective early-warning system against strangers, Beck suspected.

Yes, said Audrey. She had been here during some of the renovation. She remembered that Jericho had a terrible screaming argument with the roofer—

Jericho's buzzer sounded.

"My turn," said the nun.

When Audrey had gone, Pamela turned to Beck. "There's something I've been wanting to ask you."

"I don't have time."

"Oh, you'll make time for this one." Her voice was pitched low, the tone gentle: the voice of the peacemaker. "It's about your daughter."

Panic. Visions of Jack Notting. "Nina? What about her?"

"Her father was that lawyer you married, right?"

"Larry Vayner."

"Sean says he was a stuck-up asshole."

"He was appropriately surnamed," Beck said, voice strained as she remembered Larry's big plans to exploit her life story for money; and his fury when she refused.

"I have no doubt," said Pamela. "Now, listen. I've been doing a little studying. That file I mentioned. The one Dad kept on you. Had a chance to read it yet? I didn't think so. You've been so busy reading up on the house you're hoping to inherit—"

"What!"

"Well, anyway, you've missed the forest for the trees. The file's in Dad's desk drawer, if you want to see it. Not even locked in the safe. And, believe me, it makes interesting reading. I had no idea that his obsession was so . . . ongoing."

Beck had the sense that movement was dangerous. Besides, her limbs were frozen. A desperate, panicky part of her was ready to shriek with laughter, because Jericho, back when she was his student, had been the scourge of what he called the neologisms of nihilism—such words as "ongoing," and "tolerance," and "impact" as a verb. But the rest of her had never been more alert.

"This is what I read," Pamela continued, quite implacable. "You and my dad broke up at the end of 1995. You and your asshole lawyer got married in 1998. Asshole lawyer went back to wife number one in 2000. You were divorced in 2001. Nina arrived in 2002. That means, unless you and asshole lawyer had *another* affair behind his wife's back—"

"Get to the point," Beck hissed, or maybe pleaded, because the world was disintegrating again, and at a very high speed.

"It means that the man you're telling the world is the father isn't the father. I wonder why you'd tell a lie about something like that, a pillar of integrity like yourself. And then, I'm still in this file, and what do I find? A letter, Rebecca. From you to my father. Dated late 2001. Just after Christmas, as a matter of fact. You know. All saccharine and sub-missive. Dear Jer-Bear. All that bullshit. Thank you for the choker, it was so sweet, and it was wonderful seeing you last month in New York, et cetera, et cetera." Neither woman had budged, but Pamela seemed to be towering over her. "The choker cost ten thousand dollars, Rebecca. The receipt's in there, too, along with a fawning note from some Tiffany's flunky about their years of service to both the Ainsleys and the Hillimans. There's some other receipts, too. I don't think the choker was the only thing Dad has sent you since you left him. I think he sent you some other jewelry, too. I count about seven different items, Rebecca, and none of them were cheap."

"I gave them away—"

"To charity. I know. It's in the file. But not the choker. You kept the choker, didn't you? I was wondering why."

Beck's mouth moved. No words emerged. She saw herself on that wintry Christmas morning, at her mother's house in New Jersey, bitter and tired and ready to die, when the package arrived, delivered by a messenger in the blue Tiffany's box—

"And then Nina came along," said Pamela, implacably. "Nina Anne DeForde-Vayner, born July 2002, daughter of Rebecca DeForde-Vayner, as you were calling yourself back then, no father listed on the birth certificate. For some reason there's a copy in Dad's file. So. Nina is born in July, therefore conceived in November or December. And November is exactly when you saw my father in New York. Two nights at the Four Seasons, receipts in the folder."

"I didn't stay with him, we just had dinner—"

Pamela was relentless. "A month later, he sends you the ten-thousand-dollar choker, and this one, mysteriously, you don't give to charity. I don't think your little girl's father is the asshole lawyer, Rebecca. I don't think you think so, either. I think the reason you're here is to make sure that, whether you're provided for or not, my baby sister gets her share of the—"

Beck was gone. She had to turn her back, because the alternative was a fistfight. Things had reached that point. Gleeful Pamela at last had a justification for her years of animosity, and Beck, after being manipulated by Jericho and threatened by Jack Notting, needed somebody to hit. She marched up the stairs and, reaching the guest suite, had a good cry, then stood up and took it out on the pillow, just the way Dr. Eisenstadt had suggested. First she tried hammering the pillow right on the bed, but the results were unsatisfactory, the pillow was unscathed. So she tossed the pillow into the air and caught it with a straight punch on the way down, then did it again, and again, releasing all the anger of all those years in the wilderness of her tangled emotions and tangled existence. The one she really wanted to hit was Jack Notting, but he was surrounded by bodyguards, and, besides, Beck had no idea where he was. Then there was the great Jericho Ainsley, author of the horror show she called a life, but he was out of her league, and sick besides. Pamela, who possessed all her father's talent for derision and none of his charm, would have been a perfect stand-in. But she was bigger than Rebecca, and probably stronger. The idea was to achieve catharsis, not to earn a bed in that awful clinic down in Bethel, behind the elementary school.

A knock on the door.

Audrey poked her head in.

"Is everything okay? I thought I heard— Oh." She saw the pillow and, everywhere, the feathers.

"Sorry," said Beck, breathing hard, but feeling better, and desperate to be with her child.

"I hope that was my sister, not me," said the nun, and, grinning, departed.

But Rebecca had her measure by now. It was like dealing with a superhero from the comic books. Saint Audrey of the cloister was the public identity; the secret identity was Professor Audrey, the interrogator.

And even if Audrey herself was no longer doing what she used to, she had left a catalogue of instructions.

—*slowly breaking down the world your subject knows, and replacing it with a world of your own devising*—

Say, a house in the Rockies, where one has limited ability to reach the outside world, and a succession of threats, ratcheting up your subject's fears—

You keep him guessing, keep him off balance, keep changing the rules, until, after a while, he doesn't know what's real and what isn't. That's when he'll cling to any anchor. And you give him a new reality. A better one.

Exactly. Somebody was using Audrey's methods to break down Beck's resistance, to rewrite her world, hoping she would be desperate enough to—

Well, to do what she was doing.

Maybe it was Jack Notting, maybe it was Dak, maybe it was Maggie and Sean, maybe it was one of the other nameless countries worried about Jericho's threats. Whoever it was, Beck realized, had nearly won. They had driven her into a corner where she saw no option but to figure out what Jericho had hidden, and where.

The difference was, she had no intention of turning it over.

To anybody.

Beck picked up the pillow again. "It was all of you," she said, punching hard.

THURSDAY–FRIDAY:
THE WEE HOURS

CHAPTER 30

The Manager

(1)

Beck crawled into bed around half past two, the folders and printouts forming a mountain on her desk. Fear about Nina's safety bucked and kicked like a live thing within her, but Beck still saw no salvation other than finding what Jericho had hidden. And so she had puzzled through the documents, seeking the elusive clue. Even the knowledge that she was being manipulated into doing exactly what she was doing did not divert Rebecca from her search.

As she drifted toward sleep, her daughter's trusting face swam into focus. Beck's eyes snapped open. She whispered a sleepy, disjointed prayer, and hoped that Jacqueline had indeed taken her granddaughter to Brad's.

Beck rolled onto her side and gazed out the window at the filtering snow. Tomorrow, around ten, she would leave for Denver. She had between now and then to follow Jericho's clues, find what he had hidden, and thereby protect her daughter. She had hoped to work all night, but her energy had run out. She set the alarm for four-thirty. Two hours of sleep was all she could afford. She closed her eyes and dropped off at once, to dream about lifting a rubbery, resistant weight that seemed to grow as she hefted it, dragging her down no matter how she struggled. It was cold outside, and that was where she was, outside in the snow, and Pamela was there and Audrey was there and they were yelling about Jericho—

—about how Jericho was—

—dying—

She bolted upright. In the hallway, the sisters were screaming at each other.

(11)

Beck cinched her robe and rushed out onto the landing. Pamela was ordering Audrey to calm down, and Audrey was telling Pamela to do the same.

Their father, she gathered, had taken a turn for the worse.

"He can't breathe," Audrey kept saying. "He's not breathing."

"He's breathing fine," Pamela insisted. She alone was dressed, in her usual uniform of jeans and sweater and pearls. She did not look sleepy. "Rebecca, wait." She had a hand on Audrey's large shoulder, and now took Beck by the hand. "Wait. Listen. I'm sorry about before, but we have to work together now, okay?"

"What's the matter?"

"He can't breathe," said Audrey again.

"He can breathe, but he's coughing hard, and he can't stop. He's weak. He can't stand up. I think it's pneumonia. He should never have left the house."

"Is there a doctor he uses?"

"Yes, but I think he needs the hospital."

"Do something!" Jericho hollered from the bedroom. "Do something, you stupid bitches, or I'm fucking writing you out of my will!" A fit of coughing like an artillery barrage cut off the rest.

Pamela colored. "He's also delusional."

"I'm calling 911," said Audrey, reaching for the phone.

"I'll go sit with him," said Beck.

"I'll do it," said Pamela, brushing her aside. "You stay here."

"The phone doesn't work," said Audrey, putting the receiver down with a snap.

(III)

Pamela took charge. Nobody elected her. Nobody had to. Crisis was her element. Taking charge was what she did best. "Take your cell phones to opposite corners of the house. See if you can get a signal, even a faint one. If it doesn't work, switch corners. I'll stay with him. Rebecca, take mine." She lifted the house line and confirmed what Audrey had told them. No dial tone. No busy signal. No nothing.

"It doesn't make any sense," said Audrey.

"The storm," Pamela said, although the storm had been over for hours.

Three minutes later, they all met on the landing. No signal. Through the open door, Jericho continued to rage.

"The computer," said Pamela. "We can message somebody."

Leaving Audrey with the patient, Pamela and Beck trooped to Jericho's office, because the computer was connected to the cable modem.

Which was out.

The power was on, but the DATA and SEND lights were off.

"No connection," said Pamela, unnecessarily. The wind shook the house. Outside the long windows, shadows chased shadows in the spilling floodlights. "We reboot the modem."

"How?"

"Easiest way is to unplug it, plug it back in, and wait. If it's a software problem, rebooting will fix it."

But it wasn't.

"There's a satellite phone," said Audrey, when they met once more on the landing. "It's in the safe."

The safe was in the wall behind the desk. Nobody had the combination, although Pamela's glare said she thought somebody might be lying about that. Audrey reported that Jericho was unable to recall the numbers. "He said to leave him alone," she added, flushing, and Beck wondered how colorfully he had said it.

"The panic button," Pamela said.

Beck looked at her in puzzlement. Audrey explained.

"It's part of the alarm system. There are three portable panic buttons. You press one, the alarm sounds—not here, but at—I don't know—in Bangladesh or someplace. They call you, and if you can't come up with the security code or you don't answer the phone they call the police to check—"

"I get the idea," said Beck. "Where are the buttons?"

Again the sisters looked at each other. Neither seemed to know. Audrey held out her hand. "A little plastic rectangle, about half the size of my palm."

Beck said, "Jericho would have one in his room."

Audrey went to check, while Beck and Pamela hunted through the study and the kitchen. The nun was back a moment later, carrying the device in her hand. The back was open. "No battery," she said.

"There must be spares in the house," said Beck, looking out at the grounds. The precipitation had ended. Wind swirled light eddies of snow across the lawn.

"It needs a special kind, like a watch."

"There must be a master," said Pamela. "Attached to the system itself."

The panel was in the security room downstairs, beside the monitors. Multicolored buttons mocked them. Metal labels had been removed, presumably by the madman upstairs. There were no instructions. When Beck and Audrey hesitated, Pamela reached in and began punching buttons at random. Lights blinked on and off, but there was no way to tell whether anything else was happening.

"Maybe they got a signal," she said, but doubted her own words.

Audrey had an idea. They set the alarm—that much they knew how to do—then went to the kitchen and pulled the back door ajar. This should have set off the alarm, but they did not hear the expected clanging, or even the reassuring double tone to tell them a door was open.

"You must have turned it off," said Beck.

Pamela shook her head. "We just reset it. It should work."

"Close the security mesh," said Beck. "We know that sets off an alarm, right?"

Pamela pushed the button. The gates rattled down, but no klaxon sounded.

"Maybe it's set on SILENT," said Audrey, with tired optimism. "Maybe they're on the way."

Her sister's gaze withered her. "Maybe pigs have wings," she said.

"Leave her alone," said Beck, when the nun's mouth dropped open.

"We drive him," said Pamela, relentless.

"Drive him where?"

"Hospital in Vail. Ninety minutes away. We'll take Audrey's van. He can lie down in the back." Already on her feet, headed toward the door, because ideas were what gave her breath. "Let's get moving."

"Wait," said Beck.

Pamela waited. Impatiently.

"All we have to do is go down the mountain eight or nine miles, and the cell phones should work." Rebecca hesitated, uneasy about telling them her arrangement with Pete Mundy: that until she left town, he would be waiting within half an hour of the house. All she had to do was call. "We drive for ten minutes, we can call anybody we want."

"That's if you drive toward Bethel, not Vail."

"Then let's drive toward Bethel."

"There's no time. He needs a real hospital."

"We can work it out on the road," said Audrey. "Maybe we'll pick up a signal along the way."

"I'll get the keys."

Pamela opened the gates again, then suggested that Beck go for the van while Audrey prepped Jericho for travel. "I'll go to the study and get the papers we might need. Health insurance or whatever."

The nun smiled. "I'll get the van. Beck can take care of Dad."

"But—

"The van has so many problems, I don't think anybody but me can drive it. And Dad's prepped. I got him ready. All he needs is a coat and his shoes. Beck can do that."

Rebecca spoke up. "I'm not sure anybody should go out there, Aud. Especially alone."

Pamela ran an exhausted hand over her face. "Please don't start that again."

"We don't have a choice," said Audrey. "Either we get Dad to Vail, or he dies upstairs."

"Then I'm going out there with you—"

"Thank you, but I travel with my own bodyguard." Fingering the cross around her neck. "Now, please, honey. Let's get him moving."

Pamela, muttering to herself, was already heading for the stairs. Beck lingered, watching as Audrey crossed the foyer and slipped out of the house. Not a peep from the alarm system as she exited. Then she heard the reassuring *beep-beep-buzz:* Audrey had passed one of the proximity sensors. The system might not tell them if a door was opened, but at least they would have warning if anyone approached the house.

Rebecca shivered, hoping there was no danger, and hurried up to Jericho's room.

(I V)

He was sitting in the chair, fully dressed, trying to put on his shoes.

"Let me help you," said Beck, very surprised.

"About time you got here," he said pleasantly. He stuck out a foot. He was wearing dark silk socks, and had selected a pair of alligator loafers. His slacks were a lovely fawn twill. He might have been preparing for dinner at the club. He did not look like a man who had taken a turn for the worse; or who, just a short while ago, had been screaming threats down the hall.

"How are you feeling?" she asked, manipulating his feet into the right position.

"Saint Audrey says I'm dying."

"But how do you feel? What's the big emergency?"

Jericho shrugged. His ear was cocked, but Beck could hear nothing. "I feel great. I kept telling Saint Audrey, but she seems to think I'm going to collapse at any moment—"

He broke off. His eyes widened and his cheeks grew splotchy. His hands went to his neck, and he began to make choking sounds. Beck was paralyzed. Did he need the Heimlich maneuver? The oxygen? Or was this a symptom of something else?

Unsure what else to do as he went on hacking, she grabbed the oxygen tank, wheeled it to the chair, pulled the mask over his face, opened the cock.

He calmed down.

"Well, maybe I am," he said, voice now wet and creaky. He settled back in the chair. "Going to collapse at any moment." Another coughing bout, evidently because he was trying to laugh. "She told me not to get up. Saint Audrey. She told me to wait. I wanted to help."

"It's okay, Jer-Bear."

He coughed, and tugged at the tube. "I hate this thing."

"I know. I'm sorry. I'll get your coat."

"I don't need a coat."

"It's cold out there."

"Oh, I see. The coat's so I won't get sick. Good idea."

Working his arms into the sleeves while he sat in a chair breathing through a mask was tricky, but she got it done. She decided to take a long chance. "Jericho?"

"Yes, dear?"

"I want to ask you something. About my conversation with Dak the other night."

A chuckle. "I remember. He's leaving us. Before the roof caves in. Very wise." Cough. "Seems to me I told you to do the same."

She smiled and kissed his clammy forehead. "I'm leaving, too. With you. We're going to Vail."

"Fat chance." The golden eyes moved. "Dak was my protection. Without Dak, anything can happen."

His fantasy had reversed. "I thought you said Dak was trying to kill you."

"I never said that." He shrugged, and coughed again. "Look. You should leave me here. *You* should go to Vail."

"I am going. I'm just not planning to leave you behind."

"Silly girl." He said it sweetly.

She heard Pamela calling from downstairs. She helped him to his feet. "Jericho?"

"Yes, my dear?"

"Who's Max?"

"Who?"

"I overheard Dak on his cell phone. Somebody called him to say Max was coming. He seemed upset."

He reached up and pulled the mask away. "Seriously?"

"Yes." She saw his face. "What is it, Jericho? Who's Max?"

"If Max is coming, you'd better get moving."

But this time she would not allow herself to be played. She took him by the shoulders. "Tell me."

The eyes lost their humor. Maybe it was never there to begin with. His voice, when he spoke, was as dry as a weather report. "Max is retired. Used to be a killer. A contract killer." A sad grin. "Pretty good at it, too, so they tell me."

A chill passed through the room. "Are you saying—"

"Quit." He shook his head. "They all quit sooner or later. Except the ones who go nuts. Nobody can do that kind of work for too long without—" Another fit of coughing doubled him over. She hugged him and patted his back. He breathed the oxygen for a while, then pulled the mask off again. "Max worked for Dak. I bet he didn't tell you that part, did he? Dak knows Max. If Max is coming, it's probably at Dak's invitation."

Her head was whirling. "No. He was surprised. I heard it in his voice."

"You heard what he wanted you to hear, Beck. Dak is no fool. He knew you'd run and tell me that Max is coming. The idea was to scare me. And you know what? It worked. I'm scared."

Beck balled her fists. "Then let's tell them. We can tell them what they want to know. Where you hid . . . whatever you hid."

Jericho shook his head. "That would be wrong. Some terrible people did some terrible things. They shouldn't get away with it." He coughed. "Of course, if they've brought in Max, I would assume they disagree."

"But how—how will we recognize—"

"Nobody ever recognizes Max. The trouble comes if Max recognizes you."

"You were Director of Central Intelligence. You must know what Max looks like!"

His answer was curiously bureaucratic. "Now, that would hardly be fitting, would it? A man in my position could never have actual knowledge of matters at that level. The principle is deniability." The golden eyes grew kindly. "But I wouldn't worry, my dear. Max and Saint Audrey were pretty close in the old days, so I'm told, and I'm quite sure—"

The explosion drowned the rest.

Beck raced to the window.

Out in the forecourt, the van was in flames.

And on her hip, the cell phone was vibrating.

CHAPTER 31

The Crisis

(1)

Every crisis is the same, although later we pretend that every crisis is different. A crisis begins unexpectedly, threatens that which we value, and intensifies faster than the rational faculty can follow. A crisis is like a clever computer virus: when we believe we have guarded against its worst capabilities, it strikes off in an entirely different direction, forcing a mobilization of all we possess, in defense of all we love.

Sometimes the crisis wins.

Beck could not help herself. She left Jericho in the master suite and raced outside, Pamela at her heels, neither one capable, for the moment, of worrying about personal safety. They tried to get to the van, but the heat was too intense. Pamela kept lurching forward, screaming her sister's name, her face a mask of sweat and tears. Rebecca had to hold her back. The nun's body was there, in the flames, the broad shoulders perfectly recognizable, wrecking Beck's last hope—that, through some miracle, Audrey's bodyguard had kept her away from the wheel.

"We have to go back inside," said Beck, mouth close to Pamela's ear.

"No. No. No."

"Come on." Wrapping the slimmer woman in her arms. "Come on. We can't stay out here."

"We have to help her—"

"We can't," said Beck. "She's dead." But Pamela refused to be moved. Rebecca looked at the trees, wondering who was out there watching. *Max is a killer.* The cell phone, unanswered upstairs, began vibrating once more on her hip. She glanced at the other cars and the pickup but rejected them at once: if the van had a bomb wired to it, surely the mysterious Max would not have forgotten the others. "We have to get back inside," she hissed.

"No."

"We have to help your father."

"He's a monster. He can help himself." But the flaming car was drawing the energy out of her. Pamela slumped to her knees. Beck knelt beside her. "I told you," Pamela said. "I told you to go. But no. You had to send Audrey. You bitch."

Rebecca blinked. This was the last thing she had expected. She tugged on the other woman's arm. "We have to get in the house," she said. "We don't know who's out there."

At last, glumly, Pamela allowed herself to be led, face twisted toward the wreckage, the bright leaping flames reflected in her tears.

(11)

They were in the security room. The mesh was closed. The external sensors were on. The monitors continued to show them trees swaying in the night wind and empty lawn, and, in the forecourt, one van, burning brightly in the night.

"They'll see it from town," said Pamela, wiping her eyes.

Beck looked at the screen. She remembered the view from Main Street. At thirty miles, Jericho's property was not even a blip on the mountainside. "No," she said. "We're on our own."

"Somebody will come," said Pamela, doggedly.

"Maybe. But we have to assume—"

"They *will*."

Beck took her wrists, pulled the hands away from the pale face. "We need a plan, Pamela. We need to protect ourselves." A pause. "And your father."

"They'll come."

"Pamela, listen to me. Listen. There's a gun in my room. I'll get it, and you should get the one from yours—"

"There isn't one. Audrey got rid of them."

"You had it Tuesday night."

"Audrey took it." Tears streaming. "Oh, God. Oh, God. It's real. Oh, God."

Beck lifted her face, sought out the golden eyes, which now looked lost. "Yes, Pamela. It's real. Now, unless you want to really die, do what I tell you." She hesitated, and felt her own tears threaten. For Audrey. For Nina. Anger rescued her. She wondered if Jack Notting had known that this Max was coming, and wanted Beck to stay the night for that reason; or whether yet another player was showing its hand. "Help me out here, okay?"

"Okay." Listlessly.

"Good. Now, I'm going to get the gun and check on your father. You stay here. Watch those monitors. If anything twitches, give a holler."

She hurried from the room, knowing that, whatever she said, only one of the screens would garner Pamela's attention.

(III)

Pamela was sitting with Jericho. Rebecca was downstairs, watching as the cameras scanned the lawn, occasionally patrolling the windows. The fire in the van had burned down. They had no idea what to do next. They were in one of the wealthiest states in the most technologically advanced nation in history, and they had no way to get in touch with the world beyond this patch of mountain to call for help. They had repeatedly pressed the alarm buttons, but they doubted that anyone had heard. They had considered and rejected one idea after another. The satellite phone in the safe made the most sense, but Jericho still could not remember the combination. Beck tried various permutations of her own birthday and, for good measure, Jericho's and Pamela's and Audrey's. Nothing worked. At one point, Jericho grabbed her by the arm and drew her face close. "You should have run when I told you," he whispered, breath hot and sickly. "Silly girl. Well, now you know. Loyalty can be expensive."

After that, she left him to Pamela.

"At least let me have the gun," Pamela had begged. But Rebecca was not about to share the Glock, least of all with a woman who, earlier tonight, might have been delighted to shoot her in the back.

The peculiar part was that she saw no movement. Whether checking the monitors or peering through the windows, she saw nothing but the occasional low, skittering shadow of a forest animal. But somebody was out there. All Jericho's calculations were wrong. Somebody was out there, willing to kill the people Jericho thought he was protecting.

Wait.

She had an idea.

That business with the cell phone. Maybe it could work both ways. She picked up the phone. No bars, of course. But if a device existed to send messages, maybe it would also monitor her transmissions, bars or none. She pressed green and heard the vast emptiness of the ether.

"Anybody there?" she said. "Can you hear me?"

Evidently not.

"If you're listening, we're in trouble. We need help."

No reply, not even the hum of dead air.

Try something else.

"Pamela!"

A moment's wait, then a pale face over the banister.

"Let's switch. I have an idea."

"What kind of idea?"

"I have to talk to Jericho. You have to watch the monitors."

"Does that mean I get the gun?"

"Just go."

(IV)

Jericho sat, exhausted, in the armchair. His breathing seemed labored, though Beck was no expert. He was no longer coughing, but he was wearing the oxygen mask.

Beck crouched in front of him. The golden eyes flicked across her face. "Good evening, my dear," he said from behind the plastic.

"How are you holding up?"

He lifted a hand, said nothing.

"Jericho, listen a minute, okay? Do you understand what's happening?"

"Of course, my dear. No need to shout."

But she had been whispering, and now pitched her voice lower still. "We need to get out of here."

He managed a sad smile. The eyes were still moist, and his hands trembled. "I believe I made that point the night you arrived."

"I have an idea."

"I'm listening, my dear."

"This killer—this Max—well, he isn't here to kill us for the fun of it. He's a killer for hire. You said so. And whoever hired him wants something, right? And if we give them what they want, maybe they'll call him off."

Jericho frowned. "We don't bargain with terrorists. First rule of civilized government."

"They're not terrorists, Jericho. They're your partners. The people you're blackmailing. All they want is for you to stop."

He coughed again, eyes half shut. "Too late for that, my dear."

"No, it isn't. I don't believe that. Now, listen to me. Listen. You had your fun. You wanted the world to notice you again. Well, they're noticing. They're noticing so hard they hired an assassin." The Former Everything showed no response. "You have to tell me, Jericho. It's life or death now. You have to give me whatever you can that I can use to trade—"

"I told you already. It's too late for that. Max doesn't do deals. Max won't bargain. Max won't be reasoned with. Max does the job. Period." He smiled. "We used to have a saying around the Agency. About who makes the best assassin. We said you need somebody crazy enough to pull the trigger, but sane enough not to miss. That's Max, my dear. A wounded soul with a steady hand."

(v)

The two women sat together on the stairs, drinking lukewarm coffee to stay awake. Upstairs, Jericho slumbered.

"We should nap," said Pamela, yawning. "We could take turns."

"You go ahead."

"You're afraid I might try to pull something, aren't you? You're more afraid of me than you are of whoever's out there."

Beck rubbed weary eyes. "Believe me, Pamela, I'm a lot more afraid of Max than I am of you."

Jericho's daughter shook her head. "I've made movies about hired killers," said Pamela. "I never thought I'd be running from one."

"So far, we're not running. We're sitting."

A long silence, both perhaps thinking the same thing. It was Pamela who first put it into words. "We're not going to get out of this, are we?"

"Come on." Patting her leg. "Stop talking that way."

"Audrey was supposed to be Max's friend, right? Isn't that what my dad told you? Well, if Max was willing to kill his friend Audrey, he wouldn't hesitate to kill the two of us."

"I don't know about you, but I'm not giving up. I'm going to see my daughter again." She found a laugh somewhere. "I can't leave her for my mother to raise."

Another silence. It occurred to Beck that they were not watching the monitors. Still, the sensors should tell them if anybody approached the house. Sooner or later, somebody would.

All at once, she grabbed Pamela's shoulder. "Look. When we get out of this, please, make peace with your daughter. You have no idea how important that is."

"Peace? I love Madeira!"

"Then stop bribing her and start raising her."

Pamela's color rose. She raised a hand, and Beck saw her own father's twisted face before he struck. Then Pamela relaxed, and almost smiled. "I will. I'll make peace with her." She tilted her head toward the window. "If we get out of this."

"When we get out of this."

"When," Pamela agreed. She laughed.

Beck was about to answer when the lights went out.

CHAPTER 32

The Prison

(1)

"The backup generator will come on in a minute," said Pamela, with none of her usual confidence. They were in the kitchen, where an array of flashlights hung on the back of the closet door. Beck selected two apiece. The heavier of the pair, she said, could be swung as a club, the way the police do. Pamela laughed screechily but took the proffered weapon.

"We have to get out of here," said Beck.

Pamela looked around. The mesh still guarded all the windows big enough for anyone to crawl through, including skylights. "We should wait."

"Wait?"

"Whoever's out there, they can't get in. It'll be light in a couple of hours." Nodding jerkily as her own plan became clearer to her. "Daylight means visitors. A delivery truck, somebody from town, even another crazy journalist. You'll see."

Beck stared at her. When you have spent your life living according to whim and looking down kindly on those who cannot, it must be no easy matter to accept that you might be, even for an instant, at the whim of another. "Have you noticed that it's still dark?"

"Because it's just four-thirty in the morning—"

"I meant, the house. The generator didn't come on."

Pamela was hugging herself. "It will in a minute."

"No. It won't. No power, no generator. No security cameras, no sensors, no alarm. Whoever did this went to a lot of trouble. They didn't cut everything off to wait until morning. No, Pamela. They're coming in."

"You're wrong, Rebecca." A flash of the old airiness. "The alarms and cameras have batteries—"

"Are you sure?" Beck had not heard this before. She had not bothered to visit the security room, assuming that nothing was on. Now she brushed past the other woman, and, sure enough, the monitors were still working. The alarm lights continued to glow. The gates in the basement probably worked, too, but they were designed less for protection than to trap an intruder. "How long do the batteries last?"

"Dad always said forty-eight hours. We can hold out a long time."

"Pamela—"

"We should stay here. Shut ourselves up in the bedroom with my father, and just wait."

Beck took her by the shoulders. Pamela was taller but, at the moment, too busy trembling to break free. "Listen to me. Just listen. We have power for the cameras. That means we might be able to plot a way out. But that's all it means. They're still coming in, Pamela. They blew up your sister. Do you think that's why they're here? You think they came to kill Audrey and then leave?"

"She could have been the target." In the glow of the monitors, Pamela's eyes had taken on her own father's mad energy. "She used to be in the CIA. Maybe they came to get her. Maybe now they'll be satisfied."

"Then why did they cut the power?"

"I don't know!"

"Well, I do. They cut the power because they're coming in, and they're coming in because your father has something they want." Pamela only stared. "You told me before that you don't know what Jericho's hiding. Was that true, or was that just an act?"

The fire went out of Pamela's gaze. She looked down and shuffled her feet. "No. It was true. I don't know what he's up to. I never know." She wiped at her eyes. "If there was anyone he'd tell, it would be Audrey. She was always . . . around."

"Audrey?"

"She was the one he loved best."

"I think I understand," said Beck, with quiet wonder. A helper in town. Always around. Audrey, helping him with the fake autobiography that turned out to be a fake will, the set of materials the lawyers had carried down to Denver for safekeeping.

"Audrey," she repeated, shaking her head. Audrey, the repentant sinner, the reformed interrogator, helping her father to blackmail whoever had hired her old friend Max to put the toothpaste back in the tube. Beck still doubted that Audrey was the one harassing her with mysterious telephone calls—the nun's repentance seemed genuine—but, the rest—

Maybe the bomb had not been random, or meant for Rebecca herself. Maybe poor Audrey had been the target after all.

Beck wondered how Audrey reconciled her roles; and whether, at this moment, she was standing before her God, mumbling excuses.

"Are you sure you have no idea? Not even a clue?"

Pamela shook her head.

"Maybe something you overheard. From Jericho. From your sister. A word. A phrase." Desperation. "Maybe a joke between the two of them."

For a moment the gaze sharpened, as if the questions had focused Pamela's mind.

"You did, didn't you? You remember something!"

"There was one time," Pamela said, softly. "I don't know if it means anything. We were up here—just the three of us—for Dad's birthday. So that's October. Six months ago. They went out for a walk on the property—Dad and Audrey. I was working. What's new, right? I felt left out. I always felt left out, and—and I guess that made me work harder. I don't know. Anyway, they were gone for maybe an hour. Could have been two. When they came back, they were laughing. But

J E R I C H O ' S   F A L L

furtive, too, like they were embarrassed. Audrey especially. She couldn't look me in the eye. And Dad said—he said, 'That'll show your Mr. Gould, won't it?' Audrey shushed him. But he wouldn't stop. You know how he was. How he is."

She needed a moment.

"Then he said, 'He wasn't good enough for you.' Well, that's what he always said. He said, 'He wasn't good enough for you, but he'll be good enough for me. He doesn't have to last that long.' He said, 'We'll show the bastards.' He kept raving on and on, but Audrey noticed I was listening and told him if he didn't stop he'd blow the whole thing."

Beck asked only one question. "Did he know he was sick?"

"Dad?"

"On his birthday. Did he already know he was dying?"

A tight nod. "That's when he told us. They gave him six months to a year."

Pamela closed down again, the animation visibly leaving her body. She had reminisced, she had told a story of the old days. She had eulogized her father, and now her mind was done trying.

Beck hardly noticed. She was close now, she knew she was. But first things first.

"Come with me," she said.

"Where?"

"Just come." She took Pamela by an unresisting arm and led her, gently, back into the kitchen. She pointed outside, behind the house. The land sloped downhill, toward a culvert. "That's where we're going. Whoever's out there will expect us to stay inside. We're going to head for the creek and follow it downstream."

"We should stay here and wait for help," said Pamela, listlessly.

"We're going. Either through the basement or through the kitchen, but we're definitely going. I don't know how we'll move Jericho, but we'll figure it out." Rebecca planned as she spoke. "We'll have to carry him." True, a part of her thought he deserved to be left behind, but the rest of her, despite the events of the past couple of days, remained infused with gratitude and guilt. Besides, the mother in her would never allow her to abandon one so helpless to his fate. "We have to get him ready."

"We can't go out there."

"We don't have a choice."

Pamela stood her ground. "We should stay here," she repeated, retreating to the single unchangeable tenet of her newfound faith. "We shouldn't go out there."

"We're going," said Beck. She pushed Pamela toward the stairs. "Now, come on. Help me here. I need you to go upstairs and get your father ready. He's mostly dressed, but make sure he has everything he needs. If there's any medication, bring that." Not explaining why: that once they headed downhill they would be heading away from town, away from civilization, and into the wilderness. "And blankets. Plenty of blankets."

"Rebecca, I—"

"Just do it, Pamela. We have the gun. I'm going to see what else we can use for a weapon, and figure out the best way out of here."

The taller woman shook her head. "That's not what I was going to say." She swallowed, and began trembling again, and Beck was afraid she would begin reciting her mantra once more. "I—I'm sorry for what I said. And if—if we get out of this—*when,* I mean"—a wry smile—"I want you and Nina to come stay with me. Please, Rebecca. We have a guesthouse, and you can have it for as long as you want. You can teach me how to raise a daughter, and I—I can get to know my little sister."

"She's not your—"

"Just come. Please."

She was gone up the stairs.

(11)

Beck went back to the security room and studied the monitors. Still no sign of movement. It occurred to her that whoever had blown up the van had not come close to check. Either they were sure they had hit the right target, or they didn't care which target they hit. She bit her lip. The face she had shown Pamela to keep her spirts up bloomed with a good deal more confidence than Beck actually felt. She had the Glock on her hip, but she was no commando. She had no idea how many men were out there, whether it was the mysterious Max or an entire team, but she did not honestly believe that two untrained women and a sick old man could escape. She had liked it better when she thought Jericho might be lying about his illness.

She checked her cell phone: no bars.

In the kitchen, she put together a package for each of them, food in a carrier bag, and a selection of knives in a wrapper. She included matches, because she had always heard they were essential survival gear.

She found clean plastic bottles, which she filled with water from the sink. She stared out into the night, still scarcely able to believe that it was Audrey who had betrayed, and Pamela who had ended up, out of necessity, an ally. Audrey, with her desperate faith, her fervent need not only to believe, but to draw others into the charmed circle. Her sweetness and generosity were no doubt real, but they were not her whole. There had remained a part of her that did not belong to the world of her previous work, or to her vows, either.

A part of Audrey had belonged to her father. It was precisely to escape that part that she had fled to the convent. To no avail. Jericho had done what he always did. He had taken her loyalty and her love and twisted it to his own ends.

For a moment, Beck stopped, hunched over the sink, a pain of near-physical intensity threatening to upend what equilibrium she had found. But whatever else she was, she was Jacqueline's daughter and Nina's mother. If she lost, it would not be because she refused to fight. She splashed cold water on her face and capped the bottles, relieved that, although the power was out, the storage tank remained full enough to maintain minimal pressure, at least for a while—

She stopped.

The water continued to run, but Rebecca DeForde was elsewhere, her mind galloping on ahead of itself, as Jacqueline used to say, rushing around to make logical connections and intuitive leaps, remembering the home-improvement books she had studied, and Audrey's tale, and Lewiston Clark's ravings, and what she had seen in the basement—

And then she had it.

She had no idea how much time was left before whoever was out there came inside, but it could not have been much. She needed one more fact, and then she would be done. She needed to look at the architectural drawings for Stone Heights. She turned off the water, grabbed her flashlight and her gun, and hurried upstairs to her room.

On the way, she peeked into the master suite. Jericho was dressed, swaddled in blankets, fast asleep on the bed. No sign of Pamela. Maybe she was taking a bathroom break.

Never mind. Get the plans. They were on her desk, along with the other papers she had collected during her frantic night of research. She sat on the bed, and had begun paging through the drawings when she heard Pamela's voice, ragged and whispery, coming from the study, through the connecting bath. Beck lifted her head. Was Pamela so far gone that she was now talking to herself?

"Like *you* can criticize anybody for that," Beck muttered.

She stood up, stepped into the bathroom, peeked around the door, and froze.

The safe was open. Pamela was on the satellite phone. And the last words she spoke chilled Rebecca to the bone. "Hurry, Dak. Please hurry."

CHAPTER 33

The Window

(1)

As Pamela put down the telephone, Beck stepped into view, the Glock in her hand.

Pamela looked up in alarm. "Rebecca!"

"I see you remembered the combination to the safe."

"What?" She looked down at the phone. "Oh. No, no, I didn't remember. I figured it out—"

"And you called Dak. How cozy."

"I only got his voice mail. I asked him to send help—" She looked at Beck's hand. "Why are you pointing that thing at me?"

Beck's voice was ice. "You know why, Pamela."

"No, I don't. What's the matter with you? Put it away. You're making me nervous."

"I'm such an idiot. I don't know why I didn't see it sooner. Of course you knew the combination. Of course you called Dak. The two of you have been working together all along, haven't you? I can't imagine what he promised you, but I have a hunch that it was supposed to be me in that car. Not Audrey. I was supposed to be blown to bits, and Audrey was supposed to help you wheedle your father into giving up whatever is keeping us alive. Only, Audrey got in the car and died. So much for your plan."

Pamela was trembling. "Rebecca, no. How can you believe that? I wouldn't—I would never—"

"Spare me. Just tell me how much time we have."

"Time?"

"Before they get here. Dak and his friends. How long, Pamela?" She gestured toward the window, and whoever was outside. "Is the alarm even still on? Or did you shut that off, too?"

Pamela shook her head. She was trembling. "No. No. I don't know what you're talking about. Why would I shut off the alarm?"

Beck, on the other hand, was rock steady. The gun never wavered. Jericho had taught her to put her shots center-mass, and center-mass was where she was aiming. Just below the pearls.

"How much time do we have, Pamela? When are they getting here?"

"There isn't any *they*! Please, Rebecca, stop it. Please."

"Keep your hands where I can see them."

"I just want a cigarette—"

"No." Beck stepped farther into the room, took in the open safe, and the paper, half covered with Scotch tape, with the numbers on it. "Is that the combination?"

Pamela nodded, wide eyes on the barrel. "Yes. Yes. I found it taped under the chair. A stupid hiding place. Then you add Mom's birthday to each number, dividing the year into two parts—nineteen and forty-five—and, well, you see how it works."

"Step away from the desk," said Beck, quite unimpressed. It had occurred to her that Pamela had made a mistake. She should not have used the satellite phone in the study, where Beck might overhear. She should have shut the safe and made her call later. Now Beck could use the phone to summon help. The real kind. The kind that actually helped. "Keep your hands where I can see them."

"Yes, okay, fine. Please, don't point the gun at me."

"Relax. I'm just going to make a couple of calls."

Alarm in those clever eyes. "Who are you calling, Rebecca?"

"Just stand still. No, that's far enough. Good." Picking up the receiver. "How does this thing work?"

Pamela pointed. "Just press there and wait for the beep that tells you you're uplinked. But the battery was almost dead. I don't know if there's enough for another call."

Beck looked. A red light was flashing, and then, as she held the phone in her hand, the entire screen went blank. She pressed the power button, but nothing happened.

"How convenient," she muttered, mostly in frustration.

"It's not my fault."

Rebecca considered. "We're going to walk into the hall. You walk in front of me. Understand? And keep your hands up."

"I will. I'll do whatever you say. Please, don't do this."

"Don't do what, Pamela?"

"I don't know. Whatever you're doing."

"When is Dak coming?"

"I didn't talk to him, I just got his voice mail!"

"What was your deal?" Out at the balustrade now, inching along in the darkness. "With Dak, Pamela. Come on. What was your deal? How long after your call was he supposed to arrive?"

Again that frantic shake of the head, eyes so confused and frightened that part of Rebecca wanted to believe her. "There isn't any deal. It's just, those were always Dad's standing instructions. In an emergency, call Dak."

Then Beck had another idea.

"You stand right here," she said. "I'm going back in the study, but I'll have the gun on you the whole time. If you try to run, I'll shoot you. Understand?"

"Rebecca, please—"

"Do you understand?"

"Yes, yes, I understand, but you have it all wrong."

"Shut up," said Beck, having wanted to say those words to Pamela for years. She inched back into the study. Her theory was simple. If there is a phone, there is a charger. She went through the desk drawers, then glanced at Pamela, who stood wide-eyed in the doorway. Beck frowned. She peered into the safe, then shone her flashlight through the gloom and saw what looked like an attachment in the back. She leaned in, got up on her toes to lean farther, and then hit the floor as Pamela kicked her legs out from under her.

(11)

The flashlight went flying.

Beck was on her stomach, and Pamela was sitting atop her, pummeling her with the flashlight, aimlessly, even hopelessly, but now and then a blow would find a sensitive spot, and it hurt like the dickens. Pamela was screaming and Beck was screaming back, and the strange part was that Rebecca still held the gun, and the stranger part was that Pamela was making no effort to grab it. If Beck bent her hand at the proper angle, she could easily have shot Pamela in the chest.

Only, she found she didn't want to.

Instead, she managed to roll halfway over. Not till then did Pamela see the gun, and reach for it. They wrestled, they kicked, they knocked over the lamp, they fought for the gun and only managed to spin it across the floor and out of reach. Pamela snarled that Beck was out of her mind, and Beck snarled back that Pamela had betrayed her own father, and from out in the hall came the *beep-beep-buzz* of an external sensor, still working from its battery.

Somebody was approaching the house.

A frozen moment.

Then Pamela slapped Beck's head against the desk, Beck went briefly boneless, and her adversary scooped up the gun as if she knew how to use it and scurried off into the hallway.

Rebecca, gripping the desk, began the endless climb to her shaky feet in the whirling room, cursing herself for turning her back for even a second, but, then, Jericho had taught her only how to fire a gun, not how to guard a prisoner. She stood there, leaning against the wall, gulping air. She did not understand why Pamela had not shot her. Maybe she was waiting for Dak to arrive and finish her off.

And Dak himself! How could he turn his back on his best friend? But friendship was one thing, she supposed, and the nation's security was another.

Holding on to the furniture, guiding herself slowly toward the hall, she wondered whether any part of the story Phil Agadakos had told her was true, or whether Jericho was really hiding something else altogether. She supposed she would get the chance to ask when Dak showed up—

Wait.

Why was Pamela calling him? If they were in this together, if all the misfortunes that had struck in the past few days were the doing of Jericho's longtime comrade-in-arms, then why would she need to call him on the sat phone to tell him what was going on? Wouldn't he already know, either because he was on the scene, or because he was in touch with those who were?

Had she misjudged Pamela?

Beck heard glass shattering. Bad news. She had to get help. She turned back to the safe and dug out the charger, only to realize her stupidity. With no power in the house, there was nowhere to plug it in.

Fine. She would have to do it the hard way.

Still shaking, she stepped out into the darkness. She could not see past the bend in the hallway. The guest suite was beside her; Jericho's suite, and the other bedrooms, were around the corner. She pressed her back into the wall, trying to make herself as small a target as possible. Maybe Pamela was working with Dak, maybe she was in it for herself, maybe she was even in it for her father. The one thing Beck knew for sure was that Pamela was not in it for Beck. She inched along the hall, trying to figure out where else Jericho would have hidden guns. The master suite had to have a couple. To be sure, Audrey might not have thought about cleansing the guest quarters, but she would hardly have overlooked Jericho's room. So he would have hidden the guns well.

They would, however, be there.

At the corner, she hesitated. She did not have even the flashlight any more. If Pamela was waiting for her around the bend, she would be a perfect target. And yet there was no way out but forward. She shut her eyes for a moment, then opened them, remembering that trick from Jericho, too: shutting her eyes would widen the pupils, making it easier for her to use the thin scatters of light from moon and stars to pick out whatever was waiting for her.

She poked her head around the corner.

And did not need much light at all to see Pamela's body, crumpled on the floor.

CHAPTER 34

The Sniper

(1)

There was blood everywhere, but Pamela was breathing. She tried to talk, and even managed to wave a hand to show Rebecca where the gun had fallen. Beck nodded, retrieved it, and tried to find the wounds. The one in the arm did not look too bad. The one in the stomach was bleeding. Too low for the heart or the lungs. If it had smashed something else vital, there was nothing to be done until they could get out of here. She crawled to the bathroom, came back with towels, did her best to stuff them in place, whispered to Pamela to hold them.

Pamela tried to grab her arm.

Beck leaned in.

"I wasn't lying," she said.

"I don't understand."

A tilt of the head, both hands now busy trying to stanch the flow. "Calling Dak. Didn't do anything wrong. Trying to help."

Beck looked at her, couldn't decide. "Rest," she said, kissing her forehead.

Then, gun in hand, she scuttled along the landing with her knees bent, hoping the banister would hide her. The broken glass in the high windows told her that the shots had come from outside. The security mesh covered only the panes large enough to climb through. The clerestory windows were too small for a man, but plenty large enough for a bullet. So the sniper was perched high up Jericho's mountain. She glanced back at Pamela, already a moaning shadow in the darkness. Dak had insisted that nobody in Jericho's family could be harmed, but with Audrey dead and Pamela wounded, somebody out there had decided otherwise.

The strategy was simple, and obvious. Cut the house off from the world, shut down the power, remove those around Jericho, then come in and get him.

She wondered if the man out there shooting might be the killer Phil Agadakos had mentioned: the great Max, out of retirement for one last job. Jericho had said she would never see Max coming. She hadn't; neither had Audrey; and neither had Pamela, whichever side she was on.

Rebecca took a moment, leaned against the wall, shut her eyes. She should be with Nina now. She should never have come. Even a weekend in Chicago with Pfister had never looked so good. A week ago, she had been a nobody, raising her daughter and advising her bosses on where to put the perfume. And now the mysterious Max was out there, trying with all his skill to kill her. She wondered how Audrey would fit this little scenario into God's will—except that Audrey was gone. Max had blown her to bits, and, sooner or later, he would get Beck, too.

Pamela's groans were louder.

Eyes open, Beck measured the distance to Jericho's suite. "Move," she told herself harshly.

The motion sensor had buzzed once, and not since. How long? Fifteen minutes. Twenty at the most. She was not sure why it was so important to get in there, but she knew she had no choice. Whatever was going on—whoever was out there, trying to get in—Jericho would have the answers. Either he was awake, or she would find a way to wake him.

If she could get to the room.

She began crawling. To anybody with night-vision glasses she would be visible between the dowels of the banister, but there was nothing for it.

More glass shattered. Bullets. She had never been shot at in her life, and, crawling faster, only hoped that—

The gunfire stopped.

She looked up.

She was at the entrance of the suite. Of course. Whoever was out there was perfectly willing to kill everyone else in the house, but did not want to take any risk of harming Jericho, and a stray bullet through the door might just do it. Meaning, somebody still hoped to extract his secrets from him, no matter how sick he might be.

She reached out, shoved the door, crawled through, slammed it behind her.

(11)

Jericho was half on the bed and half on the floor. He had found a flashlight somewhere, but was too weak to do anything but shine it at her as she burst in. He looked up at her and smiled, and behind the smile was agony, and behind the agony—just for a moment—was delighted calculation.

"You came for me," he gasped, still struggling to rise. "I knew you would. Can't do what you're told, can you? Silly girl."

But over the last half-hour Beck had grown up all the way, and she had no more time for his nonsense. "Stop it," she said. "We have to get moving."

Jericho looked at her, then nodded. With her help, he made it to a sitting position on the bed. "What's the status?" he said, as if they were co-conspirators.

"Your friend Max is out there with a sniper's rifle. Pamela is wounded. Audrey"—she hesitated—"I don't know Audrey's status."

The old man made a face. "Meaning that explosion was my little girl."

"Yes. I'm sorry, Jericho."

"Oh well. It's not like you did it." His face clouded, but only for a second or two. "Well, what the hell. Saint Audrey is getting her chance to find out if all the praying and sacrifice made a difference, or if she's going to hell with the rest of us."

Again Beck refused to rise. "We need a plan."

"Not if it's Max out there. If it's Max, the best thing to do is sit and wait."

"For what?"

"Well, if you don't make Max angry, you get a nice bullet in the back of the head. No muss, no fuss."

She grabbed the lapels of his jacket. "Jericho, listen to me. Listen. It's over now. You proved your point, okay? You're smarter than everybody. You made everybody stand up and take notice. But now we're going to die. Do you understand that? Max is out there. He killed Audrey. He shot Pamela. He's going to kill us next. The only way to change that is for us to give him whatever—"

"I told you, my dear. Max doesn't bargain. You go out there under a flag of truce, beating a *chamade* on the drum, and Max will put a bullet through your brain."

"You don't know that, Jericho. Max is working for a client, right? And all his client wants is the secrets you've squirreled away. We might have a chance of making it out of here alive, but you're going to have to tell me everything."

He waved all this away. "I need to lie down."

For a mad moment she wanted to smack him. "Come on, Jericho. I think I've figured it out, but unless you confirm my—"

"I told you already. You know everything. Did you ask Saint Audrey why she left the family business?" He was up on the bed.

"Yes. She said she couldn't take the torturing any more—"

He stretched out. "And she told you everything? All about liking girls? About leaving poor Mr. Gould in the lurch to run off with some chick?"

"She said you made all that up."

"Well, then."

"Jericho—"

"You know as much as you need to know, my dear. I need to sleep."
He tugged at the blankets, and Rebecca knew she would never get him
moving. She stood up. He was waiting for Max. Waiting to die. She
would not wait with him. "Jericho, listen. Before you go to sleep. I
need to know about weapons—"

"You'll find what you need in the kitchen. Under the sink, I think.
And when they come, tell them what they're looking for is in the
garage. But don't go out there yourself."

"Listen—"

"Good night, Becky-Bear."

"Wait. Jericho, wait. Why would Max kill Audrey? Didn't you say
they were friends? And Dak told me your family couldn't be hurt—"

A yawn, then a series of coughs. "No rules," he whispered. "That's
the first rule of this business. We used to preach it to the newbies. Rule
Number One is that there are no rules. Rule Number Two is to see
Rule Number One." He laughed, then coughed again, harder. He
finally had the blankets over him. He lay there, fully clothed. "I'm
going to sleep now, Becky-Bear. Tell Max not to bother waking me."

And he would say no more.

She was alone.

CHAPTER 35

The Kitchen

(1)

The kitchen was as dark as the rest of the house. By now Rebecca knew that nobody was coming: nobody on her side, anyway. The alarm people had received no alert, because somebody had taken the system off line. The van was only smoldering now, and if the town had not sent the fire brigade by this time, it never would. Pamela was wounded. Jericho was waiting to die. She had no working telephone. She had no vehicle she dared use. If Beck was going to see Nina grow up, she was going to have to find her own way out.

And her way out began with the sink.

Down on her knees, Beck pawed through the cabinets. She found cleansers and sponges and steel wool. She found mouse droppings. She found a folder of more instruction pamphlets for the various devices in the house. She found bug spray. She found extra garbage bags. She found wires and pipes. She found no weapon or signaling device. She found no directions on how to escape from the prison the house had become.

But she found the confirmation she craved, an instruction pamphlet that matched a set of schematics Jericho had printed from the Internet. Best of all, the device bore the brand name that—

"Find what you're looking for?" said a voice behind her.

Rebecca spun, the gun waving wildly.

Slouching against the butcher-block table, hands in the pockets of her jeans, was the town librarian, Miss Kelly.

(11)

"How did you get in here?"

"I have the alarm code." The dark face was shy. "Mr. Ainsley and I are very good friends."

Beck pointed the Glock. "How good?"

"Oh, not like you mean. Not like the two of you were. I just help him out from time to time."

"I don't believe you. The power's out. You don't need the alarm code."

"The alarm runs on batteries. It's working fine. Not the part that notifies the alarm company. The part that protects the house. Please point that thing somewhere else. You're making me nervous."

Beck shook her head. "You're telling me that, just for helping him out, he gave you the alarm code? A man as paranoid as Jericho?"

"You're right. Mr. Ainsley didn't give me the alarm code. When poor Mr. Pesky took his tumble and the alarm company called to find out why somebody pushed the panic button? That's how I got it."

"You were listening in? You?"

"Somebody was," said Miss Kelly, testily. "That doesn't matter. The important thing is, I'm on your side."

Beck pointed with the Glock. "Everybody says they're on my side. You. Pete. Lewiston Clark. Dak."

"The others are lying. I'm telling you the truth." She held out her hands. "I'm unarmed. See? Now, why don't you put that gun away? It's making me nervous."

"I've heard everybody else's stories. Why don't you tell me yours?"

Miss Kelly shook her head. "No. There isn't time. You're going to have to trust me."

"Why?"

"Because any minute now that helicopter that has you so bamboozled is going to drop off half a dozen heavily armed men wearing night-vision goggles who will scoop Jericho up and fly him off to an undisclosed location before you can say Patriot Act."

Beck couldn't help herself. She backed away, peered through the window, saw no helicopter.

"Who are you?" she asked.

"Miss Kelly, town librarian."

"Come on. If you're going to show up at a time like this and ask me to trust you, you should at least tell me your name. I'm sure it isn't Kelly."

The librarian turned out to have a dazzling smile. "If you don't believe Kelly is my last name," she said, "why would you believe whatever I tell you is my first name?"

"I have to call you something. I can't just call you Miss."

The smile widened. "My name is Maxine," she said. "My friends call me Max."

(111)

Rebecca's hand wavered. For the third time on this endless night, reality seemed to shift around her. "No. No. That's not possible."

"Why not? It's just a name."

"Max is a killer! An assassin!"

A moue of disapproval. "Ouch. That one hurt."

"But—but—"

"Tell you what. Let's just agree that I get called in to do difficult jobs now and then. Now, please. Put the gun away."

"Not a chance." Beck had both hands on the grip now, just the way Jericho had taught her. "I know why you're here."

"I'm here because you called me."

"What?"

Maxine pointed toward the cell phone on Rebecca's hip. "You

called for help. You said, if anybody's listening, you were in trouble. You made a good guess, Beck. Somebody was listening."

"It was you all along." The barrel grew, if anything, steadier. "All that bullshit, those sounds, those voices, that was all you. Trying to disorient me. Manipulate me. Make me think I had no way out but to find what Jericho was hiding. That was you."

"Not me. My clients." A careless shrug. "The point is, you called for help, and I got your message, so to speak. So here I am. Ready to help."

"Ready to kill me and Pamela and take Jericho, you mean."

"That's not true." A gesture, both palms open. "Please, try to calm down. You're making me nervous with that thing."

"Sit down."

"We don't have time for these games, Beck."

Rebecca pointed toward the refrigerator and pulled the trigger. She had guessed, correctly, that she could not miss so large a target. "Sit," she snapped, waving the pistol.

The librarian sat. "Happy now?"

"I should kill you," Beck muttered. Her hand was aching. She had forgotten how powerful the recoil was.

"You can't shoot me, Beck."

Rebecca's hand trembled, but she kept the gun trained center-mass. "You blew up your friend. I'd shoot you in two seconds."

A look of pain flitted across the dark face. "You're wrong. That wasn't me."

"Bullshit."

"Give me the gun."

"Don't move."

But Maxine was not moving. She remained in the chair, hands spread wide in entreaty. "Beck, listen to me. Please. There isn't a lot of time. This isn't your world. These aren't your rules. You can still get out of this, but you're going to have to put the gun down."

"No."

"I don't want to have to hurt you."

"You can't hurt me. I have the gun."

"Wrong." Something happened very fast, a flicker, a flurry, a pain, a wild shot, and then Beck was on the floor, cradling her wrist, and Maxine was standing over her. "I have the gun."

(I V)

With Maxine in charge, they trooped into the security room. The assassin insisted. There was something she wanted Beck to see.

"Why don't you shoot me and get it over with?"

"Stop talking nonsense." She pointed. "Here. This monitor. See it?"

Beck stared, fear and fury mingling. "I see, you bitch. I see the van you blew up with your friend inside."

"Look closer. By the right rear wheel."

She looked closer. Then looked again. Without the floodlights, it was harder to see anything, but bits of the fire still smoldered, and something dark and slim—

Was that what it looked like?

"What is this?" She swung around, only to find Maxine several paces back and the gun level between them. "What are you showing me? That you blew Audrey's leg off?"

"It's not Audrey's leg, Rebecca. It's attached to a body. The body belongs to the man who blew her up."

Beck swung around to look again.

"I wasn't gentle," the librarian admitted. "Usually I try to make it painless. But, as you said, he blew up my friend."

A chilly moment as this image settled between them.

"Who is he?" said Beck. "Was he?"

"Nobody. Hired help. He's not the point, Rebecca. The point is, we have to get out of here."

"We?"

"Just you and I, I'm afraid. Mr. Ainsley and his daughter will have to wait a while. We can't carry baggage."

"Why am I so important?"

"Just come with me, Rebecca. Please."

"How are we going to get out?"

"The same way I got in."

"I'd like to check on Jericho first."

"Sorry, honey. No time."

CHAPTER 36

The Decision

(1)

Maxine made Beck go first. They walked down the stairs into the basement. The killer held both the gun and the flashlight. With the power out, even if Beck escaped, she would not be able to see where she was going.

"How did you get into this line of work anyway?" Rebecca asked as they picked their way past the pool table. "A nice librarian like you."

"Walk slower."

"I guess there aren't too many women in your field, are there? You probably get a lot of work. Maybe you could get me in."

"Relax, Beck. I'm not going to hurt you. I'm here to help you."

Rebecca snickered. "I should have guessed. All my best friends point guns at me."

"Down the hall. Slowly."

The silence was eerie. In a house, one is accustomed to the background whir of equipment, and in a basement especially. With the power cut, there was nothing but their own soft footsteps on the carpet and the skitter of mice.

"You came through the garage," said Beck, thinking about the pin lights.

"Yes."

"But the doors are padlocked—"

"Not any more. Now. Slowly. Step into the storeroom."

This was the chance. There would be only one.

"Jericho said you're retired."

"Slow down. You're walking too fast."

"If you didn't kill Audrey," said Beck, slowing as ordered, "I'm assuming you didn't shoot Pamela, either."

"That's correct."

She stopped. "You're saying the sniper is still out there."

"Presumably. Don't stop moving. We have to get going."

Rebecca had both hands on the doorjamb, hesitating as if in fear. Maxine moved very close behind her. "Come on, Beck. You can do this."

"You don't know who's out there."

"Not entirely. No. All I can tell you is, there are a lot of contenders for the prize Mr. Ainsley has hidden. They were all hanging back. Nobody wanted to set Jericho's scheme in motion. One of them got impatient, so now all of them have to close in." She gestured with the gun. "Anyway, we're safer on the move."

Beck shook her head. "I want to go back. I can't leave them."

"You don't have a choice."

"Please."

It had to happen. One woman to another. Maxine reached up to lay a reassuring hand on Beck's shoulder. And Beck, at the same instant, braced her hands against the jamb, bent her knees, and kicked backward as hard as she could. The librarian cried out in surprise and tumbled. Beck was ready for this, too. Her fingers were curled around the three buttons set inside the door. As soon as she was sure Maxine was on her back, she pressed the buttons.

The gate came thundering down.

The killer was trapped behind it.

Beck ran up the stairs, waiting for the gunshot.

Maxine bellowed, demanding to be released, warning Rebecca that she would never make it on her own, but she never fired. Beck slipped into the garage, slammed the door behind her, and cycled the lock.

(11)

She was back in the garage. No light of any kind, not from below, not from outside, and Maxine had the flashlight. Beck hated darkness but had no choice. She ran across the concrete floor, bumping into one crate after another, before finally finding her way to a door. She shoved. Nothing happened.

Still locked.

She tried the next, and it gave. She stepped out into the night air and did her sums.

First: Max was trapped but Beck did not know for how long. The night had already been full of surprises, and Maxine had been responsible for a number of them. The assassin was, by all accounts, good at her job. At best, Jericho's little trap would only slow her down.

Second: There was a sniper out there. If the sniper spotted her, she was finished. Still, he had fired from the north side of the house, and the garage was to the southeast, so there was a fair chance that Stone Heights itself would protect her.

Third: She knew where she had to go. The key was in the question Jericho kept asking her, repeating his demand so that she would sense its importance, but at the same time the listeners would not. He had asked her why Audrey left the family business, and each successive iteration of the question had embedded more and more mention of her husband. As though she had left because of her husband. Her husband had been Ted Gould. Now Beck understood the research. He had been planning all along for the moment when he would have to tell-without-telling. But Rebecca knew, because Jericho had printed the information from the Internet.

Gould just happened to be the name of the nation's leading maker of well pumps. Pamela said her father had changed the well pump. One of the documents from Jericho's folder explained how to get a pump out of the well. She had it in her jacket now.

From the architectural plans, she knew that the well was located in the ravine to the southeast of the house. She had to cross the lawn. With the brush cut back fifty yards on every side, she would be a sitting duck. But she had no choice. She took a breath, looked around into the starry night, and, giving a prayer of thanks that the power outage had killed the floodlights, ran for the woods.

(III)

She made it to the well; but getting there was the easy part.

Now she had to get the pump out.

The well was simply a hole in the ground, less than a foot in diameter, drilled as far down as necessary to reach the water. The pump was attached to the end of a heavy-duty hose, and the hose was lowered into the well. Above ground, all that was visible was the wellhead, a metal cylinder protruding just a few inches above the ground.

Stooping, she tried to pull off the top with her hands, but she had no leverage; besides, the metal was freezing. The fallen branches she tested as levers all broke. Finally, she was able to pry it off by shoving a flat rock beneath the edge and hammering it with another.

With the top aside, she peered in. She had no flashlight, but she remembered the schematics. The hose took a sharp turn, entering the house through a pipe set a few inches beneath ground level. She slid her hand in and grasped the hose. The rubber was freezing.

She began to pull.

The first couple of tugs were easy. The next couple were not too bad. After that, all of a sudden, the work was backbreaking. Beck had apparently just drawn out the slack. Removing the hose was another matter.

She tested several methods before deciding that the most efficient was to brace herself, one foot against the wellhead, the other flat on the frozen earth, and tug, hand over hand.

Rebecca tugged, and breathed, and tugged, and breathed. Little by little, the hose was coiling on the ground. It was so heavy that half the time it tugged back, and she lost part of what she had removed. She rested, and then, with a great moan, went back to work. She had mittens in the pocket of her jacket, but they were wool, not meant for manual labor. They did little to protect her from the chill of the hose, and very soon began to unravel. Her hands were chapping, and after fifteen minutes or so, she could no longer feel her fingers. But she kept on tugging. She had no choice. Sooner or later, the sniper would come, or the commandos would come, or Max would get loose. She had to get her hands on Jericho's secrets before anybody else did. She needed to protect her daughter. She kept tugging for Nina's sake, and sometimes to show her mother that she could do it. She kept tugging because she could not get back the wasted years. Jericho was right. She was ambitious, so ambitious there were indeed days when she could scarcely bear to look at herself in the mirror. She had to have whatever was at the end of the hose. So she kept tugging. She thought of all the jerks she had dated, and the jerk she had married, and tugged harder. This one for her ex-husband, this one for Jericho, this one for Sean, this one for Pete Mundy, this one for the wide receiver whose nose she broke freshman year.

Rebecca rested a bit, and tried to figure out how much she had pulled out of the well. The hose was coiled everywhere. Her palms were sore. Her fingers were swelling. Her shoulders ached. The books said the hose for a well could easily run five hundred feet, sometimes more, depending on where the water was.

Five hundred feet was nearly a tenth of a mile. She wondered how much a tenth of a mile of hose weighed.

A lot.

She took a break and leaned against a tree. She tugged off her mittens and sucked on her fingers, trying to get some sensation back into them. She looked up at the house. She wished she were in there, except that it was a death trap. Pamela and Jericho, like Nina and Beck herself, had only one chance, and it lay hidden at the bottom of the well.

Back to work.

She looked at the hose laid out on the forest floor. The looped black shadow seemed to go on for miles, but was probably no more than a few hundred feet. Beck had read that usually a team of two or even three is sent when the hose needs to be pulled up. Unfortunately, her only choice was to be a team of one.

She tugged and rested, tugged and rested, reminded herself that Jericho had once loved her, and that she still owed him, no matter what Dr. Eisenstadt thought. She conjured Nina's shining face, and the cynicism of a Jack Notting, who would get someone to kill a dog exactly like the one her daughter had been given. Tugging and resting, tugging and resting, Beck thought about Sean, and marveled at the enormity of the enmity that would so turn son against father. And she wondered whether, had Maggie Ainsley not come along to recruit him, Sean would have found some other excuse to play his dangerous game—

A massive explosion shook the forest.

Beck screamed. Animals that had been invisible ran in panic. Up on the hill behind her, the garage was in flames.

She forgot the hose for a moment, forgot the pump, forgot everything as she scrambled up the frozen verge, needing to know whose life had just been incinerated. At the top of the rise, she saw the garage ablaze and, in a panic, stumbled toward it, not away, until Pete Mundy brought her down in a flying tackle.

"Sorry I'm late," he puffed, sitting beside her on the frozen ground.

(I V)

She hugged him for longer than was decent, and probably kissed him, but later could never remember the exact details.

"What are you doing here?" she managed at last.

"Got a call about suspicious traffic. It all seemed headed this way. You were supposed to get in touch if there were problems, but I hadn't heard a word, so I took a chance." He glanced over her shoulder. "What are you doing out here in the middle of the night?" He pointed at the snow. "You left footprints. Pretty easy to follow."

In her relief, Beck actually giggled. "I was pulling up the well pump."

"Fixing it?"

"Looking for something."

He frowned. "Did you find what you were looking for?"

"Not yet."

He considered this, then shrugged. "Whatever you say, honey."

"What happened?" she asked as they moved toward the lawn.

"I think Mr. Ainsley had the garage booby-trapped." He held out a restraining hand, and Beck drew back. "I saw somebody go in there. He must have heard the rumors in town about something being delivered."

Her expression was grim. If the garage was booby-trapped, the electric eyes must have been connected to the explosive. Had Jericho not given her the code, she might have set off the bomb when she went in. Maybe he had known she was curious, and would find a way in sooner or later; maybe the booby trap was not armed at the time, and he had wanted her to see it and stay away. Whatever the reason, the code had worked. Beck had made it through the garage tonight without setting off the explosives; somebody else had not.

She remembered, shuddering, not only Jericho's paranoia; but the life he had lived before they met. Maxine, too, had navigated the garage successfully, most likely through some combination of training and prudence. A wounded soul with a steady hand.

"I think the rumors were planted on purpose," she said faintly. "I think he wanted someone to try to open his crates."

"The man who went in was one of the strangers."

"He could be the one who shot Pamela. I hope she's still alive. She's upstairs."

Pete seemed to be sniffing the air, much as Dak had done a million years ago on Monday afternoon. "He wasn't the only one out here. Somebody's moving around."

"An animal—"

"Too big for that." He put a hand on her arm, propelling her forward. He held his gun ready but angled away from her. "We have to get help."

"Pete, wait."

"What's the matter?" He was out of the woods, beckoning.

"There's somebody else in the house. Trapped in the basement."

"Who?"

"Miss Kelly."

He closed the distance between them, face bewildered. "I'm sorry, Beck. Did you say the town librarian is locked in the basement?"

"It's a long story. Look. The phones are out, the power's out—you have a radio in your cruiser, right?"

"I have my pickup down the hill. There's a radio in there, sure."

"Then let's hurry. Pamela and Jericho both need to get to the hospital."

"Okay." Again he was on the move. Beck realized that she was holding his hand. He looked at the garage. "I'm pretty sure they'll see that fire from town, though. Not like the other one."

Rebecca took her hand back. "What did you say?"

He was a few paces ahead of her, gun at the ready, eyes searching lawn and woods. "I said they'll see the fire from town. They'll send help."

She shook her head. "No. You said *not like the other one*. What other one, Pete?"

"The van. It's out front. Hard to miss."

"How do you know if they saw it from town or not?" A terrible suspicion was starting to dawn. "How do you even know when it burned?"

"Anybody can see it burned."

"Not in this darkness. Not without the floodlights."

"I examined it with my flashlight, Beck. Come on. It's the first thing a cop would see."

"And did you see Audrey's body?"

He dropped his eyes. "I wasn't going to mention that. She's kind of a mess."

She relaxed. "Pete, I'm sorry."

"For what? It's been quite a night. I still want to hear why Miss Kelly is in the basement."

"Let me just warn you. Before we let her out, you'd better put the cuffs on. She's some kind of hired gun."

"Always knew there was something odd about her." Laconic and unperturbed, as always. "You know, Beck, maybe we shouldn't use my radio. The sheriff hears all the radio calls, and, well, I don't know which side he's on."

"Not ours," said Beck, rubbing her arms. The cold was seeping in. The wind was spreading the fire toward the trees. Sooner or later, left unchecked, it would reach the house. She said, "Let's carry them, then. Jericho and Pamela. We'll put them in your truck."

The deputy thought this over. "The house is the first place anybody will be looking."

"Still—"

"One man died in the explosion. Another man is dead over by the van. But there's somebody else. I saw him, and I kept my distance. He had a sniper rifle. He's in the woods to the west. Or he was. But if we go around that way"—he pointed—"and stay in the east woods all the way to the front of the house, he won't see us. If we try to get to the house across this lawn, with the sight lines he has? We're sitting ducks."

Rebecca saw his point. Jericho's mad insistence on cutting back the brush and trees turned out to have disadvantages. But she could not bear the thought of abandoning Pamela and Jericho. "Please, Pete. We can't just leave them."

"We can send help—"

"Whoever's out there will have come and gone. They'll swoop down and take him. Maxine told me."

"Who?"

"Miss Kelly—it's her real name—she's a killer—oh, shit—"

The tension of the endless night had become too much. The pain, the fear, the flight—Pamela's wounded body. Beck nearly broke down.

Pete held her, stroked her back, murmured all the things we murmur to comfort the sobbing. But she had already decided not to cry after all, and her eyes were dry as she said, firmly, "I'm not leaving without them, Pete."

"I guess we can try," he said at last. "But you do exactly what I say."

CHAPTER 37

The Escape

(1)

They tramped through the woods to the east, keeping the bulk of Stone Heights itself between their position and the spot where Pete had seen the sniper. Frozen leaves crinkled under their feet. At first, Rebecca kept talking, explaining what had happened over the last frightening hours, but Pete kept telling her to keep her voice down and finally ordered her, roughly, to hush.

"Keep very still," he commanded, and, except for a continued trembling, half fear and half chill, she did.

They were still in the east woods. The house was fifty yards away. They were looking at the living room, and, up above, the windows of the master suite, and, at the rear, the study. There were no lights, of course. Beck thought she detected movement upstairs, but it might have been her imagination. The lawn before them was where Pesky had taken his fall.

"This is the plan," Pete murmured after a moment. "It works if there's only one sniper. If there's two, we're cooked."

She forced the words through gritted teeth. "I understand."

"Good. Now we have to split up. You stay right here, Beck. I'm going to circle around to the front, then dash across the driveway. He'll see me, and he'll shoot at me, but I think he'll be a minute adjusting, because he's watching the house, and the south woods. His rifle is on a tripod. He'll have to move it. That gives me an edge. As soon as you hear the gunshots, you run across this lawn, straight for the house. It's only fifty yards. You'll be exposed for maybe ten seconds. When you get to the house, you hug that wall and head around to the back. You go in that door. Got it?"

"What about you?"

"I'll join you as soon as I can."

"The sniper—"

"I have a gun, too, Beck. In the truck, I have a rifle and a shotgun. I can take care of myself." He paused, letting this sink in. "Are you sure you won't come with me? We can send help and sit tight—"

She shook her head. "The helicopter's coming."

"And so you're going to risk your life saving a woman who hates you and a man who's blackmailing the federal government?" But his tone was gentle. He put a hand on her face. "You're a very strange person, Beck. Did anybody ever tell you that?"

"Pretty much everybody."

"Your skin is cold."

"You noticed."

He kissed her, taking his time, leaned away, grinned. "Oh, man, when this is all over—"

They heard two quick gunshots.

Beck was on her feet, but Pete pulled her back down to the icy forest floor. "That wasn't a rifle. That was a handgun. There's somebody else out there. And unless I miss my guess—"

The flat snap of the sniper's rifle, twice.

An answering gunshot.

"I think we've kind of got our distraction in place. We should go for the truck while they kill each other."

"We stick to the plan," said Beck.

(11)

Rebecca was alone in the woods, hugging the ground as Pete had instructed. Exhaustion and fear bore down on her, and now loneliness besides. She did not understand what was happening. Dak had assured her that nobody could touch Jericho. Sure, lots of people were watch-, ing, including what Dak called a few "unofficial nations"—which Beck took to mean terrorist organizations, although, having had her confrontation with Jack Notting, she supposed that unofficial nations came in other forms, too. Dak had described a standoff: nobody dared kill Jericho, for fear of what he had hidden, and nobody dared kidnap him to make him talk, for fear that, given his age and illness, the interrogation itself would kill him. But now somebody had decided to act, notwithstanding the risk—and once the uneasy truce was broken, it was every unofficial nation for itself.

But why act now? she asked herself, breath curling whitely in the frigid air. Why suddenly swoop in tonight, when Jericho had spent weeks bedridden, there for the picking? The answer was so obvious it made her cringe.

They acted now because Beck was leaving tomorrow.

So simple. Jericho's lover of so many years ago had come late to his bedside, stayed a few days, and was off again. What unofficial nation could resist the conclusion that Jericho had summoned Rebecca for a purpose, and was sending her off to do whatever it was he had threatened to do? Because human nature is as constant for the heads of giant corporations and the most secret of secret spies as it is for adolescents and wronged spouses everywhere, all of whom believe, deep down, that whatever happens, happens for a reason; and that the reason has to do with them. And so, if Beck flew in, stayed a few days, and flew out again, she had to be carrying the secrets with her.

Meaning they could not afford to let her go. Whatever fate was in store for Jericho was likely in store for Rebecca, too.

Sitting there in the bushes, fifty yards from the house, listening to what sounded like a small battle around front, Beck saw the rest of the story, and shuddered. Jericho had known. Of course he had. That clever, twisted mind that saw six conspiracies in as many minutes would have realized at once that Rebecca's presence would shatter the informal truce: Jericho might even have wanted her there for that reason. His plan, whatever it was, was ready, and he needed only to smoke his enemies out. To Jericho, the Rebecca who had once loved him and now had her own life was simply another piece to be moved about the board. That Beck had telephoned Stone Heights when she heard the news of his condition just made his job easier; but, had Rebecca not called, she was willing to bet that a compliant Audrey would have contacted her, told her that Jericho needed her—

The shooting had stopped.

Immediately Rebecca's attention snapped to the present. Pete was out there, risking his life. She crept forward, peered toward the front of the house.

She saw him.

He had emerged from the woods and was crouching behind the burned van, near the man Maxine had killed. He did not even glance behind him, but instead sprang to his feet and raced across the gravel.

Immediately, the snap of the sniper's rifle.

He went down hard, and Beck covered her mouth to stifle her scream.

Another snap, and then an answering shot. Pete was rolling toward the woods again, out of sight, but firing.

The distraction.

She had forgotten her role. She leaped to her feet and pelted for the house. The grass was slick from frost, and twice she almost stumbled, before thwacking against the siding. She hugged the wood and headed toward the back. Out front, the firing continued and then, ominously, stopped. Beck had reached the corner, just below the windows of the kitchen. Had Pete been killed? Had the sniper? She wondered whether the man up there with the rifle had turned his attention back to the rear lawn. Even if he had, she decided, he would not be able to see her inching along. She could make it to the kitchen door. The door opened inward, so the sniper should not even notice. But there was a storm door, which opened outward, and was bound to attract his attention.

On the other hand, standing here would not do her much good. So it was either get back into the woods or get into the house.

"Go, girl," she whispered, and, still flat against the siding, turned the corner.

No shots.

A moment later she was up on the deck, and then she was at the kitchen door. Moment of truth.

She opened the storm door.

Snap, snap, snap.

The fusillade blew the storm door out of her hand, shattering the glass, and one bullet whizzed right by her head, but she had presented an unexpected target, and the sniper hadn't had time to take true aim. Now panic saved her. She dived toward the house, the door opened to her weight, and she was inside.

Two more shots hit the deck, then silence.

(111)

Beck sat on the kitchen floor, the door shut behind her. Her breathing had developed a hitch, and, evidently, so had her thinking, because she had pretty much decided that she would just sit here the rest of her life. Which might not be so long. Well, maybe her mother would raise Nina right. After all, she had not done too badly with Rebecca. She wished she could see her mom and apologize for being so hard on her all these years. She wished she could see Nina and tell her one last time that she loved her, and she should do whatever Grandma said. She wished she could stop her hand from trembling. She noticed blood on her jacket, a lot of it, and realized that one of the bullets must not have whizzed past. Well, that would explain why she was so sleepy. She shut her eyes. Her fingers traced the blood up to her neck, then to her face. She felt her cheek, found a piece of glass. Not a bullet at all, but not a tiny sliver either. A piece, a pretty big one, just hanging from her cheek. Well, she was not going to face her Maker with glass in her face. She wanted to look her best. She yanked it out, and the searing pain woke her.

"Thank you," she said, to Whoever, and struggled to her feet.

Then, as Jericho had trained her, she did her sums. First, the basement. The door stood open. She listened, but heard no shouting, and no pounding either. She wondered whether Maxine had escaped. Maybe it was Maxine who had set off the explosion in the garage. Pete said he had seen a man enter, but there was no power for the floods, and the night was dark, and if she did not get herself moving, she would fall asleep on her feet, right here at the top of the basement stairs.

Rebecca shut the door and slammed home the bolt.

From the kitchen drawer, she took a couple of knives. She found another flashlight in the same closet as before. Ready at last, she stepped into the hall.

The van had long since burned down, but the garage was still a torch in the night. One of the wide windows to the living room had burst, and embers were flaking in through the mesh. Soon the books would catch, and then the house would start. Beck ached, unexpectedly, for the loss of Jericho's vast library, but there was nothing to be done.

She ran for the stairs, blundering through Jericho's maze of chairs, not worried about stealth because there was nobody to hide from. On the landing, the cone of her flashlight picked out Pamela, no longer crumpled on the floor, but in a sitting position against the door to the hall bath. Beck crouched beside her, and found her still breathing, but unconscious. The bleeding seemed to have stopped. A fresh towel had replaced the one Rebecca had—

Wait. That was no towel.

It was a bandage. The wound had been cleaned and wrapped.

Either Pamela had somehow found the strength to unearth the first-aid kit—heaven knew from where—or else—

Shakily, Beck got to her feet. She clutched a knife at the ready. Jericho had taught her how to shoot, not how to cut, but she figured her intuition would be enough. With the flashlight pointed at the floor, she lunged for the master suite.

And found it empty.

She was too late.

(I V)

"That's why the back door gave so easily," she told Pete Mundy, the two of them huddled in the woods once more, with Pamela moaning between them as they carried her. "They'd been in there already. They went in, they got Jericho, they left."

"Funny they took the time to tape her up."

"Maybe that means the federal government has him. I hope so."

Pete found a laugh somewhere. "You have a higher opinion of the feds than I do, Beck."

He had come upon her on the stairs, as she tried to carry Pamela down the fireman's way, over her back. Pete had eased the unconscious woman from Rebecca's grip, and hefted her to his shoulder the way one would a baby. Beck was surprised by such strength in a man so slim. He and the sniper had exchanged fire for a while, Pete said, and then the sniper had just quit. Pete had climbed to the man's position and found him gone. Plenty of expended shells, but no shooter. He had gone to the truck and called for help, then returned to the house to search for Beck.

"We still have to be careful," the deputy warned, as they moved through the woods. "He could be around somewhere. I think I winged him, but I'm not sure."

Winged him. Showing off for her. Any other day, she would have laughed.

They trudged on, keeping once more to the east. "Pete?"

"Hmmm?"

"When are they coming?"

He stopped short and held up his hand, then was shoving her toward the ground. They put Pamela down so fast they nearly dropped her. But the noise was only a panicked deer, not sure which way to run from the fire.

"Half an hour, I'd guess," he said. "Maybe a little less."

"Maybe we should wait in the house."

"I don't think we should risk the sniper a third time. We can't go to the truck." He hesitated. "Beck, look. I peeked in the basement, where you stashed Miss Kelly? She's not there."

Rebecca rubbed her eyes. No Jericho. No Maxine. A sniper still active in the woods.

"We should sit tight," she said.

Pete shook his head. "I think we should go back to the well."

"The well?"

"They've got Mr. Ainsley, but maybe we can still help him if we can find whatever's down there."

She was tempted. She needed whatever was down there as her protection, and her daughter's. On the other hand, with Jericho gone, she had a hunch that Jack Notting was busy running for cover. Unless of course it was Jack who had Jericho, in which case—

"Pete, listen. You just told me the sniper's out there. Maxine is out there. Whoever took Jericho is out there. I think we're better off waiting where we are until help comes. The last thing we should do is head down the hill behind the house, which is kind of an obvious escape route." Her laugh was brittle. "And look at Pamela. We can't be carrying her down the ravine to the well—"

"I'm sorry, Beck." The gun was pointed her way. "I'm afraid I'll have to insist."

CHAPTER 38

The Pouch

(1)

Rebecca felt no surprise. She felt nothing, other than the raw, icy pain on her hands, and the sinking dullness of another failure. She had known. Of course she had known. She had known since their abortive date, and maybe since the night he tried to pick her up at Corinda's, if not earlier that same day, when he ignored the sisters and handed her his card.

They were back down in the dip, and Beck was back at work. Pete explained that he would be happy to help, except that the task would require him to put down the gun. They had left Pamela on the edge of the dip. Beck had wanted to bring her, but Pete had said no.

"You're a bastard," she muttered, tugging once again at the impossible weight of the hose. She tugged and groaned, tugged and groaned, increasingly certain that she was on a fool's errand, and certain, too, that it hardly mattered, because her mortal body would be receiving, any moment, the bullet.

"Need to rest?"

"No."

"I don't want to make this harder than it has to be."

She bared her teeth in a fierce grin. The gun was still clutched at his side, barrel toward the frozen earth. "You didn't even call anybody, did you? Or did you call whoever you're working for?" Another thought struck her. "Were you and that sniper even really shooting at each other? Or are you on the same side?"

"I'm sorry," he said, and looked away.

His uneasiness emboldened her. "Pamela could die up there, Pete. Have you given that any thought?"

"You don't sound scared."

"Sorry." She dropped the hose, took off her mittens, rubbed her hands together, blew on them. Her shoulders ached. "I'm too tired to be scared."

"I'm sorry, too," he said, and sounded as if he meant it. When she looked at his earnest face, she saw genuine pain. "I wish—well, I wish things were different." He shook his head. "But they're not, so we better finish. By the way, how'd you figure it out?" He shrugged, but the gun was steady. "You weren't surprised."

"I didn't figure it out, Pete. I'm never surprised when a guy who seems nice turns out to be a shithead instead. That's life." She pulled the mittens back on, bent to the hose once more. "So—you're the bad guy, and Sheriff Garvey is the good guy. No wonder he wanted to keep us apart. He was suspicious of you all along, wasn't he?"

"He's not as big a fool as he looks," the deputy agreed.

"And that story you told me? The men who came to meet him, the chief deputy resigning? Was any of that true?"

"Every word." He continued crouching beneath the tree, the gun pointed at the frozen soil between them. "Garvey's not an innocent, Beck. He's involved, just on the other side." A humorless chuckle. "One of the other sides, anyway."

"And you? Which side are you on?"

He lifted his head again, listened. "We don't have much time."

She almost laughed, understanding at last why the dying Jericho grew irritated at every tiny reference to minutes or days passing. "*We* don't have much time? Get real, Pete. I'm the one with no time. You're going to kill me as soon as we find out what's down in the well."

"Hurry up," he said, not meeting her eyes.

Beck cocked her ears but heard nothing. Still, she had not grown up in the mountain forest. She wondered what Pete heard that she did not.

She bent back to her work, tugging the heavy hose from the earth. It coiled around her feet like an endless black umbilical cord. A part of her did not want to know what the well would birth.

"I don't have a choice here," Pete blurted in sudden self-justification. "I know that's not much of an excuse, but it happens to be true."

Another maybe: maybe if she let him keep talking, he would talk himself out of it. She continued to heave, said nothing.

"You can stop now," he said. "I'll finish."

"You mean, after you shoot me?"

He was standing now, and closer, but not close enough. "You think I like this?"

She was breathing harder. "I'm too tired to play twenty questions. Now, you can do one of two things. You can kill me, or you can help me pull this pump out of the ground."

That lazy smile again. "And give you the chance to conk me on the head."

"I was kind of hoping, yes."

"Step away."

"Pete—"

"No, no, it's time to get real." Gesturing with the gun. "Move away from the well, Beck."

She swallowed. Her exhaustion was ebbing. The fear she had denied was seeping through. She wondered who had Jericho; and whether Pamela was still breathing.

"Pete, listen to me. Listen." Pointing. "What if I'm wrong? What if nothing's down there but mud?" The gun never wavered. "If you kill me, and there's nothing down there, who'll figure out the clues?"

The deputy thought this over. "Okay."

"Okay, what?"

"Okay, finish up." He crouched, but moved no closer. "Let's see what's down there."

JERICHO'S FALL

So Beck leaned in and gave another tug, and, just like that, the pump itself popped out, dark metal glinting in the moonlight.

Attached to the hose just above the nozzle was a plastic waterproof pouch. It was soldered shut with the same magical mastic that was used to protect the wires that ran power to the pump itself. As a rule, the plastic lasted the life of the pump.

She knew because she had read it in a book.

(11)

Now Pete Mundy waved her away. He wanted her nowhere near the pouch. "Over there," he said, and she dutifully trooped several paces off.

He bent over and tugged at the pouch. It was tightly attached, and for a moment she harbored hopes that he would have to put down the gun and pry with both hands. But Pete Mundy was a practical man. He slipped a Swiss Army knife from his belt, opened a blade, slit the bindings, and pulled the pouch free.

"What's in there?" she asked, because he was taking a peek.

"Photographic negatives. They look like copies of documents." He laughed. "Jericho Ainsley is so old-school. Nobody uses film any more." He straightened. "Are you ready, honey?"

"You don't have to do this," she said. But she was remembering what Dak had told her. Jack Notting would have left behind no incriminating document, and, regarding the least defensible of its deeds, neither would the Agency. Was the packet another wisp? Or was Jericho playing a deeper game than anybody—

"I do have to do it, honey," said the deputy. "I'm sorry."

"It's your boy, isn't it? Jack Notting has your boy in his sights."

She could not be certain, but she thought the gun wavered. Beck inched closer. Pete did not want to kill her. Hope battled terror. He was not an evil man, she told herself. She wondered how strong her own conscience would be if Notting had put the gun in her hand and told her that either Nina or Pete would die.

"You might want to close your eyes, honey," said Pete. "They say that makes it easier."

She shook her head. She had started to tremble, but still sensed his reluctance. "If you're going to do this, you're going to look me in the face and do this." The barrel wavered again. "Come on, Pete," she said, emboldened. She crept closer. "You're the police. You can call people. You can protect your boy."

"You don't know what these people are like," he said. "I like you, Beck. I like you a lot. But if it's you or Billy, I have to choose Billy."

"He'll kill Billy anyway. And you."

"Stand still," he said. "That's close enough."

"We're supposed to be the good guys—"

"Close your eyes," the deputy repeated. There was no tremor in his voice, and no waver in the gun. This time, without conscious thought, her lids dropped. Her hearing sharpened. All around were the night sounds of scurrying animals and blowing snow. She wondered if it was true what they said, that you died without ever hearing the shot. She found herself praying, desperately, that Audrey's God would look after Nina.

She waited. No shot. "I'm sorry Beck," he said. "I—I have to do this."

"No, you don't," she said gently, and, when he made no response, she realized that he was not going to pull the trigger, that he could not bring himself to kill her in cold blood. Eyes still closed, she took a cautious step in his direction. "It's okay, Pete," she said. "We'll find a way to—"

The shotgun blast shook the woods.

Rebecca opened her eyes.

Pete Mundy was a bloody mess on the forest floor. Standing behind him, a shotgun cradled under his arm, tall and strong and not at all sickly, was the great Jericho Ainsley.

"I'm feeling much better now, Becky-Bear," he said.

They stood there in the clearing, the wind whipping the fire around. So far it had not reached the trees or the main house. Sooner or later, as the late Pete Mundy had said, people in town would notice the flames, and somebody would come. She wondered how long it would take. She concentrated on all of these questions in order to avoid accepting the sheer impossibility that Jericho could be standing here with a shotgun, having just saved her life.

"What's the problem, Becky-Bear?" he murmured with the old roguish grin. "Aren't you going to thank me?"

"What are you doing here?" she said. She was shivering, as much with fear as with cold, for the adrenaline rush had not released her. "I don't understand."

"Oh, yes, you do. You're the smartest of the bunch, no matter what you pretend. You understand perfectly well."

"But you—you were—I saw you—"

"Quite."

And suddenly everything was clear. The wisp. Jericho's wisp. Dak said there had to be one, but, oh, she had never expected it to be so titanic. The only one in the house with medical training had been Audrey. The only one who could verify his symptoms. Oh, Audrey!

"You're a bastard," she said, backing away.

"Are you afraid of me, honey?" He seemed irritated. "I only did what had to be done. I had to know."

"People are dead, Jericho."

"And if I hadn't shown up just now, one of them would have been you." He coughed, still cradling the shotgun. "You haven't thanked me yet, Becky-Bear."

"Thanked you! This is all your doing, you sick bastard." She pointed to the body. "And you didn't have to kill him. I think I could have talked him—"

She stopped, cocked her head. A sound, somewhere in the distance—a sound that had become all too familiar—

"Jericho!" she cried. "Get back in the house!"

He glanced her way, the old half-smile on his face, the shotgun still cradled beneath his arm. "I'm doing okay, Becky-Bear. Don't worry."

"No. No. Listen to me. You're sick."

"I thought you'd worked it out. Things aren't always—"

The sounds were louder. Didn't he hear? "Jericho, no! You're a sick man! On the verge of death! You need to be in bed with the oxygen mask on!"

"I'm fine, honey. Really. I feel great."

She wanted to shake him, to slap him, to make him listen. "There's no time to argue, Jericho. I'm serious. You can't be out here like this! You have to lie down!"

He laughed, coughed a little, laughed again. "Come on, Rebecca. You're the smartest of the bunch. My health's not great, but I've got some years left in me. I can't believe you haven't—"

He stopped and looked up, the sounds at last too loud for even his aging ears to ignore. He lifted the shotgun instinctively, then dropped it on the ground, because two black-clad figures had his arms, and then his throat, and another was pulling Beck away as she screamed, because the night was full of a thousand floodlights and a million men. Somebody was cradling the wounded Pamela, somebody was checking Deputy Mundy and deciding to leave him, somebody was scooping up the pouch Pete had been ready to kill her to obtain, and then the commandos and the two surviving Ainsleys were soaring into the darkness, drawn upward by some kind of magic, Stone Heights suddenly empty of everyone but Rebecca, who knelt weeping on the frozen ground, flames dancing at her back, as the helicopters whirled away, the former DCI, former SecDef, Former Everything their captive.

FRIDAY: FIRST LIGHT

CHAPTER 39

The Wisp

After a while, Rebecca struggled to her feet. She looked up at the house but could not imagine going back for her things. She looked at her car but could not take the chance that it was, like Audrey's, booby-trapped. She supposed she would have to walk down the hill, and then walk to town, thirty-two bone-chilling miles through the Rocky Mountain night.

A hard trek, but a mother does what a mother has to do.

She began trudging down the driveway, the same route she had taken on Monday morning when she found the dead dog. But it had not been nearly so cold, and she had not been nearly so tired. She walked with a single goal: to get home to Nina. She would never leave her daughter alone this long again.

As a matter of fact, she would never leave Nina alone, period.

Now that she could, in a sense, look up the answers in the back of the book, Beck was pretty sure she had most of the story. Whether Jericho was dying or whether his illness was exaggerated to prevent his interrogation, she would never know. But the rest fell into place. Jack Notting had indeed robbed the investors of Scondell Bloom, and Jericho evidently worried that his knowledge of Jack's activities would put him—or, knowing how Jack operated, his family at risk. So he swept the information about what had really happened at Scondell Bloom beneath the capacious umbrella already created by his threats to expose government secrets. Poor Dak. He had been telling the truth. He had not wanted to harm his friend, but he had not believed the stories that Jericho was out to expose Jack Notting.

Dak might not even have known that Jack was a crook, or that Scondell Bloom was a fraud.

She wondered who had taken Jericho, whether the commandos had been sent by the federal government or Jack Notting's people. She hoped it was the feds. At least they would tend to Pamela's wounds. And if the government had Pamela, the combination of Sean pulling and Senator Ainsley pushing would sooner or later pry her from their grip. As for Jericho, well, once he started talking, Jack Notting would not long survive.

She stopped, and closed her eyes. With Jack Notting out of the way, Nina would be safe. That was the most important thing. Nina would be safe. Almost smiling, Beck opened her eyes again. And then she realized that she was not, one might say, out of the woods yet. Because blocking the path was Miss Kelly, the librarian: the retired assassin known as Max.

"Hi, Beck," Miss Kelly said, voice casual. There was no weapon in evidence. Her eyes were on the mountain sky, where pink was rising in the east. "I told you they'd be coming soon."

Rebecca, too, was gazing at the heavens. "Where are they going? Where are they taking them?"

"It's better not to ask. The important thing is, the terrorists were thwarted."

"Terrorists?"

The librarian nodded. "Sure. A vicious attack on the home of a long-retired member of the national-security establishment. These people know no limits, Beck. They have to be stopped."

Beck took a moment. "Were there any survivors?"

"Only one."

A shiver. "You?"

"No. I'm not even here. I'm in my apartment in town, fast asleep." She reached into the holster on her belt but withdrew only a PDA. Like Dak's, it worked fine up here. She scrolled down a few lines. "It's time to get moving."

But Beck refused to budge. She pictured Jericho, in an undisclosed location, being induced to—what was Dak's phrase?—vomit his knowledge onto the floor. He should have stayed in bed. Had he maintained the fiction, maybe they would have maintained their distance. On the other hand, Beck herself might be dead. She looked up at the burning house again, and, with a shudder, recalled the final act of *Don Giovanni*, Jericho's favorite opera, the unrepentant sinner being dragged physically down into the fires of hell. She glanced at the burnt-out van, and found herself aching: so much of life was spent counting your losses.

"Why didn't they take me?" she asked.

"They don't need you."

"And you?"

Flames seemed to leap in the dark eyes. "I don't need them," she said.

"You betrayed him."

"No."

"He trusted you, and you betrayed him."

"Jericho didn't trust me. I didn't work for him. As far as he knew, I was a librarian named Kelly." A shadow of humor flickered across her handsome features. "He even helped me get my job."

"Dak. Dak hired you, and then asked Jericho to find you a job." Again Beck looked into the brightening sky. "Six months. You were in town six months, waiting for tonight?"

"I'm good at my job, Beck. I'm very patient."

"But what were you doing for Dak?"

"Sorry. I can't tell you that. But if you think it over, I'm sure you'll figure it all out."

And she could. Now that she knew how the story ended, she could guess how it must have begun. Maxine had come to the house in response to Beck's call for help on the cell phone. But who had been listening? It had to be Dak's people. Putting aside the technological wizardry necessary to break into her phone, there was a glaring bit of evidence she had overlooked.

Jericho's voice. *Eight hundred acres. The middle of nowhere.*

Dak had told her that the Agency listened to her with Jericho. Who else would have the recordings? And armed with the tapes, all they had to do was follow Audrey's playbook, disorienting her, breaking her world down until her only choice was to do what they wanted.

She had found what Jericho had hidden, and they didn't even have to ask her. And, all along, Maxine had watched and waited.

"You're a considerable bitch," said Rebecca. "I hope you know that."

The ghost of a smile. "It's been said."

Rebecca wondered if Maxine had another gun. "Why did they take him? They had the packet. I pulled it up."

The assassin's smile was grim. "It could have been a wisp. The real guarantee against Jericho's fall could be somewhere else. Or there could be more than one. Like the one he sent down the mountain. Those weren't lawyers, Beck. They were from a private security firm."

"Did they survive?"

"Of course. But I'm afraid they double-crossed Mr. Ainsley. They didn't take his papers for safekeeping. They delivered them to another client."

Another client. Sean or his Aunt Maggie. Beck remembered Sheriff Garvey a couple of days ago, standing in the great room at Stone Heights, barking his cryptic message for Jericho, that he had talked to his friend, who was taking every precaution. Perhaps Jericho had hired the private firm at the sheriff's suggestion, thinking Garvey his man.

"Then somebody else has a copy of what was in the packet."

"I don't think so, Beck. Mr. Ainsley would have been a step or two ahead of them. Those papers were probably another wisp." A curt nod, one professional acknowledging another. "This was war for him. Never forget that."

"What was it for you?"

Maxine touched the gash on her forehead. "Well, it wasn't fun. I'll tell you that. Next time I need to remember to stay retired." She glanced at Rebecca. "You were never in any danger, Beck. I don't think Pete was going to pull the trigger. In any case, I wouldn't have let him."

"You were there?"

She nodded. "Getting out of your trap wasn't easy, but I managed. Then I had to take care of a couple of problems in the woods—you don't want to know—but, yes, the whole time you were talking to Pete Mundy, I was watching. Jericho saved me the trouble."

Even through the mists of fear and exhaustion, Rebecca caught the lie. "No. That's not it. You weren't sitting in Bethel for six months on the off chance that I'd show up and you'd have to protect me. You were here to keep an eye on Jericho. Sure, you were listening when I called for help, and you came running, but it wasn't to save my life. It was to make sure Jericho didn't fall into the wrong hands. The reason you knew that the helicopter was on the way was that you called Dak and told them to come. The reason you saw me with Pete was that you followed Jericho when he left the house. The reason you had to take care of a couple of problems in the woods was that there were other people out there, and you had to be sure they didn't get to him before your friends did."

Maxine studied her PDA. "We should get moving."

"You're not going to tell me, are you?"

"Don't make the mistake of thinking that people ever act out of only a single motive." That sudden smile. "And don't worry about your Nina. Or about Jack Notting. Everything's being taken care of."

"What do you—"

"Some friends of mine are watching out for your daughter and your mother. And as for Jack—well, Jack is going to have to fend for himself. I think the feds will turn him loose soon, and he's going to have to start worrying."

"About you?"

"Audrey was a good friend. Jack killed her just to make a point."

"That was your job, wasn't it? Waiting and watching, just in case somebody solved the mystery, then cleaning up the mess. And I played right into your hands, didn't I?"

"Right now, my job is to get you out of here."

"Dak told you to protect me?" said Rebecca, very surprised. "Why would he care?"

Max grimaced. For a second the mask slipped, and Beck glimpsed the woman inside the assassin. The professional smirk at once closed down again, and Rebecca would never know for sure, but she suspected that the decision by the commandos to leave her behind was an alteration to the original deal, that Maxine had demanded as additional compensation for her own services that Jericho's ex-lover be spared.

A trade-off, maybe, for Audrey.

"My car is just around the bend," said Max, pointing.

Beck stared at the inferno, the house Jericho had bought for the two of them; and where he had presided over his lonely, miserable kingdom. Evidently, her capacity for guilt was undiminished. She still felt she had wrecked his career.

She missed him.

"I won't get a chance to see him, will I? Jericho."

"I don't know." Maxine took her hand. "This is how life works, Rebecca. You do what you can to protect the people you love. First rule of living. Second rule? Same as the first. It's a biological imperative." She was leading Beck away from the carnage. "You did great."

"Huh."

"You did," said the taller woman, hand gentle on her back.

Rebecca shook her head, still watching the house, her past burning. The helicopter was long gone, and Jericho Ainsley with it. In the end, somebody was willing to risk doing to the old man whatever it was that they did to discover the truth.

"I want to call my daughter," she said.

"We have to get going. You can call her from the car. I can't let you use my mobile, but I have a sat phone. Now, we really have to get moving."

"What's the hurry?"

"The bad guys are on the way."

Beck looked up at the sky, her imagination tracking the invisible helicopter. Another part of her was counting the cost: Audrey and Pete Mundy and Mr. Lobb all dead, Pamela wounded, Jericho a prisoner. The enemy was secrecy, she realized. Secrecy, and the risks that secrets carried. She pointed toward the heavens. "Those were the good guys?"

Maxine grinned. "Not the great guys. But the good-enough guys. Put it that way."

"And you? Are you one of the good guys?"

"I'm just a librarian."

"Then why are we running away?"

"I told you before." Firm grip on Beck's biceps, leading her toward the car. "There are lots of ways for librarians to get in trouble these days."

Doors slammed. The engine started. The car headed down the long driveway and was gone.

And there was only the brisk morning, and the angry fire, and the vast, brooding silence of the mountain.

AUTHOR'S NOTE

This is a work of fiction. Its only purpose is entertainment. The characters, story, and setting proceed entirely from my imagination. And although I have spent a good deal of time over the years enjoying the beauty of the Colorado Rockies, the town of Bethel is an invention, not based on any actual community.

Having said that, I should add that the novel of course has factual predicates. The story Phil Agadakos relates about the death of William Colby is essentially true, although some of the public tellings embellish the tale with unlikely emendations. The problem of mental illness among intelligence professionals is often said to be endemic. Certainly the national-security community has been haunted for decades by the nervous breakdown, while on the job, of Frank Wisner, often referred to as the father of American covert operations, and the likely suicide of Secretary of Defense James Forrestal, who tumbled from his sixteenth-floor window at Bethesda Naval Hospital, where he was being treated for depression. The longest shadow, however, is cast by James Jesus Angleton, whose counterintelligence work at the Agency from the sixties through the mid-seventies was clouded by a growing paranoia that tore the intelligence community apart.

The Central Intelligence Agency pays its employees according to a pay scale different from the usual federal civil-service rate, and provides a generous pension, but the differences in scale are smaller than many believe, and have not prevented the occasional case of cheating. True, no financial scandal in the Agency has ever reached the very top, but imagining such events is what makes fiction possible.

As to the theft of assets at Scondell * Bloom * Notting, I have somewhat simplified what would have to be a more complex scheme. According to my friends on Wall Street, such a conspiracy would need not only insiders willing to fake the records and regulators willing to look the other way, but auditors willing to be fooled. No doubt Jack Notting's conspirators must have included them, too.

Many Princeton University students do indeed celebrate the Newman's Day tradition of downing twenty-four beers in twenty-four hours on the twenty-fourth of April, although the University itself has condemned it, on health grounds, and the late Paul Newman, for whom the tradition is named, did his best to discourage it. As of this writing, there is no Red Roof Inn in Colorado, but I suspect the chain will have no objection to my pretense. Readers of my novel *The Emperor of Ocean Park* might have formed the impression that Professor Tish Kirschbaum is older than she appears in the instant tale. I once thought so, too, but I was mistaken.

The CIA's Directorate of Operations, so beloved of thriller writers, no longer exists. In a post 9/11 reform, the mission of the Directorate was sightly restructured, and the institution was renamed the National Clandestine Service, which sounds like something out of a bad movie. But the name has changed before. For twenty-odd years it was known as the Directorate of Plans. Before that—best euphemism of all!—covert action was undertaken by the Office of Policy Coordination.

The Episcopal Church, although the fact is not widely known, does indeed have nuns. To my knowledge, none formerly conducted interrogations of terror suspects. I should add that Audrey Ainsley's theory about the best way to perform interrogations is widely shared among professionals, provided always that one possesses sufficient time. When the press of events creates the perception of emergency, everyone—my characters included—has trouble making right choices. This is evidence not of wickedness but of humanity.

Jericho's use of the word *chamade* is slightly over-precise. His story about paroled prisoners in the War of 1812 and the Revolutionary War is true.

I have benefited, as always, from the thoughtful advice of my editor, Phyllis Grann; my literary agent, Lynn Nesbit; and the small circle of intimates who read my work in its early stages. And, as always, I have learned much from the loving support, and generous readings, of my children, Leah and Andrew, and my wondrous and brilliant wife, Enola Aird. For their presence in my life I continue to thank God.

Cheshire, Connecticut
March 2009

ALSO BY STEPHEN L. CARTER

THE CULTURE OF DISBELIEF

Religion and its place in American public and private life is a theme
that has consistently remained at the center of our national debate. In
recent years, many political leaders and opinion makers have come to
view any religious element in public discourse as a tool of the radical
right for reshaping American society. So in our zeal to keep religion
from dominating our politics, we have constructed political and legal
cultures that force the religiously devout to act as if their faith doesn't
really matter. Stephen L. Carter explains how we can preserve the vital
separation of church and state while embracing rather than trivializing
the faith of millions or treating religious believers with disdain.

Current Events/Social Studies/978-0-385-47498-6

THE EMPEROR OF OCEAN PARK

In his triumphant fiction debut, Stephen L. Carter combines a riveting
novel of suspense with the saga of a unique family. *The Emperor of
Ocean Park* is set in two privileged worlds: the upper-crust African
American society of the Eastern seaboard and the inner circle of an Ivy
League law school. Talcott Garland is a successful law professor,
devoted father, and husband of a beautiful and ambitious woman,
whose future desires may threaten the family he holds so dear. When
Talcott's father, Judge Oliver Garland, a disgraced Supreme Court
nominee, is found dead under suspicious circumstances, Talcott won-
ders if he may have been murdered. Guided by the elements of a
mysterious puzzle that his father left, Talcott must risk his marriage,
his career, and even his life in his quest for justice.

Fiction/978-0-375-71292-0

NEW ENGLAND WHITE

Lemaster Carlyle, the president of the country's most prestigious university, and his wife, Julia, the divinity school's deputy dean, are America's most prominent and powerful African American couple. Driving home through a swirling blizzard late one night, the couple skids off the road. Near the site of their accident they discover a dead body. To her horror, Julia recognizes the body as a prominent academic and one of her former lovers. In the wake of the death, the icy veneer of their town, Elm Harbor, a place Julia calls "the heart of whiteness," begins to crack, having devastating consequences for a prominent local family and sending shock waves all the way to the White House.

Fiction/978-0-375-71291-3

PALACE COUNCIL

Philmont Castle is a man who has it all: wealth, respect, and connections. He's the last person you'd expect to fall prey to a murderer, but then his body is found on the grounds of a Harlem mansion by the younger writer Eddie Wesley, who along with the woman he loves, Aurelia Treene, is pulled into a twenty-year search for the truth. The disappearence of Eddie's sister June makes their investigation even more troubling. As Eddie and Aurelia uncover layer upon layer of intrigue, their odyssey takes them from the wealthy drawing rooms of New York through the shady corners of radical politics all the way to the Oval Office and President Nixon himself.

Fiction/Thriller/978-0-307-38596-3

VINTAGE AND ANCHOR BOOKS
Available at your local bookstore, or visit
www.randomhouse.com